Paul Toolan is the author of the crime mystery January Killing, and An Easter Killing. Set in the contemporary apple-orchard landscape of the West of England, they feature Inspector Zig Batten and the cider-friendly Sergeant Ball. The series is ongoing, but the books can be read standalone.

Other writing includes the "beautifully poignant and humorous stories" in A View from Memory Hill.

Paul was born in urban Yorkshire but now lives in rural Somerset, and cheerfully admits to being a Southern softie.

After a successful career in Colleges and Universities, he wrote book/lyrics for musicals before 'turning to crime'. He writes plays, too.

Like Inspector Batten, he enjoys walking, fishing, gardens and the occasional whisky. Unlike him, he appreciates sport and the taste of mushrooms, and loves travelling to sunnier climes, Greece in particular.

As promised, Dave.

Cheers,

Paul

THE KILLING OF QUEEN MAB

D.I. Zig Batten 4

Paul Toolan

"I hope for nothing. I fear nothing. I am free."

Epitaph of Nikos Kazantzakis, author of *Zorba the Greek*

THE KILLING
OF QUEEN MAB

PART ONE

Somerset, England

One

He hated the bloody curtains anyway.

Because of the colour? Pale blue, with a grey stripe so faint it was pointless? Or because Erin made him buy them? *'To nuance your sitting room, Zig.'*

Pitch black now, the room - despite the bare window. In the small village of Ashtree, streetlamps clicked off at midnight, for power saving.

Is that *he* was doing? Saving power? Not a light switched on, the music system silent but for a faint hum from the speakers. Had he managed to collapse at the rear of his house, the view beyond a valley of ancient trees would be Ham Hill's vast Iron Age earthworks, silhouetted against a night sky.

But this window overlooked the front and all he could see through a gap in the clouds was a paltry dab of moon above the blackness a yew hedge. In daylight the yew had a faint scent of damp wood. Here, on the dark floor, the only scent was carpet dust. He pushed away the fallen curtains, wrapped around him like a shroud. *How long have I been here?* he asked the empty room.

Daylight was done, he remembered, when he'd jumped to his feet - too suddenly - to change the CD. He remembered his hand grabbing the pale blue curtains, the curtains he now detested even more. Next, the carpet claimed both him and the shattered curtain pole, blue-grey fabric shrouding his face before blackness came. *And how many times is this?*

Four? Four blackouts? 'A couple', he'd admitted to the police doctor. Seizures, Dr Fallon called them...

'Bit of a pickle, eh, Inspector?' Fallon had an understated bedside manner. 'Though I shan't be calling you *Inspector* for a while.'

'*What?* Why not?'

'Because you won't be *inspecting*. In fact, I shall l be inspecting *you* – on your *compulsory* sick leave.' The palm of Fallon's hand shut Batten up. 'Either risk permanent damage to the stubborn organ currently attached to your neck or do as you're told. *Understood?*'

...Batten fumbled towards the lamp and switched it on, eyes rebelling

3

at the brightness. Two jagged holes, like empty eye-sockets, glared at him from the wall where the curtain rail should be. Below, chunks of broken plaster and a white layer of dust flecked the carpet.

Understood?

Yes! Of course, he understood!

But could he comply?

Two

Batten swore he heard the bar stool groan when it took PC Jess Foreman's weight. He clinked his tonic water against Foreman's pint.

'Still off the booze, sir?'

'Doctor's orders,' Batten said, his face a scowl. 'Haven't had a drink since...you know.' He tailed off, staring at the threadbare décor of The Lamb and Flag, Foreman's favourite watering-hole. Tuesday early doors, it was near-empty, and the two men kept their voices down. The worn bar stools, showing their age with no bums to obscure them, still had a good ten years on the wallpaper, its once blue tones a faded bile-green now.

'Tricky things, sir, head injuries. Best listen to the Doc. What if I sort-of drink this on your behalf?' Foreman's rich Somerset vowels clothed a smile. Draining a third of his cider, he tapped giant fingers on his glass, waiting for Batten to tell him why he was here.

'Queen Mab,' said Batten. No point saying more. Every cop in Parminster knew Queen Mab - or used to. Foreman glugged more cider, needing it now.

'Nasty business, sir. Nasty,' muttered Foreman, wondering why this particular cold case should trouble a Detective Inspector supposedly on sick leave. 'Found a collar to feel?'

Batten shook his head, though Doc Fallon had warned him not to. 'Thought I'd take a fresh look,' said Batten. The Queen Mab murder was a thick file on the 'unsolved' rack. 'You know. Time on my hands.'

'Indeed, sir. But why Queen Mab - if you don't mind me asking? I mean, it's not as if...'

'We're spoilt for choice?' They shared a nod. 'Something about it caught my eye, Jess. Something...It's complicated.'

Foreman shrugged, waving his empty glass at Winnie, the barmaid. 'On me,' said Batten.

'To oil my memory, sir?'

Batten smiled. Foreman enjoyed the 'fresh air and no writing' of his rural beat, a famed memory for detail offsetting his disdain for pen and paper. And since cider sharpened his memory, Batten gladly watched a brisk Winnie place a second pint of cider on the bar.

'You're quicker'n usual tonight, Winn,' said Foreman. 'Been sampling the product?'

'My hands need something to *do*, Jess. *Doing* makes things tick.' She tapped the gold globes dangling from her ears till they swung like pendulums on steroids. 'When my legs move as fast as my earrings, so does time.' She pottered away, staring across the empty pub at the clock, its spidery black hands barely disturbing a once-white face.

Batten followed her eyes. Time festered for him, too, each sick-leave day a twenty-five-hour grind. Like Winnie, he needed to be *doing*, to speed the clock.

'You found her body, didn't you, Jess? Sergeant Ball says so.'

Big fist squeezing his glass, Foreman swallowed a throatful. 'I did, sir. And I wish I could forget.'

Batten shuddered. He'd seen the crime-scene photographs, gut-wrenching, each one. But he needed feet-on-the-ground detail. 'Can we remember together, Jess? I wasn't around, when...'

Foreman wiped a finger across his wet mouth. 'You'd been delayed, up north, sir, as I recall?'

'Leeds Crown Court. Giving evidence, after tapping my toes for an ice-age. When I rolled back to Parminster, the new HQ still smelled of fresh paint.'

'Fresh paint and chaos, sir. Thin on the ground, we were. I spent as much time with CID as I did on patrol. And detectives, rarer than hen's teeth.'

'Still are,' said Batten, fingers tapping his glass in rhythm with Foreman's. 'And one less, now.'

'Can't rush healing, sir. Heed the doctor.'

A mean slice of lemon lurked at the bottom of Batten's tonic, the ice-cubes melting, the bubbles losing their fizz. Foreman tracked Batten's gaze and saw a detective whose fizz was fading too. He switched on his memory.

'You know, sir, not many in Parminster could tell you Queen Mab's real name. But I could. That's why it was more of a shock than...than a body usually is. Poor soul. I wish it hadn't been me, who found her.'

'I know, Jess. But you did. And your memory's famous. Remember for me…'

*

…Gone midnight, no sign of a moon through the damp mist of an Autumn night turning colder than it should. PC Jess Foreman squirmed his buttocks right and left.

'Pants riding up, Jess?' asked PC Lee, a choirboy grin cracking his cheeks.

Foreman shuffled his boxers into place. 'At least my pants got something to hold on to,' he said, jabbing a meaty finger at Lee's slender frame. 'You, Jon, dunno why you bother with underwear. Waste o' good cloth.'

Lee chuckled at his giant oppo - bulkier, more experienced than he would ever be. Their Saturday night Parminster patrol was almost done. A light skirmish outside The Farrier's Arms had switched to a love-in when the combatants formed a verbal alliance against the pigs. Crime, for now, was asleep in a night blessed by silence.

'Soon be home, glass of cider and a box-set,' said Foreman, pausing beneath a streetlamp to check his watch and adjust his pants. His giant shadow swallowed the pavement and PC Lee. 'What about you, Jon?'

Lee's mouth opened to speak – and closed. In the distance, through the midnight mist, his eye caught the crazed windmill of a flailing arm, whirling towards him. Beneath the arm, two jagged legs lurched closer, piston-feet thudding at the ground. Lee tensed when the man's teeth bared into a frozen scowl.

'Steady, Jon. Two of us, one of him. And what's he goin' to do? Bite you?'

Feet beating at the ground, the sprinting figure grew in size. Foreman raised a protective arm, easing his body, six-foot-two-in-all-directions, in front of his smaller companion.

The frantic man jerked to a halt beneath the streetlamp, the confused bat of his arm still flailing at the distance. Jon Lee's trained mind clocked a full description, in preparation for his notebook.

7

Thirty or so. Dark brown hipster beard. Black padded jacket. Five foot ten, slim build. Suede trainers, mid-green, matching the tight trousers, a strip of wet cloth running from knee to ankle. Wet splashes staining the left shoe.

Been for a crafty post-booze slash, in an alley somewhere. Half-cut, he's peed on his own leg. Though Lee couldn't make out what, the bottom of his trainers were stained with something dark.

All this in a flash of seconds.

'The...The...The...*THERE!* screamed the man - *THERE!* – his whole frame pulsing with such energy even Foreman tensed. Voice found, the hipster kept using it, repeating and repeating his one strident word - *THERE! THERE! THERE!* – to the shaking rhythm of his arm, till Foreman wrapped a huge hand round the man's wrist and gently drew it down to his side.

'Where, sir?' he asked. 'Where, exactly?'

*

'I normally stop at two, on Tuesdays,' said Foreman, when Batten placed a third pint on the damp bar. 'But under the circumstances...' He drained half his glass, cider shining on his lips like salve. 'I don't mind saying, sir, I wish Jon Lee had stepped into that alley and done what I had to do, but...'

At HQ, PC Lee was 'Choirboy', his cherubic face seeming to grow no older. In contrast, Batten thought, Jess Foreman's put on five years in the space of two pints.

'You were the senior man, Jess. We don't get a choice.'

'No, sir. No choice at all. Except to go and see...'

*

...Holding on to the man, both to support and secure him, Foreman followed his unsteady footsteps back to the town centre. PC Lee's only contribution was to write the hipster's name in his notebook. It stuttered out as '*M-M-Mark B-B-Bragg.*'

The strange procession stuttered too, through the darkened streets of Parminster, across the deserted town square, past the padlocked grills of unlit shops and closed cafes, their outlines fuzzier now in the gone-midnight murk. Jon Lee shivered, perhaps from cold, as the three men halted by the entrance to an unlit alleyway skirting the rear loading bays of the town's retail zone. Locals used it as a cut-through between the High Street and the pay-and-display car park. Though Foreman had patrolled the dark lane many a night, his legs stiffened at the thought of stepping into it now.

Mark Bragg's arm trembled towards the darkest corner, where the silhouette of a mini-skip bristling with off-cuts and torn rolls of old flooring obscured the back entrance to a carpet shop.

The smell…and, ugh, the rest of it. My shoes…' 'I don't have to…you know, show you?' he asked, his face paste white.

'No, no, sir. You stay here with PC Lee, that'll be fine.' Foreman caught Lee's eye, nodding at Bragg's arm before moving towards the darkness, footsteps grating, memory racing as his torch crept into the gloom, each flash of light reminding him what he already knew.

That the alley was Queen Mab's open-air bed beneath the stars, her favourite rough-sleeper haunt. That as her behaviour grew more bizarre, he watched out for her - not that she was easy to ignore. You smelt her before you saw her, two filthy old coats - even in summer - wrapped around a faded red dress like a pair of grey shrouds, her unwashed skin a pancake of grime and ingrained sweat. Some days, only the sweat perfumed her. More often, the sickly-sharp odour of cheap booze clung to her skin like old tar.

Foreman watched out for her because Queen Mab's baby sister, Sue, had been his classmate - and his childhood sweetheart - at Primary school. Forty years back, was it?

Stepping deeper into the alley, beyond the dustbins of Jake's Bake Shop and the steel rear door of Parminster Pets, the walls grew darker as the streetlamp spill faded. When did he last see little Sue - Sue Linnet? Decades ago? Her face flashed into his head now, despite the darkness, her pigtails waving, and him scribbling down the answers she whispered when the teacher's back was turned.

No need for flashbacks to remember Rose, her big sister. Rose Linnet, with her bone-china cheekbones and her sideways look, head cocked to one side like a teacher checking your work. But kind blue eyes and a strange half-smile, as if one side of the world was comic but the other, not.

Foreman's giant feet dwindled in his mind's eye, becoming five years old, stepping to school with Sue, her hand in Rose's left, his hand in Rose's right, and the three of them, tall and small, skipping in rhythm regardless. And Rose's golden voice, inventing stories of unicorns and far-off lands. Then in the afternoon, on the journey home, she would whisper how the story ended, but always leave enough gaps in the telling for another chapter on another day.

Sue's big sister, Rose. Queen Mab, as she became. How many years since anyone had called her Rose? When she turned up from nowhere, for her mother's funeral, Foreman was one of the few mourners to brave the rain. A different Rose Linnet walked alone behind the coffin, her blonde hair greying and straggly, her dress a faded, non-funeral red. But Sue - no sign at all.

'I'm sorry about your mother, Rose,' he'd said, because Rose she still was.

'Thank you, er…Quentin.' Her voice surprised him, the everyday accent now refined, almost posh.

Despite her mistaking him for someone else, he tried to converse. 'I was expecting Sue to be here,' he said. 'Little Sue.'

Rose fixed two distant eyes on the horizon. 'Who?' she said. 'Oh, yes. No, only myself, Quentin. Thank you for coming.'

He waited for the familiar half-smile.

Gone.

*

Foreman couldn't remember draining his third pint, till he saw the bar through it. He shook his head at Batten's offer of a fourth. Not on a Tuesday. Not even with the bad taste of Queen Mab/Rose Linnet in his throat.

'It was way before you transferred here, sir, when Gina died - Rose's mum. After the funeral, Rose moved into the empty house and stayed there, till...'

'Was she an oddball, back then?'

'She was faraway, sir, but no more'n some we come across, in our line of work. But every day that passed, her mind crumbled a bit more, and a bit more again, like that crumbling house she inherited. Before long, she was sleeping outdoors, weather permitting. I must have moved her on, her and her blankets, a dozen times - even from the porch of Parminster HQ.'

'I remember me and Sergeant Ball stepping over her once,' said Batten. 'And sharpish, to escape the whiff.'

'Whiff indeed, poor soul. Sweat, drink, and street dirt. I said to her, 'why do you want to sleep out here? You own a house, just up the road. Well, in that weird voice of hers, she says, *Yes. I do, don't I?*' For a moment, Foreman became Rose Linnet.

'You should do impressions, Jess.'

'She never used to talk like that, sir, in her younger days. When she turned up here the second time, her body was old but her voice brand new, and every word a question. She said, *the roof prevents me seeing the stars, Quentin* - God only knows why she called me Quentin - *and shouldn't we all try to sleep beneath the stars? To give us hope? To heal?*'

'Heal what?'

'This, maybe?' Foreman tapped his skull. 'I said to her, 'you've got a garden – safer to sleep there.' *Gardens?* says she. *Are they not unnatural? I am trying to forget I possess one. Please, Quentin, desist from reminding me.*

Draining the final dregs of his tonic, Batten set the glass on the bar, next to Foreman's - two empty reminders of how little they knew of Queen Mab.

'In the end I did what we all did, sir. Oh, I moved her on if she was rankly in the way, her and that red dress and those stinking greatcoats. Mostly, though, I turned a blind eye. Social Services did their best, but...'

'Who called her 'Queen Mab', Jess? First?'

'No-one seems to know, but the name stuck. I mean, you never called her anything else, did you?'

Batten shook his head. Stories of 'Queen Mab' were a popular currency at HQ. Arriving in Somerset, he inhaled her stench before he saw her, assuming her nickname was a wry reference to *Romeo and Juliet,* and Mercutio's famous speech about Queen Mab, Queen of the Fairies. But simpler by far, the nickname.

'Whatever you find, sir, you'll let me know…?'

'I'm pulling on a loose thread, Jess. No sense where it might lead.'

'Why couldn't she stay as Rose Linnet?' said Foreman. 'I'd give up cider for that. Because when He made Rose, I tell you, God was concentrating.' Foreman pushed away his empty glass.

'Hard for you, Jess, watching her decay.'

'Hard indeed, sir. Don't understand how a true beauty, a fairy queen, could dwindle to, what? A smelly, booze-ridden wreck?' He eased his bulk from the bar stool, the seat-foam breathing a sigh of relief. 'I suppose it made sense, her nickname. Broken minds, they drift, don't they? Drift away, with the fairies…'

*

…Swallowing bile, Foreman aimed his torch and his giant frame towards the rear door of *Comfort Carpets,* wondering why the automatic light didn't click on. Loathing every step, his heart battered with dread at what he might discover in the black shadow of the skip.

And the beat of his heart became the thump of his feet on the hard floor, each thud an echo in his chest, till he froze, rigid, when the ring of his boots changed to a sticky, sucking sound - and re-tracing his steps with the greatest care, because there was no mistaking now what his feet had stepped into.

Three

At least Doctor Fallon was brisk. 'Still tender here?' he asked, expert fingers teasing Batten's skull.

Squatting on the examination couch, its sterile paper sleeve doing a rat-rustle beneath him, Batten shrugged a 'not very.'

'Here, then?' The specialist pressed harder near the bony lump, making Batten 'oof' with pain. 'No further response required,' Fallon said. 'And the blackouts?'

'Not too bad,' Batten said, knowing a loaded question when he heard one. At least Fallon hadn't called them 'seizures' this time.

'Mmm,' said Fallon, who knew a loaded answer when he heard one. 'How frequent, these last seven days?'

Caught, Batten shrugged defensively. The surgery's stark-white walls closed in on him. 'Hard to say.'

'Perhaps because you'd blacked out,' said Fallon, without the smile this time. 'Bit of a pickle, eh? Pop your shirt back on.'

The doctor's cool eyes turned to the documents on his desk – the results of so much prodding and probing Batten felt like a laboratory rat. By now, he could recite the Reporting of Injuries, Diseases and Dangerous Occurrences Regulations, 2013 in his sleep. Not that he was getting much sleep.

Fallon leaned forward, gimlet eyes drilling into his reluctant patient. *He'd make a good cop*, Batten thought. 'Inspector. Should another cosh descend on that less-than-thick skull of yours, far from knocking some sense into you, it will more likely knock sense *out* of you – forever. And I *mean* forever! Clear enough?'

A whiff of disinfectant drifted across the surgery. Batten's answer was to reach for his jacket, keys in the pocket jangling like an alarm.

'Did you drive here today?'

'*No.*' It wasn't quite a lie. Batten had glazed over, seconds after backing his Focus from the garage of his Ashtree cottage. When he came to, he managed to roll the car back in, ring Sergeant Ball and say his car wouldn't start. When Ball turned up, he didn't believe him either.

13

As if in judgement, Fallon slid his fountain pen into the top pocket of his white coat. 'Good. Keep it that way. No chasing criminals, Inspector, and certainly not by car.'

Batten's sigh was canyon deep. In the absence of criminals, he'd chase his own tail. 'I can't sit and do *nothing*. I just can't.' He kept quiet about the Queen Mab casefile.

'Hobbies? Surely you have hobbies?'

Yes. Carp fishing. Books and CDs on his hand-made shelves. A glass or two of cider. Long hikes through rural Somerset. A garden. Pleasant deflections. But none of them a *passion…*

'Were *I* on extended leave, my wife would find me *hundreds* of things to do,' chuckled Fallon. '*Thousands.*'

Fallon was treated to a stare that said no Batten-wife was around to find him 'things to do'. A stop-start relationship with the green-eyed Erin Kemp had stumbled to a stop. In her new role as food and drink ambassador with the Somerset Produce Agency, she spent more time overseas trumpeting the county's goods, than in Somerset. When the blackouts began, she expressed tender concern - but didn't drop everything and fly back from wherever she'd flown to.

Fallon's expertise was head injuries. It wasn't his job to fix Batten's heart, but glancing at his patient's foot, tap-tapping on the surgery floor, Fallon said, 'a compromise, Inspector. Four weeks careful rest, anywhere you choose except Parminster CID. Your colleagues will cope without you.' Fallon's raised palm again silenced Batten's retort. 'Spare me the guff about *indispensability* – ever seen it carved on a gravestone? I shall liaise with occupational health on your behalf. *You* will convalesce. Fly somewhere warm if you prefer – but wear dark glasses and a hat. And take your medication. After a month, we'll reassess. Agreed?'

Batten leaned forward. 'Any other options?'

Doctor Fallon leaned forward too, narrowed pupils staring back. He tapped Batten's file. 'In addition to your name on a Coroner's Report?' he asked.

'I meant, *instead of.*'

Fallon closed the file with a brisk snap. '*None,*' he said.

'You shouldn't be here, sir.' Sergeant Ball lowered his voice, but not his eyebrows. 'I'd have thought one relapse was plenty, even for you. And aren't you supposed to be in Crete?' He didn't say, 'to convalesce'. Batten's hatred of the word was as clear as dry cider.

'Flight's next week, Ballie. Before you ask, I booked an airport taxi.'

'And you were searching for your plane ticket in these unsolved case files, were you?'

Ball's squat frame blocked the CID storeroom's exit, and the two men stood nose to nose amid metal racks of folders, boxes, and dust. In the harsh neon light, Batten was a schoolboy caught bunking off school. He would have sneaked away, unseen, but Ball's buzzard eyes had spotted his mud-spattered car, concealed at the rear of the police car park.

'Someone drove you in, sir?' asked Ball, with less than a smile.

Caught, Batten could only shrug. 'Chris, stop worrying, I drove like a pensioner. But I need *purpose*. I need to…' He was about to say 'work', but Ball's face stopped him. He locked eyes with his Sergeant. 'I can't spend a month squatting on a beach doing bugger-all. I can't.' He edged towards the door with the file he'd hauled down from the storage rack. Ball didn't budge. 'Chris, I just *can't*.'

'Not your strong suit, is it?' said Ball.

'What's not?'

'Patience. You're supposed to be slowing down.'

'Or resting *up*.'

'But not dancing left and right as if nothing's changed.' Ball stared at the file in Batten's hand, 'Queen Mab,' printed on the label. *Why that one*, he thought, *amongst so many*? Jabbing a sausage finger at the file, he said, 'might've been solved by now, if she'd been important.' Every unwarranted death was important, and both men knew it. 'Why her, sir?' Ball swept a hand at the overloaded storeroom. 'You're spoilt for choice.'

Batten trapped the file under his arm, not admitting this was his second unauthorised rummage in the storage room, where the 'Queen Mab' label caught his eye. Nor admitting it was Queen Mab's physical image, her red-grey shuffle remembered from Parminster's streets, that made him delve. Too much on his damaged mind to explain the deeper, personal reasons for his choice. 'We'd need a full night of cider, to unpick the why, Ballie. And I'm excused alcohol.'

'*I'm* not,' said Ball, who never was - even when he was.

'Later, Chris? But I need to be *doing*. I've taken no exhibits. Nothing courtroom, so to speak.'

'And you were going to pop everything in the boot of your car and drive home, were you?' said Ball, giving the thick file a stare. 'Even though you're excused driving, so to speak?'

Batten raised his free hand. 'OK, cuff me,' he said…

…Ball's reward for his silence, and for driving Batten and the Queen Mab file home, was a glass of cider and a promise.

''Course I won't *investigate*, Ballie. How can I, in Crete?'

'Where Queen Mab spent a good deal of her time, as I recall. Even your predecessor spotted that.' Ball settled into an easy chair by the inglenook fireplace. 'Pure coincidence, is it, you flying to Crete?'

'She went other places, too,' mumbled Batten from the sofa, arms folded in defence.

'And didn't we recover her journal? Big bulky thing, brown leather?' Ball's sharp gimlets had spotted the tell-tale bulge in Batten's coat.

'It deserves a proper look, Ballie. Have you seen who wrote the summary notes?'

Ball shook his head and sipped cider. He too had arrived late at Parminster, when the Queen Mab killing hit a CID team fresher than the paint on the walls. 'Remind me, sir.'

'George.'

'Ah.' He swallowed a throatful. George Halfpenny was the worst detective Ball had ever encountered. 'Didn't you rename 'C.I.D.', with George in mind? Corrupt. Indolent. Despicable?'

'C for 'Captive' now, thank God.' Halfpenny sold inside information to crooks at a thousand pounds a time. Collared, he was spending the time - but not the money - at Her Majesty's pleasure.

'What did it say? George's summary? I don't recall.'

'Nothing *to* recall. One paragraph of squat.' Batten imagined Halfpenny weighing the heavy journal in his hand – and weighing up the effort required to read it. 'If George glanced at a single page, then…' Batten's recovering mind was still slow on metaphor.

'Then cider's a penny a pint?'

'Penny a pint, Ballie. I'll give it a proper look, in Crete. Can't get my undivided attention in Parminster, can it? Been ordered off the premises.'

'I haven't,' said Ball, draining his glass. 'I hear you've already picked Jess Foreman's brains.'

Batten gave a guilty nod. 'You don't miss much.'

'Glad I missed the body, sir. Glad Jess found her, not me. All the same, leave the *investigation* to us, yes? Keep it official?'

Huh, you should talk, Batten almost said, with past events in mind. But the two men were comfortable now with a silent knowingness. 'I'll ring you at home, then. *Un*officially.'

'A safer bet,' said Ball, reaching for his own phone to call a taxi. When it rolled up, his face creased into a gargoyle smile. 'Oh, in case I forget, sir - enjoy your flight.'

Batten scowled. Flying. He loathed flying. Frightened to death of it.

*

With Ball gone, Batten's cottage was so silent he could hear the echo. The music system sulked on its handmade shelves but with rain drumming on the windows, switching on *The Walk to the Paradise Garden*, his go-to soother, was a waste of sound. Nor was he in the mood for music. Four slow days of silence faced him before his plane landed in Crete and he could pick up Queen Mab's trail. Bag prematurely packed, plane tickets and plastic folder of euros squatting like fretful toads on his bedside table - yet he was expected to kick his heels, and *wait patiently*? Ignoring doctor's orders, he grabbed the Queen Mab case file, and took the advice he'd be drilling into his team, in normal times. *Begin at the beginning!*

The file said after Jess Foreman raised the alarm, DC Hick was the first detective on the scene. Batten winced as he picked up the phone, praying the wrecking ball that was Eddie 'Loft' Hick wouldn't live up to his nickname today, and be full of crap.

To his surprise, Hick wasn't, and agreed to drop in after work. Batten considered nailing down the furniture but when Hick arrived, his tie matched his jacket and, for once, his shirt was neatly tucked into his trousers. Someone had bought him a crisp leather belt and made him wear it. When Hick scrupulously wiped his wet shoes on the doormat and refused a beer, Batten guessed the new girlfriend, Laura, was waiting at home. For a moment, he envied Eddie Hick.

'Nice place, sir.'

'Thanks, Eddie. You found it OK?'

'Satnav, sir.' Hick twitched in surprise at Batten's T-shirt and jeans.

Did Hick use Satnav indoors, too? Batten wondered, as he pointed to an armchair, dangerously close to the expensive sound system. But Hick navigated the carpet and dropped into the chair without breakages.

Picking the brains of Jess Foreman was a steady, rewarding process. Picking the brains of Eddie 'Loft' Hick…

'Bloody shambles, sir. Total cock-up. Dog's dinner. Pile of -'

'I get the picture, Eddie.' Batten had learnt to nip Hick's staccato verbals in the bud. 'What I don't get is the lack of evidence. Hell's teeth, I don't get the lack of *investigation*. How could Chief Inspector Jellicoe be so bad?'

'You met Fat Jellicoe, sir. Couldn't you tell?'

'I met him once, for thirty seconds, while he shovelled the contents of his desk into a bin liner.' Batten remembered running his fingers over Jellicoe's lavender-polished desktop – after moving into the cubby-hole office so tiny he was amazed Jellicoe's overblown frame ever squeezed past the door. 'Last thing I saw of him was his back.'

'Best feature *was* his back. If I'm allowed to say.'

'Not bosom pals, you two?'

'Speak freely, sir?'

'It's you and me, Eddie. We're not at HQ.'

Hick twitched a glance at Batten's old oak furniture to make sure. 'When Jelly turned up at her crime scene - you know, Queen Mab's - he smelled worse than she did. Booze on his breath. Booze *on* him and *in*

18

him. Late, too. And he *was* on call. We should've been zoning and searching, the lot, far sooner. Whoever knifed her must've been splattered with blood. Plain as a budgie's beak, to me.'

And to Batten. The casefile was an open sore of bad leadership.

'And I'm asking myself, how'd he get here, the killer? Or she, I suppose. Same way they left? Car, van, bike, shank's pony? We should've gone looksie soon as Jess Foreman called it in. It's why I got taken off.'

'Sorry, Eddie? What?' Understanding DC Hick was a practised art. Batten was out of practice.

'Taken off, sir. Off the case. Thought you knew.' Batten shook his head. 'When Fat Jellicoe turned up, I told him, to his face. Told him what I thought.'

'And?'

'And nothing. He puts me up against the wall, hard. And I'm no skeleton. Shoves his breath up my nostrils, all mints and whisky. Says, 'listen, *twat*, no wet-behind-the-ears arse wipe tells me my job. Got it?' I just nodded till he put me down. Next thing, I'm back at HQ. And George Halfpenny's taken my place.'

Halfpenny's name hit Batten like a wet sponge.

'Never got past the Scene of Crime bods. Would have been my first murder. But I'm removed, and shuffling paper.'

Batten knew how Hick felt - about shuffling paper. He'd gladly have been removed from the scene of his first murder, and each one since, all a struggle to view.

'CCTV?'

'I asked George, on the quiet. Too dark, he said. Pitch black.'

'Surely they got the tapes enhanced?'

'Still too dark, George said. Waste o' time. Same for the private security – some of the businesses clubbed together to cough up the fees – well, they did back then. One old git in a white van. At least George tracked the bugger down. '*I'm not Superman, you know!*' he told George. Turned out he was patrolling the industrial estate, other side of town, useless plonker - like George and Jelly. I don't miss either of them. Was I right? Telling Jelly what I thought?'

'You showed him up, Eddie. He wouldn't like that, drunk or sober.'

'Cuh, one drunk gets murdered, and another drunk investigates. Not that he did. Tried to fit up half a dozen homeless alkies. Jess Foreman said when he breathed on 'em, they inhaled with a smile. That's all I know, sir. It's a should've, isn't it?'

'A should've?'

'Should've done it proper, first time.'

'Yes, Eddie. Should've.'

A twitch from Hick signalled his brain was tired. 'Anything else, sir?'

'No, Eddie, thanks – but if something occurs to you…' *How often do I say that?* Batten wondered.

'Hope you get whoever did it,' Hick said, making it to the hallway without breakages. 'Not a bad old soul, Queen Mab. Despite the stink.'

As he departed, Hick's shoulder caught the door, whacking it against the frame with a paint-chipping *crack*. Batten prayed 'Loft' was safe on the wet roads as his Jeep revved away, leaving only frustration and more George Halfpenny in its wake. Queen Mab was proving a hard woman to find.

He heard the long-dead voice of his old mentor, D.I. Farrar, in his head. *Hard to find? Then bloody look harder!*

But Doc Fallon's brisk voice was louder still. *Rest,* it said. *Heal.*

Woozy-headed, Batten for once took the sensible route - an early night, in his bed this time, not unconscious on the cold floor, without warning.

Four

Next day, he went back to beginnings.

The witness who stumbled on Queen Mab's body, what was he called?... Batten delved till Mark Bragg's name and address materialised from the slew of documents, along with his witness statement. Mark Bragg worked in Martock, three country miles along the River Parrett trail. Batten pulled on hiking boots and shoved an apple in the pocket of his waterproof. *To keep the doctor away.*

Under heavy cloud, the river's dark ripples and swirling weeds held his attention till they began to feel like a warning. When spots of rain speckled his sleeves, he left the track, ducking through the neat graveyard of Martock church to the far end of the village's old hamstone streets, where he spotted the *Bragg's* sign. Maybe it describes the owner's behaviour, he thought, but Bragg turned out to be an unremarkable thirty-something hipster with a dimly lit computer outlet offering sales and repairs. Laptops needing surgery were stacked on the shelves like an NHS waiting list. Crouched over the counter, Bragg had the back off a laptop when Batten entered and was delicately fettling a tiny piece of something into the aperture.

'With you in ten seconds,' Bragg said, without looking up, and true to his word it was ten seconds before he did. 'Apologies – tricky motherboard. Mothers are, aren't they? Tricky?'

With few mother memories to draw on, Batten produced his warrant card instead. Bragg's chuckles dried up when he saw it.

'Look, it's what I told uniform', he muttered. 'How am I supposed to know a computer's stolen just by looking at it?'

'I'm not here about computers, Mr Bragg, stolen or otherwise.' Bragg was so relieved he dropped the tiny screwdriver his fingers were twiddling as if its magic might ward off crime. The relief disappeared when Batten explained his presence.

'The smell's never gone,' he said, clicking the dead bolt and flipping the 'Closed' sign into place. 'You're not going to make me re-live it, are you?'

'Not overly,' Batten said, getting down to brass tacks. 'A couple of minor things. Your statement said when you went down the alley - you know, to relieve yourself - it was dark, and no security light came on?'

'Yes?'

'So how did you know there *was* a security light?'

'Ah. None of your lot asked me that. Weekends, I go to Parminster, to a mate's. You know, a few drinks, a bit of a late-night card school. Well, that alley's between the card school and the taxi rank. Honest truth, first time I nipped in for a slash, the light came on and frightened the crap out of me. Come to arrest me for peeing on the Queen's highway?'

'No, sir. But if the light disturbed you, why use the alley again?'

Bragg rubbed a white hand through his hipster beard. 'It's embarrassing,' he said.

Batten's face said spit it out, regardless.

'That night, when…you know. Well, I'd had a few,' he said, 'half-cut and feeling cocky. Don't laugh, but I was having a game with the light.'

'A game? Floodlit five-a-side?'

'I was being stupid. Crept up on it, you know, the sensor, to make it switch on, then dashed back to make it switch off.'

'And?'

'And nothing. It didn't come on. At all. Three more goes and at 4-0, I did a victory dance. In the alley.'

'Till your bladder did a victory dance on you?'

'Almost. In the dark, I banged against the skip and snuck behind, for a jimmy-riddle and…' A stop-sign in Bragg's memory screeched him to a halt, turning his face to chalk.

'And that's when you saw…'

'Saw? That's when I *heard*. Heard the sound my shoes made, in the…'

Batten had lied. He was making Bragg re-live his nightmare - the ashen face said so.

'Should've just buggered off…but, well, you know the rest.'

Did Batten know the rest? The case report was threadbare. 'Your statement described the smell?'

'I already said, the smell's never gone. Till your lot told me, I didn't know you could *smell* blood. When they returned my trainers, you know what I did?'

'I can guess.'

'Binned them. The smell, still there, outside and in.'

Sweet...metallic...rusty iron... How many times had Batten heard a witness describe blood that way? He hated the smell too. But blood is spilled in an environment, and blends with the smells around it. 'Was it just blood? In the alley?'

'Was? *Is*, you mean.' Bragg cupped five fingers over his nose and mouth. 'In here, still. A smelly skip, old carpet, old rubber.'

The police had combed the skip's contents for a discarded weapon. Nothing.

'And pee. OK, some of it mine. Fags. Booze.'

'Fags? Fresh, you mean?'

'I dunno, nicotine, cigarette pong. *I* don't smoke.'

Neither did Queen Mab, Batten noted. 'But you saw and heard nothing?'

'Switched on my phone torch, saw *everything*. I still see and smell it. And *hear* it. If I tread in a bit of chewing gum, I'm back in that alley. The noise. Blood, sucking at the soles of my shoes like glue.'

'But nothing else?'

He shook his head - but failed to clear it. This man has had enough, Batten thought. When Bragg reached for the tiny screwdriver, his fingers wobbled like blancmange. 'I need to get back to work,' he said. 'Got a living to make.'

Leaving Bragg's shaky hand hovering over a laptop, Batten retraced his steps along the River Parrett Trail towards Ashtree. For three twisting miles, beneath storm clouds itching to burst, he wondered why he made *his* living by getting back to the dead. And to the sweet, metallic, rusty iron smell of their blood.

*

Erin Kemp no longer bothered ringing Batten before she jetted off on one produce-touting European tour or another. That evening, his lungs full of fresh Somerset air and the cruel irony of time on his hands, he plonked himself down on the sofa and rang *her,* uncertain why.

'You and Makis are sure to have a fine time in Crete, Zig. You will give him my love?'

Will you give me yours? Batten almost asked. 'Don't know about the 'fine time'. I'm supposed to be convalescing.'

'You were *told* to convalesce, Zig. But it's a red rag to a bull, telling you to do anything.'

Was there a tinge of acid in Erin's words, despite their truth? If he mentioned his blackouts, might she cancel her tour to support him through tricky times? He guessed the answer.

'I shan't wish you a good flight, Zig. I know how you hate planes.'

'*You* don't, Erin.'

After an icy pause, she said, 'Zig, travel is my new world. My fresh hope. My time pressure is like yours, now. You know, the police pressure.'

'I'm not allowed any.'

'But will be again, Zig. I won't believe otherwise. How often in our relationship did you ring to postpone? You were 'on a case'. Can I forget almost becoming a 'case' myself? I've learnt what 'responding to a serious incident' really means, and when a serious incident put you in hospital, it was Chris Ball who told me the facts, not you.'

He didn't tell her because he knew what she'd say. 'It would have worried you more,' he lied.

'*More*, Zig? I have no capacity for *more*. We each have fresh priorities. The difference is, I've told you mine - which don't involve another man, before you ask. Sian will be at university soon enough, so my new priority is unashamed *me*. As for your priorities, until you speak them aloud, it's anyone's guess what they are.'

He couldn't remember if Erin ended the call, or he did. The war between life and work clouded his mind, already full of crud from the grubby stones he lifted daily - in pursuit of a justice seeming less and less obtainable.

It wasn't Erin's voice that drifted back into his head, but the remembered voice of old D.I Farrar.

'I dig up other folk's dirt all day, Zig. I'm buggered if I'll go home and dig up mine. Mine'll 'ave to keep.'

But Farrar never said for how long. Cancer got him first.

Only when he became aware of the phone's vacant buzz did he accept who ended the call. From the sound system, Tom Waits groaned out, *I Hope That I Don't Fall in Love.* Staring at the Queen Mab files spread across the blanket box that served as a coffee table, Batten mouthed 'sod it', and dragged the lot towards him.

Five

'Two more days to kill, before Crete,' he told Aunt Daze. His phone calls 'home', to Yorkshire, were now as erratic as his memory, though he would never forget the self-sacrifice she had made to ungrudgingly raise him from the age of two.

'Are you sure time's for killing, Zig?' she said. 'In't it for *using*?'

Batten's mother-in-all-but-name had a point. He thanked her and rang off.

Crime scene photos embedded in his skull, Batten took his Aunt's advice and *used* his time - driving his Ford to Parminster in perfect compliance with the Highway Code. Feeding coins into the pay-and-display machine not far from the alley where Queen Mab slept on troubled nights, he strode purposefully towards the carpet shop where she met her end.

It felt comforting to be in something like work mode, despite the drizzle – till he pushed at the damp door of *Comfort Carpets* and found it locked. Squinting, he read the sign dangling from the glass. *Closed Wednesdays*. Cursing it, him, crime and doctors, he gave the door a petulant little tap with his foot.

Thwarted, he did the next best thing: trudged to the rear entrance and scoped the back alley. In the crime-scene photographs it looked ten times worse at night but was drab enough in the morning gloom. A rusting skip sat outside, a cardboard tube and a roll of foam-backed off-cuts sticking up from its maw like Churchill's fingers. No victory for Batten, though. The security light above the door could be broken, working or plain indifferent.

Back burner, he decided, stomping to his car with Doc Fallon's warning in his head: 'be prepared for attention gaps and fractures in your thinking.' When he'd phoned best friend Ged to share this snippet, the predictable response was, 'you had those *before* you got coshed, Zig!'

Thinking got him as far as keys in the ignition and an engine ticking over. *Is that what I am now*, he thought, *an engine ticking over?* Distracted by the swish of windscreen wipers, he snailed the car to the cheap end of town, parking beneath a forlorn sign rumoured to say *Parminster Night Shelter*. Fat Jellicoe had collared 'half dozen homeless alkies' as suspects in Queen Mab's murder, and whenever they found a home, this was it.

From habit, he flashed his warrant card at Eric, the manager – who could spot a cop at three hundred yards and was well acquainted with Batten. The gruff respect of two men doing difficult jobs passed between them, before Eric reluctantly disappeared down a corridor enhanced with chipped brown paint. Batten tapped his feet in reception, a cocktail of dirt, sweat and failed disinfectant piercing his nostrils, topped by a hint of fried onions. Today's lunch, he guessed.

Eric returned with a short, thin man who looked like he'd missed breakfast, lunch and dinner – for weeks. 'Well, well,' said the man, 'if it isn't Inspector Button.'

Batten ignored the verbal dig – familiar, almost funny. 'A minute of your precious time, Keith? Unbutton your lip for me.'

Eric hovered behind his desk, a canny witness, as Batten steered Keith McGarrigle to a pair of old armchairs set in the bay window, its blue curtains an unpleasant echo of those Batten had wrenched from his cottage wall in a seizure-triggered collapse. They lay in a charity shop bin-liner, awaiting collection.

Charity shop clothing covered McGarrigle's frame like rags on a stick, and a knowing smile covered his stubbly face as he waited for Inspector Button to speak.

'Queen Mab,' said Batten. Two words, enough.

'Hah, been sent, have you, by that fat copper, the one who got cashiered?' asked McGarrigle. 'Fat copper who tried to fit me up for Queen Mab? Here for another crack at my old body, eh?'

With a shrug, Batten let Keith natter on. Out of the ramblings...

'I told him straight, why would I cosy up to Queen Mab? She stank worse than this lot.' Keith waved a handful of bones at the brown corridor. 'Me, I had a shower only yesserday. I'm *clean*.'

Keith's reward was Batten's 'pigs might fly' look.

'Ask Eric. Did, din' I, Eric? Had a shower? Yesserday?'

'You needed one, Keith,' Eric mumbled. Without looking up from his desk, he added, 'and you still haven't paid for it.'

The mention of money silenced McGarrigle. Batten said, 'whoever killed her, robbed her too. Any thoughts?'

'Not me.' Keith shook what passed for a head. 'Didn't and wouldn't. She was kind, Queen Mab. Y'know, she once lent me a fiver?'

'*Lent?*'

'Aye, well. *But not for tobacco*, she says, all posh. Cuh, about as posh as me. Swore like a sailor when she'd had a few. Anyroad, cash in her pockets, common knowledge. And you saw her – more of a stick than I am. Blind cripple could mug her with a bottle-top, grab a fistful and leg it. Why knife the poor cow?'

Happy to let McGarrigle ask the questions, Batten shrugged.

'Overkill.' Keith chuckled at his own joke, till his smile faded to a sneer. 'An' you think I could do *that*?'

'Someone did.'

As McGarrigle leaned closer, Batten hoped he really had showered *yesserday*. 'No-one in this place, Mr Button. She wasn't one of us, true, but close enough. And what about the blood? Gonna stop off for clean clothes from our extensive wardrobe, are we, between knifing her and trotting back here?' Keith wobbled a nicotine finger first at the town centre then at the brown corridor, the gesture cementing what Batten already guessed – that much steadier hands had sliced a neat incision, left-to-right, across Queen Mab's throat. Even done from behind, hands and sleeves would be soaked in red.

'Who then? You and your chums were on the streets, out and about. No rumours?'

'Out and about earlier, yeh. But it was one of them bastard nights, starts all balmy, then in a blink you're sleeping in a fridge. 'Me and my chums' were either back here or wrapped in six layers of cardboard when Queen Mab…' As Keith leaned closer, Batten breathed out. 'Smart money's on an out-of-towner. Me and this lot' - again Keith waved bones at the corridor - 'we *liked* her. Find someone who *dis*liked her. Disliked her enough to cut the poor bitch's throat.'

Find the motive, find the killer. How often had Batten drummed that into his team? But if the Keith McGarrigle's of this world had no motive, who did? Lost in thought, Batten almost forgot Keith was there, till a phlegmy cough broke in.

'I'm afraid my business diary is wall to wall today, Mr Button,' McGarrigle said in a voice as affectedly posh as Queen Mab's. 'Might my secretary squeeze you in tomorrow?'

Batten smiled and waved Keith's old bones back towards the corridor's flaking paint. At the desk, he drew a tenner from his wallet and pressed it into Eric's hand. 'For Keith's showers,' he said quietly.

At the door, he added, 'next time, make him use soap.'

*

With McGarrigle's 'overkill' comment still in mind, Mr Button-Batten drove like a distracted pensioner in the vague direction of home, deciding at the last minute to pull into the parking bay opposite a different home: Queen Mab's. Through misty drizzle he saw a boarded-up house, its front garden swimming in an ocean of leylandii and brambles. Over the years, windborne seeds had swelled into grey-green giants.

As a working detective he would have planned his visit, teamed up, arranged access and brought the necessary kit. Today, all he could do was ease past the damp nettles ensnaring the garden gate and fumble his way down a narrow causeway, surprisingly weed-free, leading to the front door. Either side of the path, entire planets of bramble quivered in the breeze, concealing lord-knows-what. Beyond, his way was blocked by thick wooden sheeting nailed across door and windows.

Instead, he stared at the stonework. Rose Linnet's final residence was hamstone-built, like his own cottage. This was a grander house, detached, well-proportioned with a double bay front, though the hamstone was granular and weather pitted, the mortar loose. Above his head, he guessed the roof was a sieve, broken tiles lying on the ground either side of the boarded-up door.

A house this beautiful, and still worth a bob or two, why did Queen Mab let it decay? *Buy it, then*, his internal voice mocked. *All this sick leave, you'd have time to do it up!*

As for seeing inside - back burner, again. His mind threw up more questions. Did Queen Mab leave a will? Who inherits the house? No *For Sale* board sprouted from the weeds. Talk to the Estate Agents? Or did Queen Mab have a solicitor?

From habit, he turned to ask Sergeant Ball. But until the Doc said otherwise, Batten was a solo player, a one-man team.

Perhaps Cretan sun would renew him. He drove through the rain back to Ashtree.

Like a pensioner.

Six

After a lunch he couldn't remember eating, Batten flopped down on his sofa and rang the Mortuary, to pick the brains of whoever did Queen Mab's autopsy. He wished it had been Dr Sonia Welcome, more recently in post – but attractive, intelligent, and about his age. At their last encounter, her wedding ring finger was ringless…

The pathologist who did the autopsy 'has moved on,' he was informed, and all the senior staff currently occupied. Biting back *'wish I was,'* he wondered if skull damage inhibits sarcasm.

A second grovelling phone call to 'Prof' Andy Connor in Forensics went its usual way.

'Thought you were a pal?' said Batten.

'Not with a backlog up to my axillae, Zig - armpits to mere mortals like you. And aren't you on sick leave and not supposed to be working?'

'If you don't tell Sir, I'll buy your round *and* mine next time. Because I'm not supposed to be drinking, either.'

'So, are you?'

'Which?'

'*Drinking!* I know you're working because you do bugger all else!'

'Andy, for once, can we dispense with the foreplay?'

'Huh.'

After a mock-pompous reminder that though 'Prof' was acceptable, his proper title was 'Professional Officer [Science]', Connor agreed to annotate a copy of the Queen Mab report, for Batten's eyes only. '*When I get a free moment to call my own, Zig. And you will buy all the drinks next time, plus a bag of pork scratchings for my carefree molars to masticate.*'

In fact, the Prof emailed his annotations the very next day. Not from necessity, Batten knew, but from friendship. Batten stared into the laptop screen, the impersonal language of the report thankfully softened by Connor's off-the-cuff comments in a scrawl of italics.

…cross-referencing to a less than comprehensive autopsy report… 'a

blow to the base of the skull, left side, almost certainly rendered the victim unconscious…'

Batten's fingers soothed his own skull, in lieu of Queen Mab's.

'…the likely weapon is a round wooden object, evidenced by the single, round-edged depression in the skull tissue, and fibre fragments lodged in the hair and skin. The depth implies a degree of force…'

Why can't boffins say it like it is? thought Batten. Some heavy-handed bastard clubbed her!

…we heroes at Forensics checked the fibre traces, Zig, and they're olive wood. I dunno, a rolling pin, something like? Apart from olives, wooden and round, there's sod all data to formulate a hypothesis…

Batten smiled at 'Prof' Connor's mock-pompous *data* and *hypothesis*. But not when he read on.

'…The throat was severed, the blade extremely sharp, evidenced by the clean left to right incision through the hyaline cartilage structure and by the depth of the wound [see section 2, paragraph 1].' *Canny sod crouched behind the victim, my guess, to minimise blood spatter? Right-handed killer? But why, Zig? Why slice all the way from her left ear to her right? Pardon my French but isn't that a tad unzipped? I mean, blow to the head would have done, if she'd lain there till morning, getting on in years, slight frame, organs nigh-on pickled and the weather not exactly warm?*

'…traces of a bleach-based detergent [see Section 4] were evident in the wound to the throat, possibly transferred from a previously sanitised blade…'

Seems the killer's OCD, eh, Zig? Or at pains not to leave useful trace, more like. So why such a sloppy searcher? Scrunched-up twenties, still, in three pockets out of six. Clothing pulled aside, and one pocket turned inside out. Yes, she could've done that herself. Or her killer scarpered having found what he/she was looking for? But definitely searched. Probably while unconscious.

Small mercies Batten thought.

A few traces of carpet fibre in her lungs, breathed in from the skip near Comfort Carpets? No comfort for Queen Mab, alas.

Batten's fickle mind took him back to The Lamb and Flag and his conversation with Jess Foreman, the first cop on the scene. 'She liked sleeping in the alley, sir, by the carpet shop. If the temperature dropped, she'd raid their skip. Tried moving her on one night but ended up laughing my socks off. She'd wrapped herself in carpet offcuts, strips of that foam-backed stuff, coiled round her in layers, and said in that funny posh voice of hers, 'Look, Quentin! I'm a croissant!'

An image of Queen Mab's severed throat cancelled the levity. Connor's scribbles said the alley where her body lay was graced with a catalogue of substances. Cross-contaminated urine topped the list. A mix of vomit and alcohol came next, hints of cocaine a poor third. Traces of every substance were found on Queen Mab's clothing and blankets - neither useful nor surprising since they'd coincided with the alley floor.

Why can't the buggers pee and puke into Tupperware containers, pop the lids on, and scratch their name with a sharpie? Found every size of footprint, too, in the stale piss. Trouble is, they're from tom dick and harry, jack jill and jane, and a flash mob. Never known a stink like it. Given our victim's stench, be no surprise if her killer wore a mask to make the job more palatable. And keep any trace in check, of course. Good job Queen Mab suffered from anosmia, according to her wafer-thin medical notes. Maybe her attacker had anosmia too, eh?

Connor was his usual mix of helpful and playful. Batten reached across his desk for a dictionary and looked up anosmia. A loss of the sense of smell. Often triggered by alcoholism.

Found traces of nitrile on the body. Best guess is protective gloves, or similar, and since Queen Mab was no advert for hygiene, I assume the killer wore them? Don't get excited - nitrile gloves are bog-standard - medicine, arts and crafts, food industry, even tattoo parlours!

The autopsy revealed no tattoos or distinguishing marks - other than a gaping wound to the throat, like a second mouth. But speaking what?

Faint trace of nicotine on the body. The real thing, not gum or a patch – wrong chemical mixers. So, either the assailant smoked, or she did.

Queen Mab's anti-smoking zeal was legendary, as Connor knew, but he blustered aside the bizarre logic of an unwashed bag-lady with a large Parminster house, sleeping rough beneath the stars and soaking up alcohol – while warning passers-by that nicotine was Satan's breath.

So, Zig, is your killer a smoker who wears nitrile gloves? And plans in advance, and comes prepared - with an olive-wood club and a sharp, clean knife? And who didn't clobber Queen Mab to nick the ready cash from her pockets? Her body was searched alright, but if twenty quid's the reason I'll eat my microscope.

Batten shared Connor's doubts. But if not money, what?

He closed the report and phoned the Prof to thank him. 'I wish we knew why she was searched, Andy.'

'The killer knows why, Zig, always does. Find the killer and ask the bastard - on my behalf too.'

'Count on it, Andy.'

'Ring of Bells, Friday, half eight? Your round?' said Connor.

'Ah, Prof, now you come to mention it, I'll be in Crete. *Convalescing.*'

'Slippy sod. Friday after, then, and I warn you, I'll have worked up double the thirst.'

'Pity. I'm in Crete the week after, too.'

'Huh! I've been conned!'

'Don't blame me, Prof. *Doctor's orders!*'

With Connor's mock disgust still ringing in his ears, Batten picked up the questioning bulk of Queen Mab's journal. The dry leather - dry from the Cretan sun, he guessed - rubbed at his skin like an itch. He imagined himself in Crete on warm, solid earth. Seascapes. The flop of sandals in the same dusty streets Queen Mab once trod. Blue, clear light, and a fresh trail to follow.

But following her trail meant a four-hour knuckle-clenched ordeal at 30,000 feet, strapped inside the flimsy metal tube of an aeroplane. Silently, he cursed the Wright Brothers for inventing the bloody thing.

PART TWO

Almyrida, in Crete

Seven

The White Mountains of northern Crete, peaks still veined with snow, dwarfed the beachside taverna. Batten smoothed the blue-checked tablecloth, the folds merging with white-tipped waves lapping the sand at their feet, like a cat at milk. By lunchtime, tourists would fill the place, flicking stale bread into the bay to gawk at fish gorging and boiling in a silver fury.

Batten's host raised his cup in the air.

'I, Lieutenant Makis Grigoris, of the Greek International Police Cooperation Division, I proclaim this best Greek coffee I taste today!'

The cup disappeared behind a Greek moustache twice as lush as Batten's.

'And I, Inspector Zig Batten, allegedly of Somerset CID, proclaim it's the *only* Greek coffee you've tasted today!'

'So literal, Sig.' Grigoris could never pronounce Zig. Only *Sig*. 'I think you no coalesce enough.'

'*Convalesce,* Makis. And stop reminding me.'

'Ah. *Convalesce.* All the same, too literal. So, eat the breakfast, drink the coffee. Look up there, it heal you.'

Grigoris waved at the beauty of the White Mountains, framing the pretty fishing village of Almyrida where his English friend temporarily 'coalesced.'

Batten was more used to the soulful marshes of the Somerset Levels beyond his Ashtree cottage in an England he didn't yet miss. Crete was still fresh to his senses - a blue curve of bay, sunlight on lapping waves, the scent of tamarisk and wild thyme, and snow on the White Mountains. 'Those peaks look mysterious, Makis. I wonder if Queen Mab gazed at them from this very spot.'

'You certain she live here?'

Batten patted the leather-bound journal, staring up from the table with its eyebrows raised. 'This says she did.' He pointed over his shoulder at the steep hill above the beach. 'She lived up there.' When he unhooked the rusty metal clasp, Queen Mab's journal fell open at a faded ribbon marking the last page he'd read.

Bus dropped me in Almyrida - hardly recognised it. Still a breath of fresh air after those shitty folk at uni.

Rented a cheap little house, up the slope above the sea. Huge brass telescope on a tripod by the window. Focused it on the harbour, people watching. Well, man-watching.

Been alone too long, since…

Spotted one handsome body, squatting on the rocks. Maybe he hasn't moved in ten years! Still had a fishing rod in one hand, a cigarette in the other, paintbox beside him, and a paperback. I could even make out the title.

Ten years back, or more, was it, when me, Mum, and Dad lived on the boat? Dad often docked here. Would I have been twelve or so? Dad sailed off again, lord knows where, and me and Mum lounged on the beach. Told her I'd seen Dad talking to this tall man with a fishing rod. He's handsome, I said, and she snapped at me, keep away from him!

Why? I said. Dad took him out on our boat, I saw him. He knows Dad.

Exactly, she said. Mumbled it. What do you mean? I said, and she hissed at me - he's more than twice your age!

You're not much more than twice mine! I hissed back – she slapped me so hard across the face I could feel a red bruise forming. When Dad came back, she said I fell. He shot her his sneery look, hard as steel. She turned the same colour as my cheek. We know what to expect, Mum and me.

Ten years? Feels like a hundred.

In Almyrida tonight, he was at a table, by himself, the same man, in the next taverna. The waiters speak Greek to him and seem pally. He looks, I don't know, deeper? Or are we just older, both of us? He's reading Jack Kerouac's 'On the Road'.

If I ask to borrow it, he might remember me.

Then who knows?

Batten ran his finger down the page, discoloured by, what? Raki? Ouzo? Red wine more likely, from the stains. The leather binding was dry and cracked, from being left in the sun. For all the sense it's made so far, he thought, it might as well have been left in the snow, up in the White Mountains. He pushed the journal towards Grigoris.

'I look, Sig, before.'

'You *glanced*, Makis. There's three hundred pages. She kept a journal, on and off, for years.'

'And you must read *all*?' said Grigoris, hands in the air in mock-horror.

'Every word,' said Batten, with a moustached smile of his own. 'Only two hundred and ninety pages to go. It's evidence.' The smile faded. 'And there's sod-all else.'

'Except her copse, Sig.'

Batten didn't correct him. A corpse is a corpse - all Queen Mab could be. A dead corpse, with the dead fairies, and he had to know why. In the silent lull of morning, his foot tap-tapped, faster, on the sandy taverna floor.

*

Breakfast over, Grigoris straggled after Batten on his convalescent walk along the beach by the tiny harbour, where a scattering of pleasure craft rocked at anchor beside a forlorn fishing boat, paintwork a faded blue, nets coiled on its deck like piles of old rope. Batten caught the faint whiff of salt and fish. Despite his hat, salty sweat prickled his forehead and neck.

'To coalesce, Sig, you must walk in the *sun*? You crazy as the weather!'

Grigoris refused to understand the English walking cure, sighing in mock dismay when Batten turned up the track leading to the clifftop.

'Hill is for walking *down*, Sig, not up! This man who knock your head, he waste his time. Your brain, it already *kaput*!'

Instinctively, Batten fingers touched the bone mound on his skull, a permanent reminder of damage done by a steel cosh. He shook away Doc Fallon's warning - that another sharp crack to the skull would knock him out of CID forever, and maybe out of the world. If as Grigoris said, he was *coalescing*, Crete was a fine place for it. Batten had fallen in love with the island the first time he stayed with Grigoris, after the two men worked on an extradition case.

'I find place for you to sleep, Sig,' the rich Greek voice had said down the phone. 'An apartment, in Almyrida. It overlook the sea.'

Batten had mentioned 'Almyrida' cropping up in Queen Mab's journal, with no expectation his Greek friend's *xenophilia* would find him somewhere to stay there.

'Almyrida, very fine place, Sig. Near Souda Bay. Small, pretty. Sea before, White Mountain above. Apartment my cousin's. He away in Thessaloniki.'

'I've lost count of how many cousins you have, Makis.'

'Ah, cousins, Sig. *Useful.*'

Gazing across the bay at the flat calm of the glass-smooth sea, Batten said, 'you should move here, to this very spot, Makis. What a view...it takes my breath away.'

'This *hill* take *my* breath away, Sig. And I must move? Why so? Sea is sea. Same sea in Panormos. You been. You know.'

Twice, Batten had enjoyed Cretan hospitality at the Grigoris family home, near Panormos, twenty miles to the East. If not for building repairs, he would be staying in Panormos now. But Almyrida was where Queen Mab lived, all those years ago. Why this place, when the same sea cloaked the entire coast of Crete? Grigoris read his thoughts.

'You so...transparent, Sig. This thug who knock your head, he spoil your brain! You think, my Queen Mab, she stand in this very place. She say, *ah, look, beautiful marvellous wonderful blue-green sea.* Tuh, you so English! Sea here always this colour. But you, you stare at blue-green sea like it a unicorn!'

'Maybe she did stand here, Makis. And maybe the unicorn was a horse.'

Batten pointed across the road to a walled enclosure. Ears and a scruffy mane poked above the parapet. On his daily walk, Batten brought an apple-core for the ragged-maned creature. Stroking its stubbly neck was soothing to both beast and detective. Grigoris spotted a mound of loose hay and a water bucket, shaded by the wall.

'Horse already fed, Sig. You fly all the way to Crete, with...what you call it? *Pudding?*'

Batten's apple-core disappeared in a single crunch. 'Living things, Makis. They need care. You and me, we spend too much time with the dead.'

Grigoris shrugged his broad shoulders. 'Dead or alive, Sig, your Queen Mab not feed this horse. It not born when she in Almyrida. It not even a fool.'

'A foal. You mean a foal, Makis.'

In his appalling cod-English accent, Grigoris drawled, '*my deepest apologies, old chap. A genuine error on my part, don't you know.*' His own rich voice added, 'and *you* mean 'Kalimera' in the taverna today when you speak to waiter. No wonder he stare at you when you say, 'Calamari'. He expect 'Good Morning' – but you, you order fried squid!'

The horse's ears twitched as two old friends chuckled like schoolboys. 'I'm feeling better.'

'Good, Sig. Because this journal, this *book* - three hundred pages! Maybe you think, ah, on page two hundred ninety-nine, Queen Mab she dip a finger in her own blood and write who kill her? You crazy! Maybe later you read it. Or maybe we go for lunch, read menu instead.'

They laughed all the way back to the beach, the horse staring after them in equine disregard, pushing its nose at the bucket to sluice up water. It was far too young to have lifted apples from the palm of Queen Mab.

But the previous horses, dead now, had chomped apples from her hand, whinnying as she fluttered her fingers through their manes, untroubled by glints of sunlight flashing from hands adorned by six silver rings.

'Shhh,' she'd told the horses, her head cocked sideways, half-smile on her lips. 'Shhh, now,' her voice liquid silver. 'Be thankful for apples and sun. And look, down there, a blue-green sea to bring you hope. And to heal you.'

*

Sergeant Ball glared at the sea of files on his desk. If only I smoked, he thought, I'd carry matches. Could set fire to this lot. Reaching for the topmost file, his hand veered off to grab the ringing phone.

'Yes?' he snapped. Reception had taken a call, they said. *Oh, really?*

41

How unusual! A woman, they said. Sounded old. Needed to speak to a detective. *I'm not a detective, I'm a filing clerk!* Yes, they'd taken her details. How urgent? Moderately, she'd said. In that case, not today! He clattered the phone back on its receiver.

CID HQ was quiet as a grave, everyone out chasing crooks, except him. *Today,* he was a Sergeant-Inspector-Detective Constable-filing clerk. And could say goodbye to lunch – just like *yesterday.* He dragged his stare from the sea of files to Batten's empty office. Beyond the glass, a bare, polished desk stared back at him.

Convalesce faster! he hissed, dragging the topmost file towards him.

*

Much to the dismay of his Greek friend, Batten said no to a long, slow lunch.

'You filled my fridge with an entire Mediterranean diet, Makis. I shan't starve.'

'It is this *book* of hers, Sig! You in love with it! Maybe you in love with *her*!'

'She's a 'copse', Makis. Too dead to love. The journal may tell me why, tell me who she is.'

'*Is*, Sig? *Is*? Your Queen Mab, she is a *was!* And I, Lieutenant Makis Grigoris, *I* know who she really was. Was *English!* So, she *thin.* She just like you - not *eat!*'

Batten pulled a key from his pocket and unlocked the heavy door. 'Lunch tomorrow?'

'Tomorrow, I am dead, from hunger.'

'Afroditi won't let that happen. And give her my love.' Grigoris had married 'best cook in all of Greece.' There was some truth in the claim.

When they shook hands, Grigoris held on to Batten's fingers, his eyes serious, the familiar smile gone. 'Sig, you promise me to rest, endaxi? You get well, yes? Not stay up all night reading of your Queen Mab? Some time, we must stop being police.'

Batten's smile faded too. 'That's my fear, Makis - *stopping being police.* It's all I know. What else would I do?'

'You move here, Sig!' smiled Grigoris. 'My cousin, he find you job!'

'Greece is my *second* favourite country in the world, Makis, but…'

'But, Sig? But? Always a but, with you! *But,* tonight, do not read three-hundred pages. Is crazy. Rest, sleep. *Heal.*'

'Don't worry, Makis. I will.'

But when Batten closed the door, both men had their doubts.

Eight

On the balcony of the little apartment in the cool shade of a canopy of vines, Batten spread his long frame onto a cushioned recliner and reached for the off-the-shelf reading glasses he'd bought in Chania - without telling Grigoris. Approaching his fortieth birthday was bad enough, and a dangerous lump on his skull far worse. But admitting he needed specs? *To Grigoris?*

He would have bought prescription glasses but for a fear of medicos in white coats who blew air at your eyeballs and made you read letters aloud, like at Primary school. Queen Mab's handwriting, despite its neat loops and curls, was tiny, and strained his eyes. Slipping on the specs, he opened the journal.

In his cubby-hole office in Parminster, a clamour of phone calls, keyboards and CID bustle would have surrounded him. Here he was alone, foreign, with only the rustle of birds and the faint susurration of the waves below. He wondered if Queen Mab heard the same sounds when she covered fresh white paper in tiny whorls of script.

Andros let me go with him again today, fishing. Only fisherman who would. Almyrida is even more beautiful from the bay. The White Mountains rising and falling in the distance. I love the little boats and the smell of the nets.

Hate the yachts though. Below-deck tight enough to crush me. And at night, that slap-slap of the sea against the hull – you're close to the deep, says the slap. Little boats seem closer to the sky, a promise of stars.

A little boat, me.

Watched Andros from the tiny wheelhouse and poured foul-tasting raki for him. Ouzo better, he said, but cost double. I'll buy him a bottle, as thanks.

He catches every size of fish but only smiles at the big ones. Ask what they're called, he says money-fish.

Time stops, on the sea. No sense of the past, thank God. I need to be

free like Andros, but it's men who run the boats. Women in the
kitchen, here. And, of course, the bedroom.
I wonder when Daniel will return.

Batten couldn't remember reading this before. He jotted down questions.

Daniel who? Ever identified? Still in Almyrida?
Andros, the fisherman? Still alive?

Tomorrow, he would ask Grigoris, who knew everyone. And since everyone knew Grigoris was police, they were quick to cooperate – which made a change. Batten had begun to wonder if GMT really did mean Greek Maybe Time.

Unhooking the specs to rub sore eyes, the sunlight flashed, burned, and blurred his vision, without warning. Sudden darkness turned his eyeballs whiter than the journal's pages. Under the canopy of vines, he tumbled to a place somewhere between sleep and trauma.

The darkness of dream floated him back to a pitch-black English Easter and the *thwack!* of a cosh gripped in drugged-up vengeful hands…till Doc Fallon's fingers entered the dream, pressing down so firmly his shoulders jerked up at the sharpness of the hurt. Then the acid ache dulled to the thrum of an aeroplane, his dream spinning him back to the flight to Crete, strapped into seat 9F, sipping fizzy water from the overpriced bottle bought in Departures…

…Warned off strong spirits, he shook his head at the stewardess and watched the drinks trolley rattle between the plane's half-empty rows towards the raised finger of the passenger in the seat behind.

Queen Mab's case file lurked in the backpack at Batten's feet, but he could hardly peruse crime-scene photos here, with the man behind mere inches away. So repugnant were the images, a single glance would curdle gin.

Instead, he kept at bay the cold sweat of flying by opening the journal. He was pushing boundaries to have it, the stained pages almost shameful, like every unsolved case he'd ever touched.

Three years ago, when the Queen Mab murder fizzled down a Somerset road to nowhere, the journal was a brown leather brick, ignored. Now, he firmly agreed with the opening line.

Soon as I learned to write, I should have kept a journal.

Had Queen Mab recorded her beginnings, the investigation into her end might have progressed. *Then progress it!* he told himself.

He scanned pages at random, because 'at random' was Queen Mab's method, too. After the hopeful tone of page one, she seemed to open the journal at whatever blank page coincided with her thumb and inked in a jumble of thoughts of the day or memories of the past. Batten searched for any kind of flow - dates, events, places, names - and spotted Parminster.

Dad's disappeared.
Don't know what I'm supposed to feel. Him and his boat went down and Mum swears she doesn't know where or why. Doesn't care, she says.
She's ditched Crete and moved me and Sue to England. But Somerset? And Parminster? We don't know a soul there, and no-one knows **us.** *Can't wave your arm without colliding with an apple tree - but sod-all else. My classmates, even their A Level essays have a yokel accent!*
Mum says, things will settle down. Huh, **I** *won't. Can't stop me leaving, now I'm 18. Even uni's better than here. In the vacs she'll mistake me for germs and take to her bed. Me, cook, bottle-washer and Sue's child minder. Again. Happy families – what crap.*
Sue's from another world. She's got a beau - five years old and she's fixed up! Took him to school as well. Sue and her big chunky lad called...his name's gone already. My made-up name for him is Quentin because a Quentin he's defo not! Wish I'd had a broad-shouldered beau to protect me, when I was five.
Wish I still had one, a beau.

Beau. What a starry word.

The next few entries rambled between Greece and Somerset. Would Queen Mab pop up in Batten's native Yorkshire too? On the next page, it was Greece.

Fourteen when my beau first laid me down. At the school, in Crete.
*Well, not **at** the school – the staff would've turned purple!*
Sneaked down to the beach, where it meets the trees. Our private bed,
under the stars. So dark, the trees, that night.
But the stars. Oh, the stars, the stars.
My first beau, Darren. Darren Pope. Made up a name for him too -
The Dazzler. A bright star above me, pressing down. Saw every
diamond-white star in the universe, that night - every star shining
just for me.
I needed Darren, the starry Dazzler. Dad couldn't stomach him.
Little wanker - Dad's name for big Darren, in his sneery voice. I'll
take the shine off you, you little wanker!
When I was fourteen. Fourteen. Gone.
Hated it.
And who took the stars?

The twenty-something stewardess flashed a lips-only smile as she rolled the drinks trolley back up the aisle. Batten automatically clocked the frontier on her neck where foundation had failed to blend in, the flat cheekbones and bottle-blonde hair. Barbie pushing a pram, and doing her best, he thought, but no Rose Linnet. What did Jess Foreman say? *When He made Rose, I tell you, God was concentrating.*

He tried switching off detective mode, but within seconds the aircraft's hum switched him back on, and soon he was scribbling:

Rose, age 14 – at school in Crete? Rose age 18 - A levels in Somerset?
Mother – why leave Crete? Why Somerset?
Father – disappeared?
Two kids. Rose and Sue. What happened to Sue?
Darren Pope, Rose's 'beau' – where?

When Batten cross-referenced to the police files, the father's name popped up in the search for Queen Mab's next of kin – then popped permanently down. Abe Linnet was officially presumed drowned, in the Mediterranean, the report said.

Batten wondered if Abe's body lay beneath the patio in the Linnets' crumbling house in Parminster, but he disappeared long before Mrs Linnet - Gina – moved to Somerset. The cack-handed investigation failed to ask why Gina suddenly fled from Crete, or where she found ready cash to buy a detached hamstone house in Parminster. Nor why the house fell into disrepair at much the same rate as Gina Linnet.

In the buzz of cabin noise, Batten's mind buzzed too, turning to the list of persons of interest - a short read, with Gina dead and Abe presumed so. Apart from Sue Linnet, only Darren Pope warranted a mention – and not because his name appeared in the journal George Halfpenny barely glanced at.

Searching Queen Mab's rotting house, the police found a grubby envelope written in Rose Linnet's unmistakeable hand, and bearing Darren's name, No letter, just an unstamped, unsent envelope, with an address in Australia. Batten stared at the photocopy, another teaser in the pile – but a detective more diligent than George Halfpenny had contacted someone called Brad, an Australian police liaison officer.

That address is rubble, said Brad's reply. But the follow-up had possibilities.

Darren Pope, born in Crete, Greece. English parents. Emigrated to Sydney, age16. Big fella. Now wanted for knife crime and ABH. No recent sightings. File flagged as 'approach with caution'. Whereabouts unknown.

The same diligent detective must have ploughed on because Batten found a follow-up. 'If he's such a *big fella*, why no sightings?' Brad's reply was a single terse line: 'Have you any concept of the *size* of Australia?'

Well, I'm not flying *there*, thought Batten, glancing through the window at mountain tops below and fighting off an image of the plane spiralling unstoppably towards them, his white knuckles clamping an oxygen mask to a face made entirely of screams. To fend off fear, he closed his eyes, trying to conjure up an image of Darren Pope.

Had such an image appeared, Batten would have seen a six-foot-and-plenty giant of a man, older now but muscled. And had the police photo ever been filed, Batten would have seen a pair of hard steel eyes in a once handsome face. Though Batten did not know it, the liaison officer's 'approach with caution' was sound advice even before Darren went on the run, when his stamping ground was the dubious Sydney underworld…

…So brown with age the letter, Darren could barely read it. But he'd read it so often he knew each word by heart. *Heart? Huh!* He opened the door of his ute and spat the thought onto the road. Sliding the flimsy paper back into its envelope, he revved the engine.

The Sydney traffic was worse today, stop-start, a crawl of bored elbows jutting from windows, the air sandwiched between tall city buildings, thick and hot.

'I love you, Dazzler…'

A tailgating car blared its horn as Darren dawdled. When he turned in his seat to flash two steel eyes at the driver, the horn shut its mouth. How many letters had he written to Rose? Or at least to Lucy, Rose's friend in Crete, who said she'd pass them on?

'Lost count,' he said to no-one.

Write to me, Rose. Write to me in Australia. Explain. One letter, from all their time in Crete, him and Rose, and what did it matter if they were young?

The letter's tiny curls, shabby with age, haunted Darren's face in the rear-view mirror.

'I love you, Darren, I need you…to protect us, me and the baby…'

Love? Kisses and love? Then why did suspicion still gnaw at his innards? He did not have the words to explain his doubts. If muscle was his strength, words were his weakness, always. *WHAT DID YOU DO TO MY BABY, YOU BITCH?*

He spat the word *love* onto the road, the driver in the adjacent lane almost gibing a comment. When Darren's storm-cloud face warned him off, in came the elbow, up went the window, eyes on nothing but the road ahead.

'Kiss, kiss, kiss…your Rose.'

If Rose came here to Sydney, he'd kiss her alright. Kiss her so hard she'd never wake up. He spat *kiss* on the road this time, shoving the one letter the bitch ever wrote back into his jeans, the brown tattered words a boiling cauldron. *I could've had a life*, Darren snarled to himself. *A child! I could've been a family – whatever that is!*

As the traffic crawled forward, drivers either side pretended to ignore an eighteen stone giant with a face like rock, and what looked like anger carved into his eyeballs.

They were wrong.

It was revenge.

An over-loud tannoy message warned of imminent turbulence. Seat belt already pulled tight, a flimsy comfort blanket strapping him in, 30,000 feet above solid ground, Batten screwed the cap back on his water bottle and closed his eyes…

…When he came to, confused and prone on his padded recliner, he imagined he was still in the clouds, flying. Only when a Cretan sunset haloed the far headland did he remember he was in Almyrida. Dazed, he watched the sea bleed orange and red before turning a deep grey-green as night sneaked into the sky.

He gulped down cold water. Queen Mab's journal lay on the floor, open at the random page he'd been reading, next to the scribbled notes he could barely remember - a list of people who bumped up against Queen Mab, only to disappear. So far, Gina Linnet was the sole person with a standard death certificate. He scanned the other names.

Sue Linnet?
Abe Linnet?
Daniel Somebody?
Darren Pope?

Like Queen Mab, were they 'with the fairies' too?

Before he knew it, the journal was back in his hands and he re-read the entry.

Told Daniel I went off sex for a while. I've buried the reasons.
Completely fooled me, he said – so I pinched him, hard.
Shall we more pleasurably continue? he asked. I pretended to think about it. He fucks like he speaks. Cultured, educated, even after wine. I copy his voice sometimes, like the girl from Pygmalion - for gender equality, of course!
Paint me with your biggest brush, I commanded.
But is the canvas prepared? he said. Those artist fingers, tingling my skin.
Oh, just a canvas, am I? Yes, says he, and aching for paint?
Stop waffling then, I said, and paint. Painted each other, all night.
Then began again.

Batten snapped the journal closed, locked the balcony doors and staggered to bed, alone.

Nine

More dreams disturbed his sleep. The soft mattress became Erin, before shapeshifting into Dr Sonia Welcome. When she in turn morphed into Rose Linnet, he woke in a sweat, sunrise taunting the curtains.

A staccato ring on his doorbell was unmistakably Grigoris, who had two levels of insistence: a breezy Greek bustle which Batten could flick away with an eyebrow; and an unsmiling ultimatum, impossible to refuse. Today, the latter.

'No police-police for you, Sig. No staring at wonderful-marvellous-blue-green-sea, or big Queen Mab journal that make your eye hurt so much you buy spectacles!'

Batten sighed. Grigoris missed nothing.

'I am your taxi. We go to Ancient Aptera, it not far. You will see beauty, Greek, Roman, more. To take off your mind.'

'A school trip is it, Makis? Will there be a test?'

'Test? Yes, there will be lunch, after. You don't eat, you fail!'

A laughing Grigoris bundled Batten into his big Nissan and off they went, climbing through stony hills clothed in wild herbs, blotches of oleander in dark-pink and white, and ubiquitous lines of one olive tree after another.

'You know how many olive trees in Crete, Sig? Thirty-five million! We not run out.'

'Counted them, have you?'

'Ena, dio, tria, tessera, pente – ah, I think I miss one!'

The irresistible force of Grigoris eased Queen Mab aside and they laughed all the way along a dusty, straight road beyond the modern-day village of Aptera to an entrance kiosk framed by mountains and sea. The vast archaeological site was almost deserted. Batten handed over a few euros and in they went.

For twenty minutes Grigoris's claim that Ancient Aptera 'will take off your mind' proved blissfully true. Batten dreamed his way beyond massive stone cisterns, built by the Romans over earlier Hellenistic structures, which in turn lay above Minoan origins.

'You sit here please, and wait, yes?' Grigoris pointed to a curve of stone seats, rising up and around the open-air Romanised theatre, recently excavated from the hillside. Batten sat, while Grigoris crossed the dry sand of the theatre floor. Reaching a stone plinth at the centre, he whispered, 'You hear me, Sig?'

Batten shot to his feet, looking for the microphones. The natural acoustics made the bare whisper ring like a tuned bell.

'You hear me now?' This time, Grigoris raised his voice to engage an imaginary full house, declaiming half a dozen lines of pure poetry, in rich-sounding Greek. 'That was from Sophocles, Sig. Famous Greek playwright, two thousand and five hundred years ago. At school, we learn by heart. I choose it, especial.'

'Makis, it's all Greek to me.'

'You do not know *Oedipus? Oedipus the King*?' Grigoris turned away in a mock huff. 'All civilised person know *Oedipus the King!*'

'I don't know it in *Greek*, do I? Can't you translate?'

'Of course I translate! I speak Greek *and* English! You, you speak only Yorkshire!'

When the laughter stopped, Grigoris explained, 'King Oedipus is talking with Creon, his brother-in-law, about the previous king, who was killed. But they do not know the reason.'

'Or the killer,' said Batten, twigging why Grigoris brought him here.

''Is so. You will see why my choice. Creon speaks first. Listen, please.' Once more Grigoris became an ancient actor, arm pointing at the sky, accented English hammy but crystal clear.

'The gods command it.
We must bring the unknown murderer to justice.'

With a wink, Grigoris added, 'then King Oedipus, he say,

'But where shall he be found? What trace may we uncover
Of that far-distant crime?''

Batten smiled at the wily Grigoris, wrapping a 21st Century killing in an ancient Greek play.

'Then, Sig, this Creon he answer,

'Seek, and ye shall find. For what goes undetected,
Must be *unearthed*."

The ironies teemed out, in this excavated city where Nature's sound system rang with the poetry of Heroes, Gods, Kings and Queens. And me, what use am I? Batten thought. Not even a lowly detective just now. He applauded Grigoris, who gave a mock bow and enthroned himself on a stone seat.

'We Greeks have much culture, Sig. You English, you steal it, like your Lord Elgin steal our marble statues from the Parthenon!'

Batten smiled, despite Queen Mab's unearthed riddle echoing round the theatre. If only its stones could whisper the name of the 'unknown murderer' who slit the throat of an ageing eccentric sleeping beneath the stars by choice and - body odour apart - doing harm to no-one.

An elbow nudged him. Grigoris pointed to the plinth at the amphitheatre's centre. 'And now is your turn, Sig.'

Batten pulled a face. 'Dramatics? Definitely *not*. Definitely not my sort of thing.'

'Thing? *Thing?* I give you Sophocles, and you give me *thing*! Stand! Speak!'

'I'm not an actor-detective like you, Makis. Right now, I'm not even a detective. I'm...sort of private.'

'*Private*? You like to know the history of these people, yes?' Grigoris flipped an arm at the invisible population of ancient Aptera. 'These Greeks, these Romans, who build this city and live and die here? You want to know of *them*, but not want others to know of *you*? Because your history, it *private*? Humph.'

Shamed, Batten wondered if Grigoris was right. Too private a man in a public world, where lives - and deaths - were too much on display? Was he a shadowy archaeologist, unearthing the secrets of others - or a plain and simple voyeur? Blowing out his breath, he loped across the sandy floor and stood in the centre. 'Here?' he asked, his voice immediately reverberating up the slope and beyond. 'Oh, wow. You're right, Makis. The acoustics are *amazing.*'

'Then speak, Sig. No-one is here.'

It was true. Batten stared all around. They had the entire auditorium to themselves, in windless morning sunshine.

'This audience, he is impatient, Sig,' said Grigoris, folding his arms.

'I've forgotten my Sophocles, Makis.' *But I'll get my own back.* 'What about Shakespeare? Do you know *Romeo and Juliet*? I did it for A Level.'

'*Romeo and Juliet*? Of course! I see Leonardo Capricornio, in the movie! Twice! Now, speak!'

Batten cleared his throat. The Queen Mab file, gathering dust on the 'unsolved' rack, first caught his eye for literary reasons. Snippets of Mercutio's famous speech, mocking the love-sick Romeo, came back to him. With a jibe at Grigoris, he spoke what he could remember.

'O, then, I see *Queen Mab* hath been with you.
She is the fairies' midwife, and she comes
In shape no bigger than an agate-stone
On the forefinger of an alderman…'

He'd forgotten what followed. 'Wait…wait.

'This is that very Mab
That plaits the manes of horses in the night…Er…"

With a flourish, Batten declaimed the last few lines he could recall.

'Her chariot is an empty hazelnut…er…
And in this state she gallops night by night
Through lovers' brains, and then they dream of love.'

'She gallop through *your* brain, too, Sig - what brain you have left. I bring you here, this place of much history, and what you do? You dream of your Queen Mab!'

What Batten 'dreamed' was a question: through whose brains did Queen Mab gallop? Darren Pope's, wherever they were? Or Daniel's, whoever he was? Or someone else? Did Rose Linnet make them dream of love - or was it the other way round?

'Sorry, Makis,' Batten said, his voice bell-like in the remarkable acoustics, 'but Oedipus the King's not the only tragedy. Queen Mab's a tragedy too, and I don't like the ending. Sophocles was right – *the gods command it, we must bring the unknown murderer to justice!*'

Grigoris gave a gentle nod of understanding, before turning his back in mock disgust and pretending to vex himself towards the car. Over his shoulder he sniped, 'and now, Sig, the gods command we *eat!*

Ten

While Grigoris and Batten drove to their lunchtime taverna, Sergeant Ball sweated without a break at his Parminster desk, a half-chewed apple and a mug of cold tea by his elbow - beside a mountain of folders and a spinning clock. The unsolved 'Queen Mab' casefile sat untouched by his feet.

'I'm running out of hands,' he told himself – as DC Hick's sharp finger jabbed him between the shoulder-blades.

'*Hickie! I've got ears!* Even you can manage a short sentence when your mouth's not full of bacon sandwich!'

'Sorry, Sarge. There's someone needs sorting, in reception.'

'*Then sort!*'

'Can't, Sarge. I'm on a call. Sheep-theft-with-violence. Near Stembridge.'

Hick collided with a waste basket and disappeared. Ball scanned the silent desks. Nina Magnus, seconded to a squad tracking crooks with a liking for Land Rovers. DC Hazel Timms, due back soon from compassionate leave, having buried both her parents in the space of three weeks. George Halfpenny's still-empty desk, awaiting a new owner. Ball glared at Batten's cubby-hole office – empty, silent, door closed.

He phoned reception. It's the old lady who rang before, they said. The one you promised to contact. With a tinge of guilt, he trudged to meet her, but when he set eyes on the bent, spectral frame of Maud Cotter, he thought twice before ushering her to an interview room. A hospital ward might be best. Or a morgue.

'I apologise, Sergeant, for disturbing you,' she said, in a thin, breathy voice. 'I should have volunteered sooner, and in truth, cancer has decided for me. I lack the time for procrastination.'

His visitor's resemblance to a ghost explained, Ball relaxed the fists he couldn't remember clenching, and pulled out a chair for her. She sat down in slow motion, took in the chipped table and puke-green walls without comment, and began telling her story. In the middle.

'You see, old Mr Billingham died at the same time she did. That's the reason I felt I must come.'

'Sorry, Miss…Cotter. Who are we talking about?'

'Why, Queen Mab. I only know her as Queen Mab. I never knew her real name. Nor anyone in Parminster who did.'

Ball knew. Rose. Rose Linnet. 'Queen Mab' only when her real name ceased to be any use to her. 'And Mr Billingham?' he asked.

'Yes. A lovely man. I worked for him. But he died, suddenly, the same week *she* died. Well, killed, wasn't she? I read about it. And with the storage facility in chaos…'

'Er, storage facility?'

'Oh, I worked for Billingham's Self Storage. Perhaps you know of it, near Langport? I worked there, well, till I couldn't. I should have said something at the time, but it was turmoil. Indeed, it's no longer Billingham's. The son, William, took over. He never liked the name. It's Camelot Self-Storage now. William, I'm afraid, lives in Glastonbury.'

'And you came here today because…?'

'Oh. Conscience? Or is it memory? I sometimes think they're the same. Do you see?'

All Sergeant Ball could see was his desk with 'urgent' gouged into the wood.

'Regardless of Mr Billingham's passing, I'm not sure I *could* have said anything. Because of confidentialities. After all, people pay good money for their privacy. But if I break a confidence now, you'll have to be rather sprightly to prosecute, won't you?'

She managed a half-smile. Ball began to like her.

'Um, saying what you know?'

'About your Queen Mab. More or less in her right mind when she came into Billingham's, to rent her storage unit. Her behaviour not *very* disconcerting and no air-freshener required so she must have made the effort to wash. Normally, you could smell her from the other end of the High Street, poor soul.' Maud Cotter gazed into space for a moment or two. 'I smell now, sometimes,' she said, 'but that's the cancer, and frankly I don't care.'

Big hands gripping the chipped table, Ball swerved round the awkwardness. 'Queen Mab rented a storage unit, you say?'

'She still does, in a manner of speaking. She paid in advance, in cash. Five years, as I recall. So, not yet spent up, if my maths is correct?'

'Five years? And she paid up front?'

'Oh, sometimes they do, to secure a unit. People working abroad, for example. Or if they're uncertain of the future. *Mine* is rather too certain.'

Ball allowed a moment's silence to hang, for decency's sake, wondering why Queen Mab might have been 'uncertain of the future'.

'Is it normal to pay in cash?'

'Not unheard of. And her unit was a cupboard really, with a reinforced door and a light switch. Mr Billingham always insisted on good value. Young William, humph, he doubled the tariffs, overnight. Before, hers was eight pounds a week, as I recall. Hardly a fortune.'

Ball did the sums. Five years at eight quid a week...Two grand, in cash. Where did it come from? And why store *anything,* when you live alone in a house with enough empty rooms to start a storage facility of your own? Maud Cotter's stick was tap-tapping on the floor, from tremor, not impatience. All the same, Ball hurried up. 'Whatever Queen Mab stored at Billingham's -'

'At Camelot. William renamed it.'

'Camelot, sorry. But whatever she stored, it's still there?'

'I imagine so. Unless the legal profession has reclaimed her chattels. I sometimes liaised with probate lawyers and the like. Otherwise, a unit remains secure till the money runs out. Naturally, we warn the owners well in advance. In her case, alas... You'll get a subpoena or something?'

Ball had no wish to subpoena a cupboard. A search warrant was added to his list, and a dig into Queen Mab's last will and testament. If he ever found the time.

'How would she have got in and out? Of the storage unit?'

'Young William is threatening to update the system,' she replied, with disapproval. 'Electronic switches, tuh, modernity. But renters have a little brass key. I imagine hers is still around, somewhere?'

'And they just drive in and out, do they?'

'Goodness, no. Can you imagine the chaos?' Maud Cotter managed a small chuckle, which immediately became a dry, sad cough. 'No, they book a time, show ID and the security guard checks them in.'

'CCTV?' Ball's eyebrows rose in hope.

'Her stick twitched. 'Not after all this time…'

'And who controls the gate?'

'Whoever is duty security. It's an agency.'

'But the security man -'

'- Or woman.'

'The security *staff*, they'd be able to identify whoever entered Queen Mab's unit? Assuming it wasn't her?' He knew he was clutching at straws. So did Maud Cotter, who shook her head.

'Hundreds and hundreds of people, Sergeant. And different guards. None, I imagine, with a photographic memory?'

Silently, Ball piled more legwork onto his list, with an obvious concern. A search warrant could only reveal what Queen Mab locked away if it was still there.

When Maud Cotter saw the distant expression on his face, she pushed down on her stick and struggled to her feet. Ball would have mumbled the standard phrase, 'in future, should anything occur to you,' but at the sight of her doomed frame… He helped her from the chair.

'I appreciate you grappling with your conscience, Miss Cotter, even if it meant breaking a trust.' In a conspiratorial stage whisper, he added, 'between you and me, I don't expect we'll prosecute.'

She managed a dry chuckle and made to limp away.

'How did you get here?' he asked. If she drove, he might *have* to prosecute.

'On a pair of buses, Sergeant. A kind lady told me the numbers and I hopped on. Except of course I didn't *hop*.' She shuffled towards the door till Ball gently touched her arm.

'I'll make sure someone drives you back.'

When he ducked his head into the CID office, it was empty.

'I'll bring my car round,' he said, swallowing a sigh.

*

Grigoris pretended to breeze through life, when really he worked like a ferret. The following day, his finger on the doorbell spoke of how well he understood Batten's need to pull on a loose thread. Not only had he tracked down Andros Antonakis, Rose Linnet's fisherman-friend, he knew where best to tackle him, and when.

'Late afternoon, Sig, is *ouzaki* time, in Crete. I learn he is fond of ouzo, this Andros. Our chance to oil the witness?'

When Grigoris pointed him out, in the dusty kafeneion at the far end of Almyrida, Batten saw one old man amongst several, dressed in faded clothes, sandals on bare feet, iced coffee or glasses of wine or ouzo on the wooden tables before them. The speckled grey stubble on Andros's chin could be a beard or an aversion to razors.

Andros Antonakis had claws for hands, scarred by nets and salt, his fingers twirling a set of worry beads, ends held together by a blue glass charm in the shape of an evil eye. When they shook hands, the sea seemed to burst into Batten's veins and flood them with brine.

Grigoris warned that Andros spoke some English but didn't care to. 'I will translate, in good faith,' he said. 'But first, ouzo.'

When the added water turned the ouzo milky-white, Andros nodded his head in approval, crinkling eyes fixed on the glass. When his lips followed, a smile of pleasure lit his face. Grigoris had ordered the good stuff.

Short sentences croaked out, punctuated by ouzo and nibbled olives and cubes of feta.

'Andros remember Rose,' said Grigoris. 'She beautiful. Speak with him when others not. He take her on his boat, she sail well. He say she have silver hands. A silver ring on every finger, except the...?' Grigoris waggled his fourth finger at Batten.

'The pinkie?'

'Ah, yes, pinkie. Six big silver rings. Hands that sparkle when she move. Andros say the waiters, in the taverna, they joke she a silver witch.' More ouzo-scented Greek spluttered out. 'But she no witch, he say. Kind, soft. Skin not like iron, not salt. Not like his.'

Andros put down his glass and gently raised a hand to his face, speech slowing. 'Before she leave, she touch my cheek, here, he say, like no-one ever touch.' A flash of something tender glinted from the old fisherman's salty eyes. 'I want to drown, he say, to stop time, always to remember her touch.'

Did Rose gallop through the brain of Andros, too, Batten wondered, and make him dream of love? 'Were he and she, um, you know?' he asked, forgetting that Andros understood. A splutter of coarse laughter led to a shake of the head, followed by a slow, melodious trickle of broken English, so fond Batten heard the poetry in it.

'She young, I too old. She honey, I salt. She paint, I fish. I Greek, she not.'

Andros stared at his glass with regret – perhaps because it was empty, perhaps because of Rose.

'Did you call her Queen Mab?' Batten's direct question triggered more puzzlement, and a return to Greek.

'He not know this name, Sig. He call her Rose, sometime call her Linnet, when on the boat she sing to him.'

Queen Mab and Rose Linnet. English rose. Songbird. Away-with-the-Fairies Queen. Batten wanted to know which it was. 'She sang to you?' he asked.

Andros nodded. 'On the boat,' he said. 'English songs. Her Greek not so good.' With a sound like ouzo on a rusty hinge, Andros gave a short rendition of the old Chris de Burgh hit, *Lady in Red*. At the next table, a clutch of Greeks, ancient and modern, became a gentle mocking chorus, grinning as they swayed to the rhythm, croaking the wrong lyrics in accented English.

'Lay-deee in ree-eed
Plee-eese dance with meee
Nobod-dee elllse
Just you and meeee…'

Ignoring the ragged applause, Andros said, 'Rose, she sing this song many time.'

'Did Rose wear red?' asked Batten.

'Red? Much red. Later, less,' said Andros. 'She never say why.'

Not the only thing 'she never say', thought Batten, wondering who was on her mind when the song promised never to forget the way you look tonight.

Tapping a leather hand on his chest, Andros stuttered out broken English. 'Here, in the heart, Rose is much sad. When she sad, she not sing.'

'Sad for what?' asked Batten.

Andros shook his head. 'On the boat once, sea calm, flat like this table, she almost tell.' He rubbed a scarred hand on the tabletop. 'Eyes want to speak, tears almost words. But no words come. 'Too long ago,' she say. 'How long?' I ask. 'Too long,' she say. And she pour me raki. For her too. She not like raki. But this time, she drink. And then she drink more.'

When Andros pushed away his empty glass, Grigoris flicked a finger. The three men stared silently at the scrubbed wooden table as the waiter came and went.

'You call her Queen?' asked Andros. 'Rose, she was a *Queen?*'

Grigoris explained her nickname.

'Ah,' said Andros. 'But she could be a Queen. She so…' He found the word in Greek.

'Poised, Sig. Like royalty.'

Andros nodded. 'Royal, yes. Like this.' He held his arm upright. 'But, some days, she stand like…' Dragging himself from his chair, he angled his stubbly chin to one side. 'She lean her head, and her mouth it almost smile, as if I say maybe a joke, maybe not. Rose is sunlight, on the sea, when all is…*chrysafenios?*' He looked to Grigoris for help.

'Golden. Your Queen Mab was golden, he say.'

'Ah, yes. *Golden.*' Andros sat back down, smiling his approval, till the smile faded. 'But sometimes, gold become grey, the sun black, and this same sea, it can drown us.'

'And something was drowning Rose?' asked Batten.

Sipping ouzo, Andros considered the question, tapping a leather finger against his head. 'Rose, in here, is storms.'

'Storms? Caused by what?'

'I think is many things.' Once more Andros tapped his skull. 'But for Rose, there was also a man.'

Before Batten could ask, Andros spat out *Daniel*, gnarled fingers tightening around his glass. 'He English, like you.'

'What, he looked like me?'

'No, no. This man tall, yes, but no moustache. He look like…' Andros reverted to Greek.

'Like an actor, in the movies, with a little cigarette in his fingers,' translated Grigoris. 'Everyone can see he is English. Walk like the English. And not so much younger, then, as you now, Sig.'

'I'm 39. So this man would have been older than her?'

Andros understood. 'Older, yes. Ten years, twelve, more.' After a rueful sip, he slowly set his ouzo on the table. 'But not so old as Andros.'

'Who *was* Daniel?' Batten asked. 'Did he have a second name?'

Andros pondered. 'I not know his other name. He sit on the rocks, he fish. Paint pictures. Some days there, some days gone, like big fish in the sea. You sail close, but not catch him. Everyone know Daniel's name. But nobody know Daniel.'

'Did Rose?'

The shrill laughter of old men from the next table distracted Andros. He looked away, in thought, before turning back, his voice low. 'They lie on beach. I see them from the harbour. They laugh. Kiss. They lay hands, his on her, she on him.' Andros crossed himself. 'I jealous,' he mumbled, scarred fingers clicking his worry beads. Pushing away his half-full glass with something approaching reverence, he gazed up at the two detectives. 'And I think, because you are police and ask so much, I think there is trouble for Rose?'

Grigoris gently placed his hand on the old fisherman's arm, explaining the circumstances in quiet, careful tones. Andros grabbed his ouzo and drained the glass. When Batten made to ask more questions, Grigoris shook his head.

'Slow, Sig. The Greek way. I think an ouzo more, before we talk again.'

While Andros shuffled off to the loo, a journey lengthened by a string of gruff-sounding conversations at every table on the way, Grigoris went to jabber in Greek to the kafenion's owner. Alone, Batten scanned the nearby tables, where groups of Cretans enjoyed the *ouzaki* ritual. At the kafenion's fringes, two or three older men sat alone, one bearded man limping away on his walking stick, its brass tip beating a *click-pause-click* into the pavement, almost in rhythm with Batten's tapping foot.

The noise brought Batten back to life and he slid Queen Mab's journal from his backpack to find the 'Andros' page he'd read before.

We sailed out in flat calm this morning. The chug of the little engine, it feels like sleep, to me.
Is it too calm for the fish? I asked Andros. As usual, a shrug for an answer. Even shrugs while drinking raki, and never spills a drop.
Calm sea, the White Mountains looking down, limestone towers, snow on the peaks. I almost told him.
Used to live up there, I said. A long time ago.
Cold?
Cold even when it was warm. My feet frozen, even in summer. I remember the first time the ice got into them. And never went away..
When? he says.
I wanted warm tears to release me. But the tears pricked my skin like daggers of ice. No words.
When? Andros said.
Long ago, I told him. Long ago. I won't live in the mountains anymore.
Another shrug and he wagged his raki glass. I filled his and the one he keeps for me, that I never use, but I did.
Sharp like tears, the raki, hot in my throat. Such tiny glasses I filled them again. Will raki burn the ice from my feet?
After four more glasses, didn't care.

When Grigoris returned, Batten tucked away the journal to avoid a telling-off. The loo must have swallowed Andros. In England, a witness on a 'comfort break' always irked Batten, but here in Almyrida's dusty warmth, rather than drum impatient fingers on the table, he did what Cretans do: watched the daily parade of humanity strolling by - with a running commentary from Grigoris.

'That big-belly man, there, Sig, is the baker. The fine bread he bake, he also eat - his trousers say so. While we sit here in the sun, he go home, to sleep.'

Batten sympathised, his own sleep patterns upside down since a cosh met his skull. Three middle-aged men, dressed for work, stared at the two cops as they shuffled past, lips moving in mumbles.

'Talking about you, Makis?'

Grigoris rewarded Batten with a look of disdain. 'Sig, Sig, why cannot your ears speak Greek? These men, some others, they talk of me for days now. And also of you!'

'*Me?* I've never seen them before in my life.'

'In this small place, Sig, one policeman is cause for rumour, yes? But *two*? And two *detectives*? One *foreign*? Those men, others, they think we from Europol. Tell everyone we chase smugglers. Think we chase *them*!'

'But not those two?' said Batten, pointing at an older woman with a worn face, trotting in the wake of a teenage boy, his sandals noisily slapping at the ground to make the dust fly up.

'Ah, no. That is Mrs Tsomakis and her son. He is Iannis, poor boy. His head, it was hit by…the lever that steers a boat?'

'The tiller?'

'Ah, yes. The tiller. He is not so good now, Iannis, in the mind.'

'I know how he feels,' Batten said.

'Mrs Tsomakis is a saint, to cope. Poor boy, he is a trial for her. And a thief.'

'Then arrest him, Makis.'

'No, Sig, no. Poor Iannis, he is not so good, in the mind. All is free, he thinks. And so, he help himself. His mother gives back what he steals, or she pays, and tries to smile. Here, the people have much patience. Not like you.' With a smile, Grigoris pointed at Batten's tapping foot, as Andros Antonakis, emerged from his ablutions.

Grigoris had set a fresh glass on the scrubbed table, but Andros stared through the clear liquor, not adding water to turn it milk-white, not drinking. The news of Rose Linnet's death had soured his relationship with ouzo. Snapping out of his trance, he came to the point. 'It was the man, Daniel?' he said. 'Who kill Rose?'

'We don't know,' said Batten. 'We really don't know much, at all.'

'This Daniel, he leave. Before Rose did,' said Andros, pushing aside his glass. 'I watch him go. Maybe someone chase him. Maybe big fish eat him.'

'Or maybe he drowned?' Batten said.

'I not catch him,' said Andros, 'in my net. No-one catch Daniel. He borrow Leon's van – Leon from the bar, you know it?' Andros jabbed a twisted finger in the direction of the beachfront. Batten had sat in Leon's bar a time or two, sipping slow beer, pretending it was whisky.

'Leon, after, he say Daniel load the van with paintings. Many, many paintings. He drive it over there.' This time, Andros pointed across the bay, to Akrotiri, where planes and ferries left for dozens of destinations.

'Did he have luggage?' Batten asked. 'You know, bags?'

'His fishing rods, Leon say he tie them to the van, to its roof. Daniel either paint, or he fish.' Andros gave a look of horror. 'But he never bring big fish home! *He say he put them back in the sea!*'

Batten didn't tell Andros he too was a sports fisherman, returning every catch to the water.

'He have a…' Andros babbled in Greek at Grigoris while tapping the plastic drainpipe that ran from the canopy by their table into a soak-away.

'A stiff plastic tube, Sig. To protect the rods.'

Andros nodded. 'And a big bag like…' More Greek.

'Like a kitbag, Sig. Leon says Daniel struggle to lift it.'

Before Batten could ask, Andros said, 'I not see Rose. Not see her say goodbye. Daniel go, alone. Never see him here again.'

'What did Rose do?'

'Rose? Not sing. Never sing *Lady in Red*. Drink, not eat.' Andros stared in hard silence at the greying sky, as if Rose's troubles had stained it.

'Sig?' said Grigoris, cocking his head, inviting more questions. But Andros waved both men away, his face that of a fisherman whose boat had sunk. His shoulders sank too, and he stared at the dust.

All Batten could do was pay the bill, shake hands with Grigoris and a silent Andros, and leave. A puzzle of vans and boats, and a faceless painter called Daniel Somebody jangled in his head as he trudged back to his apartment, the hill now twice as steep as before.

*

Ball had to help Maud Cotter into his car and click her seat-belt in place. As soon as they set off, he understood why she needed two buses to get to

Parminster HQ. She lived seven miles away – the bottlenecks frequent, the traffic slow. Now, he listened to her sharp breathing, wondering if his car was in fact an ambulance. After five stop-start miles, her lungs recovered.

'Memory is a fluttering bird, Sergeant, don't you think? Your car, it's reminded me. She drove into the storage unit in a little car. Queen Mab, I mean. One of those car-hire firms. The name has gone, alas. I remember her opening the boot. There wasn't much in it - a large folder. With handles. You know, architects and artists use them, for drawings and suchlike?'

'Just a folder?'

Maud Cotter closed her eyes. *Please God, let it be temporary*, Ball prayed, before her eyes opened with a start. 'Of course. How could I forget? *Two* folders. One in each hand, because she lifted them in the air and pressed down on the boot with her elbows, to close it. Most ungainly. But effective.'

'Two folders? Two artists folders? Nothing else?'

'Nothing else I *saw*. The office was busy. Ah, my street. You're very kind.'

As Ball helped her from the car and saw her into the house, a faint tremor disturbed him. Only when he'd driven away could he identify where he'd felt it before.

It was at the last funeral he'd attended.

Eleven

At least I'm not alone, thought Batten, when the evening mosquitoes began to find him attractive. Moving from his balcony to the little sitting room overlooking the sea, he scanned page after journal page, despite the tiny writing turning him half-blind. Propped against the window frame he sipped cold water, Alymrida bay his backdrop. Head full, glass empty, he was about to give up – when his eye caught the word 'Daniel'.

> *Daniel just disappears.*
> *First time, I go to his rooms, no sign. Tramp across to his studio - door locked, giant padlock for good measure. Four days later, he's back. Fishing? He never smells of fish. Working, he says.*
> *Next, it's a week, no warning. Then two, three. Once a blue moon, a postcard. He returns, we start afresh. Anger, then passion. And him, refined lust. That's Daniel. Behind his refined words, lust.*
> *I should hate him. Should be Lysistrata. To my stupid shame I'm faithful bloody Penelope.*
> *Where do you go, on your little odysseys? Same answers drawl out - as questions – between puffs on those naff cheroots I wish he wouldn't smoke.*
> *Oh, grubbing around, paying the rent, Rose? Some valuation, for the auction houses?*
> *Where?*
> *Where euros accumulate, Rose? Athens? Etcetera?*
> *Etcetera? Where the fuck's Etcetera? Typical Daniel! Invents a new Greek province and buggers off there! Or is Etcetera a she?*
> *Then his artist fingers, bare flesh. Anger, passion. Don't want my skin to tingle when he touches me.*
> *But it does, the bastard.*

When Batten rested his eyes, it was his feet tingling - with suspicion. Who *is* this Daniel, and what was he up to in Athens - if that's where he went? After five more pages, 'Daniel' re-emerged.

Couldn't believe it, Daniel's bought me a dress! A red dress. A
sweetener, I bet. Never bought me clothes before. I wear mum's old
stuff and he likes it.
Been singing Lady in Red to him, he must have remembered.
Stripped off to try it on – but we adjusted our priorities!
Wore it today. Perfect fit. But he's an artist, good at anatomy. A lady
in red, me, dancing, cheek to cheek.
Just my cheek, though. In the mirror. Because Daniel left, early.
Athens?
Or Etcetera? he said. Couldn't stop myself laughing, stupid cow.
Dark now. Me in my blood-red dress. Might sleep in it. Tell myself he
won't forget the way I look tonight. Wherever he is.
Athens, or Etcetera, or fuck knows.

A weary Batten crawled into bed. Tomorrow, he too would 'adjust his priorities' – and bump Daniel to the top of the list.

*

As far as Batten could tell, Almyrida had three populations: the tourists; the seasonal workers; and the locals. Andros Antonakis, the old fisherman, was local from his chin-stubble to his sandals, and proved it, when Grigoris and Batten re-visited the kafenion where he seemed to live. The mention of Daniel's name drew dark shrugs and a high-pitched chink as Andros rattled his worry beads against his coffee cup.

'Sometimes, I see him, *Daniel*, in the street, when he go to Rose. She rent a small place, there.' He pointed uphill. 'I see him go to her house. When it grow dark, he not leave.'

'Which house?' asked Batten.

'It gone now. To make bigger house. For the tourists.'

At least Andros didn't say, 'tourists, like *you*'. Batten's dismay vanished when Andros added, 'the owner, I know. She old,' he said, in a tone suggesting Andros wasn't, 'but she remember.'

When Grigoris translated the address, Batten smiled at the irony.

Queen Mab's one-time landlady lived a few hundred yards from his temporary home, on the hill overlooking the bay.

Grigoris introduced Batten to Clio Demopoulou as 'Mr Sig', then took his leave. Batten sat with his new acquaintance in Clio's walled garden, in the shade of a tamarisk tree, sipping cool white wine made from the family grapes. He feared the light breeze might snap her in two, but she had a quiet strength and a strong memory, her English almost as good as Batten's.

'I travelled much, in the past,' she said. 'Now I travel…less. You like the wine?'

He raised his glass. 'Nectar,' he said, and she smiled.

'She enjoyed wine, too,' said Clio. 'I remember her, of course. Rose…She was like me.'

Rose Linnet was a fair-faced blonde. Clio Demopoulou's salt and pepper hair straggled across skin darkened by birth and sun. She caught Batten's glance.

'Yes, yes, like me, because lost, both of us. She travelled to Greece to find herself. Me, twenty years before, I travel the other way, to England. Perhaps we should have done a…what do you call it?'

'An exchange?' asked Batten, and she nodded.

'An exchange, yes. Life is an exchange, one thing for another?' She gazed through pink fronds of tamarisk, eyes examining the sea.

'You said Rose was lost?'

She thought about this, tapping a swollen finger against her mouth. 'In English, you have a saying? 'It takes one to know one?''

'Yes.'

'Well, from the moment I saw her, I know Rose was lost in the eyes. I recognised the look, from my youth, from my mirror. Always Rose stared - at the sea by day, the stars at night. Like me, searching, for something lost. And so, I agreed to rent her a little house I owned. It is gone now.' Her hands mimed a collapse. 'How do you say it?'

'Demolished?'

'Ah, demolished. To build a bigger house, for the tourists. Then, the tourists were few and we did not know if we should trust them. But Rose

71

was English, and we still remember the English from the war. Rose, yes, lost in the eyes.'

'Did she find what she was searching for?' asked Batten. Did Clio? he wondered.

'She found what women often find. She found a man. And, foolish perhaps, relied on him.'

Batten felt told off, but at least Clio had opened a door. 'The man was Daniel?'

'Daniel. All the village knew his name. But nobody knew Daniel.'

Andros, it seemed, was not alone in thinking so.

'Rose and Daniel were lovers, of course. But both foreign, so it did not matter. It was fortunate he found Rose here. Before she came, Mr Sig, some…Cretan women tried to fall in love with Daniel. Years ago, here, more dangerous.'

'But not dangerous for Rose?'

Clio paused to give Batten a stare. 'Ach,' she said. 'Passion. Danger. Are they not the same?'

With an eyebrow, Batten reflected back her question, drawing a rueful laugh.

'The same, yes. Rose, me, we travelled the same journey, in our different ways. I knew…men like Daniel. Passionate men. Dangerous.'

'Violent?'

'No, no, not how a policeman might mean. The English word is… *irregular*? Not constant? And Rose, she hoped for passion, yes, but to be constant. Foolish, perhaps, to wish for both?' Clio dismissed her own question with a wave of her hand.

It was Batten's turn to sip wine and ponder. If every bout of lovers' inconstancy led to murder, the earth would depopulate. He needed detail from Clio, not cul-de-sacs.

'Do you know Daniel's full name?' So far, nobody seemed to - including Clio Demopoulou, who stared in puzzlement at her tamarisk tree, as if the answer lay engraved in the bark. After a moment, she fluttered a bony hand at the door behind her.

'Mr Sig, I give you permission to fumble in my drawers,' she said, with a well-travelled smile. 'In the kitchen, there is a little chest, by the fridge.

In the top drawer, a scrapbook, with a blue ship with white sails on the front. You can bring it to me.'

When Batten returned, she tapped the cover. 'I painted this ship,' she said, 'many times. But too many years ago and…ach!' Dismissing the thought, she flicked through the scuffed pages till she found a clipping from a magazine, the captions in Greek. If it had once been in colour, none remained. 'Almyrida Art Exhibition,' she translated. 'All those lost years ago.' She thrust the scrapbook at Batten as if it had misbehaved. 'You will need to look hard at the clipping.'

Looking hard revealed a whitewashed room, its walls hung with paintings, and a group of artists staring at the camera. Peering closer, he spotted two non-Cretan types - Rose Linnet and a much taller man, his face in shadow. Rose, by contrast, was a half-smiling blonde-haired beauty.

'There.' Clio jabbed a brown finger at the list of names beneath the photograph. 'We called ourselves artists,' she said with a smirk, 'and we hired this space to exhibit. Exhibit! We were *terrible*!' Coughs of laughter shook the tamarisk tree. 'And you know who was worst, by a hundred miles?'

Batten politely shook his head.

'*Rose!*' she said. 'But the next worse was me! Daniel was the only artist amongst us. Much, much skill, with a brush in his hand. Though even he was a copyist. And later, his own work - what little he let us see - it lacked a soul. Fine paintings, but empty - as maybe Daniel became.' Clio pointed at the scrapbook's painted ship, shaking her head at it. 'Daubers, all,' she said. 'We called ourselves *primitives*. Because when you are primitive, why care about technique, or learn perspective?' Clio Demopoulou laughed till she coughed, waving her glass at the wine-carafe for a refill.

Sipping, she said, 'it mattered less than a grain of rice, because people with full wallets and empty heads, they bought many paintings! Alas, we became encouraged, and painted more! Art is strange, you agree?'

'Art *and* life,' said Batten, embarrassed to slip on his spectacles in the presence of this puzzle of a woman with eyesight twice as sharp as his. He read the names. Yes, Rose Linnet, an English version of a Greek goddess. And a shadowy tall man called Daniel…? The faded print was tiny, testing Batten's eyes, till a dry chuckle from Clio made him look up. She had produced from her pocket a gold-rimmed magnifying glass.

'Here, Mr Sig,' she smirked. 'You are a detective, yes? So, now you can be Sherlock Holmes!'

Smiling, he peered at the newsprint. Daniel…*Flowers* stared back. The botched investigation, made no mention of him at all. Flowers. Daniel Flowers.

'How could I forget?' said Clio. '*Flowers*. Like the flowery words that came from his mouth. And, sometimes, a weed or two.'

'A weed or two?'

'If weeds are evasions, yes. Daniel spoke Greek badly but English like a lord. Fine words. And with Daniel, it was mostly fine words - questions, never answers. Daniel the *man*? Humph. I can tell you he was English and an artist. After that…' She batted Daniel's unknowns into the sky.

'But you must have spoken with him?' asked Batten. 'About art - and life?'

'Spoken with him? Yes. We spoke. Of course. We spoke. Of art, yes.'

'But not of life?'

The dark knuckles of Clio's hand carefully replaced her empty glass. Eyelids suddenly heavy, she gave a Greek shrug, as if finding evasions of her own. 'Some other time, perhaps, Mr Sig. I am tired and have things I must do with what energy my age has left me. You know where I live, and I am mostly here. Take this, as a gift.' She handed him a green bottle sealed with a cork. 'Olive oil,' she said. 'The best in Crete, from my family's olive trees. It has healing powers - perhaps the reason I am still here.' Once more, she coughed out a grim laugh. 'Alas, it did not work for Rose.'

'Er, that's kind,' said Batten, still surprised by the sudden change. Did 'some other time,' mean never? He would have to find out *some other time*. Now, all he could do was return the magnifying glass to her brown, bony fingers, and thank her for the gift. With reluctance, he closed the door on Clio Demopolou, and on Daniel *Flowers*.

Retracing his steps, he wondered who disappearing Daniel was. A painter? An angler? A lover? And 'irregular' at them all? A man who spoke Greek badly but English like a lord - whose flowery words curled themselves into questions, when what Batten needed was answers.

Juggling with keys, he hoped Daniel's surname might open a door.

*

'Ballie? This a good time to talk?'

Batten was on speakerphone, one hand clutching a glass of water, the other fiddling with Queen Mab's journal. An Almyrida moon threw silver shadows on the polished boards. Over a thousand miles away, in the village of Stockton Marsh, streetlamps did for Sergeant Ball what the moon was doing for Batten.

'I'm fed, dog-walked and sipping cider, sir. And Di's next door, watching meerkat mating rituals on BBC2.' Before Ball could mention Queen Mab's storage unit, Batten steamed in a different direction.

'Do you remember warning me not to *investigate*, over here?'

Wish I hadn't, thought Ball, sensing what was coming. 'Er, vaguely, sir.'

'So, can *you* dig up the whereabouts of a Daniel Flowers?' Batten spelt out the name. 'British, but also lived in Greece. Try European Arrest Warrants - we might strike lucky. He's some sort of artist -'

'Date of birth?'

'Sorry, Ballie, unknown. At a guess, in his sixties now.'

Ball's evening of domesticity slipped away. A missing sixty-something male with a common name, some sort of artist, no date of birth? 'A suspect, is he? In the Queen Mab business?'

'Depends what you dig up, Chris. He seems expert at keeping it to himself. Only just dug up his full name.'

'At least give me some idea where he *might* be?'

'Unknown, again, sorry. He could be in England. Or in Etcetera.'

In Etcetera? Was the boss having a relapse? 'Look on the moon, do I?'

'The Earth, Ballie. I know you yokels think it's flat. But he didn't fall off the edge.'

'It'll have to be when time allows,' Ball said, spirits diminishing as the workload climbed. He kept the news of Queen Mab's storage unit in his back pocket. One mention, and Batten would have him chasing that as well. 'And what about you, sir? In Crete.'

75

'What, did I fall off the edge?'

'Well. In a manner of speaking. *Did* you?'

'I'm behaving myself, Chris.'

Ball pretended horror. 'Not even cider?'

'God's truth, I'm drinking water.'

'In that case, sir, I'll pour two ciders, and down the second on your behalf.'

When Batten rang off, Ball kept his promise. Raising the second glass to his absent Inspector, his eyes fell on the notepad where he'd scribbled *Flowers, Daniel Flowers*. 'Cheers - and thanks a bunch,' he said, through gritted teeth.

Twelve

By the time Chris Ball popped two empty cider glasses in the dishwasher and switched off the downstairs lights, an exhausted Zig Batten was fast asleep. When a case got under his skin, it entered his dreams. Tonight, a shadowy English figure, tall, refined, artistic, flitted into the dreamscape – and out again, leaving behind a face still in shadow.

Had Batten been able to go back in time, as dreams can, he might have dreamed another 'D' in the life of Queen Mab - 'Dazzler' Darren Pope, his silhouette a dark tall shadow too. Inside the darkness, Darren's hatred of Rose Linnet - of all the Linnets - burned like a beacon. And beneath the smoke, a fiery past crackled and flamed...

...Darren Pope's boot clipped the man's knee, hard. If he'd wanted to smash the kneecap, it would be in pieces. Eighteen stone, Darren, mostly muscle. The rest, unforgotten hate.

Sydney was teeming with punters tonight, and so was the Club, which was how Darren preferred it. Muggy, the boss, preferred it that way too, the cash rolling in - legal, and the other kind. Darren's job was weeding out 'freelancers' like this piece of crud, cringing on the alley's concrete floor, hands clutching a swollen knee.

'Dazzler's too thick to know the brain's a muscle,' Muggy told Brent, Darren's sidekick. 'But he thinks bonzer with his other muscles, so who gives a shit?' Muggy was chuffed with Darren. Armour plate. A wall. Catching rats, and the first year doing it well.

The second year, Darren did it better. But just for Darren, now.

Darren's brain wasn't made for fancy thoughts, but a deficiency in words hid canny skill in numbers. His job was to rough them up any rogue dealers and pass the confiscated cash and stash to Muggy. Darren got a tidy ten percent, no tax, no questions.

These days Darren could sniff a rogue two streets away. At twenty yards, he knew the high rollers from the chaff. Once in a while, he'd 'miss' a high-roller and let him deal - till the guy tried to exit with the profits. Why hand the cash to Muggy, for a measly ten percent, when snaffling the lot meant a growing nest-egg? Which is what he'd squirrelled away, for long-distance travel. And a long-distance reason for needing it.

Darren knew all the CCTV blind spots. He was standing in one.

'Empty 'em!' he snapped at the dealer. The threat in Darren's voice shifted the man's hands from a swollen knee to his pockets. 'Slide it over,' hissed Darren. A decent return, he guessed, pocketing the roll of bills. He threw the remaining bags of white powder back at the dealer. 'You can have those,' he said. 'Never touch the stuff.' As the man scrambled for them, Darren planted a size twelve into the man's ribs. 'You can have that, too,' he said. 'And this.' He stepped back for a head kick.

'Please! No! *Please!* I've got a kid,' said the punter, protective hands in the air. 'She needs me. *Look!*' He held up a photo. 'You've got your money. I'll stay away. Leave me with a face that won't frighten her. *Please!*'

Boot pinning down the hand, Darren grabbed the photo. A blonde baby smiled up at the camera, and at Darren, like a cherub. One glance became a long stare. Old tremors stirred in his gut, reminding him of his own loss, of the hole in his life. The black bile of hate fizzed in his throat.

Size twelve boot pressing harder on the dealer's fingers, Darren snarled, 'If this kid was *mine*, I wouldn't be scrabbling in an alley for bags of white powder, and whining, *please, please!*' He pulled back for a head-kick but wavered when his eyes again flashed across the photo he'd forgotten he was holding. Two baby eyes, innocent, angelic, flashed back at him. He wished she was his.

'*Get up!*'

The man shot to his feet like a coiled spring, plenty of artificial juice still in him. Darren flipped the photo into the air and the man caught it. 'Fuck off back to your kid, while you *can!*' He watched the dealer hobble into the shadows. Cash in his pocket, but mind off the pace, Darren turned his back and headed for the club.

'Pathetic bastard,' he hissed, a second before he heard faint uneven footsteps and saw the raised arm and shiny knife glinting in the dealer's hand, beneath the chemical wildness of eyes hardened by experience.

…Darren looked down and saw the blood. His sleeves were covered, wet with the stuff. Not his. All the same he hated the sticky metallic smell, hated it on his skin. Squirming from his jacket, he turned it inside out and towelled blood from his fingers. The dealer clutched his gut, groaning and writhing on the alley floor - but from more than a kick to the knee.

Darren's mind hissed - *car keys, where?* Fumbling in his trouser pocket, past the dealer's fat bankroll, his stained fingers found them. 'Come on, drive!' he said, aloud.

But Brent's on the door. Should be two of us. He'll use the headset. Have to. And then?

A single word was the answer. *Muggy.* When the police arrived and Muggy had a meltdown, Darren would end up in the bay. Shark food.

The knife's thin blade glinted on the ground. He had no memory of picking it up, till he felt the red wetness in his hand. Wiping it on the soiled jacket, he folded the blade into its handle. Later, he'd soak it in bleach, kill all trace of blood.

And keep it sharp.

Darren Pope slid the knife into the child-sized bundle in his hand and ghosted to the car, his mind on escape but his craw burning with the sharp tang of revenge.

Thirteen

Sleep broken by shadowy dreams without substance, Batten woke unrested and later than usual. Leaning on the balcony rail, sipping coffee, he gazed long and slow at Almyrida's curve of beach, scanning the blue-green sea beyond in the vain hope a Daniel Flowers might sail into the bay.

Frustrated, he did what he would have done in England - strolled out for the English walking cure, despite the Cretan heat. He wore shorts, a hat, sun cream and dark glasses, the habitual sandwich and apple in his backpack replaced by bottled water - and Queen Mab's case file.

By the time he reached the shoreline, a poultice of sweat plastered his shoulders where the backpack sat. Why, he asked himself, am I carrying this *stuff*, in this heat, like a snail lugging somebody else's house? He paused by the little harbour to stare at the boats, mostly small caiques, which reminded him of Andros Antonakis, the old fisherman. Out in the bay, a bright-white ocean-going yacht breezed along, mysterious, brooding, like a white shark's fin. His thoughts flashed from Andros to Daniel Flowers, from Darren Pope to Abe Linnet.

Didn't the journal mention Abe having a boat?

Too hot, here, to delve into his backpack and read. He trudged to the nearest taverna and flopped down at a table in the shade. Despite Doc Fallon's warnings, he would have loved to sip the aniseed tang of an ouzo, early though it was. Settling for a Mythos beer, he silently communed with the white lap of the waves, till the journal's itch became too strong.

Each page was a mantrap-maze, a caprice of words. Rose, a smashed Jack Kerouac one day, was Jane Austen the next. Batten's glass was almost empty by the time he unearthed the flowery passage about Abe Linnet's boat.

I was young, but one day we didn't have a boat, next day we did.
We'll be living on it, Dad said – no explanation, no choice. In a
blink, our few worldly goods were stowed aboard and, like it or not,
Dad steered mum and me across the bay, the White Mountains

shrinking to hillocks as the prow sliced beyond the headland into open water.

I remember feeling tiny, the sea vast around me, the waves turning white then rippling back to blue darkness - a pair of arms, one wrapping me in white protective shimmers, one dragging me down to bottomless blue.

Then, and forever.

The first night, we anchored in a cove off Souda Bay. Tried to sleep. The sea, rising and falling, the low roof, so close to my head. Afraid it would crush my skull like an egg. Wanted to be aloft, beneath the stars, free. But each plank a prison, creaking in the blackness. Never-ending noise. That nasty slapping sound of water against the hull. The sound of Dad's hand hitting Mum's face. And when we fight back, he slaps again and twice as hard, and then again.

In me, that slap of water on the hull, then a silence till the waves slap again. And then another slap, and another.

Grew used to boats. But the slapping sound rattles in my skull. Every da-

The writing fizzled out in Batten's hand. An angry line of ink stretched from 'da-', almost cleaving the paper before tailing off into white space. He turned over. A manic, cross-hatched doodle gouged the top of the page, the thick black lines as deep as an engraving. Then below, Queen Mab's tiny loops began again, the present tense returning, and the fear.

Hate that slapping sound. Loud, beating at the hull. Some days, beats so loudly I think the waves will shatter the planks and drag me down. Some days, I wake and they do.

Rose was 'young' and no stranger to Abe's violence, the entry said, but gave no clue why Abe acquired a boat and had to live on it, *in a blink*. Escaping from something, or somebody? Were Gina and Rose a front, Batten wondered, Abe's window dressing - the law-abiding family man at sea? Gazing past the boats in the harbour to the empty horizon, Batten itched to know what Abe carried, below deck, other than two frightened women.

When he stuffed the journal into his pack, Batten's hand fell on the crime scene photographs. Against his human instincts, he viewed them again. If Rose's early years were opaque, the photos capturing her too-definite end were in technicolour.

Had he ever seen images as brutal? Any naïve view of rural Somerset as a Garden of Eden - its crime somehow pastoral, genteel - crumbled to dust as he scanned each frame, one after another, thirty-six in all.

After half a dozen, he wished they were in black and white.

Queen Mab lay on the alley's concrete floor on an old rubber yoga-mat, jammed between the back door of *Comfort Carpets* and a skip full of old lino and discarded underlay. Dishevelled blankets snaked across her body, pointlessly warming what would always now be cold. But it was the concrete floor that almost made him gag into his beer.

A blood-red lake had seeped unstoppably from Queen Mab's throat, as if some depraved carpet-fitter had trowelled a thick red screed over the cold ground. Against his will, Batten looked again to check how far the lake had bled. In the police arc lights, the ground glistened like oil.

The silver rings on her hands were silver no more, tainted by a varnish of brown-black blood. Numbered references on each photo coolly noted whose footprints were etched into it: Scene of Crimes officers; PC Jess Foreman; Mark Bragg, who discovered her body. Whoever the killer was, he or she left no footprints, striking from behind with deliberation - and finality.

A voice in his skull hissed, *you already know the end. You're wincing at thirty-six versions of it! Find the middle, find the beginning!*

An approaching waiter became Batten's excuse to thrust the photos into his backpack. Despite glugging down cold beer, hot sweat still prickled his brow.

'Another Mythos? Something else?'

Ouzo was for sharing, and later in the day. But Batten ordered a glass, pushing aside the ice and water. Alone, he swallowed the ouzo neat, and staggered off.

*

82

In the bar opposite, a tall, bearded figure in mundane clothes sipped iced coffee as Batten tramped away. In the close communities of the Apokoronas peninsula, rumour travelled fast. The presence of not one but two policemen in sleepy Almyrida was much discussed, for they were not mere police, but *detectives,* and one was *foreign.*

Big man detective, fine moustache, from Crete. And a tall English, moustache less good. Two detectives? Looking for him? The man came to Almyrida, in disguise, to see.

They had questioned the old fisherman, Andros Something, pickled in ouzo, but whatever tales were told, the bearded man was too far away to hear. He scratched his bristling chin, impatient to shave off the unfamiliar beard with its constant itch. Old clothes, hat pulled down, dark glasses jammed in between. A safe disguise, though no-one in the whole of Crete would recognise him now. The walking stick helped, and some days - today was one - he needed it. The slow gait was a new disguise, but all too real.

Yesterday, the Greek cop left, but the English cop lingered. And always with a backpack full of files. Do those files contain my name? wondered the bearded man, dropping a few coins on the table.

Unhurried, casual, he eased from his chair and limped along with the parade of locals and tourists, to the rhythm of his brass-tipped stick, click-pause-click, click-pause-click. He followed the tall English, moustache less good – a safe fifty yards behind.

Fourteen

The sun now intense, Batten stayed in his apartment most of the day, cursing the journal's random bones. He checked to see if Queen Mab had taken a razor blade to it, but no pages were missing from the paper puzzle. For a puzzle it was.

Men. People who go away.
Feel safe with Andros. He chugs out, catches fish, returns. Not Daniel. Ask him where he's been - up hill and down dale, Rose? Like a bloody frisbee - but I need a boomerang, don't I? My God, begun to write questions. Am I becoming Daniel? See, another question! I am!
Today, on the boat with Andros, calm sea, blue paint. I fall into…a talking dream? About Daniel. Don't expect a reply, but Andros says, 'Daniel, he is big fish. The fish I only see like…' He snaps his fingers, once. 'Fish I never catch.'
Who does?
Some big fish, they smell the net. Andros rolls his shoulders up and down then pushes at the tiller and the boat heads for shore. You've hardly begun, I said. Why are we going back?
Another Greek shrug, damn him, and he points at the horizon.
Hadn't felt the wind change but a black bank of cloud swirls towards us, some dark creature of the sky. As we dock, the wind's a banshee howl. Huge globs of rain, spattering the boat.
I walk home uphill, the longest route, tramp through the deluge, hoping the rain will heal me. Soaked to the skin when my key turns in the lock.
But no Daniel.

Rose's *people who go away*, brought Erin Kemp's overseas departures to mind – and Batten's own sudden departures to one crime scene or another. Unlike Daniel, he and Erin gave clear reasons. The next entry did have the feel of truth, because a shadowy Daniel ebbed, and a known figure flowed – Gina Linnet, dead and buried in Somerset now, but real enough when alive.

Rose, you only possess old clothing?
That's what sarky Sofia asks me today. Struts past Leon's bar, bag of tomatoes in her hand. A large glass of white in mine, far better. Picks at my red kaftan as if the cheesecloth might bite her. If she tries it again – it will!
Snide cow's right, though. Most of my wardrobe was Mum's. In the mirror, I could be her, from her hippie days. Got her old Afghan coat somewhere, mum's name inked on the lining. Plenty of snow, in the mountains.
Can only think of Mum as bruised, never young. And we've switched places, hah. I'm back in Almyrida, she's hidden away in the middle of Nowhere-Bloody-Somerset. Sent her one email so she knows I'm alive.
Sofia, I said, these clothes are nearly as old as you! And I wear them for Daniel! That shut her up. Fancy a glass of something? says I. Drink mine yourself! So, I did.
But is she right? At a crossroads, am I, looking back? Say what you like about the past, you can hold it in your...fist.
Screw Sofia. I'll wear the red kaftan Mum loved. And Daniel still does.

Batten stared at the page, not sure where Gina Linnet fit in the puzzle, nor what a kaftan was. An evening stroll by the sea will help me think, he told himself. And a large Mythos.

Given the threat of Doc Fallon, the second large beer was unwise - the third defiant. Twilight was deepening when a woozy Batten plodded back towards his apartment, away from strolling tourists, glad to have the silent hill almost to himself. '*Kalispera*, good evening,' he said to old Dimitris, tapping his tiny frame in the opposite direction, empty shopping bag in one hand, the other gripping his stick.

Not far behind, a tall man limped along on a stick of his own, his face no more than dark glasses and a bushy beard. Batten's backpack - carried like a snail's shell - grew heavy as he climbed the slope in growing darkness. Shifting it from his right shoulder to his left, he shuddered at the thought of being old, his long restorative walks through green Somerset inhibited by a tapping stick.

Behind, closer, gripped in the tall man's fist, the stick's heavy brass tip made a clicking sound when it met the street - *click-pause-click, click-pause-click.* Batten failed to register when the noise crept nearer, nor when it abruptly ceased - nor did he feel the change of air as the stick rose up from the ground and into the sky. Head a-buzz, all Batten heard was the sudden slap-slap of footsteps moving closer, faster, closer.

Danger! yelled his police training, but he was woozy tonight, his focus on the journal's maze, on Gina Linnet, on Daniel Flowers. In a Mythos haze, he turned - just as the slap-slap of footsteps caught him up, and a shrill scream ruptured the sky.

'*IANNIS! IANNIS! Come back here! IANNIS!*'

Batten jumped to the side of the road as Mrs Tsomakis puffed past in pursuit of her speedier son, his sandals slapping the dust as if stamping it to death, hands gripping a brand-new model yacht with white sails. Into Batten's mind flashed the scrapbook holding Daniel's surname, with Clio Demopoulou's painted ship on the cover.

'*IANNIS! PLEASE!*'

What had Grigoris told Batten, days ago?

'…That is Mrs Tsomakis and her son. She is a saint, to cope. He is Iannis, poor boy. His head, it was hit by…the lever that steers a boat?… He is not so good now, Iannis, in the mind. All is free, he thinks. And so, he help himself. His mother gives back what he steals, or she pays, and tries to smile…'

Would Mrs Tsomakis catch her son and retrieve today's theft? Batten doubted it. The hill was doing to her what it had already done to him. And the tall man with the beard and clickety walking stick had stuttered home or given up altogether.

Iannis, though, sailed on.

'*IANNIS! Iannis! Obey me! IANNIS!*'

Mrs Tsomakis reached the hill's brow. With Doc Fallon in mind, Batten didn't shake his head at the spectacle, and by the time he unlocked his apartment, the street was empty. Iannis, his boat, and his long-suffering mother had disappeared into the night.

Concealed behind an old van parked halfway down the slope, the tall, bearded man leaned on his brass-tipped stick, out of necessity, and cursed his luck. The attempt to stun the *tall English, moustache less good* had taxed him, the backpack's contents still a mystery. A second attempt? Or was his time in Greece over? He cursed again, at the pressure of time, at the reasons driving him on.

Pressing reasons, to end this *business,* and end it well. He had to get himself to England, and he had to do it now.

*

Cool air from the open fridge revived Batten, but not its contents. He hacked a slab from yesterday's moussaka and shovelled it down, cold. As he dropped his fork and plate into the sink, his phone buzzed in a seizure of its own. Tapping the green button, he listened…

…Face drained of colour, Batten sank onto the bed. The phone slid from shocked fingers and slammed into the floor. Grim reasons filled his head, forcing him back, now. Grim reasons, forcing him back, to England.

PART THREE

England

Fifteen

Bristol Airport basked in a midweek lull as Batten trundled his case towards the exit, past the gaze of a Customs and Excise man slumped at his desk like a bored slug. Is it still called Customs and Excise? His dislocated mind couldn't remember. He edged by, despite a suitcase containing only dirty washing and an unread book. But the crime scene photos in his backpack...

To his relief, no finger tapped him on the shoulder and the taxi driver was the silent type. Batten lost himself in the roadside verges and grey sky, an image of Queen Mab hovering in his vision - till the thought of Fallon's white-walled surgery ejected it.

Even Fallon was a side issue now. The return to England, sudden, unplanned, was because of the phone call.

As the taxi snailed along the A38 through speed-trap warning signs and cloned commuter villages, Batten drifted back to Crete, feeling the phone buzz in his hand, hearing again the breathy words whispering from it.

Aunt Daze, his mother in all but name, hated telephones but managed to ring him - once Mrs Yeadon, her neighbour, had looked up the international code. The conversation burned in his memory.

'Zig, I'm a bit ill.'

On a hot Cretan evening, Batten had turned cold, skewered by Aunt Daze's sharp icicle of understatement. In Yorkshire, *'a bit ill'* meant seriously ill indeed.

'Ill? What do mean, ill?' You're fit as a butcher's dog,' he cajoled.

'This dog had to see the vet, Zig. I'm in Jimmy's.'

Jimmy's was St James, the vast hospital complex on the edge of Leeds. As a young DC, he'd interviewed many a bandaged witness there. Now...

'I'm coming, Daze, first flight I can get.'

She didn't say, 'no, don't be daft, I've only sprained my ankle.' 'That'd be best, Zig,' her breathy voice murmured into the phone.

Tomorrow, three trains and a taxi would carry him north, to Jimmy's. She'd told him which building.

Oncology.

Batten's return to his northern birthplace defied Doc Fallon's warning: *ensure periods of rest between journeys to and from anywhere.* One convoluted journey north would soon become three, four, more, each trip non-negotiable.

Aunt Daze's condition was 'concerning', the consultant said. And since she was the nearest thing Batten had to a parent, he spent almost as much time at St James Hospital as she did.

He, though, sat in a plastic chair in the Chemotherapy waiting room. Aunt Daze shuffled herself inside. He watched the doors slide open and her faded red dressing gown straggle through. Then felt the speeding of his heart as the doors hissed closed, and she was gone.

The Queen Mab casefile had no place here. Instead, he ploughed through discarded newspapers, drank powdery coffee from the machine in the corner, and willed the silent clock to jigger its snail fingers from two-o-clock to three.

Typically, he fell into daydreams – not of Queen Mab's lost youth, but his own. Through the window, sharp-edged buildings of brick and concrete sprang from worn tarmac. Memory returned him to the childhood tarmac he'd pretended was a football field, the football almost as big as he was, and where his real name, Zbigniev, fell victim to the abbreviation of his peers. *Zig* replaced it.

Pass it, Zig! Oi, you, watch my shins! Good goal, Zig!

After the game, he'd asked Aunt Daze, *'why won't they call me Zbigniev?'*

She'd sat him down, no-nonsense. 'Because they can't pronounce it, Zig.' She didn't say *she* had trouble pronouncing it. But he got the full story now, of her dead sister June's two brief husbands: Yevgeny, a Polish-Russian trawler skipper, Zig's invisible real father; and Ronald Batten, a gentle, unassuming postman, the stepdad Batten could barely recall. Drink and a force nine gale killed the first. The M1 motorway polished off the second, when Zig was two years old.

The same car crash took his real mother, and he had no choice but to breathe out his old life, breathe in the new. June's older sister, Aunt

Daisy, became 'Daze', not 'mum'. But he never once thought of her as anything else.

She touched him gently on the shoulder. Lost in his own thoughts, he hadn't seen her return.

'Any better, Daze?'

'Oh, well. No worse.' She leaned on his arm along the now familiar corridor, towards the 'Exit' sign. At least they were allowing her home. For now.

On his third trip north, in the taxi back from Jimmy's, she curled her tiny arm around his, and in her own no-nonsense way repeated the doctor's bleak prognosis.

Batten couldn't speak. When he did, anger spiced his words. '*Terminal?*' he said. 'You're only seventy-three! It's...it's not *fair!*'

In the calm, steady way he'd always remember, she corrected him. 'I'm seventy-*two*, Zig. Don't go wishing my life away.'

They began to laugh, quiet chuckles becoming cackles of irony then crescendos of desperate, shoulder-shaking hoots - which would have turned to sobs had the thirty-seven years of life with Aunt Daze been anything other than a journey of growth. Tracking the sound in the rear-view mirror, the taxi driver's eyes opened wider and wider till they were a pair of golf balls.

Neither Batten nor Aunt Daze noticed him.

Sixteen

The ungrudging shuttle between north and south became a lonely slog, the gut-slicing fear of loss Batten's only companion. In Somerset, he tried 'keeping busy', catching up with home maintenance even as the idea of *home* crumbled away. Spots of white emulsion flecking the backs of his hands, he inspected the newly painted sitting-room ceiling, and decided he'd earned an Indian takeaway. When he reached across the sofa for the phone, the perky thing chirped at him.

Sergeant Ball thought news of Queen Mab's storage unit might provide a much-needed distraction for his saddened boss. His Somerset burr got straight to the point. 'Could have a hot lead for you, sir. On Queen Mab.' He didn't admit the hot lead - like Batten himself - was growing colder by the day.

'A lead?'

'Seems she rented a lock-up, in a self-storage unit, out Langport way. Despite having a house big enough to start one of her own.'

Batten slid his feet off the sofa and sat up. 'Why, Ballie? What for?'

'Give me a chance, sir - just about managing the day job. Half the time, it feels like I'm -'

'-Storing her gin collection, was she?'

Ball began to wish he'd kept his trap shut. 'Don't know *yet*, sir. Just updating you.'

'I could take a look?'

'Er, not with you being *unofficial*. I can handle the Area Super in my ear, but I don't want him on my back.'

'Sorry, Chris. Leaping in. Can't stop myself.'

'We *will* get to it. Just wanted to give you a boost.'

Both phones fell silent, echoes of unspoken thought. Ball was fond of Aunt Daze. When visiting Batten, she'd twice been to dinner at their house in Stockton Marsh. He and Di had taken Daze and Zig to quiz nights in The Jug and Bottle. Afterwards, Di said, 'it'll be a sharp sword that severs the bond between those two.' Well, Ball thought, cancer is a sword alright.

'A boost, Ballie? Need one, do I?'

Long and vocal, Ball's pause, 'Yes, sir. You do. I'd say you do.' It was all he needed to say. 'Leave it with me, eh?'

Ringing off, Batten slumped back on the sofa. A boost? Did he need a boost?

Tasks serious and trivial stared at him, undone. Replace the phone. Find out why Queen Mab needed a lock-up. Order a curry. Read the poker-bending journal. Put the dust sheet in the garage.

Food first, he decided, just as the phone rang in his hand. Hoping for a soft, female voice, he heard instead the northern vowels of best pal, Ged, calling from Leeds CID.

'Wish *I* was on convalescent leave, Zig!' *No*, thought Batten, *you don't.* 'Spent the day chasing wife-beaters and drug pushers – even chased a fly-tip merchant. D'you know, up here, we've got entire firms charging punters for waste-disposal, then dumping the truckload in a country lane!'

Chasing. How Batten craved to be *chasing.* 'I do know, Ged. You've phoned three times to tell me.'

'Feeling better, then, Sarky-Sod? Not that you were a laugh-machine before.'

'Sorry, Ged. Never liked facing a crossroads.'

'Thought you weren't supposed to drive?'

'Funny. Had the operation, then, to remove your metaphors?'

'Had 'em out years ago, Zig. Harsh reality, me.'

And me, thought Batten.

'So, how far've you got?'

'With what?'

'Pack it in, Zig. Your nosy snout's stuck in an unsolved. Who was it, King Kong?'

'*Queen Mab*, Ged, and stop messing about. I've a list of names. Slow.'

'If D. I. Farrar was alive, you'd get an earful.'

Farrar was Batten's first mentor on the force. And Ged's. '*Slow?*' he would have snapped. '*Bloody speed up then!*' Ged had a point.

'I'm up in Leeds this Friday, Ged, if you've an hour free?'

'I can be in The Victoria? 'Bout half-seven? Your round.'

If Ged said it was, it was. And Batten would need a beer. And a friend.

'Daze, again, is it? St Jimmy's?'

Batten sighed into the phone. 'Afraid so.' Both men tiptoed round the harsh reality. Flecks of white paint on Batten's hand conjured up the white-coated staff in Oncology. The smell of emulsion triggered the sickly carbolic scent in Chemo.

'Want to stay at mine?'

'Thanks, Ged, but Daze's house is empty. Not even a small queue for the bathroom.'

From nowhere, an image of Daze's tidy little house shivered into Batten's head. Tidy still, but an echo. Without her, it ceased to be 'home'. Her worn sofa, once soft and yielding, felt lumpen now. From his own sofa, he noticed the dust sheet he'd forgotten to put away. Rolled up, it looked like a small pale corpse.

To kill the thought, he shook his head with too much vigour, triggering a stab of pain and a familiar slow spinning of the room. Enveloping darkness dragged him beyond the sofa's edge and down into carpet dust. The last thing he remembered as the phone tumbled from his white-speckled hand was his eyeballs rolling upwards and a fleeting view of fresh white emulsion on the ceiling.

'Zig, you still there? *You* stop messing about, Zig… *Zig?*'

Batten woke, stiff from lying at an awkward angle on the floor, the room grave-black. Hands on the walls for support, he struggled into the kitchen and splashed cold water on his face. When the feeling returned to his bones, he sent Ged a reassuring text.

Queen Mab's journal lurked on the coffee table. He pushed it away, cursing the scribbles of a soul from a lost world - while cancer threatened *his* world and the most important soul in it. The rolled-up dust sheet lay interred on the carpet, like a warning.

Dragging himself upstairs, he slept the sleep of the dead.

Seventeen

Next day, for the first time in a run of grey days, a brazen sunrise lit the curtains. *Stop moping!* it seemed to say. *Move, walk!* With breakfast calories in him, he laced up his hiking boots and tramped through the tree-lined landscape.

Trees. Policing urban Leeds, he'd viewed trees at a distance amid whirls of tarmac, concrete and glass. On escapes to the Yorkshire Dales, he breathed in the beauty of ancient trunks and towering branches.

Now, hiking along the Parrett Trail, Batten enjoyed the native tree-shapes he was learning to identify. Oak, beech, sweet chestnut, willow nodded back as he strode on, heel and toe, the beat of his boots settling to a steady rhythm of reflection. The River Parrett his guide, he arrived at a familiar hiker's moment, when steps and heartbeat harmonise. Clouds, fields and farmsteads drifted into the background, memories replacing them.

The beat of his feet walked him back to his time as a young Police Constable, treading the pavements and alleyways of old Leeds, the smell of fog and traffic in his nostrils and a faint whiff of breweries on the wind. And his first Sergeant, Lenny 'Pig-eye' Ross, sidling up to him at his first major crime-scene and calling him 'Son' - because he'd either forgotten his name or couldn't be arsed remembering it.

'Son, if I told you to talk to the neighbours, what'd you say?'

'I wouldn't say anything, Sarge. To you. I'd be talking to the neighbours.'

'Good answer, lad,' said Pig-eye, eyeballs just visible in his pig-fat sockets. 'Your newbie pals all said, 'talk about what, Sarge?' Brain bypass, every one of the buggers. Off you trot, then. Don't keep the neighbours waiting.'

And Batten did, trotting from door to door with focused questions, listening for the half-truths of reluctant witnesses, probing and reporting back with ready-to-use information. CID signed him up faster than a greyhound on speed.

Pig-eye's question was still on his mind when he stepped onto the footbridge at Thorney Mill, the river racing beneath his feet and hazy hills in the distance. Halfway across, he stopped to gaze down at the boil of silver spray, silhouetted against dark water, a kickstart to his brain.

Neighbours, the froth-clad river seemed to hiss.

'Neighbours!' he said aloud, the word lost in the river's roar as a splash of Queen Mab's case file skittered into his head. Rose Linnet's neighbours had been visited and interviewed, yes – but by George Halfpenny, the laziest detective in Somerset. There, in the middle of the narrow bridge, Batten spun on his heel and hoofed it back to Ashtree, fast, to the car he wasn't supposed to drive.

Talk to the neighbours, you prat, he told himself. *Talk to Queen Mab's neighbours. Properly! Now!*

*

It came as no surprise to see strong fences on both sides of Queen Mab's overgrown house. Whoever said good fences make good neighbours, it was pointless asking the neighbour to the right. When Batten peered through the window, an empty room peered back. By the front porch, a 'Sold' sign grew from a flower bed like a wooden foxglove.

Perhaps from long experience of Queen Mab, the ageing neighbour to the left had sacrificed half a metre of his own lawn to erect a stout, second fence. He introduced himself as Elliot Paine. A finger swollen by arthritis jabbed at the arid gap between fences one and two, which implied a weedkiller so pungent Batten was tempted to check its legality.

'At least she stopped throwing things over the fence,' Paine said. 'Oh, I'm sorry. I meant she stopped before…before she was no longer able to. Oh dear. That's what I meant.'

Batten was doubly puzzled now. Queen Mab rented a private storage space, yet freely discarded 'things' over her neighbour's fence?

'Any particular reason why she started in the first place, sir?'

'She *started* the day of Gina - Mrs Linnet's - funeral. Why? Grief, I surmise. And because drink had been taken? Later that evening I heard noises, thuds, from the garden, and when I stepped out it was raining *things.* I had to dodge some of them.'

'Things, sir? Can you be more specific?'

'I can be entirely specific. I collected all the *things* and boxed them up. The following day, when I tried to return them, she met me - I had barely set a toe on her garden path - with an expletive-heavy tirade, advising me to 'something' off. I did, rapidly, but retained the *things* as evidence, in case of boundary disputes. Gina had always been strange, but quiet, at least. Sue much the same. By contrast, Queen Mab - *Rose*, I mean - was strange and *unpredictable*. The drunken shouting began that night, and came and went until she...well, until her demise.'

'Shouting at who, Mr Paine?'

'At first, I thought she was shouting at me, except my name is Elliot, not Daniel. At least I think it was Daniel. Alcohol rather blurred her tongue. 'Daniel' seemed to slur, into - Dazzle, perhaps? I don't recall. The threats I *do* recall, yelled at the heavens. And such piercing cries of the heart. Daniel or Dazzle this, Dazzle or Daniel that, day and night, in that plummy voice of hers. Pretend posh, surely, because she could be rather crude.'

Batten was familiar with Rose Linnet's ramblings - plummy, crude and otherwise. The streets of Parminster grew used to them. Elliot Paine lived too close for that. And seemed reluctant to invite Batten *in*.

'These *things* she threw over the fence. You still have them?'

'I do. When she was...when she *died*, I showed them to the detective who came here enquiring. He glanced into the box for two seconds and said, 'hold on to them for now. In case.'

'In case of what, sir?'

'He didn't enlighten me. He seemed in a hurry. Now, can I recall his name?'

'Detective Constable Halfpenny?'

'Of course! I *knew* the young man's name was something to do with coinage,' said Paine, smiling at the memory.

Batten hovered on the doorstep, silently cursing George Halfpenny, whose whole being was to do with coinage. Rotten-apple George, and still proving it.

'Er, do come in, Inspector.'

When Batten's stepped into the clean kitchen, he was assailed by walls hung with dozens of photos of Morris dancers and Wassail ceremonies, and a faint scent of fresh baked bread. Next door, Queen Mab's old house smells a whole world different, he guessed.

'Mr Paine, the box?'

'Of *things*?'

'Yes. You kept it?'

'I did, in case of further disputes - should more…more *Linnets* appear. Young Sue used to stub her cigarette butts on the old fence and flick them over, onto my lawn. Far too young to be smoking, but with Gina as a parent, well…' Elliot Paine threw his hands at the air. 'Sue departed years ago, but if Rose could return then why not Sue? Strange, the Linnets, all of them.'

'Yes, sir. Could I see it?' Batten's foot tapped the floor, fast.

'The box?'

'The box, Mr Paine. If you would? *Please*?'

Did Batten's hands shake from over-exertion, fear of loss, or because of Queen Mab? When his gloved fingers delved into the cardboard box on Paine's kitchen table, the answer emerged with the contents. He listed each item in his notebook:

Four empty gin bottles – the supermarket variety.
A scuffed pair of shoes, tiny, too small to fit even Queen Mab.

'Sue's?' he scribbled.

A photograph of Gina Linnet, in a cheap wooden frame, a young Sue Linnet on one side, Rose in her late teens on the other, half-smile on her lips, head turned slightly away from the camera. Sue and Gina stared at it, sullen faced.

He wondered who took the photo, and where, but the background was an out of focus blur, the glass cracked into three jagged shards.

A stained red dress, its hem ripped and dangling.

Did George Halfpenny bother with *any* of these? Batten thought. He'd certainly not glanced at the final one. If he had…

Batten fingered the stained object. Had someone spilled - or *thrown* - wine on it?

'Did you open this?' he asked.

Elliot Paine wrinkled his nose at the thought. 'I retrieved each *thing* from my lawn using gardening gloves, dropped them in this box, closed the lid and put it under the stairs. It came out for the young detective, then I rapidly put it away *again* – with gardening gloves *again*. I have not the slightest desire to touch any of it - let alone *delve.*'

Good, Batten thought. Delving is my job. Sliding the final object into an evidence bag, he imposed receipts on reluctant Mr Paine and, against procedure, eased Queen Mab's discards into his Ford for the trip to Ashtree.

All journey long, his eyes crept from the road to the thick brown bible on the passenger seat - a second leather-bound journal, the twin of the first.

Rose Linnet's tiny, copperplate script covered every page.

Eighteen

In Batten's study, its walls lined with prints and artworks he'd bought at auction, two wine-stained journals lay side-by-side on the oak desk. He stared at the first – then at the tantalising bulk of journal number two.

Don't, he warned himself. Ease up, before Doc Fallon gets his hands on you. And why didn't you log it in at HQ?

To deflect the question, he turned to household duties. Dust lay like ash on his TV, and he couldn't remember when he last wiped it – or when he last *watched* it. He checked to see if it worked.

Flicking past cheap reality programmes, he sat down to watch a repeat of *Time Team,* with its quirky bunch of archaeologists on a three-day search for the nation's deep history, partly because the site in question was a suspected Roman villa near Dinnington, a few miles down the road. This team and *his* team - when he had one - did much the same job: digging.

'How ooold's this piece of glaaass, Towwny?' asked the archaeologist with long hair and a West Country accent you could shovel into a bucket.

'Let me guess,' said Tony. 'Roman?'

'*Rowman*? Nooo. They never gaaat round to bottlin' lemonade!'

Hoots of laughter, then a return to meticulous digging. Like at Parminster HQ, where Batten craved to be. He grabbed the remote and switched off, his mind hissing, *you find evidence by digging for it!* In unsolved cases, time blurs old loyalties. With age, witnesses discover a conscience not fully formed in youth. Lost details emerge - lost journals, too.

Get your bloody trowel in the ground, Zig!

Steaming hot coffee in hand, and defying Doctor's orders, he flopped down in his study and stared at the second leather-bound brick. Did Queen Mab discard it because she no longer kept a journal – or because it reminded her of the Rose Linnet she used to be?

Expecting revelations, he was dismayed to see more random entries. Worse, the journals had no sequence. Rose Linnet must have grabbed whichever of the two was to hand and attacked its pages with ink. Only after a scrabble of bleary pages did he unearth a snippet of early life biography.

Mrs Howe-the-cow, my art teacher, she says I'm lucky.
Lucky? Surrounded by Somerset yokels in the back of beyond? Lucky,
she says, because the school offers Art History. State schools rarely do.
Lucky for Howe-the-cow, then, bovine bitch.
Art History's the only thing I like - I'm not telling her. Nor telling her
I'm better at looking than painting. Given her snide comments, she
already knows.
So, Art History at uni. Try Bristol, advises Howe-the-cow. How far's
Bristol? I ask, and she says, sixty miles. Huh, only just far enough.
Went home and told mum. Didn't ask her, told her.
Could do Swahili, in Timbuktu, she wouldn't give a shit.

The entry reminded Batten of his own maturing journey from school to university – in his case without moving out of the Leeds home Aunt Daze had lovingly made. He remembered the literature she bought him, lined up neatly on his bedroom shelves, *The Adventures of Sherlock Holmes* in pride of place. His treasured works on Yorkshire artists, jammed between polar opposites, *Civilisation,* and *Ways of Seeing.* He could almost touch the misty moonlight in the work of Atkinson Grimshaw, the tactile curves of a Henry Moore.

By contrast, a rebellious Rose named not a single artwork, and the 'family' she described was dysfunctional at best.

Twice as many nerves as the rest of us, Mum. When I'm in the house,
I get on all of them.
When I go out, she has to shift her drunken arse and look after my
little sister. If she's as bad at raising Sue as she was raising me, God
help all three of us.
She calls Crete a prison. Huh, Somerset, school, this house – one
giant prison to me. Nobody speaks. Sue sits alone in her room,
jabbers at a ragdoll. A cork says 'pop' when Mum opens one more
bottle of booze. Shouldn't have had either of us. The one thing she's

good at is filling a glass. Oh, and emptying it. Two things, then.
She hides bottles everywhere. I snaffle a swig, dream of Crete. Darren
on the beach. A trillion stars.
Fat chance.
Calendar on the wall, want to tear off the days, make time shoot
forward, so April's September
At uni in September.
Couldn't give a shit about uni.
But it gets me out of here, before the sky falls in.

Batten checked the sky beyond the window-frame, dark now, and starless. He thought of Darren Pope and Rose Linnet, on a Cretan beach beneath a trillion stars. For the briefest moment, the image morphed into Zig Batten and Sonia Welcome, her earrings like stars of gold, her fantasy fingers gently brushing his cheek.

Fat chance. He fell asleep in a bed big enough for two, with only the hard fingers of a different doctor, Doc Fallon, haunting his dreams.

*

Had Darren Pope entered his dreams, or those of an older Rose, the dreams would have turned to nightmares …

… 'Darren! *Darren!*' No answer. 'Wake up, you lazy bastard! Muggy's screaming blue murder. He says get your arse to the club!'

Silence. Brent's fist pounded harder on Darren's door.

'Darren! Dazza! Daz! You fat snail!'

Still no reply. Brent ran through his list of insults, settling on, '*Open up, slug!*' The only jibe he never threw at Darren, was *wanker*. He had, once. And could still feel Darren's fingers on his throat, and the air being squeezed out of him.

Despite the insults, Brent liked Darren - eighteen stone of brooding muscle though he was, and something dark inside him. They were the hard edge of Muggy's muscle-heap but the cash-in-hand was ripper and the pair of them got beery days off, to fish for barramundi or black marlin.

No fishing today. Upset Muggy, your reward's two concrete boots. Brent reached into his pocket for the other reason the boss paid him: his lock-picks.

'Daz, open up, man, or I'm through this door! Don't care if she's a prozzie or the Queen of Sheba. She comes and goes right now. *DARREN!*'

Not a sound. Brent put his skilled fingers to work.

Click, said the lock.

'*Shit!*' said Brent.

Darren's room was always a mess. Daz and mess were made for each other. But when Brent got past the ingrained stink of nicotine, no size twelve boots poked from the cupboard, and not so much as a grubby sock lay discarded on the cheap vinyl.

Brent dragged open the wardrobe door - a jangle of bare wire hangers, no holdall. The bathroom stank of Darren, but all Brent found by the chipped sink was a white ring where the toothpaste used to be.

'You stupid bastard, Daz,' Brent said to the empty room. 'What've you gone and done? You're not the first to knife a punter. I told you, face it down – he'll live. Muggy'll sort the Blue-Heel boys, grease a palm or two.'

Or feed Darren to the sharks.

He winced at his watch. 'He'll feed *me* to the sharks, if I don't get a shift on.' Climbing into his ute, Brent joined the slow lines of Sydney traffic and said goodbye to his day off. He'd be the one to tell Muggy about a disappeared Darren, and when Muggy's face turned purple, spite was never far behind.

At last, the traffic parted. He gave the accelerator an angry kick, spinning the ute into the club's car park and clambering out in dread. No fishing for Brent, this week.

But then, he'd never liked fishing on his own.

Nineteen

Breakfast at the kitchen table seemed days ago, and Batten's broken sleep a forgotten history by the time Doc Fallon's fingers got to work.

On the examination couch, boxed in by cold surgery walls, Batten pretended the tapping and prodding was painless, till a second barrage had his teeth doing a tap-dance.

'Impressive tan,' said Fallon, settling himself behind his desk, forefinger beating on Batten's medical file, like a clawhammer on a nail. 'Crete, you said. Never been.'

Wish I'd never come back. Batten kept quiet about Leeds, and his arduous return trips to a different hospital.

'And you claim the blackouts are a thing of the past?'

'Mostly,' lied Batten.

'Bit of a pickle, then. Shirt back on.'

Batten rapidly buttoned up, to prove he always obeyed doctor's orders – but the prosecution evidence was too strong.

Fallon dropped his pen into the top pocket of his white coat and gave his patient a stare. 'Cards on the table, Mr Batten. No return to active duty yet.' He raised a flat palm before Batten could open his mouth. 'Your wish to do your job is admirable. As is mine - and you are on my turf. So. Light duties. Mental and physical exertion dialled down to a minimum.'

'*Light duties?* What, answering phones, filing, making tea? I can't do that.'

'Then do nothing at all. And not at HQ. Make up your mind.' Only Fallon's Southern vowels stopped him passing for a Yorkshireman. His directness matched Batten's - deliberately.

'For how long?'

Fallon flicked a glance at his screen. 'A further month - depending on how much of my advice you actually *follow*. Light duties at HQ does at least mean mixing with colleagues – which I trust is a boon?'

In Batten's head, DC Hick collided with a filing cabinet. 'Mostly,' he mumbled.

'Or go back to the healing sunlight of Crete - but no driving. It's not

106

the *where*. It's following my *advice*. Until then…' Again, Fallon's flat palm stopped Batten's retort in its tracks. 'Don't. You are not Mr Invincible. See sense.'

*

See sense! How could Batten 'see sense?' In the taxi home, glowering through the window, he saw the premature end of a thwarted career. Sick to death of seeing the inside of taxi cabs and trains and hospital waiting rooms, how soon would he tire of seeing his CID colleagues wholly seeing to their business, while he blinked like a speccy lost boy on the fringes? *Light duties, my arse!*

In the hallway, the postman's daily junk mail delivery was treated to a kick. Batten's shoes followed, flying across the kitchen and slamming into the back door. In stockinged feet, he stomped to the study and flicked on the sound system. Queen Mab's second journal lay on the desk, like a fat, brown question-mark. He yanked it open at a random page.

The erratic punctuation almost made him close it again, but as Bob Dylan sang *Tangled Up in Blue,* a few flakes of narrative emerged – not least about Daniel Flowers.

Savage heat last night. Daniel drank even more wine than me —
always does when something's on his mind — never says what.
We lay in bed, not even a sheet — after my degree, I said, didn't want
to do anything at all — still don't.
Moved to Cornwall after mine, to St Ives, he says, wine leading his
tongue. Used to go across the peninsula, to Marazion. Stroll over the
causeway at low tide, from Marazion to St Michael's Mount - in the
footsteps of history? A fairy-tale castle, rising from the sea. Up on the
battlements, in every direction, the stuff of paintings. Enough
paintings for a lifetime. Land, sea and sky. Cornwall. Inspired whole
colonies of artists, you know?
He reels off a long list — went on and on about Ben Nicholson.
Never told me you'd been to Cornwall
Oh? he says.

ceiling fan, schoom-schoom, pointless air blowing across us
Daniel goes silent — I thought, ah, Ben Nicholson must've poked his
head round the door, told us to keep the fucking noise down!
What did you paint in Cornwall?
Paint? Oh, goodness. Anything and everything? Cornwall. Inspiring.
Inspiring what?
Well. Refinement?
What's that supposed to mean - and why St Ives
Why anywhere, Rose?
I count to ten.
Oh, the deceptive simplicity of the art...?
Deceptive? No reply, count to twenty.
Rose. The fat-wallets, who buy art, how hard do they look? Mm? Give
them something with status and they'll sign a cheque, deceive
themselves, and hang their new-found status on the nearest wall.
His sulky tone for when the world offends him — or I do.
People who can't paint, Rose, can they truly see the depths of a work?
People who can't paint - meaning me? No answer. Falls asleep or
pretends to.
Blood-hot room. My hand a fist — want to hurt him.
Can't.
Growing up, saw what a fist can do.

Noting more hints of domestic violence, Batten listed the real places
Daniel Flowers said he'd been. St Ives, Marazion, St Michael's Mount – a
trail to follow?

In the next Daniel reference, Rose seemed to wobble between Virginia
Woolf and Adrian Mole, the entry sober, in both senses.

Thursday morning, alone to Chania, the little streets a joy. I'm short
of joy. Daniel's stopped disappearing, won't say why, behaves like a
recluse. Hides in his studio - hides - and when he does leave, on goes
the padlock.
I bought paints, watched the tourists ignore the best tavernas to over-
pay in those with good views and worse food. Put me off, the throng

of idiots. Caught the early bus back to Almyrida, for a cool shower.

In the bathroom, first thing I see is an empty hook. Daniel's dressing gown's gone. In the bedroom, his clothes, books - gone too.

Searingly hot, yet icicles of pain. Dash through the back of the village to Daniel's apartment and hammer on the door. Nothing. In a sweat, run to his studio. He'll be there, he will.

He is.

Leon's van's parked outside, stuffed with canvases – all wrapped in thick brown card. Lashed to the roof rack, that bloody plastic tube protecting his precious bloody fishing rods.

The studio padlock, key still in it, dangling from the hasp. I walk in unannounced - and that's a first. Sun blazing off the white walls, blank now but grey outlines of dozens of oblongs and squares. Daniel doesn't notice, staring at the empty shapes, as if the walls were hung with Rothko's.

Before I can speak, he gives me his sulky glance, as if I don't share his bed as if I'm the bloody landlord and he's explaining why the premises are being vacated.

To Etcetera, he says, before I even ask.

Am I coming? Don't know what else to say.

Shakes his head. Difficult, Rose. You know how I work.

I wish I did! Do you need money? Are you in trouble? Tell me! I stare at him, a different Daniel, his refined little question-mark sentences...gone. I'm the questions now. Him, decisions.

Daniel shrugs. That Greek shrug, that Greek flip of the shoulders, when a Greek male can't be bothered uttering one grudging word to a mere woman, from the stingy store at the back of his brain!

In the blood-hot studio, I'm shivering, with anger, is it? Fear? I whisper, are you coming back?

This time, at least, he looks at me. Complications, Rose.

A...disturbance. External pressure. Unexpected.

What does any of that mean? I shout. He shuffles to the door and pulls it to. Oh, do close the bloody door, Daniel, we wouldn't want the neighbours to hear! I'm screaming now. He shuffles past me, a wait-a-minute finger in the air.

I left the van doors open, he says, goes outside in a jangle of keys.
I spin round to follow but see the empty room. Strips of muslin
discarded on the daybed, all the walls bare. None of Daniel's canvas
knives on the rack. I might have grabbed one…
I expect him to come back, padlock the door, but the van's engine
turns and rumbles, and I rush outside. He's in the driver's seat,
window rolled down, waiting. How does he find it so easy to leave?
Icicles in my throat. I can only gape.
Intended to write, Rose, naturally.
Oh, that's alright, then! my lips shout. But no sound comes out.
Pressed for time, he says. His face, the face I'd held so often in my
hands, like a delicate Greek vase, closes to nothing. A glance, then no
expression at all.
Are you coming back? I ask. This time the question struggles past my
lips. But when it does, the van's disappearing down the road. Only
reply a rasp from the old engine, rumbling towards the sea.
The vacant padlock still dangling from the studio door.
Daniel has no further use for it.

*

Beyond the study window, the day was fading. Batten didn't remember switching on the desk lamp, but the journal was mottled with light - and with shade, like Daniel. Impatient for answers, he grabbed his phone, and disturbed Chris Ball's hard-earned domestic bliss.

'Sir?' Weary, Ball's voice. Batten almost reconsidered, but the journal egged him on.

'Ballie, I know you're rushed off your feet, but…Daniel Flowers? Any luck?'

The noise of Ball's two-pounds-of-sausage fingers scrabbling through paper covered his long sigh. 'Do you know how many Brits called Daniel Flowers are still alive, and in their sixties right now?' More paper noises crinkled down the phone. 'And not one on a European Arrest Warrant, so you can shove that line of enquiry up an orifice of your choice. Nearest match so far is a Daniel Flowers from your neck of the woods.'

'What, Ashtree?'

A louder sigh. 'I'm brain-dead, sir. Lost track of where you are. No, Greece. Same bloke, maybe?'

'Greece? So it's Athens?'

Ball treated Batten to five seconds of silence. 'Sir, if you already *knew...*'

'A guess, Ballie. What's he up to, in Athens?'

'Maybe nothing *now*, but a Daniel Flowers is listed in an old Arts Services Directory – which happens to be in Greek *and* English, or I'd be in the dark. It says he's a valuer, whatever that means.'

The remembered voice of Clio Demopoulou said: *Daniel did some valuation...for the auction houses.* 'Paintings, Chris. If he's our man, he values paintings.' Batten paused, trying to connect the dots. 'And well done. Um...is this recent?'

'Ages ago. Not a squeak after. Thank God.'

Batten wanted to ask about Daniel in Cornwall, but not even his brass neck could ignore the fatigue in Ball's voice. 'I'm grateful, Ballie. I promise I'll deal with the rest myself. Soon as, you know...'

Loud silence filled both phones now. It was Ball's turn to pierce it. 'Is she any better?'

For a second, Batten was back at the hospital, watching Aunt Daze's red dressing gown totter past the *Oncology* sign. 'Same, Chris. Chemo, still. And chemo's still a bastard. But no breakthrough. None.'

Ball kept his reply simple. 'You know where we are, sir, me and Di. I won't say more.'

'No need, Ballie. Loud and clear.'

Both phones went down at the same time. That's how wavelengths should work, thought Batten.

He opened the second journal. Queen Mab's wavelength would only appear if he dug for it.

A single page was all he managed before sleep took him. Inevitable dreams followed, this time of his old Leeds mentor, D.I Farrar - oiled by Tetley's bitter, elbow glued to the bar in The Victoria, jabbing home his point with a wave of a whisky chaser.

'*Any cop worth his salt smells a villain at two hundred yards! And any villain worth his salt smells a cop!*'

Batten's dream brought back the journal, and Daniel telling Rose he left because of *external pressure…unexpected.* Were the forces of the law about to sniff out Daniel? Or he them?

At least knife-man Darren, the other 'D-for-Disappeared', had concrete reasons to sniff out the police and make himself invisible. All those years ago, if The Victoria had been not in Leeds but Australia's Northern Territory, Farrar's nose might have twitched at the burly bulk of Darren Pope, now 'Daz Parry', elbow on the bar, chilled glass of Foster's in one giant hand, cigarette in the other, an ocean of wary space around him.

Spelling was never Darren's strong suit, and 'Daz Parry' chose the outback town of Batchelor, noticed it on a map, because he was a bachelor too. No wife. No family. No child. No baby to raise and care for, to compensate for the dry desert of his own early years. When the time - and money - was right, Rose would pay.

She had failed him. Failed his baby. And still that niggle in the misty part of his mind, that vague grain of doubt, about Rose. He struggled to find the right words, to explain it to himself but words were a weakness. Hate would have to do.

Batchelor was a safe two thousand miles from Sydney, 500 souls to its name, and mostly minding their business. 'Daz Parry' took a job, no-questions-asked, in the abattoir, despite its rancid stink. Darren's hard side enjoyed the stun gun. And the knife.

'Never seen a bloke carve a carcass faster, Daz,' his boss told him. 'Productive, you, mate. Keep up the good work.'

'Work?' Darren might have said. 'I'm *practising!* He'd weighed the knife in his hand and sliced into meat.

Across the bar, a crowd of young teachers shared after-school jokes about dunces. 'Got a sprog in my class, tried to scratch his head – and missed!' The group's harsh laughter drilled into Darren. School. Hated it. Hated teachers as much as he hated his parents. And at school he met Rose.

Picking at the callous on his hand where the stun gun rubbed, he looked forward to grasping a knife.

Twenty

After his daily call to Aunt Daze, Batten swallowed a faraway breakfast. Rose Linnet's second journal lay beside him, open at a strange, drunken entry:

Not coming to find me is he
Shall have to fetch him — How I'll do it is
Has he gone back to C

Wish I could dispense with question-marks, Batten thought. He almost snapped the journal shut – till, lower down the page, another 'Daniel' turned up.

SHE has an Art History MA, does Margaret — keeps reminding me
— Opens doors, an MA, Margaret says
Might open MY door
Hate uni — but safe
Which one — Bristol, no — not twice
— Nottingham Leeds St Andrews — prospectuses —options, staff, the whole shebang
What the fuck's a shebang

After four more drunken entries…

Decided — MA Art History
Should go to university every ten years, everyone — like it or not — even if not
Should make it a law

Turning the page, Batten hit the star prize:

FOUND YOU — HAH
Found Daniel

Leeds Uni prospectus — staff column —HAH
Daniel Flowers — Dr Daniel Flowers
Never said you had a Ph.D. — why why — what a stupid secret
Buggered off to Etcetera — and Etcetera is bloody Leeds —
Tell you what hasn't buggered off — secret somethings — secret somethings
locked away behind MY padlock
Can't paint but know how to look — how to look at your canvas secrets
Want them back — eh — Or shall I show them to the wrong people —
Hah-HAH — Hah-HAH — Silence costs.
an MA, Daniel — with you — in your la-di-da-department
Didn't fetch me — I'll fetch the pair of us
My MA — and we'll see what else

Batten's confusion deepened. Secret somethings? Canvas secrets, locked away? Was Rose shape-shifting from Queen Mab into a blackmailer? And who the hell *is* this anonymous artist, Daniel, who hides away in Cornwall and Crete, disappears to 'Athens etcetera', then turns up as *Dr* Daniel Flowers, an academic at a northern seat of learning?

Might Daniel still be there, all these years later? The university's central tower of white Portland stone pricked the Leeds skyline a few miles from St James Hospital, where Aunt Daze endured chemo in faint hope of a cure. Where, tomorrow, Batten must travel.

But with a second reason now.

Twenty one

Despite being more or less a detective, Batten struggled to find the Senior Common Room in Leeds University's bustling mix of campuses. He'd studied for his own degree at what used to be Leeds Metropolitan, down the road, without ever gracing the 'proper' university. It took no time at all to find the object of his visit, because Kendrick Merry, Emeritus Professor of the Arts, was the sole 'oldie' in a near-empty room studded with worn armchairs bizarrely grouped around shiny tables of imitation wood. And compared to the professor, the barista was a schoolboy.

Merry spotted Batten instantly. Try to look less like a policeman, Zig, in this hall of academe.

They shook hands. 'How do you take your coffee, Inspector?' asked Merry, slight frame easy in an open-necked shirt and well-worn linen jacket, intelligent eyes a-twinkle. His Yorkshire vowels came as a welcome surprise. Batten had primed himself for cut-glass Oxbridge.

'Er, straight black, for me, thanks.'

'I rarely drop into the Common Room these days,' Merry said, with an apologetic smile. 'In semi-retirement, the place seems a little…young. Nonetheless, I am intrigued to be contacted by Somerset CID – represented by a Yorkshireman, unless my ear for an accent is faulty?'

'It's not. Leeds, born and bred.'

The coffee arrived and Merry sat back against a worn cushion, slowly sipping. Batten was more accustomed to being hurried along.

'I want to ask about Daniel Flowers,' said Batten. 'Dr Daniel Flowers. He worked in your department. Early 1990s?'

Merry raised a wary eyebrow the moment he heard the name, before closing his eyes in a ritual of thinking. 'Or thereabouts. Yes. Art history, decent at it. Here for the best part of three years, I'd bet a second cappuccino on it. Brain like a filing cabinet, that's what they used to say. About me, I mean, not Daniel.'

'So, his brain wasn't? Like a filing cabinet?'

'A different brain, Daniel's.'

'In what way different?'

The Professor had assessed too many research questions not to spot the angle of Batten's. His eyes narrowed. 'Has Daniel committed some sort of crime, Inspector? Is that why you're here? No names or pack drill were mentioned on the telephone.'

'It's a 'don't know,' I'm afraid. I'm investigating an unsolved death, in the West Country, and Daniel Flowers knew the victim. To be frank, that's the only connection. I'm fact-finding.'

Merry sipped his coffee, dabbing milk-foam from his upper lip with a paper napkin, which he twirled into a cylinder, till it looked like a question mark. 'Different,' said Merry. 'Yes. A different brain. 'Great wits are sure to madness near allied', are they not?'

"And thin partitions do their bounds divide?' Alexander Pope?'

'Merry nodded his approval, while failing to conceal his surprise. 'Close, but no coconut - John Dryden, in fact. All the same, in Daniel's case, an apt quotation. Perhaps too great a wit for his own good – he rather fuelled the myth of the creative artist carrying the seeds of his own destruction.'

'The myth?' asked Batten. 'Van Gogh, Edvard Munch?'

'Oh, do add more, Inspector - de Sade, Rothko, Sylvia Plath, Nietzsche, Edgar Allan Poe. But many creative artists produced the goods perfectly well, while somehow contriving to stay sane. Sane is dull, I expect. 'Our interest's on the dangerous edge of things?"

Batten retreated from the battle of quotations, only half-sure this was Robert Browning. 'The dangerous edge?' he said. 'Where Daniel teetered?'

'Daniel was 'edge' personified. Not a man to follow a rule if he could circumvent it. Though his students learned a great deal - when they bothered to listen.'

'You make him sound like a baggy-trousered academic, lecturing his own shoes,' said Batten.

To Merry's credit, he laughed. 'I know such academics, Inspector, and a far greater number who meld engaging personality and pedagogic excellence. At his best, Daniel could glisten with the arcane. A man full of questions. Though in these hi-tech days, students prefers answers, instant ones.'

So do I, Batten thought, wondering if Merry had touched on his reasons for retiring.

'When Daniel failed to elicit the wished-for response, he did tend to sulk, toys tumbling from the pram. No lover of technology, Daniel. Mid you, googling isn't thinking, is it?'

Batten was thinking about what Daniel was thinking. 'Sounds like Daniel had a lot on his mind?'

Again, Merry smiled. 'If he hadn't told me himself, I would have guessed. When not teaching, Daniel was a painter who dreamed of becoming as great an artist as those he explicated.'

The voice of Clio Demopoulou came to mind. 'Daniel had much skill…but even he was a copyist.' Batten sipped cold espresso. 'Did his dream come true?'

'Here, no. He left, presumably to chase it.'

'Left for Greece, perhaps?'

Merry's hands flicked a 'perhaps'. 'Wherever he went, we received not so much as a postcard from him. I still check for his name in exhibitions, but if after leaving he exhibited a 'great work', then it was incognito.'

In the Professor's filing cabinet mind, was Rose Linnet also incognito? Pulling her passport photograph from his pocket – a pale gold Rose, young, beautiful, not yet 'with the fairies' – Batten asked if Merry recognised her.

Donning a pair of half-moon spectacles reminding Batten of his own, Merry peered and nodded. 'Well, in fact, I think I do.' Once again, academic eyes closed in thought, and Merry tapped a finger against his lips in a ritual of memory. 'Would you mind waiting here for me, Inspector, while I rummage in what I laughably call 'my archive'? An ancient pile of bumph. Should have recycled it decades ago.'

On Batten's nod, he got to his feet and strutted off. Batten did the same, but only as far as the Common Room's tall picture-window. The vista beyond was a Leeds he hardly recognised. Shoe-horned into awkward gaps, new buildings climbed towards the sky, obscuring the city of his childhood. Hardly a brick to their name, these new glass facades bristled with shiny aluminium and stainless steel. On the far horizon, the chimneypots and slate of 'old' Leeds lived on, at least for now.

'It changes, year by year, you know?' Batten wasn't aware the Professor had returned. 'The view, I mean. I roof-gazed from this very spot almost every day, for what feels like a century,' said Merry, a thick folder under his arm, the contents reined in by two enormous elastic bands. 'In my office, I quantify and qualify, you see. Here, I merely gaze, in freedom. Shall we sit?'

With a comic thwack, the elastic bands released Merry's file of ancient paper. He flipped through one document after another, muttering, 'no...no...no...where are you hiding?'

Batten fiddled with his empty cup, assuming a wasted visit, till the triumphant Professor raised a white paper rabbit from a crumpled hat.

'Ahah! The filing-cabinet-Professor strikes again!' He selected a typed document and studied it. 'And I have a strange feeling I've seen this lady elsewhere, too... No matter.' He pushed the document across the table to Batten. 'But this is her, surely?' Stapled to the top corner was a headshot of a blonde beauty, head tilted slightly to one side.

Kendrick Merry had interviewed Rose Linnet for a place on an Art History MA, and Batten held the official interview report in his hand. 'Ms Linnet displays significant knowledge gaps,' he read. 'Rather awkward discussion of the Modernist debate. Engaging personality/some potential – but too high risk...Decline/send polite letter of good wishes for the future etc.'

'You remembered her because she was high risk?' asked Batten, his cup pushed aside.

'No, no, not at all. I remembered her for an awkwardly specific reason. But I'm struggling with my appalling handwriting.' Peering at a dog-eared page of handwritten notes, he read aloud: 'had to practically drag answers from her...Lives in St Ives yet mentioned only one St Ives artist, Ben Nicholson.'

'St Ives?'

'Her address says - said - St Ives. I know no more than that,' said Merry, reading. 'On edge, throughout...unable or unwilling to articulate coherent opinions." Merry pushed away the notes. 'She couldn't really explain why she applied. And given the fierce competition for places, well.' He raised his coffee cup, but it was empty. Too experienced to break the moment by offering a refill, Batten tackled the obvious.

'If such a weak candidate, how come she made it to the interview stage?' Primed by Queen Mab's journal, he guessed the reason.

'That's precisely why I remember her. I put the same question to Daniel, who'd given her a glowing - and highly inaccurate - reference. He turned red, whether from embarrassment or anger at the failure of his plan I'm still unsure. Both, perhaps.'

'What, Daniel wangled an interview, for Rose Linnet?'

Merry gave a simple nod and lowered his voice. 'It rapidly became obvious he'd written her letter of application, too.'

'Isn't that a bit…?'

'Irregular? Yes. Unprofessional? Certainly. A soupcon of private influence was not unheard of, back then, and Daniel did have persuasive charm. Even so… We exchanged strong opinions, he and I.'

'Who won?' asked Batten with a smile.

'Moi. Bien sur,' said Merry, in comical Yorkshire-French. 'Un coup de grace.'

Batten pointed to their empty cups and Merry bowed a thank-you. While the barista's machine hissed, Batten juggled his thoughts. Whatever Rose had on Daniel Flowers must have been significant. He blithely gambled on inveigling his ex-lover onto an MA whose demands she would struggle to meet, in his own Department, and behind the back of his professor. Wrote an untrue reference, then chanced his arm by writing the application too. Was Daniel a born chancer?

'That's not why Daniel left?' Batten said, inhaling the aroma of piping-hot expresso.

'Shall we say it contributed?' said Merry, inhaling his own. 'Why Daniel should even dream of shoe-horning Ms Linnet into an MA programme beyond her ability, he refused to say. He sulked, in fact. Perhaps he was in her debt – though for what I haven't the slightest idea. If for her 'favours', well, good luck, since he was living in the frozen North and she in the toe of England.'

In St Ives, Batten noted.

'In any case, I doubt she would have been Daniel's sole bed-mate. Frankly, he was notorious.' Merry again dropped his voice. 'Not just his prettier colleagues. He plucked flowers from the student body, too. Very fond of a student body, was Daniel. Dubious morality. Dangerous. The dangerous edge of things.' Milk foam once again speckled Merry's top lip. This time, he ignored it.

'Sounds like you marked his card?'

A group of colleagues wandered into the Common Room, glancing curiously at Merry's unfamiliar guest, their research-data minds quantifying his significance. Merry postponed them with an articulate wave, his dander well up now. Leaning towards Batten, he lowered his voice further still. 'I most certainly did. It's a pity Personnel failed to spot the irony of his name.'

'Er…?' Batten said. He hadn't spotted it either.

'Daniel Flowers?'

Batten could only shrug.

'Daniel Flowers. On his Personnel file as D. Flowers? Well, the rogue spent three years de-flowering half the attractive females on campus!' Merry gave a brief chuckle. 'Taste, full marks. Morality, nil.'

'And Rose was his taste?'

'You've seen her photograph. These days, an unreconstructed male student would doubtless term her a babe. Intelligent – but not intelligent enough. Daniel feasted on brains as well as bodies, but I doubt it was her brain that attracted him.'

Merry stopped in his tracks, replacing his cup on its saucer with the gentlest of clicks, his dander receding. He gave Batten a more guarded stare. 'Bodies. Oh, dear. My ageing mind is slowing up. Brains - and bodies. This unsolved…death you're investigating? Not Rose?'

An apologetic nod was all Batten could offer.

Staring at Rose Linnet's photo on the application form, Merry once more broke into quotation. 'Such a waste – 'Brightness falls from the air.'' Batten watched Rose's interview documents disappear into the file, and the thick elastic bands replaced, soundlessly this time. 'Poor girl.'

From habit, Batten wondered what else lay within the file resting on Merry's knee, but the Professor's candour was receding.

'Inspector. I hope you are not implying that Daniel is a suspect? Devoted to himself he may have been, but he clearly made a considerable effort - unprofessional, yes - on Rose's behalf. I won't believe he would do her harm.' Leaning forward in his chair, Merry's tone sharpened. 'And perhaps I should make it clear. I wish nothing I've said to be interpreted to the contrary.'

Noting the change, Batten kept the complex theories to himself. 'Perhaps you were right, and Daniel couldn't face the commute between Leeds and St Ives? You said it wasn't her brain that attracted him. Perhaps he grew tired of her body?'

'Mm. Inspector, in my younger days, I grew tired of half a dozen female bodies - or they of me - before walking down the aisle with number seven. But I felt no urge to commit six murders before saying, 'I do.'

'Six sounds on the low side, for Daniel?'

'Nevertheless…' Glancing into his half-full cup, Merry pushed it away.

How often do I put people off their food and drink? Batten wondered.

'I ought really to be badinaging.' Merry pointed at the group of colleagues, earnestly in debate at a table by the rooftop view. Whatever the topic, it was suddenly more appetising than anything a policeman had to say. The Professor climbed to his feet.

Batten did the same, on a final question. 'So, what happened? To Dr Daniel Flowers?'

Turning away from his colleagues, Merry quietly said, 'resigned, Inspector. Jumped before being pushed. His resignation ensured a reference - which, in fact, he seems never to have used. I always feared Daniel might become an embarker.'

Wishing the Professor's metaphors would land on solid ground, Batten asked, 'an embarker? What, he sailed off into the sunset?'

'In a manner of speaking. Embarked on his search for the holy grail within. And I imagine without doing without, if you take my meaning? He sailed away, Inspector, into the blue unknown.' With that, Merry said an abrupt farewell and, with undisguised relief, headed for the more palatable badinage of his peers.

With a final glance at the rooftop view, Batten made his way downstairs and trudged through a campus teeming with youth to the old Micra he'd borrowed from Aunt Daze, omitting to mention he too was excused driving. The rhythm of walking often helped him get his ducks in a row but by the time he reached the car, they still swam in circles, quacking their questions as he drove away.

What 'blue unknown' did Daniel Flowers sail into? Did Rose join him, for a second time? If not, where did she go, before a dark alley in Parminster became her final 'home'?

At home in Aunt Daze's house, Batten whipped up an omelette but only remembered eating it when the empty plate stared back at him. From the CD player, Robert Johnson barked, I Went Down to the Crossroads, as Batten fell asleep in the chair.

Twenty two

After signing enough paper to replant a forest, Inspector Zig Batten once again stepped through the doors of Parminster CID, feeling like a trespasser.

Wallingford, the Area Superintendent, had produced a thin list of 'light duties' and when Batten loped into his cubby-hole office the white page of warning was the sole document on his polished desk. Paper-clipped to 'light duties', a depressingly long list of forbidden ones glowered up. He flung them down, as Sergeant Ball squeezed himself and two mugs of tea into the tiny space.

'Grand to have you back, sir. Really grand.'

'As what, Ballie? *Filing clerk?*'

'Now, now, sir. Intelligent man like you can surely see beyond a bit of filing? Didn't Mr Wallingford kindly instruct you to streamline the file-storage system, for efficiency's sake?' A wry smile lit Ball's face - Wallingford's favourite words were *efficiency* and *streamline.* 'Well, how you can streamline a file without reading it?'

Batten chinked his mug against Ball's. 'Do you know, Ballie, when you're at your slyest, I feel sorry for the criminals. I do sense a touch of efficiency coming on.'

'Wonder if I can guess where you'll start, sir?'

Dropping his voice, Batten said, 'I'll start by returning the stuff I'm not supposed to have. And adding the few morsels I've unearthed.'

'To the Queen Mab file?'

'Sergeant Ball, I refuse to answer without my solicitor present.'

'Not required, sir. And I've already added morsels of my own. I'll have it all copied for you.'

Eyes twinkling over the top of his mug, Batten said, 'Not required, Ballie.' He jabbed a finger at the papers on his desk. 'One of the duties bloody Wallingford says I'm allowed to do...is *photocopying!*'

Laughter shrieking from Batten's office made DC Eddie 'Loft' Hick glance up from his laptop screen. If the Doc put *me* on light duties, he wondered, would I have to give up bacon sandwiches? He shuddered at the thought, as Batten headed for the storeroom where the rest of the Queen Mab evidence lurked.

*

Photocopying the Queen Mab casefile did more to tease the knowledge gaps than fill them in. Drumming hesitant fingers on the phone, Batten twice picked it up and put it down. On a deep breath, he dialled the number he would have dialled before, had his professional and personal hopes been less confused. Dr Sonia Welcome had undoubted skills in dissecting the dead, but how mutual was the living attraction he'd felt the first time he met her, and would gladly feel again?

Her phone voice was too professional to tell, but she agreed to give the Queen Mab autopsy report a once-over, and to meet him.

Office hours. At the mortuary.

Better than nothing, he thought.

No scent of fresh coffee caressed him from the dim mortuary corridor or the glass cubicle of Sonia Welcome's office. Formaldehyde and disinfectant stung his nostrils as he sat by her desk, opposite the eyes and soft skin he remembered from last time. Her boss, Doc Benjamin Danvers, was a fine practitioner, but much given to riddles. Batten preferred the female version.

Sonia Welcome was as focused as ever, though when she looked up from her notes the same unfathomable half-smile softened her working-hours face. For a moment, he wondered if she'd borrowed it from Queen Mab.

'Trust you to bring me a dead case. Not noticed I'm surrounded by the dead? Anyone else, and I would have said a crisp, 'No', Inspector.'

Anyone else? Queen Mab - or Zig Batten? Chancing his arm, he said, 'strictly speaking, for now, I'm just plain Zig.'

Her half-smile stretched into full. 'Yes,' she said, 'I think perhaps you are.' And she reached across her desk with mock formality to shake his hand. 'Sonia,' she said. 'As I think perhaps you know.' They both laughed, and her eyes suggested she didn't mind when he held onto her hand a second longer than necessary.

124

He watched the same hand move to a file on her desk. '*Professionally*, I am embarrassed by this,' she said, tapping the file. 'The Queen Mab autopsy was carried out by my predecessor. I didn't know at the time, but the vacancy I filled was…enforced. What he left in his wake showed a woeful disrespect for the dead.' She gazed at the document lying shamefully on her desk. 'This could be a training exercise. 'Spot the omissions."

'Can you spot them for *me*?' he said, almost adding, 'before I take you to lunch.'

'The important ones, yes. We'd need to put an hour aside to list them *all*. Alas, I have but twenty minutes, before…' She twiddled a forefinger at the Pathology Lab.

Batten had seen her use the same gesture at crime scenes – a sanity-preserving shorthand, to deflect the unpleasant. *Twenty minutes*, he thought, as lunch disappeared. *Life, measured out in coffee-spoons.* He clicked his pen.

'In fairness,' she said, 'the autopsy was broadly competent. But the main report is a riddle of arcane language. Whoever wrote it overdid the medical jargon.'

'Whoever wrote it?'

A frown clouded Sonia Welcome's face. 'I suspect it was hurriedly 'farmed out' to an underling, last-minute, by my predecessor. And, given he was later cashiered, others clearly agreed.' She tapped the report harder this time, her left hand still ringless. Unless, Batten wondered, she removes her rings at work, before she…?

'The conclusion has alarming gaps of significance.'

'I thought it was thin, but -'

'Thin is polite. Will my scribbles do for now?'

'Anything,' Batten said. 'Mostly, there's nothing.'

She peered at her scribbles, gold earrings flickering in the desk lamp's light.

'Alarming gaps, you said?'

Sonia Welcome's earrings nodded and flashed. 'I'm afraid so. Did you bring the Queen Mab photographs?' Batten pushed them across the desk, each shot a glistening lake of blood in a midnight alley. 'Good. Now compare them against these from the autopsy.'

He was relieved to see the photos she set down were from the autopsy's early stages, before the scalpels and saws got to work. 'Look, there.' Dr Welcome's delicate finger pointed to the first photo, showing the still-clothed body of Queen Mab, the forensic bags removed from her hands which lay palms down, knuckles up.

The next two were close-ups of the left and right hand, Queen Mab's ringed fingers shining not with silver but with the black-brown spill from her own carotid artery.

Unclear what he was supposed to see, Batten could only gape till Sonia Welcome shuffled through his own pack of photos and drew out a print. Once again, he was relieved. It was blood-free, an older black and white photo of Rose Linnet, found when her crumbling house was searched.

'Look at her hands, and compare,' Welcome pointed to the photo of a younger Rose, late thirties, standing by a canvas clamped to an easel, a reluctant expression on her face. Her crossed hands gripped a paintbrush and pallet-knife, knuckles towards the camera. Batten recognised the loose parody of a Frieda Kahlo self-portrait. 'Count,' said Welcome.

No need. An 'alarming gap' stared back at him. The younger Rose Linnet wore six silver rings, three on the hand gripping the brush, three more curled around the pallet-knife. Years later, as Queen Mab, she continued to wear them. Batten remembered six flashes of silver being shaken in his face when she and her smelly blankets were 'evicted' from the porch of Police HQ. In Almyrida, the waiters called her a silver witch.

Now, in death, the much-photographed hands of Queen Mab - in the Parminster alley where she was killed, and in close-up on the Pathology slab - sported only five. *Five* blood-covered silver rings.

'Given the amount of blood, I can *almost* forgive my predecessor not noticing a dirt-gap on her finger. But I spotted it because I took the trouble to *look*. A trained practitioner, failing to spot a missing ring, perhaps stolen? In a criminal case involving theft?'

Batten stopped listening. If someone yanked a ring from Queen Mab's finger, trace evidence would be left behind – was this why Andy Connor detected faint hints of nitrile and nicotine on the body…?

'Zig?'

'Er, thinking. Sonia.' He looked up, caught her eye, then peered again at the photograph. 'Do you have a…'

Sonia Welcome produced a desk-magnifier with an integral lamp. Under the strong lens, Batten scanned the older, black and white photo. On Rose Linnet's left hand, three rings of different sizes were engraved with the letter 'L', in an English font. On her right, all three rings were in the shape of a triangle. Grigoris had cajoled Batten into learning the Greek alphabet, and since Rose must have acquired her rings in Greece, Batten guessed the triangle he stared at was the Greek letter D, or Delta.

He checked again. In the autopsy photos Queen Mab's right hand sported only two rings. A Delta-shaped ring was missing from her first finger.

He closed his eyes, forcing his mind to catch up. Was the 'removed' ring lost, discarded, or stolen? If the latter, why steal one ring and leave five behind? The price of the silver alone would keep an addict grinning for a day. When Batten opened his eyes, the magnifier's harsh light made him nauseous, his forehead tightening to fend off the haze of a blackout.

'I can see your cogs turning,' she said, mistakenly.

In half-truth, he said, 'I'm trying to focus on likelihoods. As ever.'

'The likelihoods being …?'

'Simplistic, perhaps, but let's say the three 'L' rings on her left hand are the Linnets? Gina, Abe, Sue. Mother, father, sister. Despite the chaos, they were family. She had sod-all else.'

'And the right hand?'

'I think the triangle could be a Greek Delta, a D. Her journal says she likes names beginning with 'D'.'

'D, for what?'

'Two of her men, perhaps. Darren and Daniel - she met them in Greece. They figure in her journal. In her *life*.'

'And the missing 'D'?'

Batten pulled a face. A third 'D' in Rose's life had yet to appear. 'Not a clue,' he said. 'Another man, who gave her the ring?'

'And who took it back?'

He offered her the Greek shrug he had picked up from Grigoris, willing her to switch off the magnifier before the harsh light made him drop to the floor in an embarrassed heap. When she didn't, he pretended to need the loo, shuffling past gold earrings and a scent more pleasant than formaldehyde.

Cold splashes on his face revived him, but water circling down the plughole said 'rings'. One missing ring, a D, import unknown. He dried his face with a paper towel, threw it at the bin and missed.

When his reflection in the mirror looked more human, he slunk back into Sonia's office. She asked if he'd like to continue another time, but pride made him say no. He winced as she slid a further print from his pack under the sharp light of the magnifier. It loomed up like an apparition.

More recent, more official, this photo – it had a Social Services date stamp. Queen Mab's social worker had caught her charge on a good day and persuaded her to pose, hands on hips, head tilted in suspicion at the camera, eyes unreadable. Her two filthy greatcoats, a cliché in Parminster's streets, were nowhere to be seen. Without them, Queen Mab's frame still clung to a hint of shapeliness. She wore a dubious red dress, open at the neck, a gold chain dangling down. The skin of her throat was intact, un-torn.

Despite the throbbing in his skull, Batten peered closer. And the next alarming gap peered back at him. 'Her necklace?'

'Correct.'

He gave Sonia Welcome an admiring glance. She was damn good at her job, and he was drawn to people who were. He focused on the necklace looped around Rose Linnet's throat, a single charm dangling from the chain. Eyes blurring, he couldn't make it out.

'The necklace and charm are clearly visible here,' Welcome said, 'but missing in the autopsy shots. And no mention in the inventory. Gone.'

'Gone where?' asked Batten.

Sonia Welcome raised and dropped her shoulders. 'The main report, for all its faults, does mention an abrasion to the skin at the back of the neck – where the chain was perhaps yanked off? If it was gold, it would have value. No tissue samples, alas.'

'And skin abrasions are circumstantial. I don't suppose Queen Mab was a poster-girl for moisturiser.' He pushed the lens towards his host.

'Your eyes are better than mine. The charm? On the necklace. Can you make it out?'

The smoothness of Sonia Welcome's neck, as she bent over the magnifier, said she *could* be a poster-girl for moisturiser. He fended off an aching need, a deep desire to stroke the softness of her skin, his fingers tingling with failure.

'I can tell you what I think it *was*,' she said. 'The collar of her dress is in the way, but I'm seeing a circle - with a cross attached to its outer edge?'

'A circle with a cross? What, the female symbol?'

'Indeed. Adopted by feminism in the 1970s but derived from astrology. It's supposed to represent Venus. You men get Mars, of course. In the shape of a phallic arrow.' She glanced up from the magnifier and when she caught Batten's eye neither of them looked away. 'A circle-with-cross is also an obsolete symbol for copper. So perhaps we are looking at copper, rather than gold?'

'I wish I knew *what* I was looking at, 'he said, looking at her. 'More's beginning to mean less.'

'The symbol's deeper history may help. As an educated man, I presume you're aware of the Linnaean system of classification?'

'Carl Linnaeus? Eighteenth century? Order, genus and species?'

'That's him - the Linnaean method of classifying living organisms, from microbe to Man. And a source of the symbol in question. Pertinent perhaps, because if this charm *is* what we think, Linnaeus in fact employed it to denote a hybrid plant's female parent...'

Batten's brow tightened. 'Female parent? What, and the charm's some kind of memento? Of her *mother*? Queen Mab wore a symbol of her *mother* round her neck? That's a bit of a stretch. She and Gina were two cats fighting.'

Sonia Welcome let the idea hover. Batten gazed at the photograph, struggling with Queen Mab sporting *any* symbol of parentage. At least, he thought, it wasn't the long-buried Gina who ripped the charm from her daughter's neck and dragged a knife from one end of her throat to the other - even if in the distant past she might have been tempted. 'I don't buy it,' he said.

'Perhaps because there's more to 'buy'?' Sonia Welcome's smile disappeared. 'I'm hesitating because it pains me to criticise a fellow pathologist. I might have said nothing at all, were you not someone to be trusted.'

Despite the lack of smile, Batten sensed warmth in her eyes. His cheeks glowed red with the praise - and its imagined possibilities. When her official tone returned, he sank back into his shoes.

'Let me put it so: my predecessor demonstrated more interest in his private medical research than the defenceless bodies which fuelled it - and I do not approve. And when I say *private*, I mean *unofficial*.' As Sonia Welcome paused to juggle her ethical stance, Batten eased aside the 'unofficial' nature of his own research.

'My predecessor's vices may be of use, regardless. His handwritten notes - sloppily included in the file by mistake, I assume - betray his focus. You won't have heard of microchimeric cells?'

Batten shook his head, though it hurt to do so.

'Gobbledygook to the layman, of course, but *microchimerism* is basically to do with genetic markers – those preserved in the cells of an organism. In this case, the cells of a person. A common reason for their presence is the two-way transfer of cells from mother to foetus, and vice-versa.'

She had Batten's full attention now, despite his throbbing temples.

'Microchimeric cell research is an oblique field, and I shan't burden you with the science. *However*, in pursuit of his research our man seems to have examined the victim's pubic symphysis and sacroiliac joints - his jottings say so.' She caught the puzzlement on Batten's face. 'Think of them as pelvic joints, for simplicity?'

'I could use a bit of simplicity,' said Batten.

With a half-smile, Sonia Welcome pulled a textbook from the shelf above her head, flipping through the pages till a large black and white photograph of a pelvic bone emerged. She traced her finger along it. 'You see the tiny pockmarks, there? And the pitted bone, here? Well, in the female of the species, they may indicate childbirth…'

In Batten's head, the snare-drum rattle became a trombone. 'Are you saying what I think you're saying?'

'Not saying. *Inferring.* From limited evidence. Because there's an obvious downside.'

'There always is.'

Again, she smiled. 'The downside is our man's jottings are incomplete. Perhaps he was interrupted by a superior who reminded him what happened to Burke and Hare. So, alas, no photographic record of the victim's pelvic bones. As for the bones themselves…'

Cremated. Batten cursed in silence, as the burnt dust of evidence blew away on the wind. 'Let me get this straight, you're *inferring* Queen Mab wore a sort of mother-symbol round her neck, not as a memento of Gina Linnet – but because she'd *given birth*?'

'Possible, if not provable.' She smiled when he pulled a face. 'I suppose you'd like me to say how many children, their gender, eye colour, current address, and next week's winning numbers on the National Lottery?'

'The *when* might narrow it down.' He conjured up a young, nomadic Rose and the later version at her mother's funeral. 'But I don't see her lifestyle ever having room for a kiddie.'

'If there was a child, you're assuming it lived. Nothing in the autopsy report can prove it either way.'

'So, we're talking about, what, a *maybe-baby*? Immaculate conception, was it?'

'No science to support such a miracle, I'm afraid. Nor, in this case, to name the father.'

'Might need another miracle for that.' Batten blew out a sigh, as two possibles emerged from the past. A young *big fella* called Darren Pope. And the 'refined lust' of an artist called Daniel Flowers. Two 'D's, whereabouts unknown. Or a third 'D', commemorated in a third silver ring?

A loud rap on the door jerked Batten back to the present. Sonia Welcome nodded through the glass at a burly male technician and gave Batten an apologetic shrug. Her own diary, not Queen Mab's, was the focus now.

Controlling as best he could the gathering darkness behind his eyes, Batten climbed from his chair, too proud to risk a blackout in front of Sonia Welcome, despite her ability to deal with it. She rose too, and they faced each other, he wanting to kick aside the desk that lay between them.

'Progress, all the same?' she asked. 'Isn't it? Zig?'

'A step forward,' he said. 'If sort of going backwards. Sonia.'

In the lamplight, she flashed a smile as bright as her earrings. 'Progress' hung in the air like fog. Erin Kemp's words came back to him: *As for your priorities, Zig, until you speak them aloud, it's anyone's guess what they are.*

'Another time, perhaps we might…?'

'We might,' she said, with a lesser smile. 'Might, may, could. Handy words.'

'Still recovering, up here,' he said, tapping his head in apology, 'but I'd like it if we might, may, could.'

Before she had chance to reply, the technician returned, a gloved colossus in a plastic apron. Batten thought he saw a look of regret on Sonia Welcome's face. With a disappointed thank you, he wobbled to the car park, hoping to arrive before waves of nausea hit.

Driving was out of the question. He phoned a cab before descending into darkness - whether from the war between work and relationships or the new puzzle of evidence, he was in no position to decide.

His eyes opened only when a taxi pulled up, horn blaring like a siren.

*

Back at HQ, motherhood mysteries continued to occupy Batten - but not because of Queen Mab.

About to share Sonia Welcome's insights with Sergeant Ball, he was interrupted by Eddie 'Loft' Hick's wrecking-ball knuckles clattering on the office door.

'Yes, Hickie?'

'Phone call for you, sir.'

'And?'

'Er, Reception wants to put it through.'

'Hickie, they get paid to do that.'

'*No*, sir. I mean, *yes*. But, sir, they said it's private.'

'Well?'

'Well. They want to know.'

'Want to know *what*?'

'Want to know if they should.'

Batten took a deep breath. 'Ask them to put it through, Eddie. *Please?*'

Hick did so on the way to his Jeep, and another cack-handed interaction with a farmer who'd counted considerably fewer sheep in his fields today than yesterday.

Which is why Hick failed to witness Batten lift the receiver to his ear or hear what was said. And why he failed to see Batten's face turn the colour of wax.

Nor watched the receiver drop from his frozen hand and slam onto the desk.

Nor saw Sergeant Ball drive Batten home, to pack a dark suit and a black tie for one more journey to the Leeds of his birth.

Twenty three

'The funeral people, Zig,' Aunt Daze had joked, 'you will make sure they choose a nice plot? Just in case?'

Despite trying to resurrect Queen Mab, Batten didn't share Daze's faith in the process. He carried out her wishes all the same, wandering down the vast cemetery's sombre lines of gravestones to check the grassy mound soon to be her resting place. He hoped it would do.

Beyond the graves, a cram of rooftops and chimneys filled the valley of the River Aire below, its waters tinged red by the last dregs of sun. Scanning the landscape for the lost Leeds of his youth, he spotted the art-deco tower of Leeds University's Parkinson Building, its white Portland stone turning almost pink in the far distance before clouds rolled in, spreading a dull dark grey on the tower, the river and him.

How often had he told himself to stop hanging around where dead bodies are?

In the gap between the passing of Aunt Daze and her funeral, Batten struggled to fill the grave-deep hole in his sense of purpose. Best pal Ged dragged him to The Victoria and fed him a lunchtime pint of Tetley's with a chaser of northern advice.

'Just now, Zig, you're sort-of a survivor. Think what *you*'ve told survivors, many a time, eh? Grieve, you've said. But don't mope.'

'Hard not to, Ged. I've lost my roots. I don't know what I'm *for*.'

'Deep down you know, Zig. You mostly know.'

'Oh, I do, do I?'

Ged flipped a beer mat in the air and caught it. When he went to flip it again, Batten slapped it with his hand, trapping it on the table. Ged softened his words with a smile of understanding.

'Zig. You're for two things. Work, and a woman. It's all you've ever been for.'

Batten stared at his pale flat beer. 'I'm not allowed to work, Ged. And I've lost the finest woman on earth.'

Ged drained his pint. 'Two things, Zig. First, you're not allowed to work, but your snout's in an unsolved. Second, if Daze is looking down, she's saying, 'I'm not the *only* woman on earth - find another!' Right?'

Snap, Snap, went the beermat, as Batten's fingers flicked it against the table, unaware. *Find another*? An image of Sonia Welcome filtered into his head. *Snap, Snap*. He felt somehow disloyal, but the image remained. *Snap, Snap, Snap*, harder and harder - till Ged silenced the beermat with a gentle hand.

'Right, Zig?'

Batten looked up at his old friend – valued, direct, clear. A nod.

'Good. Now, drink up. It's your round.'

*

Sergeant Ball would kill for a pint of cider. He'd needed a pee for the last ten minutes and only just made it to the loo. As the door closed behind him, Detective Constable Hazel Timms paused in the CID car park, prayed her funeral memories would behave, and shuffled inside. The first person she saw - almost collided with - was her Sergeant, emerging from the gents.

'Hazel,' he said. 'Clean forgot you were due back.' Jerking a thumb at the loo door, he added, 'I make an appointment now, for a jimmy-riddle. Never been so far behind – I need to take a week off to catch up.'

Ball's bluster postponed a mention of her compassionate leave – and how she felt about burying both father and mother, with nary a pause for breath between.

'I should've phoned,' said Hazel, 'but…' She glanced across the room at her empty desk, clean, polished. CID's ready for me, she thought, but am I ready for it? Nor was her return fuelled by the prospect of living on half-pay. The empty house where she nursed two dying parents, a house echoing with only the clock's tick, decided for her. At HQ, human voices and ringing phones might silence the ghosts.

She pointed a finger and a Batten-like eyebrow at her Inspector's office – glass partition sparkling, desk as empty and polished as her own, door firmly shut. Ball explained why Batten was in Leeds.

'The boss, too?' she said, as if funerals were part of the job description. Well, she thought, they often are.

'I suspect he'd rather be in Crete, Hazel. *I* would, right now. We're overrun.' Ball was doing nothing for Hazel's re-entry. He shut his trap, and Timms stuck a pin in the silence.

'Sarge. Just give me something to *do*. Yes?'

Relieved, Ball found his workaday voice. 'Sorry, Hazel. There's plenty.' His hand hovered over a stack of files. 'Do you remember Queen Mab?'

Timms shrugged. 'Before my time, but I remember the gossip. Nina Magnus said if I'd met her, I'd remember the smell.' *Like mum and dad's house, in the final days.*

'One job to add to your list, then,' he said, rummaging for his Camelot Self-Storage notes. 'Haven't the foggiest idea why, but Queen Mab rented a unit, near Langport, and seems she locked away a couple of those big artist's folders. I was thinking, with your background…'

Timms had worked in the Art and Antiques Squad. A downside was every cop at HQ assumed her desk was *Antiques Roadshow* and wanted a 'valuation' of their worthless tat. All the same, she knew her stuff.

'The folders could be empty, but if you get a moment, nip to Langport and have a gander?' Ball didn't say, *it'll give Zig Batten a boost.*

She took the thin file to her desk and went through the details, as her relieved Sergeant shuffled more documents from his paper mountain into a Hazel pile. Within a minute, Timms was tapping Ball on the shoulder. 'Sarge? How do I get into her unit?'

Ball sat up in his chair. Didn't Maud Cotter mention a brass key? 'Hang on.' He reached for the Queen Mab casefile at his feet, rummaging through the inventory of victim's possessions.

No key.

'She wasn't carrying a brass key when she was… Just a house key. And no other keys in the rubbish tip she called home, according to this.'

Timms nodded. 'But your notes say the storage unit opens with a key. She couldn't have got in without one.'

'She couldn't, Hazel. You're right.' Ball stared at the paper mountain on his desk. 'Been so busy, I…'

'Don't worry, Sarge. I'll sort it.'

'Er, not till you've shifted this week's crime, Hazel. My desk needs stronger legs, to take the weight.' He stabbed a meaty finger at the files he'd shuffled together. 'You did a domestic violence refresher, didn't you? Plenty of that.'

Timms swallowed. Plenty of that in her history, too, when her dementia Dad's flailing arm whacked Mum across the face. And if he remembered liking the sound, he did it again. Serves me right, asking for something to *do,* she thought. 'Fine, Sarge. Pass it over, I'll make a start.'

First, she jotted down the Camelot Self-Storage phone number. The artist folders intrigued her. She could take a peek, couldn't she, in her own time? More or less what Ball said Batten had been doing in Crete? And what's good for the goose...

At their desks, Timms and Ball busied themselves while silently thinking the same: what did Queen Mab lock away in a storage unit? And what happened to the key?

Twenty four

Three days later, Hazel Timms arranged the visit.

After tapping her feet, Batten-like, for an age, she was met by an ancient security guard at the gate of Camelot Self-Storage. According to his badge he was a Ray and his lips moved when he read her warrant card. Tall he might have been, but his miserable face said he should have retired twenty years ago. His hair - like Hazel's - could use a pint of conditioner.

'Where are the master keys kept?' she asked.

'New here myself. I suppose you want me to show you?'

Timms' eyebrow told Ray he was no ray of sunshine. He led her to the rear of an office, unlocking a reinforced door to a windowless room containing a desk, a clipboard, and a safe. 'Apart from the Manager, only duty security has the key. Today, I'm it.'

Timms pointed at the safe. 'And the master keys to individual units are inside?'

Ray nodded, jangling a brass key in a fist of knuckles. 'Manager said you were coming. Here's one we prepared earlier,' he said, with no hint of a smile. 'It's recorded.' He jabbed a finger at the clipboard. 'Linnet, R, Unit 44' was inked beneath the date and time, above a squiggled signature that could have been written by a chimpanzee. 'Have to sign again when the key's put back,' said Ray, with a bored glance at his watch.

Glancing at her own, Timms pretended to think, and took her time doing it. She'd borrowed the technique from Batten – his way of retaliating to jobsworths. Notebook and pen in hand, she pointed at the name badge. 'Does Ray have a surname?'

'Yeh,' he said. Her eyebrows pinned him. 'Breeze.'

Breeze? Timms almost laughed. *Hardly a hurricane!* She was tempted to write down 'Breeze*block*,' but he was watching. 'Well, Ray Breeze, kindly jangle your key at Unit 44.'

After despatching the sullen guard, Timms surveyed the fruits of her labour. The windowless unit felt like her parents' bedroom, in the final days of their lives - an all but empty prison. In the far corner, its entire contents lay propped against the wall like a pair of buttresses: two large, bulging artist's folders. If she had a pound for all those she'd riffled through, at Arts and Antiques...

Squatting on the floor to untie the first, she found twenty of the worst amateur paintings she'd ever seen, all naïve, all in the same limited colours - mid-green, yellow, blue, a few in oils on cheap canvas, the rest watercolours on paper and card. All were the same: the seashore; a harbour with a naïve boat; a curved bay; islands in the distance.

When she unzipped the second folder, another twenty daubs tumbled out – a grey palette this time, twenty identical versions of an offshore island with a make-believe castle at its peak. She'd seen many such daubs, in tourist shops and on cheap birthday cards. Piss-poor derivatives of the untrained art of an Alfred Wallis or his ilk, without the charm.

Shuffling through them, hoping in vain for signs of improvement, her hand fell on half a dozen canvasses held together by strips of muslin, printed with Greek lettering. All Greek to her.

Untying them, she was treated to six ambrosial paintings, each an eye-punch of painterly skill.

A cubist still life - loaves, bowls, and saucepans. A pair of modernist seascapes, identical except the second was even better than the first. Three versions of the same abstract painting of circles and squares, the muted tones enlivened by flashes of colour – a small block of red, a fawn band, a strip of black. Each version was finely done, each an improvement on the previous attempt. The third version, she saw, was an entire gallery better than the rest.

Holding each painting closer to the overhead light, she thought they looked like early Ben Nicholson's. Copies? If so, painstakingly accurate. But the originals, she'd bet, were not locked away in a storage room in small-town Somerset.

Timms peered at the bad amateur daubs, presumably by Rose Linnet, and again at the 'Nicholson's'. Without question, a different hand was at work. A gifted student, honing technique by copying the well-painted work of others? Opening the door to view the paintings in daylight, she jumped in surprise when the tall bulk of glum Ray Breeze confronted her.

'It's my tea break,' he said. 'Need to lock up.'

Nosey sod jobsworth, she thought.

'Fifteen minutes. Need to make an inventory.' She could manage it in five but fifteen would piss off Mr Ray-Of-Sunshine. She'd doubly piss him off by commandeering both folders as 'materials pertinent to an unsolved crime' and making him sign the receipt.

As he slumped off with a scowl, Timms scrutinised the finely painted abstract under daylight. Yes, too mature for student work, the composition and brushwork superb, each strip of colour just so.

She flipped the painting over, and on the back found a blank square of canvas clipped to the frame. When she eased it away, far from blank, the underside was covered in scrawled signatures – over thirty of them, the top few incomplete, the lower versions finished with a confident flourish. Some were followed by the year, in the same hand. 34, she read. 46. 52. She'd seen this combination of elongated signature and date before. 'Nicholson', it said, in a distinctive hand. It was how he generally signed his work.

But when Ben Nicholson signed a canvas, he didn't need to practise thirty times.

Scanning the paintings and 'signatures', she mouthed the question asked daily in Arts and Antiques. *What's the difference between a copy and a fake?*

'Intent,' she said aloud. 'Intent to defraud.'

Like Batten, Hazel Timms doubted a drug-mugger murdered the ageing Queen Mab, whose only offence was to the nostrils. These six near-perfect fakes added six more layers of doubt. Queen Mab certainly hadn't painted them. So who did, and how did they end up with Queen Mab?

Timms laid all six on the ground, the practice signatures beside them, and clicked her phone-camera.

Sergeant Ball had reminded her not to bother Batten, while he recovered from his Leeds bereavement. All the same, he'd need to take a close look at these.

Twenty five

Aunt Daze had paid for her funeral in advance and the undertaker was warm and efficient. Even so, the pre-interment days became an age of slow time. Half his purpose gone, Batten wandered through the silent rooms of his dead Aunt's house, trying to conjure up the 'home' it used to be. On the old sideboard, Daze had placed a defiant framed photograph, her bald head wrapped in a scarf, eyebrows gone. When she was alive, he'd chuckled when she returned from the hairdresser, her short curls clamped in place by hairspray stronger than iron.

No chuckles today. He returned to the safer haven of work, to back-burner questions about Daniel Flowers, a man who lived mostly off the map, yet at least left an imprint on the University of Leeds.

Might a second visit to Professor Kendrick Merry add forgotten details, despite his distinctly cool response when an *academic* was vaguely implicated in the death of an English Rose? After dithering, Batten did what his old brass-neck self would have done right away: grabbed the phone, rang Merry, and bluntly asked.

*

In preparation for their meeting, he flicked back to two curious journal entries Rose must have scribbled down when the gin was flowing.

> *Think that's it, Daniel? Just go away do I — because you snap your fingers*
> *Told him — I want money. — Buy myself a new red dr-*
> *Dropped through the letterbox, the cash. Not enough, I said. Send more — a rainy day.*
> *Spent it, on a safe place — all locked up — and I've got the key-hee-hee.*
> *Paid with your money, Daniel — what d'you think of that*

Flicking ahead, Batten found the second, more disturbing entry.

Watching me — Someone is. In the distance — twice
A bearded man — was it — couldn't see his face.

The entry fizzled out. A bearded man? Just the drink talking?
Or Daniel?

*

When again he found his way to the rooftop view in the University's
Senior Common Room, Merry was already there, half-empty coffee cup
on the table, and six inches of bumph piled on the adjacent armchair.

'Double espresso, black?' Merry asked.

'Thank you, yes. Well-remembered.'

An articulate wave to the young barista set the machine hissing. The
two men sat in awkward silence till the coffee arrived.

'I may have been a little short, Inspector, last time we met. Most unlike
me, and I do apologise. Daniel Flowers left a more negative taste in my
mouth than I remembered, and perhaps I didn't want to remember at all.'
He patted the pile of bumph sitting beside him. 'As recompense, I have
returned to my archive, on your behalf.'

Batten wilted at the size of the pile, but before he could open his
mouth Merry was off again, one hand waving a thick, bound tome, like a
weightlifter showing off.

'A copy of Daniel's doctoral thesis,' he said. *Cornwall and Modern Art,
in the Decades before and after World War Two.* You asked, on the phone,
about Daniel's connection to Cornwall? To St. Ives? This is it.'

Batten winced. *I didn't ask to read the bloody thing.*

To his relief, Merry flipped it back onto the seat, with an air of disdain.
'Sound,' he said. 'But dry. Daniel himself was more…moist. I imagine he
enjoyed his time in St Ives, researching this.' He gave the thesis a clip
round the ear. 'Or more likely reserved his 'enjoyment' for more physical
preoccupations.'

'Either way, it got him a university post.'

'Mm, not of itself, no. Without his artistic travels, I doubt we would
have appointed him. He brought additional perspectives, you see, on

142

contemporary Greek painting and the European art market. And excellent references from Greek auction houses. Modernism was only one string to his bow.'

Batten pointed at the thesis. 'If the abstract is *very* short, I could take a shufty.'

'No need, Inspector. I shall gladly summarise. Daniel focused on Ben Nicholson, famous giant of the St Ives school. And on Nicholson's dream of abstract art as an international language. A worthy aim, in Cornwall certainly, pre-war. Till Hitler and Mussolini marched across Europe and destroyed all hope. Daniel's concluding chapters are marred by what I can only call *annoyance* at their audacity. A characteristic of Daniel's - the tendency to sulk when dreams failed to come true.'

'And when brightness falls from the air?'

'Ah, Inspector. Yes, Rose *and* Daniel. Both. Both.'

'Two litanies, in a time of plague?'

'Touché!' said Merry, approving. 'You've been reading your Thomas Nashe. Admirable.'

When Merry dropped 'brightness falls from the air' into their previous conversation, Batten's competitive pride made him look up the source - Nashe's *A Litany in Time of Plague*. Merry might carry it around in his head, but Batten's was too full of Aunt Daze and Queen Mab. Was Rose the litany, and Daniel the plague? He moved the conversation along.

'You were uncertain where Daniel went, after he *embarked*. Any further thoughts?'

Merry pursed his lips in doubt. 'A place with good light, to paint his great work? Though where one goes to do so...'

Or where one finds the cash to pay for it...? Wherever Daniel went, did he return - like a plague - to murder Rose? Before he could ask, Merry drilled into his bumph and drew out a pack of photographs.

'These may inform, Inspector. They're from Daniel's interview presentation, for his lectureship. His artworks were too delicate to bring. But these give a snapshot of his skills and range. Your CID vision may spot *clues*.'

Leafing through the dozen frames, Batten saw enough to agree with Clio Demopoulou's view – *Daniel was the only artist amongst us.*

'Certainly fond of the abstract,' said Batten, peering at half a dozen flat-planed, vaguely cubist works, and a Ben Nicholson-style relief of squares and circles on a grid of white card. In a pair of Modernist seascapes, impossibly large boats floated on impossibly small bays. Batten held them up, eyebrow raised, testing Merry's reaction.

'Quite consistent with his doctoral thesis, Inspector. To the St Ives artists, traditional rules of perspective were a straitjacket. Ben Nicholson himself claimed an artist should convey complex ideas with only minimum means.'

'Achieve that, did he?'

Merry shrugged, academically. 'The eye of the beholder, etcetera. Traditionalists were horrified when the St Ives School made the vanishing-point, um, *vanish*!' he said with a chuckle.

Batten was fed up of things and people vanishing. 'Isn't that a cheat?' he said. 'I mean, if you ditch perspective, don't you leapfrog an entire skillset? Painting's not supposed to be a doddle, is it?' He was provoking, he knew.

Professor Merry had heard it all before. 'There is no single 'best' way to make a statement on a canvas,' he said, with a quiet smile. 'Neither does vanishing the vanishing point *ignore* perspective entirely. Pairing objects of different size and significance…the intersection of horizontal and vertical lines…tonal colour to give depth – these create a perspective, unencumbered by rules of geometry.'

Is he describing Daniel, Batten thought, or my approach to policing? Question the rules, assess significance, check the lines of intersection. 'But vanishing Daniel never reappeared?'

The Professor shook his head. 'Never. But I did see Rose again, in a manner of speaking. *Yesterday*, in fact, when delving into my archive.'

Merry's joined the joust, thought Batten. When he made to speak, a flat palm stopped him, as Doc Fallon's had done. Merry produced another photo of a Daniel painting and passed it across.

'At interview, we asked Daniel how prepared he was to teach Renaissance art – a core programme. He supported his case with that very photograph. Can you spot the pastiche?'

Batten wanted to remind Merry he was educated too. 'Botticelli,' he said. 'A key artist of the Renaissance.'

'Yes! *The Birth of Venus*. It's in the Uffizi Gallery in Florence -'

'I've been. Seen it.'

'The Botticelli, yes. But not this version.' Merry pointed at the pastiche of the Renaissance original, its trees and jagged shoreline replaced by a contemporary curve of seashore, with a little harbour and dots of islands in the distance. Leaning across to tap the photo, he said, 'Daniel modernised the background, see?'

Batten allowed himself a victory smile. *It's Almyrida, in Crete, but I bet the Professor doesn't know.*

'And replaced Venus, too. Look.'

When Batten did, he saw the face of Venus was instead the face - and presumably the very naked body - of Rose. Exquisitely done, highly sensual, almost anatomical, the entire painting a hymn to skill.

'Of course,' Merry said, 'I'd never clapped eyes on Rose when I saw this. But last time, when you showed me her photo, I could have sworn I'd seen her before - before her interview, I mean. And, voila, I found her again. Immortalised, rather beautifully.'

'In a photo,' Batten said. 'Did you see the actual canvas?'

'Never, alas. Be no surprise if Daniel sold it and sold it well. Before he left, I asked after the model herself. He gave a tiny roll of his shoulders - Daniel was far too refined to openly *shrug* - and said, 'Kendrick, isn't everything of its time?' Merry clinked his empty cup into his saucer and glanced at his watch. 'Speaking of which, I have a departmental meeting - oh, joy. Feel free to keep the photo.'

Batten nodded his thanks, in some ways relieved the lecture was over. St Ives, Almyrida, and Daniel Flowers were fizzing in his head.

'And perhaps Daniel had a point?' Merry was saying. 'How moribund our existence if new ideas failed to challenge the norms of a previous age. Which was Daniel, all over - no kow-towing to 'natural' rules. To *any* rules, damn the man.' Merry stood up.

Batten rose to his feet more slowly. Merry's speculations were luxuries he couldn't share. *My rules are the Statute Book. I can't juggle existential questions and wait for applause. Rose Linnet existed, flesh and blood, till Daniel - perhaps - defied natural rules and made her vanish.*

They shook hands and Batten took his leave, Queen Mab throbbing in his skull with every tread of the staircase. Or was it Aunt Daze? Crossing the campus and unlocking the little Nissan, worthless now to his mother-in-all-but-name, he spoke the answer aloud.

'Both,' he said. '*Both*.'

A clutch of passing students, messenger bags across their shoulders, stared in brief amusement at a sad moustached man wittering to himself in a university car park. And then went on their way.

Twenty six

A lone mourner this time, Batten breathed in the Leeds skyline as he crunched his feet along the graveyard's cinder path. *Returning to the scene*, he told himself.

Days before, at the funeral of Aunt Daze in the dark church, his internal voice whispered '*disloyalty!*' when Rose Linnet drifted into his head - a red-dressed Rose, at her mother's interment in Parminster, years before her mind drifted away with the fairies, and her own murdered bones were cremated.

Staring down at the spade-cuts, grass and lumpen earth of Aunt Daze's grave, Professor Merry's musings on perspective came back to him. Plenty of depth here, he thought. Plenty of intersecting lines and gradations of colour. His mother-in-all-but name lay beneath the rough folds of brown clay and green turf. Her headstone would only be slotted in place once the ground firmed up - a notion he found disturbing. But Daze had insisted on a burial.

'Never fancied cremation, Zig,' she'd said, after the doctors confirmed her fate. 'Makes your eyes water.'

Her faint, defiant chuckle reminded Batten of Professor Merry, and he saw what these two old Leeds-dwellers had in common. Both managed to blend, in true post-modernist style, the traditional and the modern, while retaining the better values of each. Batten managed a faint chuckle of his own, imagining Daze's response if he told her she was a post-modernist.

'I'm a *what*?' she would have said. Merry's views on perspective were artistic, informed. But perspective came as naturally as air to Aunt Daze. She was still passing hers to Batten, even from the grave. He stood a while longer, thanking her for a priceless inheritance.

This cold Leeds wind, he told himself, it makes your eyes water.

He was standing here, he knew, for two people - himself and Uncle Russell, Daze's brother, and last blood relative. Russell had arrived late for the funeral because, Batten guessed, he was sleeping off whatever he'd pumped down his throat or up his nose. Russell, an ageless shirker with a tidy income but no identifiable job - and three drug-dealing convictions already to his name.

'Don't be hurt, Zig, when I tell you I've left my little house to Russell,'

Daze had whispered from her hospital bed. 'You don't need my Premium Bonds, but I've left them to you, all the same, to make up for it. I know he's here today, gone tomorrow, our Russell, but some people are just…*wanderers*, and Russell's one of them. I'm hoping the house might help him settle. Give him firm ground, a steady place to live. A *home*, to *grow* in. Like you did, Zig.'

Touched, Batten couldn't speak.

'I shan't need an 'ouse, shall I, where I'm going? And you've already got one.'

Was Batten hurt? Not for long. There was wisdom in Aunt Daze's bequest. Other 'wanderers' entered his thoughts – Daniel Flowers, embarking on a journey into the unknown; Darren Pope, perhaps still wandering in Australia, an 'approach with caution' flag on his police record. Sue Linnet, failing to wander back for her own mother's funeral. And Queen Mab, the saddest wanderer of all, who inherited a crumbling house but chose to sleep beneath the stars - till an unknown wanderer put a knife to her throat and ended her existence.

Batten had done what he could never do till after the funeral. Eyes aflame, he'd shoved Uncle Russell against the green flock wallpaper of the sitting room in 'his' house - and spat out a stark warning. '*Your* house, now, Russell. The house where I was raised. You can live in it, yes. So long as you keep it clean. And when I say *clean*…'

Russell dared not speak. His wide-eyed stare said he knew Batten too well, knew his resolve – and his police connections. If you make a promise, you keep it. Aunt Daze had drilled that into 'young Zig'. For Uncle Russell, her perspective had vanished into nothing.

The cinder path made the sound of slow waves on shingle as Batten trudged away from the grave. When he reached the gate, he took a last look back, down the geometric corridors of headstones, hundreds of them, to where they disappeared on the far horizon. In a flash he was in a different corridor, at St James, watching Daze hobble towards Chemotherapy, her compact body silhouetted by harsh neon. Refusing a wheelchair, she'd insisted on walking, independence unbowed. She'd passed the same stubborn independence onto Batten.

Here, in the graveyard, he conjured up her silhouette again, red dressing gown wrapped about her like an overcoat a size too big; trim and slight, curled hair cut short, as in the photos of June, her dead sister - Batten's dead mother.

A second image crept into his head - a different silhouette, yet the same in size and shape, the same hobbled gait, hair cropped, body clad in an old red dress and swaddled by a pair of stinking greatcoats wrapped about the bones like shrouds.

When we dig into the past, he asked himself, what do we dig for? Deep in his gut, he always knew why his hand pulled the Queen Mab file from the rack of unsolved cases. Now, he accepted it. In silhouette, Queen Mab could have been Aunt Daze, or June, the birth-mother Batten could only meet in photographs.

Tiny figures, all three, leaving giant footprints in their wake. June, taken too young by a drunk driver on the motorway. Queen Mab, drinking her mind into fairyland. Aunt Daze, with enough strong-mindedness for the three of them.

All were buried now, vanished.

But Batten was digging, still.

Twenty seven

Hazel Timms copied into an email the report of her visit to Camelot Self-Storage, and the paintings Queen Mab had locked away. After attaching photos of the six dodgy canvases, her finger hovered over the 'To.'

'Sarge? Do I send the Camelot report to the boss, or wait a bit longer?'

Ball looked up from his swamped desk. He'd visited a gaunt-looking Batten yesterday, in daylight. The Ashtree cottage was a sad place still, curtains and windows tightly closed, no fresh air. Ball wasn't offered cider – not even tea.

'Not yet, Hazel. It's hit him hard.' Harder than a cosh, Ball thought. 'When he's ready, I bet you a pint of cider he'll rings *us*, and complain we've kept him in the dark.'

Timms stared again at the six photos, still unsure why Queen Mab had them. If Batten sees for himself, he might come up with answers. But she did as Ball instructed, moving the email to her *Drafts* folder, for later. Then with a sigh, she pulled another domestic violence file towards her.

Had Batten been back in Somerset four days, or five? He couldn't remember, each day an internal tug-of-war between grief and lost purpose.

In his Ashtree cottage, the sound-system was hot with overuse, Tom Waits' rasping vocals grating from the speakers. On repeat, *Time* played and replayed, reminding Batten how finite time is. He let the music fill voids deeper than any he had known, his cottage a cell, the sofa his bed, the thick new curtains tightly closed. In his study, Queen Mab's journals lay discarded on the desk.

With the system at full pelt, he failed to hear the phone, only saw it flash. Hesitant, he turned down the volume and stabbed at 'answer'. To his surprise, it was not Ged, ringing to check on him. The female voice was soft, concerned.

'Andy Connor told me of your loss, Zig. I'm so sorry.'

Sonia Welcome only ever rang his home number to give an update on a dead stranger. Now, the dead stranger was Aunt Daze, whose thankfully un-incised body lay not in the mortuary but in a grave on the fringe of

Leeds, waiting for the ground to settle.

'It's a while, Sonia. Less raw.'

'And what are you up to?' Welcome guessed Batten's time ticked slowly.

'Trying to get in *The Guinness Book of Records* for thumb-twiddling. Mostly doing that.'

'What wonderful thumbs you'll have, once you're back in harness.'

He wouldn't tempt fate by speculating when. Or if. 'How are you?' he asked, to deflect, and they swapped niceties.

'We never did have that drink,' she said. '*It's good to talk* is a poor cliché, but I'm free this evening if it would help?'

Would it 'help', he thought, to sit close to Sonia Welcome, instead of mourning the loving woman who raised him? It felt disloyal to even consider it, till he sensed the Yorkshire vowels of Aunt Daze. '*A lovely lass like her, Zig? You'd be daft as a brush not to.*'

He looked round the sitting room. Clean enough. Even in grief he was tidy. Open the windows, air the place? But his energy levels… 'I've been warned not to drive,' he said, without mentioning the times he had.

'*I* haven't.' she said. 'Assuming three points on my licence doesn't count as a warning?'

'Ninety in a thirty zone?'

'Forty-six, in a forty. But technically you'll be consorting with a criminal…'

At the funeral, Mrs Yeadon, Aunt Daze's neighbour of thirty years, whose first name was still a mystery, had kissed Batten on the cheek and gripped his arm in comfort. Some of his old Leeds colleagues gave him hugs of consolation, and Ged's emotional, bear-like clamp squeezed the air from his lungs.

Now, in the soft lamplight of his Ashtree cottage, in the gentle arms of Sonia Welcome, Batten drifted beyond comfort and consolation and fell into the abandonment of grief. She held him to her with quiet strength, feeling no need to speak as tears dripped from his cheeks onto her cashmere top. When at last he raised his head, she eased a tissue into his fingers, and he dabbed his eyes.

'I'm sorry,' he said.

'I should hope so. Northern male detective, expressing his feelings? Shabby.' Her smile softened the words. 'Let your humanity show, Zig. Grief works better if you unscrew the lid and release it from the jar.'

To his surprise, she reclaimed the tissue, wiped away a lost tear from the tip of his nose, and kissed first one eye then the other. 'Grieve,' she said. 'Emotions exist to be drawn on. And now is the time.' She pressed the tissue into his fingers. 'And time for me to go,' she said. 'It's late. Still have to work tomorrow.'

Batten was strangely relieved, his tears and her understanding melting the stone in his heart, despite his Northern male embarrassment. Walking her to the car, he thanked her simply and truly. Sonia Welcome wrapped her arms round him and kissed his cheek so gently he imagined a stray leaf had wafted from his cherry tree and brushed the condolences of Nature onto his skin.

Ten years ago, the two wine glasses on his coffee table would have been re-filled a time or two - not left untouched like tonight's. And ten years ago, a misplaced urge might have tempted him into post-funereal sex-on-the-sofa, in the soft light of a table-lamp. Tonight, the only fluids passing between them were his tears and the soft moisture of her lips on his cheek.

Exhausted and grieving, he was pleased to watch Sonia Welcome's rear lights grow smaller till they disappeared, without complication, at the bottom of the lane.

But doubly pleased she now knew the way to his home.

Twenty eight

A downside to easing his grief, Batten realised, was recycling the pile of takeaway food cartons - and confronting his empty fridge. He hated supermarket shopping with a vengeance but gritted his teeth till it was done. While emptying bags and re-filling his cupboards, he heard the letterbox clatter. Today's post, a flat brown package, landed on the hall carpet, address written in the unmistakeable block capitals of Makis Grigoris.

Better not be a third bloody journal. He yanked out the contents, eyes widening as official Greek documents tumbled onto the old pine table, dragging him in a blink from Ashtree back to Crete. 'Grigoris, you're a star,' he said, scanning official pages of Rose Linnet's personal history. Grigoris, his nonchalance a breezy pretence, had scoured one municipal agency after another for documents bearing Rose's name, translating key moments into scribbled English.

Batten took the whole pack to his rear porch with its distant view of Ham Hill and dropped it on the bench beside him. Sunlight mottling his fingers, he flicked through glimpses of Rose's youth - a Chania Prefecture document enquiring about her schooling; enrolment forms; school reports; a School Counsellor's letter.

On the horizon, clouds came and went, the long bulk of Ham Hill easing from grey into honey and green. Two thousand years ago, ancient Britons had fortified the hill, and lived there - till the Romans turfed them out, quarrying the golden stone for their more opulent villas. Leaning back against the porch's hamstone wall, he was struck by the scale of history, the births, marriages and deaths of generation after generation – till he realised what was triggering the thought.

In his hand, he clutched a copy of Queen Mab's birth certificate, Greek wording translated in the margins. Rose Linnet, it said. Born in the Prefecture of Chania, in Crete. Registered parents, Gina and Abe Linnet. The registry stamp made the dead Rose somehow solid, renewed, her birth a new beginning.

Ham Hill, a view he loved, still glimmered in the distance, but he saw the colours of a different view - of Almyrida village, beneath the White Mountains. Blue checked tablecloths, the golden crunch of sand on the curved beach, the scent of the Cretan Sea, where stubby blue boats swayed at anchor in the tiny harbour. He could almost hear Rose sing *Lady in Red*.

Somewhere in that Cretan landscape, histories lay hidden. Gina Linnet and her two daughters. Abe, Darren, Daniel. Perhaps another 'D', as yet unknown. And Rose, whose throat would never sing again.

At the bottom of the birth certificate, Grigoris had scribbled, 'till more recent, these records are sometimes false.' Batten stared at the warning, unfinished business elbowing its way into his head. He shuffled the papers together and went back inside.

The curtains were pulled back now, the fridge and cupboards full, his phone sitting up like a dog awaiting dinner. But the phone had been the agent of too many condolence calls – well-intended but each a sad reminder. Sonia Welcome apart, he was not ready to face more - nor to face the living, breathing bodies behind the voices. Could he face Parminster HQ, where before Aunt Daze's death he craved to be?

Not yet, he told himself, and made a snap decision. Though convalescence was his bane, it would serve as the public excuse. His private reasons were a flight from condolence, and an itch to dig that had never gone away.

Without another thought, he grabbed the phone - and booked the next available plane to Crete.

PART FOUR

Almyrida, in Crete

Twenty nine

Cloudless, the flight. Batten stared down at the sea, a hazy blue, disturbed by faint white specks of waves. He could just make out the black dot of a ship and the carved trail of water at its stern. Seatbelt pulled tight, he followed the black dot's progress, far below. In minutes he was dozing...

Five years before, feet still on solid ground, a different traveller had contemplated a different sea – but saw only biting waves of hatred. Dragged up by feckless parents, Darren Pope lacked the skill to self-reflect. Instead, he squeezed his childhood hate and hurt into a ball - and handed the ball to Rose. Rose would unravel it, wouldn't she?

But Rose failed him. Worse, she failed his child, his recompense, his dream of a different future. *I need you, Darren,* she'd said - but left him with the taste of doubt on his tongue.

Under a moon shackled by cloud, Darren Pope wondered if the boat had somehow slipped past him, unseen, in the starless night. But so silent was it, he would have heard the splash of oars, let alone an engine. Squinting and listening, hidden in a clump of rocks, he curled up on the tiny beach and continued to wait. He craved a cigarette, but they'd warned him - no lights on the shore, or else.

He itched to leave this shore behind. The job at the abattoir bolstered his savings, but he'd grown to hate the work. Stun gun. Knife. Stun gun. Knife – six days a week, the stink of blood and viscera tainting his clothes and hair. Enough was enough. Now, having saved enough, the job was history.

But so was his baby. Not even a headstone or a lock of hair. And Rose? One letter - only ever one. Lucy, Rose's friend, sent nothing but disdain and bad news. Stop bothering me, Lucy's final letter said. Rose has gone. She left Crete. They took her away, to England.

'That's right, I'm heading for Sydney,' he told his abattoir workmates at his leaving 'do'. 'Heading south, to Sydney.'

Alone, in darkness, he headed north, to this tiny beach. And waited.

Darren's watch said 2am, his bones said he was cold, but his ears said 'engine', the faint chug creeping closer. Then stillness, as the engine died, and a dinghy drifted in silence to the beach.

'Say your name,' whispered a voice.

'Daz. Daz Parry,' he whispered back.

'You have a code?' hissed the same voice.

'4-3-6-1.'

'And what else?'

Darren held out a fistful of banknotes.

The voice grunted, grabbed the money, counted it in hooded light of a pencil torch, then grabbed Darren's backpack, and him. Out in the dark bay, as arranged, a larger boat hovered. Darren would pay the rest when Australia's Northern Territory was astern, and the boat made a clandestine drop in East Timor. From there, he hoped, to the Philippines, then England.

In his pocket, he fingered the Daz Parry passport - convincing, because expensive. And the knife, purloined from a Sydney drug-dealer, bleached and sharpened, ready to flip open if his smuggler 'friends' tried to take their money early and feed him to the sharks. The two smugglers sitting opposite were dark-skinned and small-framed, Darren's muscled bulk a strong deterrent. Extra insurance, the knife.

Glancing over his shoulder at the fading beach, he shrugged goodbye to his hopeless parents, to Brent, to Muggy, to Australia. He never wanted to leave Greece in the first place. But who listens to you when you're barely sixteen? He could still hear his young voice shouting *I won't go!* when Mum and Dad dragged him to Oz – after a good kicking from Abe Linnet. Abe was also on Darren's list. A pair of Linnets, Abe and Rose. Two birds, one hard stone.

The beach disappeared as oars kissed the sea. In the silence, a voice he had loved echoed in his memory. He heard Rose say, *Yes*. Heard her say, *Yes, Darren, yes!* on that different beach. *Look at the stars*, she said, on that darkest night, *look at them, shining, for us.*

Us? Me and the baby? *You killed us,* he hissed in silence. *First the baby, then me. Sliced me like a carcass at the abattoir, a knife into dead flesh. A hole in my gut, that's all you are!*

Soon, the Pacific Ocean would be the English Channel. *Other seas, other fish*, thought Darren. When the dinghy bounced against the side of the larger boat, he clambered aboard, readying the knife, just in case. A knife can get you out of trouble, he knew, brushing aside the trouble it had got him into. *Scores to settle,* he told himself.

Extra insurance, a knife.

Thirty

Batten's plane landed without ceremony on the island of Crete - a neutral zone, where he hoped to deflect the awkwardness of condolence. Already in debt to Grigoris, he flew in unannounced, fuss-free.

Not that flying was fuss-free to Batten. Though the tarmac of Chania airport seared the soles of his shoes when he escaped from the plane, it was preferable to the soggy English tarmac he'd teetered across to board. Sonia Welcome, not Chris Ball, was the last familiar face he gazed at on English soil. And, thankfully, it was not Chris Ball's long goodbye kiss still tingling on his lips.

'Cut back on the Greek coffee,' she advised. 'And not *too* much sun. You're supposed to heal, not fry. And I'm jealous of your all-over tan.'

He re-lived her soft fingers, tracing the frontiers on his naked body where pale skin met brown.

'Come with me, then,' he said, knowing she could not.

'If you ask again, Zig, and I say yes, will it happen?'

It will, he promised, but silently.

Now, hot tarmac under his feet, he prayed hope might subdue history. In the snail-like Arrivals queue, he gazed at his passport photograph, taken six years ago. Who would he have asked, six years ago, 'come with me, then?' The queue stuttered forward, the remembered names a stuttering biography. Marie. Rhona. Erin. Three failed relationships. Some might have succeeded, he admitted, if...

As the taxi sped past Souda Bay, it was not Souda but Sonia on his mind. 'Might, may, could.' Words he and she had used. Now, the words that came to mind were clichés. *When I crack this case... When I'm back to normal...*

The taxi dropped him not at a 'spare' apartment but at the Aloe Hotel, in Almyrida – his treat. In reality, he booked it because it was adults-only, a perfect haven of much-needed peace. He told himself he could work *and* convalesce, with peace surrounding him.

By late afternoon, he was at peace on his hotel balcony, overlooking the sea, with the documents Grigoris had unearthed, and two leather-bound bricks of scrawl. On the plane, an entry from the second brick had piqued him, and did again now.

Daniel never lets me in his studio. Never been inside the place. Calls it his painterly cell. Full of great works, I suppose - that no-one's allowed to see...

The 'secret somethings', the 'canvas secrets' mentioned in the journals – were they relevant here? Ball needed to get his finger out. He texted his long-suffering Sergeant. *You keeping me in the dark, Ballie? Not been to Queen Mab's lock-up yet?*

Too sharp? No, Ball was used to his Northern bluster. He pressed *send.*

Returning to the journal, he wondered why, since Rose and Daniel shared a bed, they did not share a studio. Or at least co-visit. Batten riffed through more pages.

Clio's turn to host the Almyrida Artists' monthly gathering. Her studio's tiny, eight of us squeezed in. No Daniel, again, but plenty of wine. Clio's experimenting with pallet knives - she showed us. Sofia let slip it was Daniel who showed Clio - how to sharpen the edges, so the paint slides off. Silly cow, hers are like scalpels. Cut myself on one of the bloody things.
Didn't like her new stuff either, sharp knife or not. If she paints that bloody blue ship with the white sails again I shall scream.
When Daniel got back from Etcetera, I said you missed another studio night. He rolled his shoulder. I mentioned the pallet knives. You showed Clio, didn't you?
Clio? he said. A surfeit of enthusiasm? Then straight to sleep.
*Wish **he** had a surfeit of enthusiasm, nights like this.*

As the sun began to wane, Batten rang Clio Demopoulou, with studios, Rose - and Daniel - in mind.

'Tomorrow, if seven in the morning is not too early for you?' Clio said. 'I wake early these days, but I am abed early too. Please do not think me rude, Mr Sig, but the waking hours in-between, they are my precious time. So, come early, or not come at all?'

Cretans reminded Batten of Yorkshire folk. Direct, clear, not dancing to the false music of 'politeness'. Rather than thinking her rude, he admired her ageing energy. Tonight, too exhausted to walk a hundred yards to a taverna, he ate a lazy meal in the hotel instead. Half-way through a chicken souvlaki, his phone beeped as Ball's email arrived. Typically efficient, old Ballie. The Area Super should be proud of him.

Mind elsewhere, Batten scrolled through Timms' report of her visit to Camelot Self-Storage, too tired now to open the attachments folder.

He drank only water, and was 'abed early too', Daniel's lost enthusiasm salting his dreams.

Thirty one

This time, no carafe of wine met Batten in the blue-painted kitchen of Clio Demopoulou's tidy house. The rich aroma of Greek coffee floated from the brass *briki* on the stove, its olive wood handle heavy with age and use. He was grateful for the rich brew, kicking him as awake as Clio.

'Either Crete has drawn you back, Mr Sig,' she said, 'or Rose has? If you came to enjoy my body, you waited too long!' Her gently mocking laugh morphed into an ominous cough and a walking stick with a shiny metal tip dangled from the back of her chair.

'All three,' he said, and she laughed again.

'My old body is here, and you are in Crete. So, that leaves only Rose.'

No mention of Daniel. Batten wondered why.

'You like the coffee?'

Batten nodded, raising his cup in genuine thanks for the tarry concoction with its tiny bubbles of froth. 'In her journal, Rose mentions the Almyrida painters.'

'So, world-famous artist Clio Demopolou is given an accolade?'

He could hardly mention Rose's dismissal of Clio's *bloody blue ship with white sails*. 'I'm afraid the journal's evidence,' he lied. 'But can I ask about 'studio nights' - here in Almyrida, I mean?'

'Studio nights!' Clio's laugh became a cackle. 'We were amateurs, young. We thought we knew everything of art. We knew nothing. The Almyrida Artists, we called ourselves. And, yes, on the first Saturday of every month we took turns to host a 'studio night', to pretend to talk of painting.'

'Pretend?'

Clio considered the word. 'We shared what little knowledge we had, yes. But we shared cigarettes and wine and raki more. And we shared each other, sometimes, you know, being *avant-garde*?' Her eyebrows danced, their meaning clear.

'It was Daniel's 'sharing' I was interested in,' he said.

Clio's eyebrows fell back to earth, in silence. 'Daniel,' she said, at last. 'An Almyrida Artist, yes, and he had a studio, yes, and if not away on a mysterious 'journey', he came to some of our nights. Some, not all.' Her face screwed itself into a ball of deep memories. 'In fact, few. A pity, as he had something to teach. A brush technique. How to find new colour.'

'How to use a palette knife?'

A tiny sideways flick of her chin was Clio's only response. 'Many things. Daniel had skill. Me, I had little. But I had fire, and kept it lit. Daniel, I think his fire was going.'

'Going? Where?'

Clio shrugged. 'When fire goes out, who can say? Into the air, as smoke? To the ground as ash? Or smouldering, hidden?'

'Hidden?'

'Puh, with Daniel, there was always something hidden. If I knew what, he would have failed to hide it!' Her chuckle triggered another round of dry coughs and she reached for her cup, empty but for coffee grounds. 'Ach,' she said. 'More coffee, I think,' and tried to struggle to her feet.

'I'll make it,' said Batten.

'*You?*' she said, laughing. 'I meant *Greek* coffee.'

He crossed to the stove. 'I have a *briki* at home, in England.' A Christmas gift, from Grigoris. Batten had learned how to make Greek coffee by making it badly too often. Now, he made sure the water was cold before spooning in the coffee like a Greek, setting the briki on the stove as Clio watched in amused surprise.

'Twenty years ago, maybe you *could* have had my body, Mr Sig,' she chuckled, and they shared small talk as the briki heated up. After sipping, she said 'quaite naice,' in a mock-British accent, and they laughed like a pair of youngsters.

'Was Rose's fire going out, too?' Batten asked.

'Ach,' she said, tutting. 'You cannot have my body after all, Mr Sig. You are not *romantic* enough. Can you not see? Rose - for a while, at least - was Daniel's *muse*. If you had seen his portrait of her - oh, such a portrait, her whole body on display. He brought the painting to a 'studio night', just once. But what a work. A true work, the only true Daniel work we saw. Rose refused to let him sell it.'

'Sell it? Surely he gave it to her?'

Clio paused again, the sideways flick of her chin returning. 'I know it is gone.' She waved her free hand at nothing.

'Good, was it?' He kept quiet about Professor Merry's photo of the Botticelli pastiche, currently in his suitcase at the Aloe – with Rose the centrepiece.

Clio Demopoulou put down her cup. '*Good?* Beyond *good*. I told you before, he had great skill. You know Botticelli's *The Birth of Venus?*'

Batten nodded, encouraging Clio to talk.

'Daniel's portrait was a copy of that painting, but the background was this, here.' She waved seaward, towards the bay. 'And, oh, the Venus. The Venus was not Venus. It was *Rose*. Rose's face and yes, her body, every naked inch of it. His skill, her fire, they met on that canvas, as if the sun, up there, had exploded.' Clio jabbed at the yellow light of morning, adding with a cackle, 'Sofia, from our group, she whispered in my ear, "he didn't use a brush, he used their bedsheets!" Clio's cackles faded to a sadder note. 'But that was the only true one, ever.'

'The only one?' asked Batten.

Clio sipped her coffee, thinking. 'After the Venus, his works had skill, but no soul. And his final daubs, what few he showed us, were seascapes. Not a *human* in any of them, as if he grew tired of humans - of us, at least, the Almyrida Artists. I tell you, someone had called the fire brigade, and put him out. He was all technique again. But no flame.'

'He grew tired of Rose? Is that what you mean?'

'She had eyes. Daniel's message was there, in those later paintings. Blue sea, without people. Blue sky, without Rose. As plain as the moustache on your face! But Rose, did she want to see?'

'Love is blind?'

'Humph. *Rose* was. I told you, I liked Rose. She reminded me of me when I was young. But I grew up.'

'And Rose didn't?'

Her gnarled fingers set down her cup, the wicker chair rustling beneath her. She seemed to find an answer in the early flickers of sun, speckling the blue walls of the kitchen, a war of light and shade.

'The child in Rose was troubled. And strong. When I grew up, I grew a middle. I grew…substance. But Rose? Where was her substance? Not in her self-portraits, for sure!'

'Self-portraits? Were they any good?'

Clio's throaty laugh emerged again, her head shaking. 'They were neither good, bad nor terrible – because Rose never painted any! How can you paint self-portraits if you do not *know* yourself? Where was her substance? She was other people! She was the Daniels of this world. I watched her, many times, at studio nights, tavernas, bars. At first, a glass of wine or two. Soon, three, four, more, the glass never full enough. Wine, to keep the moment, to stop the years. Poor Rose, like one of those shiny suits of armour in a museum - empty. An empty suit of armour, protecting nothing from something. But before you ask, I do not know what.'

Someone does, Batten thought.

'Then later still, wine became raki, which she did not even like. And always a parting glass, with whoever was host that night.'

'Which was never Daniel?'

'Puh. He came rarely to our gatherings. And never hosted one, not one. Always, an excuse.'

'Did you ever go to his studio?'

She pondered the question, staring across the kitchen as light trembled through a glass lantern hanging in the window, throwing jagged spikes of shadow on the blue wall. For a moment, Clio gazed at the sharp-edged patterns, shimmering in a faint breeze from the sea.

'Yes. I went there. Twice. And only twice.' She raised her coffee cup, saw only dregs remaining, and clattered it into the tiny saucer. 'To my shame, I went there not for art, but for Daniel. I told you, we were free spirits. *Avant-garde.* And, yes, not as moral as we might have been.'

Batten put down his own cup, the movement seeming to wake Clio Demopoulou from a sleep of memory. She treated him to a long look. Somewhere between guilt and regret, he thought.

'The *second* time, he did not let me in. Not into his life, and not into his studio. He stood in the doorway, one of his little cigarettes on his lip, arm across the frame, like a guard. What are they called, those big men who stand outside bars?'

'Bouncers?'

'Yes! Like a bouncer – though Daniel was handsome – with hair on his head!'

166

'And he slammed the door in your face?'

'No, no, never that. A gentleman, always, and spoke like one, even when his meaning was less gentle. Even his cigarette was…graceful. But always a question for an answer. 'Do you think, Clio,' he said, 'we should consider the…further complications?'

'Further?' asked Batten, more briskly than he'd intended.

Clio rewarded his question with a Greek shrug. 'Further, yes. Though for Daniel it would not have been much further, I suspect.'

'I'm sorry, I don't…'

'You don't understand? No. Why would you? Daniel did not let me into his studio a second time, no. But the first time…' Her eyes stared at the woven rug at her feet. 'And I had already let him into mine.' She looked up, meeting Batten's gaze. 'You see? You see now?'

Batten nodded, a slow-witted pigeon. He had no right to judge Clio, he knew. Yet, her meaning clear, he felt absurdly protective of Rose and angry with the Daniel he had never set eyes on. 'So, you considered the further complications?' he asked.

'I did. I considered myself. I considered Rose, even though she was too young for Daniel - who considered *me* too old for him. Daniel needed to be always young, and in Rose he had youth and beauty. Until, like me, she grew older?'

'Sounds a bit…opportune.'

'Opportune? Ach, such an English word. The only word to describe Daniel is *Daniel*! Skilled, yes, but mostly at considering the wants and needs of *Daniel*. I saw this, that same day. Maybe the day I grew up.' She stared at nothing for a moment. 'Rose saw it too late, if she saw it at all.' Clio thrust an arthritic hand at Batten. 'Help me walk, please, before my old bones fuse together.'

She tottered into the garden, one hand on his arm, the other on her stick, and looked down at the sea. Boats chugged in and out of the little harbour. Vans made loud deliveries to the bars clustered round the bay. 'You know, Mr Sig, Rose painted this bay of ours, over and over, as if she would always be here, she and her Daniel, as if there was nothing else in the world to paint?'

Batten tried not to smile at the thought of Clio Demopoulou painting a blue ship with white sails, over and over. Do we grow up when we stop repeating ourselves? he wanted to ask.

'What was so special about Daniel's studio? Since he never let anyone in?'

Clio slowly drew her eyes away from the sea. 'We all had studios, and pretended they were stuffed with great works of art. We let people in because we hoped for praise, for sales. Or because deep down, we knew our daubs were hopeless, so what did it matter? No need for a 'bouncer' on the door.'

'But Daniel?'

She gave Batten a glance of...embarrassment? Something else? He found her dark eyes and hesitations hard to read.

'I told you, I did not go to his studio to look at art. I waited in shadow, as he removed the padlock on the door - a padlock bigger than a *briki*! Inside, the walls were covered in paintings, but every painting covered with a cloth. To protect? To hide? I did not ask - about paintings. And early next day he went to Athens.'

'Athens? As a tourist?'

She waved his words into the air. 'A tourist? Daniel? Puh. He had already wandered through the world. But always tight-lipped about Athens. He came back with money in his pocket, so... He did some restoration, I understand.'

'Mixing cement for the Parthenon?'

She tapped his arm playfully. 'Cement for the Parthenon, indeed! Restoring *paintings*, Mr Sig. And valuation, too, for the auction houses. Daniel had much skill.'

'And when he left, he padlocked his studio. Skill that needed protecting?'

They had walked the garden's perimeter now, and something more than tiredness was etched into Clio's face. 'Maybe he did have great works of art inside. He was the only true painter in our group, so, possible. And maybe his great works were unfinished? Or he had lost his fire? Or maybe, behind the padlock, he kept his soul?' She stared at the glassy blue of the sea, as if Daniel's soul might leap into the air astride a dolphin. 'No more questions, please, Mr Sig. They tire me.'

Batten pointed at the garden chair, shaded by a tamarisk tree. 'Do you need to sit down?'

'No, no. I have things I must do. But I will tell you one last secret. My bedroom upstairs' - she gave Batten's arm another playful tap - 'where in different lives, different times, Mr handsome Sig, who knows, we might have 'dallied', it has many paintings on the walls. But not a single work by me. None of my blue ships with the white sails, worthless daubs, all of them.'

'Surely not,' he tried to say, but she dismissed his attempt.

'The moment comes when we must choose how to be remembered. Your moment will come, soon or late. If you fail to choose, the world may remember only the worst of you. So, last year, I burnt every one of my paintings. Come, look.'

She steered Batten to the far corner of the garden, by a stone wall, where a charred patch of ground was covered in ash. Gazing down at the dead embers, he imagined Clio piling one painting on another and putting a match to the lot. Oil, canvas, and wood. Quick to catch fire. He could almost see and smell the flames. Ever the detective, he wondered what else she might have burned.

'Because I liked Rose, I kept one of her paintings of the bay. It hangs in my bedroom. I hope she had the sense to burn the rest, for they were worse than mine.' Clio's quiet cackle faded as she stared at the burnt patch of ground. 'But I tell you, my walls, they have nothing by Daniel. Nothing. And in the whole of Almyrida you will not find a single work of his. Maybe they hang in villas in Athens? Or maybe his flame went out and he threw away his paints? Or did Daniel's moment come, when he too chose how to be remembered, and so he built a bonfire of his own?'

Batten opened his face and fingers into a question, but Clio shook her head, 'No more. Please.'

On Batten's arm, she hobbled into the kitchen and hooked her brass-tipped stick on the back of her chair, the wicker creaking as she struggled down. For a moment, she gazed past the tamarisk tree to the blue waves beyond, as if creating memories.

'If you find out,' she said, 'and I am still alive, I invite you to make Greek coffee in my *briki*. And tell me of the paintings hidden by cloths behind his padlock. Because, Mr Sig, if you do, you will discover what I went there to find. You will discover *Daniel.*'

*

As a puzzled Batten strolled towards the sea, Clio Demopoulos stared through her kitchen window at the deep blue waters of the bay. What worlds of truth must the sea contain? Everything she had told the handsome detective was true. But she had not told him all. Not quite. Staring at the rippled sea, she knew her reasons.

Jealousy, for one. She shrugged. All the artists were jealous of Daniel, the men *and* the women because he had skill and they - mere daubers. But the women were jealous because…because they desired Daniel in three dimensions, not the flat two of a canvas.

And Clio was jealous of Rose, who fed on Daniel - and he on her - each time he returned to Almyrida. Clio had tasted but a morsel and yearned for more.

'*Rose is too young for you, Daniel!*' Clio had told him. Closer to the truth was, '*Clio is too old for Daniel.*'

Despite her pride, she admitted this to the English policeman. So why could she not tell him what she saw, fleetingly, in Daniel's studio, when he let her in, that one dark night, not for the sake of art? When he led her to the couch at the back of the room, and his arm brushed against the muslin draped over a painting, and the muslin fell… The briefest glance because Daniel swiftly replaced the painting's clothes - and began removing hers.

In half-shade, a glimpse, when other senses were at work. All the same, a glimpse of something Greek on a canvas, modern Greek, surely? But a Greek painting, when Daniel was English to his fingertips…? The moment ebbed away as English fingertips tingled her Greek skin.

And might she have told Mr Sig what old Dimitris saw and heard, from his balcony, on the day Daniel left for good?

And what Mrs Tsoumakis told her, later?

Clio kept it all to herself because of jealousy. Rose, a modern Venus, drew Daniel to her side by being beautiful, and young. Clio, for all her siren calls, had failed to conquer him and was ashamed of the sly pleasure she felt when he abandoned Rose.

Once more, she pieced together, half-remembered, half-imagined, what she should perhaps have told Mr handsome Sig…

'Iannis! Iannis! Where is that boy? *Iannis!*'

Ireni Tsoumakis lost him every day. Ten years ago, when his head collided sharply with the tiller of his father's boat, 'lost' became a permanent state of mind for Iannis. *Fifteen now, but does he even know his age, or that I am his mother?* If only she could ask her husband who, lacking her strength of will, swiftly deserted family life for unknown seas.

Now, it was Iannis who'd sailed away, into the streets, *again.* He would reappear soon enough, she knew, his arm in the firm grip of one of the patient shopkeepers of Almyrida. When Iannis lost his mind, he also lost his sense of ownership. *You are a trial, Iannis!* Ireni would say – when she found him.

The voice in Iannis's head says, *Help yourself!* To fruit, to sweets, to a baseball cap from the tourist shop, a comic from the minimart. The day Iannis helped himself to a solid gold signet ring from the jeweller's, Ireni began to lock him in the house.

Iannis, though, was a climber. He climbed out of windows, down drainpipes, across rooftops, in and out of shops, tavernas, delivery vans. 'What am I to do?' she asked one complainant after another? 'Chain him up, like a donkey? Like a goat?'

So, blind eyes were turned, and goods recovered or paid for.

'*Iannis!*' No reply. When he *was* here, he could talk well enough. But making sense, that was different.

'Here! I stand here, in the street! Why can you not see me?' Iannis, four hours gone, and wandering home as if he'd popped out for a bag of peaches.

'What is that you are carrying?' she asked. Not a comic or a baseball cap, this.

'A painting,' said Iannis, as if he'd just finished sloshing oils onto canvas.

Ireni had stopped asking, 'whose?' Iannis would only say - '*mine.*' And if he really had 'borrowed' a painting, he'd borrowed more than one. The package under his arm was bulky, sealed with thick tape. Perhaps several paintings without the frames, she thought, before her mind screamed, *does it matter how many?*

Instead of 'whose?' she'd learned to ask 'where?'

Iannis pointed upwards, to the narrow road which curled above the village, overlooking the shore. 'Daniel gave it to me.'

'Gave'. Another word she'd learned to ignore. 'Show me,' she said, taking Iannis by the arm and marching him up the dust-covered hill.

The road bent sharply, curling past old Dimitris' house near the studios where the crazy village artists did their daubs. Ireni thought she saw a bundle of old clothes on the pavement - till the bundle moved. It was the English girl who drinks too much, slumped against the wall, head down. In the heat of the afternoon, she was alone, worse for wear. Ouzo, Ireni supposed, as if it mattered. She tried to remember her name.

'*Rose!*' shouted Iannis. Every word a shout, these days. Rose glanced up, recognising the voice, and briefly swished at her face with a hankie. When she turned back, she wore a half-smile. Another crazy artist, like Daniel, Ireni told herself. But at least the pair of them *talk* to Iannis – in awful Greek, yes, that makes Iannis cackle like a hyena.

But no hyena with Rose. Her presence calmed him, quelled the tannoy of his voice. Iannis smiled back at Rose, leaving the words to his mother.

'I am sorry…Rose. But Iannis, he has borrowed again.' She pointed at the package, still jammed beneath her son's arm.

'Daniel gave it, Rose,' whispered Iannis. 'A painting. From his van. He left the doors open, for me, yes?'

Ireni shrugged. Rose nodded back. The village understood what Iannis meant by 'gave.'

'Daniel gave you a painting, Iannis?' said Rose, staring at the bundle. A long silence. 'He gave me a painting, once.'

To Ireni, the words came out like fingernails on a blackboard. 'I think more than one painting, Rose, see? A whole pack? We are returning them to Daniel.' She gave Rose a practised smile of apology. 'You know how it is.'

'Returning them? Daniel's gone,' said Rose. After a tight pause, she added, 'he drove away. He drove away to Etcetera.'

Ireni had no time for riddles. She yanked the package from Iannis and pushed it forward. It was heavier than she thought and almost fell onto the dusty road. 'Please give it to Daniel, Rose. When he returns.'

'Returns?' said Rose, her unblinking stare on the paintings.

A bored Iannis, his package reclaimed, wandered down the hill towards the minimart, slapping his sandals at the dust devils thrown up by a wind from the sea.

'I must go,' said Ireni. 'Before Iannis…you see how it is. Please return the paintings to Daniel. I am sorry. We are sorry, again.'

And Ireni disappeared into the whirls of dust, leaving Rose propped against the white wall of Daniel's empty studio, clutching the package his own hands had carefully sealed.

'*Return them to Daniel?*' she shouted at the empty street, her words slurring. '*Where? In Etcetera?*' Hearing the commotion, Old Dimitris popped his head around the pink bracts of bougainvillea shielding his balcony, to see Rose searching the package for a label, an address.

Peering closer at tiny letters inked along the edge in Daniel's hand, Rose made out two short words, 'St. Ives.'

'Not to Etcetera, then!' she yelled, as if words screamed at the sky would reach the ears of her departed lover. 'St. Ives? Heading back to Cornwall, Daniel?' Her words reached only the ears of old Dimitris, hiding, intimidated - on his own balcony - by this *crazy Rose*. 'Why St Ives?' she screamed at the street. 'You've already been!'

Easily, she mimicked Daniel's cultured voice. His voice, implanted within her, was all that remained of him. '*Why travel anywhere, Rose? A station on life's rich journey, mm?*' Louder now she yelled, 'you changed the subject, didn't you? Questions! Always questions!'

Old Dimitris watched her rip at the package, but the tape was too strong for her fingers. The last thing he saw was Rose tucking the parcel under her arm, much as poor lost Iannis had done, and wobbling back to her rented house. In her wake, dust devils spun in the air, whipped up by a breeze fast becoming a storm…

Slumped in her kitchen chair overlooking the bay, Clio Demopoulos imagined the rest. Imagined Rose Linnet ignoring the storm because storms of her own boiled within. Imagined her tumbling into the little house she rented from Clio and crossing to her kitchen worktop and the heavy wooden block, studded with knives. Perhaps she chose the thin, razor-sharp knife for boning fish. Perhaps she gripped the hard, cold steel of the handle in her angry fingers, the blade slicing not into Daniel but his mystery package.

What does it contain, Rose would wonder - as Clio did - this package Daniel needed to conceal? And why did Daniel write 'St Ives' on the wrapper, in the neat, flowing hand Rose would never purge from her memory?

Because Clio had only a faint inkling why, she chose not to say 'St Ives' to Mr Sig, nor tell him of the Greek-looking canvas she glimpsed in Daniel's studio, that hot dark night when lust, not art, removed the padlock and she slipped inside.

Instead, she shuffled back into her garden, to stare again at the charred patch of ground by the stone wall. In her mind's eye, the ash and dust re-formed into smoke, the smoke into flame, the flame emerging from the daubs she had piled there and burnt, without regret. As she stared, she saw again the previous object to catch fire, the object Rose left behind in the little rented house that once stood a few doors down.

In daydream, a younger Clio was there again, at the old house, taking the keys from Rose's hand, as the taxi drew up for Rose's final departure.

'I've left it spick and span, Clio,' Rose said. Clio nodded. She knew Rose would. 'I broke a wine glass, so please let me pay for it.'

Full, or empty? Clio wanted to ask. 'Ach,' she said, waving away the offer. 'One glass. A thing.' The two women looked at each other, two mirrors, two reflections of jealousy and respect, trust and suspicion. 'A forwarding address?'

Rose shrugged. 'I'll write, once I'm sure,' she said.

'From Athens?' asked Clio.

'*Athens*? I'm not going to Athens.'

'But I thought...'

'Daniel's not in Athens, Clio. Wherever Daniel's taken his shadow, it's not Athens. I'd feel it.'

The keys jangled in Clio's sceptical hand. She slipped them into her bag as the taxi driver, impatient now, climbed from his seat and opened the boot, his hand waving a question at the two suitcases on the pavement.

'Efharisto,' said Rose. 'Thank you.' The driver picked up both, left hand and right, before putting the left one down and struggling to load the other.

'All my worldly goods,' Rose said to Clio. 'They weigh more than me.'

Clio nodded, glancing with envy at the slim curves of Rose Linnet, before her sense of care returned. 'You will be safe? Wherever you go?'

Rose considered the question. 'Safe? Hope to be,' she said. 'Safe in Cornwall perhaps. Daniel was there once. So, I'll find *something* of him, won't I?'

With a meaningful *clunk*, the driver slammed the boot and yanked open the passenger door. Wordlessly, the two women hugged, whether from concern or relief Clio was unsure. As the taxi rolled away, she knew it was both. Rose neither waved nor looked back.

Unlocking the door, Clio reverted to owner, inspecting cupboards and worktops, curtains, balcony, all spick and span as Rose had promised. At the bedroom door, she hesitated before entering, feeling an intruder in the house she owned, memory and regret seeming to rise from the floor like mist. On the bed, she saw Rose had left her a present. A bulky rolled canvas, secured by a muslin strip tied in a neat bow, but no card or message. *If she's left me another daub of Almyrida bay, I shall take a knife to it!* thought Clio, untying the bow.

As if alive, the canvas uncurled across the bed, revealing Daniel's pastiche of *The Birth of Venus*, Almyrida the background, and Venus replaced by Rose, her anatomical glory on public display.

Clio slumped down on the bedsheets.

Had to.

Rose would never 'forget' a work so precious, before departing on a search for even *something* of Daniel. Is this 'gift' a message? *Clio, we've **both** been inside Daniel's studio!* Did Rose guess?

Clio flattened out the canvas, shocked and shamed as the naked figure of Venus-Rose draped itself across the bed. When Daniel had proudly displayed it, Clio never *studied* the work. A glance or two and she'd studied the wasted desire in her own heart. Now, beneath the painterly skill, she saw what Rose must also have seen and, in a breath, she understood why Rose left behind her only portrait.

What Clio stared at was the triumph of the artist over his model. With acute technique, Daniel had imprinted his own assumptions on the canvas, like a surgeon slicing into a helpless patient. The structure of the work was Daniel's alone. Rose, the subject, mere scaffolding, her eyes fixed firmly on the artist. And the brush gripped in Daniel's hand betrayed what he really valued - her youthful naked beauty, her physical form.

Clio's shaking hand caressed the varnish Daniel had used to fix in place the vanities of his world. She stared at Daniel's Almyrida, Daniel's Venus, *Daniel's* Rose. The soul of Rose was missing, because only her body beguiled him. Each exquisite dab of paint defined the flesh Daniel thought he owned – until such time as he chose to cast it aside.

Shamed, within the now empty house *she* owned, the house she had rented to Rose, Clio grew up for a second time. Unworthily, she had wanted to own Daniel, too. Yet Rose, in her naivety, was prepared to search for his shadow.

Re-tying the canvas, Clio knew what must be done. Without hesitation she walked the painting back to the other house she owned, the house she lived in, walked it to the far corner of her garden by the old stone wall, and struck a match. In the dry heat of the day, oil and canvas became an instant pyre. Rolled into a coil, Rose's naked body was at least invisible as it charred, flamed, and turned to ash…

…Staring now at the blackened ground in her garden, framed by the honest blue of sea and sky, Clio wondered should she have told Mr handsome Sig the fate of Rose's only portrait? And told him of that other curious painting, Greek, modern, glimpsed in the darkness of Daniel's studio when something more than art was on her mind?

No. This burnt patch of ground belonged to her and was many things. The ashes of her own worthless daubs. The blackened embers of Rose. And, in a way, the dregs of Daniel.

Flicking at the ash with her stick, she pitied Mr Sig, a driven dog if ever she saw one, scratching in the dust for old bones.

Some things need to burn.

Then be forgotten.

Thirty two

Almyrida village was still stretching its arms when Batten stepped away from Clio's house into the shadows of morning. Rather than have breakfast at the Aloe, he decided to stretch his legs along the clifftop and down to the beach.

He wondered why the sea drew him, as a boat lolled at anchor in the little harbour, and gentle ripples ebbed and flowed across the sand. When Batten kicked at a stone sticking up from the damp beach, it shifted an inch and settled back. *A measure of progress?* he wondered.

From distance, the tablecloths of his favourite taverna were still blue and white – but as he drew closer, his face turned an embarrassed red. At the nearest table, a familiar face gave a mock, flamboyant wave of greeting.

Grigoris.

'How the hell did you know I -'

'Sig. You receive in the post the papers I send? And we are friends, yes?'

'Good friends, Makis.'

'And so, to follow these clues, I know you must return. And you have no false passport? Your real name, it is on your ticket for the plane, the taxi, the hotel?'

'Of course, Makis. I'm not a smuggler.'

'And yet you try to smuggle yourself into Crete? And not tell Lieutenant Makis Grigoris of the Greek *International Police Cooperation Division*? Your friend who is on leave? And bored? I am disgusted, Sig!' The mock-stern Grigoris broke into a grin as a waiter brought two Greek coffees. 'I see you on the beach, I order for you. But your turn to pay.'

Batten had no heart to tell Grigoris this would be his third cup of the morning and he'd be a jumping bean for hours. Nor tell him Sonia had advised him to cut back on the caffeine. He raised his cup in greeting, the White Mountains raising their wrinkled brow at him.

'We Grigoris cousins, we have been busy, on your behalf. We do not need to be asked, not even informed of your arrival. We know you are

English-polite.' In his best cod-English accent, Grigoris added, '*wouldn't want to be a burden, old boy.*' But the laughter was brief. 'Next time, Sig, remember please your friend is *Greek*-polite? And it is *not* polite to refuse Greek hospitality! *Agree?*'

Shamed, Batten mumbled a 'yes' and sipped redundant coffee. Then as if nothing had happened, the puzzle that was Grigoris pitched right in - but not with news of Daniel Flowers.

'I am sorry, Sig, but Abe Linnet's boat, I cannot find.'

'No surprise, Makis.'

'But the mooring records of the boat, not so hard to discover.' Grigoris managed a smug nod. 'In Alimos Marina. He kept it there, many time.'

'Alimos? Never heard of it.'

'Ah, it is quite close to…Athens, yes? Maybe ten of your English miles?'

Almyrida. Alimos. Batten imagined Abe's boat sneaking between them, before he hit the road for the short hop to Athens, Greece's bustling capital. To do what?

'In Alimos, he is one sailing boat, lost among boats like his. You know how many boats, at Alimos? *One thousand!*'

'Then I'm amazed you tracked him down, Makis.'

'Would be hard, Sig. Except he still owe three-month harbour fees!'

'I doubt the Port Authority will see the cash.'

'Is so. But - they send these to me.'

Grigoris handed over two photographs. The first pictured an impressive white boat, broad-beamed, a surprise to Batten, who expected a stubby fishing boat like those in Almyrida harbour. This boat was sleek. 'How many cabins?' he asked.

Grigoris pointed to portholes at stern and prow. 'Two cabin. Four berth.'

Batten stared at the photo. Even before little Sue was born, Abe Linnet had returned to a life on land - yet held onto a four-berth seagoing yacht? 'Why keep the boat, Makis? Not cheap.'

'Who can say, Sig. But with a boat, you are free. Can sail here, go there.'

'*Which* here or there, though? And where's it gone? If it sank, wouldn't there be wreckage?'

Grigoris pointed at the sea's vastness. 'A little piece of boat, in all of this?' he said, dismissing Batten's question with a shrug and nudging the second photo.

An old mooring ID, Abe Linnet's mugshot in the top corner, stared up at Batten. Abe's features were so nondescript the ID could have been an advert for sun-cream – but little else. If Abe bore a resemblance to anything, it was a horse, with long teeth and mane-like hair pulled back in a ponytail. Whatever once attracted Gina Linnet was lost on Batten.

Turning back to the photo of Abe's boat, Batten struggled with the Greek alphabet before deciphering the name stencilled on the hull. *Aura?* Tough guy Abe Linnet christened his boat *Aura*? Batten found the idea laughable. 'Makis, does 'Aura' mean something different, in Greek?'

Grigoris gave his mock-pitying shrug, eyes to the heavens, palms splayed upwards. 'Why you not learn my language, Sig? I learn English, you hear me speak it, every day, yes?'

'Makis, I'm trying. I've learnt the alphabet, haven't I? Just tell me what it means.'

'Sig, your schools, your universities, they do not teach of Greek myth? *Aura* is one of the ancient Titans, a Greek goddess.'

Batten shrugged away the irony of Abe Linnet, his boat an escape from women, naming it after a *goddess*? 'Goddess of what?' he asked.

'Many things, Sig, but mostly goddess of the air, the wind, of the breeze. Now, drink this fine coffee.'

Batten pretended to. The rich, tarry liquid was strong enough to tingle his veins, but it wasn't coffee tingling the soles of his feet. *Breeze.* Where had he come across *Breeze* before? Eyes screwed closed, his recovering mind flashed an answer. Scrolling through his phone's 'saved documents' folder, he found Ball's email. Last night, he'd flicked through Hazel Timms' report in a daze.

'You need to see what's in Queen Mab's storage unit for yourself, sir,' it said. He scanned the account of her visit.

'*Ray Breeze!*' he said, so loudly the four tourists at the next table stopped chewing their breakfast and stared at him. Grigoris too. Batten ignored them all, punching numbers into the phone. He walked along the beach a little way when Timms answered. The background noise of Parminster CID could have been from another planet.

'Anything wrong, sir?' she said.

'Depends, Hazel. Describe Ray Breeze to me.'

Is this some kind of 'welcome back' test? she thought. 'What, that decrepit security guard? At Camelot Self-Storage? Should have been superannuated years ago.'

'Yes, yes, but what's he look like?'

Timms sighed into the phone. Ray Breeze didn't look like *anything*. 'Lank hair, grey. Tall. Muscled, I suppose, but going to seed. Looked ill, to me, despite a suntan. Big teeth. And glum - but that could've been disdain for the police, especially the female version. How I'm doing, sir?'

Batten stared at Abe Linnet's photo ID, then at the waves creeping up the sand and ebbing back into the bay. In, out. In, out. His eyes followed the white furrows as they rippled back towards the little harbour where the solitary boat still bobbed like a wayward cork in a blue bucket.

'*Sir?*'

'Sorry, Hazel. You're doing fine. Can you track down a photo of your Mr Breeze? The security company will have one. And run a check on his comings and goings. If he has a passport and it's genuine, I'll eat the bloody thing. But do it on the quiet. Don't want Ray Breeze getting wind of it.'

'Yes, sir,' said Timms, wincing at the bad pun. Despite more work, she was piqued now. 'Any particular reason?'

The waves flowed back, darkening the sand and dowsing Batten's feet. He didn't notice, eyes still fixed on the boat swaying at anchor, as if signalling.

'Maybe, Hazel. Maybe a very particular reason indeed…'

Grigoris gave a resigned sigh when Batten sat down and yanked Queen Mab's journal from his backpack.

'Apologies, Makis, but I'm struggling to connect the dots. It's something I read, early on, when I was even more fuzzy headed than I am now. It's all this Greek coffee you're making me drink.' Flicking through page after page, he found the entry his memory had pushed aside.

Bus dropped me in Almyrida - hardly recognised it. But a breath of fresh air after those shitty folk at uni.

Rented a cheap little house, up the slope above the sea. Huge brass telescope on a tripod by the window. Focused it on the harbour, people watching. Well, man-watching.

Been alone too long, since...

Spotted one handsome body, squatting on the rocks. Maybe he hasn't moved in ten years! Still had a fishing rod in one hand, a cigarette in the other, paintbox beside him, and a paperback. I could even make out the title.

Ten years back, or more, was it, when me, Mum, and Dad lived on the boat? Dad often docked here. Would I have been twelve or so? Dad sailed off again, lord knows where, and me and Mum lounged on the beach. Told her I'd seen Dad talking to this tall man with a fishing rod. He's handsome, I said, and she snapped at me, keep away from him!

Why? I said. Dad took him out on our boat, I saw him. He knows Dad.

Exactly, she said. Mumbled it. What do you mean? I said, and she hissed at me, He's more than twice your age!

You're not much more than twice mine! I hissed back – big mistake. She slapped me so hard across the face I could feel a red bruise forming. When Dad came back, she said I fell. He shot her his sneery look, hard as steel - she turned the same colour as my cheek. We know what to expect, Mum and me.

Ten years? Feels like a hundred...

The handsome man with a fishing rod, and a box of paints - clearly Daniel. But *'Dad took him out on our boat, I saw him. He knows Dad.'*

'Sig, your face. You have won the European Lottery, yes? Your Queen Mab – she told you the numbers!'

'She told me something, Makis. Told me Abe Linnet and Daniel Flowers were well-acquainted, a long time ago. And the two of them sailed off together in Abe's boat. I don't believe for a moment they just went 'fishing', so what else did they catch?' He tapped the photograph of *Aura*. 'It's a puzzle, this boat.'

'The boat that disappear?'

Batten blew out his breath. Not easy, in the 21st century, for a boat to disappear. For people, harder still. But Abe and his boat had managed it. Daniel Flowers, too.

Dammit, where?

Thirty three

With the afternoon sun so strong on his hotel balcony it stung his eyes, Batten moved inside as the brooding boom in his skull became a warning. Inside was cooler, the dressing table as good as a desk – better, with no phones or clacking keyboards threatening the peace.

Boat, boat, boat, he mumbled to himself, shuffling through page after journal page in search of *Aura,* without success. He turned to the email attachment Timms had sent - the photos of the six modernist paintings Hazel thought were Ben Nicholson copies. To his frustration, they were thumbnails, too small to show much detail. Despite having a pair of Ben Nicholson prints on his study wall in England, he was no wiser about these.

Balked, he returned to the leather-bound bricks. Sipping cold bottled water, half-tourist, half-native now, he picked at the lush red tomato from a room-service Cretan salad while letting chunks of onion soak a little longer in the olive oil and oregano. By the time he snapped the journals shut, he'd polished off the onion too.

Sighing, he pushed aside a scribbled note from Grigoris saying, 'Sig, I will keep my search for the boat.' Will it be found?

In search of connections, he switched to the documents Grigoris had posted to England, and a Prefecture letter enquiring about Rose's home-schooling. What dry wells of wisdom did Abe and Gina dip their buckets in, to teach their daughter anything at all beyond the lessons of Nature - a blue sunlit sea, the white peaks, and a blaze of stars at night?

He wondered if the same thought struck them too, till he read the Prefecture's official warning which triggered the thirteen-year-old Rose's enrolment at the Theodoropoulos Private School in Chania. Batten had no idea home-schooling was illegal in Greece. While her enrolment details were clear enough, less clear was the source of the money to pay the fees. And Abe's compliance - Batten would bet cider on it – was not from respect for the law, but to avoid the law's scrutiny.

Comparing school documents and journal pages, he spotted one name that cropped up in both. Malcolm McTay had taught Literature at the

Theodoropoulos school, and Rose Linnet was one of his pupils. Copies of her glowing reports had McTay's signature at the bottom. He clearly made a strong impression on Rose because her journal said so, more than once. And she called him 'Malkie'.

Malkie's off sick, again. Got that woman with the mole on her chin instead, yuk. — Whines on about there being bugger all worth reading after Homer's Odyssey. I said, The Odyssey was originally for **reciting***. She aims her mole at me, her eyeball a gun. Hope Malkie doesn't die. Couldn't stand being taught by Old-Miss-Mole, instead of Malkie.*

The retired McTay still lived in Chania. Though Batten could now tell *kalimera* from *calamari* he still needed Grigoris to help him converse with a true Cretan, so it was a relief to hear a British voice on the phone.

'Do you know the street called Chalidon?' asked McTay. Batten did. 'Near the far end, going away from the sea, there's a cafe called Funky's.'

'*Funky's?* Doesn't sound very Greek?'

'Pizza and chips, but welcoming. Excellent coffee. And very close to my flat. I'm afraid I struggle to walk.'

Batten reminded himself McTay was no spring chicken. Will I ever talk to a *young* Cretan, he thought, one who isn't a waiter? Next morning, at eleven, McTay suggested.

Thirty four

Chania was hot. Funky's small, young, and buzzing. Within seconds, the din triggered a knock of warning in Batten's skull, easing when they moved to an outside table set back from the road and the whine of scooters – and tasted the excellent coffee.

McTay's retained Scottish burr almost had Batten checking for a kilt, despite his host's plain blue shirt and linen trousers. 'We choose our destinations for a reason, do we not?' McTay said, raising his cup.

Then why, Batten wondered, in my thirty-nine years on the planet do I bumble from one destination to another?

'I miss being amongst the young, now I am considered old,' said McTay, tapping his fingers on the collapsible walking stick in his lap, beneath a shock of grey hair and a beard out of Tolstoy. Whatever scholars are supposed to look like, this man is it. Memories of an ex-girlfriend's voice told Batten the soft burr was Edinburgh.

I loved my work,' said McTay, 'I miss it.' He glanced at his stick, for the briefest moment. 'I miss all my students, whether bright, beautiful, ugly or damned.'

'And Rose Linnet, which was she?'

McTay laughed. 'Rose? All four!' His laugh faltered to a dry wheeze which he lubricated with coffee. 'From time to time, a teacher meets a pupil more rewarding than the norm.'

'And she fit the bill?'

'She had *potential*. Articulate, and a sharp eye. Are you familiar with Nikos Kazantzakis?'

'Didn't he write *Zorba the Greek*?' Batten had seen the movie but couldn't remember reading the book.

'*Zorba*, and more besides. *Zorba the Greek* is big business here. The Theodorakis film score is quite wonderful, of course – the first three hundred times?'

Batten laughed. In every taverna, the famous Zorba theme, all bazoukis and mandolins, sooner or later sneaked out of the speakers, slow at first, before speeding to a frenzy, as if hypnotising diners then telling them to eat fast, pay faster and vacate their table for the next lot. 'Wasn't the film version made round here?'

'Yes, alas. One tires of giving directions to Stavros beach, on Akrotiri, where Zorba - played by Anthony Quinn - famously dances the *syrtaki*. Did you know Quinn was not Greek at all, but Mexican?'

Shaking his head, Batten wondered where all this was going.

'The novel, though, has merit - despite some tougher parts. I set my class a creative project: to write a journal, as if Zorba was the writer. Rose's version vibrated with Zorba's energy – and a good deal of her own. Not fourteen, yet she wrote with spark and at great length. I regret not keeping a copy.'

I've got her journals in my backpack, Batten almost said. He smiled at the man who inspired Rose to write them.

'She submitted but one problem assignment the whole time I taught her,' said McTay. 'And even that was remarkable. Curiously, it was based on Kazantzakis. His grave is in Heraklion, you know?' Batten didn't. 'The epitaph is thought-provoking.' McTay's hands framed the words in the air:

"I hope for nothing. I fear nothing. I am free."

'I set my class the task of evaluating these sentiments – and looked forward to a sparkling effort from Rose. To my surprise, she thrust two terse sentences at me, black ink carving the page. I shall never forget it: '*All three statements wrong. No further comment.*' Nor would she. I began to wonder if she was the Rose I knew, or a proxy.'

'So, which was it, who hoped for something, feared something, and *wasn't* free? Rose, or her proxy?'

'Alas, both, perhaps.'

'That's how she could be beautiful and ugly, at the same time?'

McTay shrugged a maybe. 'I was being more literary than literal, but, yes, in a way. Physically, Rose was anointed by Aphrodite, goddess of beauty. Alas, it was Zeus, god of weather, who governed her behaviour – which could border on the meteorological. Without warning, storms obliterated her sunshine. The change was…ugly. Yes. Apt.'

Selecting words and stringing them together was something McTay clearly enjoyed. From experience, Batten let him do what he was good at, while he did the same - listening.

'We were on a field trip, once. Greek schools *love* field trips – museums, beaches, historic sites. We visited Ancient Aptera, in the hills, not far from Kalyves. I don't suppose you know it?'

'As a matter of fact, I do.' Batten relived his awkward recitation of Mercutio's 'Queen Mab' speech from *Romeo and Juliet,* what little he remembered - in the very public middle of the restored Roman theatre there. With a playful Grigoris egging him on.

'Then, you'll appreciate Aptera's wonderful setting? And those magnificent vistas above the sea?' Batten nodded. 'Rose appreciated it too. Adored the tree-clad hilltops, the ancient stones, the open sky. Her face *glowed.* I was basking in the glory a teacher feels when a bright student responds to his pedagogics.'

'Nothing ugly about that,' Batten said.

'No. Until I led the class to the ancient Roman cisterns. A feat of massive stone engineering, 2000 years old, yet way beyond the plumbing standards of modern Greece – if I may be allowed to poke gentle fun at my chosen homeland?'

A smiling Batten was enjoying McTay's Scottish lilt and quirky delivery, just for itself, and imagined 'Malkie' holding a class of learners in the palm of his hand. He was teaching Batten, too, about the young Queen Mab.

'If you've seen the cisterns, you'll remember. Vast, yet feeling small. Not fully underground - yet seeming so. Chambers, dank water, green mould on the thick stone walls, and a deep, dark contrast to the golden sun outside? The class were fascinated by them. And may still remember that Rose - was *not.* The school did not tolerate profanity, in or out of the classroom. But Rose's father. Mm. A little…ugly in his language, and the habit passed on. *Get out of my effing way!* Rose screamed - at her classmates, and at me, too, her teacher. And not 'effing', but the full epithet. *Get me out of this effing place!* And she was gone, all elbows, screams and panic buttons, face whiter than marble.'

Batten put down his coffee cup. McTay drained his.

'I, Mr Batten, was lost for words. *Me!* And Rose's classmates…' McTay threw his hands at the air in bewilderment. 'We followed, of course, but she must have stolen the winged sandals of Hermes because we failed to find her. After an hour, with the bus-driver apoplectic at the unpaid overtime, she was discovered squatting against the twisted trunk of an olive tree, on the far fringe of Aptera, ghost-white and shaking.'

'What, claustrophobia? Something like that?'

"Something *like*'. I have experience of students with a fear of confined spaces. This was deeper. Relevant questions were posed, services offered - it's a caring school. Rose refused to respond. Her parents - when eventually we tracked them down - seemed unconcerned, which left an ugly taste in my mouth. And Rose continued to react in ugly ways.'

Before Batten could ask, McTay counted off nearer-to-home examples on his bony fingers. 'Flatly refusing to enter the sound-proof booths of our language laboratory. Insisting she sit by an open door in the blackout of a film show. Revealing herself in creative writing classes, but only ever through an invented persona.' McTay shook his puzzled beard. 'When asked to express a personal view in open discussion – stubborn silence.'

The journals were hardly silent, Batten thought. Perhaps the only places she felt safe to express herself?

'Of course, in one so physically beautiful, 'ugly' behaviour seems more pronounced. But the ugly face of Rose could have been the head of Medusa.' McTay broke off, pale, as if seeing the ugliness again. Glancing at his watch, he said, 'Pill time. I shall fetch a glass of water.'

When he struggled to rise, Batten waved him back down and wandered to the counter. The waiter was young, he noted, but a waiter still.

'Most grateful,' said McTay, swishing down three tiny pills, yellow, red and green, like traffic lights. Batten wondered what each was for. They sat in a silence broken by a scooter whining up to Funky's and squeezing in at the kerb, the show-off owner revving his engine to the delight of a group of teenage girls. Batten thought about borrowing a crash helmet, to protect his throbbing head.

'I'm grateful to you, Mr McTay -'

'Malcolm, please.'

Not 'Malkie', noted Batten. 'I'm grateful, Malcolm – but one more question?'

McTay's hands invited it.

'You've talked about bright, beautiful and ugly. But you also said Rose was damned?'

McTay paused. He locked eyes with Batten – gently, but with the practised power of a teacher commanding a classroom. 'The phrase you used on the phone, was, 'the police are trying to find Rose. *You* are trying to find Rose?'

'Trying, yes.'

'But now, given the depth and nature of your interest, do I sense Rose is in danger?'

Where's my subtlety gone? Batten thought. *I'm becoming a priest. Or an undertaker.* He explained, as gently as he could. 'I wasn't sure whether to tell you. I'm trying to find out why. I'm trying to find *Rose*. It's a broken trail.'

Placing his empty cup on its saucer, McTay pushed it slowly across the tin table and closed his eyes in what seemed like prayer before he spoke again. 'I'm annoyed with myself, for not guessing. Rose did lack...*continuity*. When I said 'damned', perhaps I meant 'doomed.''

'Damned is the word you chose, Malcolm. You don't strike me as a man who struggles with language.'

McTay dipped his head at the compliment. 'My words are chosen with care. We are discussing a past pupil, and I have professional ethics to consider.'

'Yes, but mine's a different profession. Is there room for leeway?'

'*Leeway*? Because words cannot harm the dead? Mm. Don't forget, I make my home amid the rich mythology of Greece. Here, between Elysium and Hades, there's a god for almost everything - and Greek gods are traditionally quick to take offence.'

'Even the god of Truth? Veritas, is it?'

McTay shook his head. 'Veritas is the Roman god of Truth. The Greek version is Alethea, with perhaps a dab of Apollo thrown in. But I take your point.' After a long pause, he appraised Batten. 'Died? Or was killed?'

'Malcolm, I work for the CID...'

With a sigh of recognition, McTay withdrew into the chatter from nearby tables, the rattle of cups and plates, the intermittent babel of traffic. Batten feared 'Malkie' had clammed up, and their meeting was over, but when the retired schoolmaster spoke, he did so with vehemence.

'I think, because it is Rose,' he said, 'I will choose to speak directly and from the heart. I can trust you to ignore any statements valueless in a courtroom?'

A nod of encouragement.

'One doesn't choose one's parents. I was lucky. Mine were wide-minded and nurturing. Yours the same, I imagine.'

Memories of Aunt Daze jabbed Batten in the gut, bitter tasting coffee rising in his throat. He said nothing.

'But Rose…Oh, dear. Abe, her father? 'Full of strange oaths', like the soldier in Shakespeare - and twice as vicious. I still recall him looking over his chin at me with a vile sneer, on the rare occasions he bothered to turn up at the school. And the long teeth of his false smile. How could a man with such an unprepossessing appearance sire a creature as beautiful as Rose?' When McTay shook his head, his grey beard and hair trembled from side to side. 'Her mother - Gina?'

Batten nodded, happy to nod all day to keep McTay talking.

'Gina attended more often – along with a distinct whiff of alcohol. Sans husband, she conversed with intelligence. When *he* was present, she spoke nary a word. Twice, she arrived wearing make-up - unusual for her - but it failed to hide the bruises. A punchbag, Mrs Linnet, I suspect. A ball of anxiety. She passed the ball to Rose, I fear.'

'Her folks 'damned' her? Is that what you're saying?'

'Abe damned her by being Abe. I'm convinced he was a crook. There, I've said it. The rumours were rife.' McTay leaned forward, voice hardening. 'Abe, full to the brim with cunning – I tell you, *crook* was engraved on one eyeball, and *cunning* on the other!'

McTay stopped in his tracks, caught, as if school inspectors had walked in. For a moment, he gazed at the youthful faces coming and going between scooters and tables.

'My apologies. By vocation I nurtured the young, you see, and when older minds destroy the progress made…' His knuckles were white on his folded stick, as if he ached to bring it down on Abe Linnet's head.

'And Abe was a destroyer of progress?'

'Oh, without doubt. At a consultation evening, I overheard him tell Rose, in no uncertain terms, to keep her effing opinions to herself. And she did. Though being Rose, she made a fist of rebelling.'

A fist, Batten thought, how apt. 'Perhaps to the end of her days,' he said.

'At the school, however, her rebellion did more harm than good. Her classmates grew wary of her. She had but one true…companion, in my class -'

'Darren Pope?'

'Ah. You *have* been finding Rose. Yes, Darren. His nickname - Dazzler - carried a certain irony. Oldest and slowest boy in the class - old enough to be in the class above had he kept up with his studies. Like the Linnets, his parents cocked a snook at the State and chanced their arm at home-schooling, despite a dearth of aptitude. The Linnets, the Popes, the whole lot of their group arrived in Crete via the hippy trail and hid away in the White Mountains, to ignore their social responsibilities.' Catching Batten's look, McTay added, 'I am not being dismissive. It may surprise you to know *I* arrived on the shores of this fine island via the hippy trail. I was fortunate. Unlike them, I packed a little spare humanity in my rucksack.'

Batten kept the focus on Darren Pope. 'You called Darren her *companion*. Not her friend?'

'Oh, both. But they were…close. I'm being unnecessarily coy. They were *intimate*, plain as day, despite their youth. She, and poor Darren - a lost boy if ever I saw one - playing out a familiar trope from literature: the 'star-crossed lovers.' Lost souls, tragically colliding. When Rose left, Darren was a cauldron. The anger and the pain, goodness me.'

'A tragedy, alright.'

'You already know what happened, then, between Darren and Rose?'

Batten nodded, not saying he'd gleaned it from Rose's journals.

'The pregnancy? The miscarriage?'

Batten gave a CID nod, agreeing with the witness in hope he might say more – despite his story contradicting the journal pages Batten had read that very morning. McTay tapped his walking stick in disappointment.

'But I'd like to hear your version. To corroborate. If you've time?'

'Malkie' watched the late morning sun creep across their table, a sundial of shade and light. 'Time? Most days, I've little else.' He double-checked his watch and struggled to his feet. 'But we have conversed the time away, I'm afraid. Literature has its share of physicians, and I have an appointment with mine. I'd prefer him to be Dr Zhivago, but he's somewhere between Jekyll, Hyde, and Frankenstein. Beneath this shirt, my skin is a patchwork quilt of post-operative scars.' With a practised turn of his wrist, McTay switched his folding stick to the 'on' position. 'Nevertheless, assuming I survive my doctor, I shall be back here at eleven tomorrow, for my daily coffee, and to absorb the sound of youth. This evening, a rummage through my memories, on your behalf.'

With a wave, the old teacher leaned on his stick and limped away a little sadly, as if, in losing Rose, he'd lost part of himself. Tomorrow, Batten would be here at eleven, amid the buzz of scooters and the animated language of the young, in hope of unfinished business. Because *if it's not ruled out, it's still ruled in.*

Wandering towards the bus stop, pangs of guilt prodded him. Rose's journals sat silently in his backpack throughout her resurrection and McTay deserved to know they depicted him as valued and caring. But given their less wholesome content, best leave both journals tucked away?

Hardly. The half-empty bus back to Almyrida travelled less than a mile before Batten's twitching fingers drew the second leather-clad bundle from his pack, and he flicked through the pages that had led him to 'Malkie'.

Poor Dazzler. When he got B+ for his essay on Greek drama, Malkie gave me a look, eyebrows in the air. He can't prove I wrote it, and it means Darren stays in my class.
Like a big tree's branches, the Dazzler's arms.
I shall need Darren, to protect me.

From what? Batten wondered. He searched for reasons in the glimpses of sea, flashing like strobes between gaps in buildings and clumps of roadside oleander, till the flickers of light nudged him to a place between seizure and sleep. He knew nothing more till the bus driver shook him

192

back to daylight. 'Almyrida?' he asked. 'You want Almyrida?'

Familiar streets came into view. 'Yes. Sorry. Er, nodded off.' He climbed down, and struggled up the hill to his apartment, backpack stuck to his shirt like glue.

Thirty five

After a cooler-than-expected Greek shower, he was on his hotel balcony, eyes dancing between the sea and the journal-jigsaw of Rose's early life. Birth, boat, White Mountains, education. In the light of McTay's curious reference to a miscarriage, Batten flicked back through the entries about the school, where Rose and Darren Pope swapped literature for biology.

> *Sent a secret letter, and Darren sent one back, via Lucy, from my class. Made her read it, over the phone. If Darren sent it to me, Dad'd burn the bloody thing - and call Darren 'that little wanker' for the millionth time. And wouldn't stop there.*
> *Lucy was squeamish, reading it. Read me every word, I said. And all the kisses.*
> *I need to be lying on the beach, with the Dazzler, under the stars. I need to be.*
> *My feet, blocks of ice.*

Ice, thought Batten, filling a glass with cold water from the minibar, instead of ouzo. He forgot about the water when he found the entry he'd been searching for.

> *Mum already knew. Said she knew before I knew.*
> *Never seen her so angry. Against the White Mountains she turned purple, and more besides. Called me a stupid cow, warmed to the task and called me worse, yelling and screaming. Flopped down against the wall in tears, sob-screams shuddering out of her. I thought she'd burst, spray blood across the white walls, turn them scarlet.*
> *Mum, Mum, I said.*
> *Idiot! she screamed. That's what you're going to be!*
> *What?*
> *A MUM! she said. At fourteen! Have you lost the sense you were*

born with? How many times have I told you, don't copy my mistake?

I AM the mistake! I wanted to scream. But I squatted down next to her, cold stone between us. Mum, I said. She slapped my hand away and I was crying too. Blubbed together, us and the wall.

That's when she put her arms round me. Never does, but she squeezed so tight I couldn't tell if it was love or hate. When she hugged me to her, I knew.

Mum. There's going to be a baby in the house.

She didn't reply, at first. Then she mumbled, not one, Rose. Two.

TWO? I'm not having twins!

No. We're sharing the load. A baby each. Because we've both lost the sense we were born with.

Put her hands on my shoulders and looked at me. What she saw I couldn't say. Both of us blurred with tears. Didn't know if I was sad or glad for her. Then she saw the clock on the wall. Oh God, I haven't made dinner!

Starts rattling frantic pans in the kitchen. A bare table when Dad gets home, it sets him off again.

When she told him, he went ape, smashed a chair with his bare hands, kicked the pieces across the room. Don't know who he was furious with, her or me. Heard them, after, arguing about getting rid. Mum's, mine, or both, I don't know. Mum wasn't having it. Heard them fighting till she screamed like a banshee and Dad stormed off into the night.

If he hadn't, God knows.

Gone, a week or more.

Our bumps began to show, mine and Mum's, like a pair of balloons. Dad moved us up into the mountains, hired that old hag-midwife. Huh, midwife? Prison guard.

Didn't see a soul apart from her.

And then the snow came.

Batten read the last few lines again, the lines he'd been looking for. *Our bumps began to show, mine and Mum's, like a pair of balloons.* Why did Rose say so if, as Malcolm McTay claimed, her miscarriage had already made it impossible?

The next entry said who was right.

Never heard a man scream before.

Only women scream.

Darren screamed. Turned scarlet. Don't know what else because he ran up the beach, scattering pebbles, and into the woods. Saw his back and his strong legs, pumping at the wind, getting smaller. Till the trees took him.

Lucy said Dad kicked in the door to Darren's house, punched his lights out. Darren's dad tried to stop him, got floored too. Dad has a power. Frightens people. Us.

Darren's folk are upping sticks. Australia, overland on the hippy trail, a campervan. I bet Dad scratched piss off! on the bodywork. Taking my Darren with them. My Dazzler, my star.

Don't see the stars now. Just dark trees, above the beach, and Darren's wide back running into them and the branches are some other woman's arms, not mine, and he disappears.

The mountains. Still a prison, even with old witch Maddy gone. If I live to be as old as her, let no evil spikes of hair sprout from my chin. Hope she drowns or burns or whatever they do to witches.

Shouldn't have been on the beach, but Dad's away, I sneaked out, flagged down the bus. Darren put his giant arms round me. Crush me to death, I wanted to say, so I won't need to care. Soon as his fingers touched my stomach, flat now, I knew they hadn't told him. Saw it in his face. He didn't know what happened, to the baby he'd never seen.

They're carting me off to Australia! he said. They won't let you and the baby come! Flops onto the beach, his legs jelly. I won't go, he said, the words squeaking out of him. Giant limbs, but his voice like a hinge on a broken door. We need a plan, he said. You, me and the baby. They can't do this! It's…illegal!

It's Dad's law, up in the mountains. Why can't there be a law that makes them tell Darren? Why me?

I blurted out a babble of rubbish, us being too young. My parents,
yours, they don't think we're...Almost laughed. Mum was sixteen
when she had me.
I'M NOT TOO YOUNG! Darren yells. They'll soon find out! I'M
STRONG!
He is. He's a tree.
I'm not. So I blurted it out. Darren, I said. You have to listen! Can't
tell you how sad and sorry I feel. But...there isn't a baby anymore.
There isn't.
Darren's face...dissolved. Dragged his legs towards his body, surged
to his feet, a tree - branches, trunk and roots - bursting from the
pebbles and sand. Gapes at me, like I'd cut him in two, sliced him
into separate people. A non-son and a non-father, I suppose.
Couldn't stop my tears. Been stopping them, best I can, because when
they start, they pour out of me till I'm sand. I might blow away in the
wind, to nothing.
There is no baby, Darren. The baby didn't live. Our baby.
Darren stared at me. I stared at my own space, remembering Mum,
after, telling me what I'm telling Darren now.
Your baby was stillborn, Mum said. Stillborn. You were out of it.
Both of us. A mess, the whole thing. I called my baby Sue, a short
name, didn't expect her to live. That monster - a midwife, her?
Drugged us up to our eyeballs, stupid hag. Buried your baby, nearly
killed mine. Nearly killed you and me into the bargain!
I wouldn't believe what Mum said – wouldn't. Buried her? Buried
her where? Mum couldn't look at me. WHERE? She waved at the
White Mountains. In Nature, she said.
Wanted to run up the mountain and thrown myself off. Mum locked
me in. But when Mum's new baby cried I heard every tiny murmur.
My baby couldn't cry. I cried for her - a girl, like Mum's. I drained
myself.
Rose, you gave birth. At fourteen. I'm proud of you, Mum said. To do
that, so young. I know what it's like.
But you gave birth to me and I'm alive! Me, I gave birth to a death!
I'm yelling at her. HOW DARE YOU BE PROUD OF ME? HOW?

*She looked up at the White Mountains, where they'd buried my
baby.*

After 'baby', the ink tore at the page in a zigzag of gouges, the white
paper a black sea. Batten's humanity felt the sting of Rose's pain, but his
cop mind wondered what Greek law said about unregistered births, death
and burials. The next page was a drunken scrawl, as if to match the
content.

*Stared up at Darren — he doubled in size — a huge rock from the
beach above his head
— a rock the size of a cradle.
Knew, there and then, it didn't matter. Wasn't afraid. Pound my
skull with the rock
make me a ruin of dry veins — barren blood. Like the baby.
To make him do it, told him what I'd told Mum. I gave birth to a
death, Darren. I'm worthless.
Such anger, such a stare. Never looked at me like that before. Lifted
the massive rock above his head like a pigeon's egg. Closed my eyes,
wanting to feel my skull split
one egg splintering another.
A woosh of air and a rock the size of a cradle burst the sea. Opened
my eyes, boiling waves, Darren staring, his pain slapping the water
But his eyes — felt the echo of his scream in my empty womb.
That's when he ran up the beach — and the trees took him. They
took Darren away.
Took the stars.*

The water in Batten's glass was lukewarm. Throat dry as sand, he
glugged it down, tapped in the international code and rang Ball at home.
'Ballie? Did Eddie Hick squeeze in another call to Australia?'
'About Darren What's-his-name?'
'Yes, anything?'
'Hang on, sir, he left an unreadable note. It's next door.'
When Ball put down the phone, Batten shook away the guilt at

disturbing his Sergeant's domestic normality. Chris Ball, glass of cider in hand, yanked from his armchair and whisked back to CID. *Domestic normality.* Did Rose and Darren ever experience such a thing?

'Found it. From Brad, the Wizard of Oz.'

'*What?*'

'From Australia. Hickie can't spell liaison. Calls their liaison officer the Wizard of Oz.'

'Hope the Wizard sent magic.'

'I'll read you the gist, sir, once I've deciphered Hickie's scrawl. Er, it says, 'Darren Pope still wanted in Sydney, for knife crime, still on the run. Jungle drums say he's run your way.' I suppose that means England. 'Can't miss him, six foot four, built like a brick dunny.' A dunny, sir? What's that?'

'A toilet.'

'Ah, a brick toilet. Anyway, it says, 'if he turns up, wear armour.''

'That's comforting, Ballie. Bloke's six foot four, can handle a knife and might be in England. When did he go on the run?'

Ball knew what his boss was asking. 'A goodly while before someone cut Queen Mab's throat, sir.'

'We're thinking the same, then?'

'Afraid so. England in his sights. Feasible timeline. Pope's a suspect.'

Batten remembered Rose's description of the deep hate in Darren's eyes. 'That's dandy, eh? An armed giant with motive and means. Anything else?'

'Brad says, 'search continues.' Nothing since.'

The search always continues, Batten thought. Darren Pope. *Big fella*, in Australian parlance. 'No sightings in Parminster, Ballie? At the time? No giants spotted near the crime scene?'

Once more, Ball batted back the question. 'It was a dog's dinner, sir. If we had the manpower, I suppose we could revisit door-to-door, but…'

'I heard the 'if', Chris. Don't worry. When I get back, I'll do some delving of my own.'

'Unofficial, I hope?'

'The Doc's put a stop to anything else.'

'Can't stop delving, though, can you?'

No, thought Batten, *I bloody can't.*

He ended the call and swallowed warm, flat water. Impatient for the Edinburgh burr of Malkie McTay, he pored over the six thumbnails, the 'canvas secrets' Queen Mab had locked away, but his eyes rebelled. Instead, he tap-tapped his finger on the open journals, two booze-stained, leather-bound towers of Babel.

Thirty six

This time, McTay wore a green check shirt and grey faded trousers, his lap cradling the same folded stick. Someone had neatly trimmed his hair and beard. Before Batten could ask, or savour his coffee, McTay's need for speech took over.

'When looking at the world, Mr Batten, exceptional people see the breadth and depth of it, while the average person sees only clutter, distractions - *things.*' McTay lowered his voice and pointed at a young man two tables away. 'His mesmeric mobile phone; the shiny crash helmet hooked over his knee; red trainers with transparent soles and heels; a snake tattoo, slithering from elbow to wrist.'

McTay's finger panned left and right across more phones, shoulder bags, necks hung with gold and silver chains, and at the café's edge, spindly blood-red geraniums sprouting from dry soil in a row of rusty olive-oil cans. 'Interesting accoutrements of the world,' said McTay. 'But not the world itself. And each object exists beneath this.' His finger pointed upwards, beyond rooftops and the black hedgehogs of aerials and wires, to a sky more cloudless than yesterday, wrapping everything beneath it in a shawl of blue.

Foolishly, Batten looked up, wincing at the strength of the light before easing McTay from philosophy to his ex-pupil. 'Rose was exceptional – and saw the wider world? That's your point?'

'Rose *might* have. She had potential.'

'Sounds like a line from a school report,' he said, bringing a smile to McTay's face.

'I continued to see hope in her. Though, not long before she left, I said, 'Rose, when you look at the world, you tilt your head to one side. Why is that?' I expected a zippy response, but in a hard voice, quite unlike her own, she said, *'To keep one eye on the vultures,'* and walked away without a word.'

'Vultures? Meaning what?'

McTay's shrug returned. 'Her teachers? But not me, I hope. Her classmates, her parents? Whoever made her afraid? Before I could ask, she left, without warning. Oh dear, my discourse grows sloppy. Not *left*. She was *removed*.'

'By Abe Linnet?'

'By both Linnets – an enforced harmony, I'm sure. Not that Abe had the grace to give reasons. No matter. Corridor rumour became rumour in the staffroom too. Eventually the facts drifted down from the White Mountains. A classroom romance. A teenage pregnancy. A retreat to the hills, away from public gaze. A miscarriage, as you already know. And after that, silence.'

Once more, Batten pretended to agree. *A miscarriage? Not a stillbirth?* Did Abe Linnet feed 'fake news' about a miscarriage from his lair in the White Mountains - to keep the officialdom of birth, death and burial off his shifty back?

McTay broke into his thoughts. 'More coffee?'

'Er, yes, but I'll get it.' Batten loped to the counter, amid crash helmets, youth, and the aggressive-sounding babble of Greek friends warmly greeting one another. Despite the puzzle of McTay's account, Batten let the rich scent of espresso waft away his doubts - for now.

'While you were at the counter,' McTay said, 'I asked myself if I should have intervened on Rose's behalf, other than through school channels. But even *finding* the Linnets in the White Mountains, well… have you been up there?'

'No, but I'd like to. They stare down at me, every morning. Untapped beauty.'

'Then stay on the roads. Or take a guide. At three thousand metres, according to tradition, you may discover the throne of Zeus, god of gods. In the war, the Cretan resistance gave the Germans the slip daily, up there. You need to be a goat.'

'The Linnets weren't.'

'Indeed. *Abe* looked more like a horse. I suspect living in the mountains made him as difficult to find as when he lived on his boat.'

Batten was of the same opinion. 'When Rose left, Darren Pope didn't. Not right away. Did you…?'

'Intervene on *his* behalf?'

Let McTay do the talking, thought Batten, with the tiniest nod.

'I tried. The Popes were a witless pair. Poor Darren. A colleague described him as a giant version of The Scarecrow, in *The Wizard of Oz*. *'If I only had a brain.'* Whether he found one...' McTay shrugged and sipped coffee in silence. They sat at the same table as yesterday, and once more the sun crept round, creating a pale frontier where it met the shade.

Batten was thinking of Eddie Hick's Wizard of Oz, the Australian police liaison officer. McTay's concern for a young Darren Pope didn't keep the adult knifeman off the wanted list.

'When Rose left, Darren was incendiary. Only after much counselling -'

'By you?'

'And others. We hoped he might turn a corner. But his rumbling volcano erupted. Three of us had to physically restrain him. For his age, that boy had the grip of a Goliath - a screaming Goliath. Young males rarely scream, but Darren... I have never experienced such anger in one so young - hissing out like steam, turning his face a raging purple, at the mention of a name.'

'Rose?'

'Rose. In the School Counsellor's somewhat facile view, Darren was traumatised by the loss of his unborn child - and why would he not be? Darren, she claimed, himself an abandoned child, searched for lost happiness in a fantasy future. And Rose, he convinced himself, killed it off.'

'That doesn't seem to square with your view of Rose.' It didn't square with the journal, either, but Batten knew when to keep his mouth shut.

'*Rose* did not hurt Darren! Dragged from the school by her parents – with no choice in the matter? At fifteen, she could hardly decide to stay. And pay her own fees? Neither do I suppose when asked what she wanted for Christmas, she said, 'a miscarriage please, Santa!'

In keeping his voice down, McTay resorted to a hiss, which had the effect of contorting a face unused to anger. Let the conversation cool, Batten decided. He finished his coffee and glanced around, hoping the true world might appear if he stared through the transparent heel of the red trainer crooked over a knee, two tables away. When McTay blew out a long breath, Batten said, 'all the same...'

'Mr Batten -'

'Zig, please.'

'Zig. Zig, yes. *All the same*, I feel now as I did then - trapped in quicksand. I told the counsellors - in no uncertain terms - that trauma is far too facile a word. If we wish to be facile, I said, let's plump for good old revenge, as Darren seemed to. He was dangerous. I tell you, for that reason alone I was glad the Linnets yanked Rose from the school. Could we have guaranteed her safety, given Darren's fury at the mere mention of her name? He would have had her by the throat.'

Maybe he did, thought Batten, nudging one more duck into the row.

'I breathed a sigh of relief when his parents decamped. Whether to remove Darren or to satisfy their idle wanderlust, I couldn't say.'

I could, Batten thought. The Popes legged it to escape Abe's wrath, if the journal is true. But why wrath, exactly? As McTay twirled a regretful spoon in his coffee, Batten imagined himself inside Abe Linnet's skull, unpleasant though it was…*Crazy Rose is drawing attention. Hide her away…Then disappear myself.* And is that what happened?

McTay pushed aside his cup and gazed in silence at his version of the world. Batten guessed it was memories he saw, somewhere between age and youth. He sensed Batten watching him.

'I'm sorry. Chasing demons. Are you any closer now?'

'To Rose's trail?'

'To her trail. To Rose herself.'

'Some. And, thanks to you, Malcolm, I'm a tad closer to Darren.'

'Then this may help.' From the pocket of what looked like a Greek version of a cardigan, McTay drew a photograph of a young basketball team. With a wistful glance, he handed it to Batten. 'Yours to keep. It will quickly become obvious which is Darren.'

A line of players, all tall for their age, scowled at the camera, challenging the opposition. At the far left, two vacant eyes stared out from the head of a giant. Darren Pope was six inches taller than his tallest classmates. Both ways, Batten saw. 'I hadn't realised he *looked* so big.'

'A colossal sore thumb is an apt description. Because the poor boy stuck out, everywhere he went. Always to feel conspicuous? I dread to think what became of him.'

So do the Australian police, thought Batten. 'The size of the lad, I'm surprised he didn't tell his folks to stuff it when they dragged him away from Crete.'

'Muscle is but muscle. Heart and mind…different creatures.'

'And Darren lacked them?'

McTay's nod had sadness in it. 'I suspect Darren needed Rose to be his heart and mind. But she left him only muscle.'

If the journal is to be believed, Rose needed Darren's muscle. With her one eye on the vultures, whoever they were, was Darren the other eye? And when he was removed…? In the photo, Darren's face had the look of a lost boy, a Scarecrow Giant who grew into a failed father and a knife-wielding fugitive from the law. 'Whatever turns up,' Batten said, 'I'll let you know.

'In which case, best not tarry.' McTay added a crooked smile.

To change the mood, Batten said, 'I know it's a trivial question, given all we've discussed, but I was wondering…who cut your hair? I could use a trim.'

To his credit, McTay laughed, fell suddenly silent, then laughed again. 'I go to the barbershop, in the next street,' he said, pointing. 'You know the Greek alphabet?' Batten nodded wryly. McTay didn't bother asking if he *spoke* Greek. 'Look for the shop sign, it's quite small. It says, 'koureio".' He spelled it out in Greek and English. 'The barber there is cheap, and quick. Afterwards, though, I suggested he visit an optikos.'

Even Batten got the joke, opticians much on his mind. Abruptly, McTay's laughter ceased, and a fond voice replaced it.

'My wife used to trim my hair. Now, the barbershop.'

Guilt jabbed at Batten. In Crete, a thousand miles from HQ, ingrained police habits dictated. He was conducting an interview. McTay was reminiscing. Worse, Batten had already assumed Malcolm was gay. He backpedalled.

'You lost her?'

'Alas. Many years ago.'

'I'm sorry.'

'Helena, too. My young daughter. In the same car, on the same road. Greek roads are better now. But then…'

Cymbals clashed in Batten's head as McTay's deep contempt for Abe

Linnet fell into place. And perhaps the reason Rose was such a tender subject for him.

'You didn't remarry?'

A shake of the head. 'The school supported me. Everyone there became my family. And each pupil I taught was a son or a…daughter to me. I kept in touch with many, heard news of most. Alas, there were exceptions.'

Without adding, 'Rose and Darren', McTay struggled to his feet, drew a business card from his wallet and handed it to Batten.

'Ignore the title. It's an old card. I am 'Senior Tutor' only in memory, but the email address will serve. Whatever you discover…'

In response, Batten handed over a card of his own, wondering if, age 39, he was a Detective only in memory.

They shook hands, both men regretting their conversation was over, though for different reasons. McTay deftly flipped open his collapsible stick and shuffled past tin tables, empty cups, crash helmets dangling from handlebars, and brassy gaggles of youth, all oblivious to another old grey man disappearing into the crowd.

The bus to Almyrida had gone. With an hour to kill, Batten chose to escape the energy of youth. *I'm not even 40*, he reminded himself, *and I don't need a stick.* He bumped his way down Chalidon past a mixed bag of tourist shops and phone stores to the stunning horseshoe bay of Chania - a favourite place, despite the squeeze of tavernas, café-bars and selfie-loving tourists. Deep green ripples on the shallow water drew his eyes along and up to Venetian buildings encircling the bay, beautiful still, whether repurposed for culture or for profit.

Had Grigoris been here, they would have eaten a long seafood lunch on Salpidon, by the old harbour, where the hordes of day visitors ventured less. Today, the seafront crowds swarmed around him in a phalanx, and he retreated to the back streets of the old town.

On his first visit here, he quickly became lost in the narrow lanes beneath iron balconies decked with washing lines, cats and geraniums, and had to dash past thin tavernas and hibiscus flowers to catch his bus in the nick of time. Now, he wandered dreamily. If he missed the bus, he'd catch the next, or fork out for a taxi.

His distractions were what McTay called the accoutrements of the world, the *things* in it. Things for sale were everywhere. Pale gold leather bags and Greek sandals of every size, piled high on hooks above shop doorways. Paintings and ceramics, some exquisite, some tourist tat. Red and green herbs and spices piled up in baskets, their scent enticing the nostrils.

He stopped to buy a pack of Cretan Mountain Tea. Clio Demopolou had recommended it – 'to calm your head. But not your bladder!' she had laughed. 'It is a diuretic!' Grigoris had wrinkled his nose at her advice – '*it will taste like you boiled your socks!*' Batten bought thyme honey, too - the taste of Crete - and wandered towards the bus stop, senses dancing to the joy of things.

Till he reached the last street before the old town met the new. The shop confronting him - sunlit windows straddling a metal-grilled door - sold nothing but knives. Thousands of knives: Swiss Army knives, hunting knives, kitchen knives, tiny fruit knives, heavy serrated knives with thick bone handles and, above the counter, three glistening Samurai swords on a carved wooden rack. He gazed in shock at the shine of metal, the stack on stack of silver blades.

'Have everything,' said the shopkeeper. 'All the knives from the world. You look, please.' He waved an inviting arm.

Batten looked, seeing not the sparkle of knives but the sparkle of a young Rose Linnet, bright and beautiful, the way McTay described her. As he stared, the brightness tarnished, Rose fading to a bedraggled Queen Mab in an old red dress and a pair of dirty greatcoats - then a torn throat in a back alley, a thousand miles away in midnight Somerset. And it was not the shine of silver he saw, but the brown-black glisten of Queen Mab's blood.

The things of my world, he told himself, hurrying off, the shopkeeper's arm dropping to his side in disappointment.

Turning the corner, he watched his bus pull away in an iron-grey cloud of noise and diesel.

Thirty seven

Batten stared at an eight-o-clock sea – eight in the morning, the air still, and the beach undisturbed by the faint in-out of calm water that might have been molten glass.

Sated with coffee, he ordered fresh orange juice and lounged in silence with Grigoris in the empty taverna, breathing in the colours of Crete. Deep blue skies, pink bougainvillea, the White Mountains above, and the jade-green silence of Almyrida bay at his feet. 'You know, Makis, when Crete is this peaceful, I could almost live here.'

'Then I am sad to bring you these, Sig. Because I am certain they send you back to England. And then, peace or not, I must talk only with my shadow!'

A smiling Batten envied the contacts Grigoris happily milked, with a mix of authority and charm. He was almost afraid to sift through the documents his Greek friend dropped on the table. *Hellenic Civil Aviation Authority,* said the headings. On each flight manifest, Grigoris had underlined the name, *Ray Breeze.*

'He was in Greece?'

Grigoris spread out the papers. 'And flew to England. Or *a* Ray Breeze flew to England. See?'

Batten saw. If Abe Linnet and Ray Breeze were one and the same, their dubious passport flew from Athens airport to Bristol and back again on several occasions – one of them a year before *someone* took a scalpel-sharp knife to Queen Mab's throat.

'He change his name, Sig, this Abe. Buy new passport. Clever, bad.'

Batten stopped listening. He stared at the most recent flight. It was one-way, Athens to Bristol. He double-checked, but no return flight was recorded. 'Makis. Whatever he's calling himself, he must still be in England.'

Grigoris gave his customary shrug. 'And you, Sig, you will return, to find him.'

Silence was Batten's response.

'Silence betookens consent, Sig? I read it somewhere. Plato, I think.'

'Betokens, Makis. Silence betokens consent.'

'Well?'

'It means if we don't speak out against outrage, our silence becomes approval. How can I approve of Abe Linnet? I won't consent.'

'So? I am right? You go back?'

Eyes smiling at Grigoris, Batten savoured the last breakfast they would share for some time. The smile faded as he zipped the flight documents into his backpack.

*

Unknown to Batten, 'Ray Breeze' was not the only false passport with sights on a journey to England.

Unlike 'Ray', Darren Pope - Daz Parry now - floated not in the clouds but on the sea. Not till salt water splashed into his mouth and brought him to his senses did Darren accept this was no dream. In the gloom, he continued to float, relieved the water was warm. He listened for the sound of waves breaking on land - nothing. Worse, the boat's engine had faded into silence.

It was pitch black when the smugglers dumped him overboard. Now, the faintest glow of morning lit the distance. His left leg had crashed against the hull as he went over the side, and it hurt to tread water. They should have hit him harder - he was bigger than expected. But why, *why* did he turn his back? If the water had not shocked him to consciousness, he would be at the bottom of the sea. His head felt tender from the blow, but no broken skin, no blood in the water. If sharks found him, blood or no blood, he'd end up as a carcass in the sea's abattoir.

From the gloom, a Voice - his own - whispered thoughts.

'The smugglers will be going through your rucksack, Darren. The concealed pockets, they'll be empty now, your bankroll in their greasy fingers. And your spare clothes, huh, too big to fit that set of squat little bastards. A fire, that's where they'll end up. But it's water for you.'

My passport? he asked the Voice. *My knife?*

'In your pockets, Darren,' said his Voice. 'A passport's the least of your worries. And the knife? Useless - because you turned your back. A slow learner, you.'

He touched his fingers against the shape of the knife, remembering the knives in the Northern Territory abattoir, and the drug-dealer's blood in Sydney. A past and present of knives, was Darren.

'*Why couldn't I stay in Crete!*' he screamed at the sea. '*I had a life there!*'

'On the boat they'll have found the letter, Darren,' said the Voice. 'Tucked away in that rucksack of yours. And the envelope, with your real name. Traceable. Tut-tut. Hope they burn that too.'

Even treading water, he could almost feel the creased paper in his hand. Rose's only letter, faded from reading, again and again. *Kiss, kiss, kiss, Rose.* Three kisses to remember.

And return.

Darren spun in the water, searching the darkness, like the darkness on the beach near Chania, when he was just sixteen, when he and Rose made the baby. She begged him, despite his doubts, because he was strong, she said, and she needed his strength, to protect her.

'*We could've had a life!*' he yelled.

'Could've had three, Darren,' the Voice replied. 'You, Rose, and the baby. But she took the baby from you, let it die.'

I'd have killed for Rose. And she killed my baby.

Darren spluttered sea water back into the waves. *Rose Linnet!*' he spat. '*Abe Linnet!*

'*Oi! Wanker!*' Abe's voice, when he kicked down Mum and Dad's door. Big, muscled bastard, with his poison sneer. 'Take a walk, wanker.' *I've been walking ever since!* Darren's lungs craved a cigarette. He would kill for a cigarette.

When faint grey light fell on a mound of land, Darren struck out towards it. In one pocket, the Daz Parry passport. In the other, his sharpened blade. When he reached land, the knife would find him money.

And money would find him Rose.

He put his giant arms to work, cleaving the water, advancing towards the light, driven on by the Linnets, and by the sixteen years of his ruined youth, swimming through his veins like a fury.

Yellow light from the bedside lamp gave Batten's hotel room a jaundiced air. His suitcase packed and his passport ready for tomorrow's flight, he itched to get his hands on Ray Breeze. Till the thought of Doc Fallon's hands gave him the sweats.

Would Fallon declare him 'fit for work'? Would hope triumph over expectation? He recalled McTay's story of the Kazantzakis epitaph: *I hope for nothing.* Rose had rejected it, Batten too. *I hope to collar Ray Breeze – or whatever Abe's calling himself!*

Yellow lamplight brought Sonia Welcome to mind, her earrings glinting gold. Dare he also hope for a life beyond duty?

He stepped onto the balcony for a final dose of moonlight on Almyrida bay, aching to see Sonia Welcome gaze at the moon's beauty, and the moon gaze back on hers. When he turned to look, his only company was mosquitoes.

Shutting them out, he slipped on his reading glasses. On the bed sat journal number two, next to his Kindle. Before his conscious mind kicked in, the leather-bound brick lay open in his hand...

Tucked me away in a little private hospital, Mum did, after the baby. Stuff in my arm, from a drip.
Asked her if Darren could visit, she turned white. If I'd asked Dad, we'd have both turned black and blue. He's moving us on, again. Do I get a choice? She stared at me. Rabbit-in-the-headlights eyeballs, her face a stretched balloon. I remember when she was so beautiful. Three nights I was there. No Darren.
Used to be a Chinese woman at the commune, only had one eye. She did that Chinese medicine where they boil up bits of tree and a slice of old skunk and drink the liquor. Mum used to take me to her 'for healing'. I thought, if Chinese medicine's so good, why have you still only got one eye? Fingernails black with something. Skunk, probably. Used to want my hands to be clean. Don't care now.
Here, everything is white - white pills and walls, white sheets and uniforms - like I'm living inside somebody else's soul. Because souls

are white, aren't they? But what I truly want is a soul of my own. My soul went missing. It went missing when the baby died. I search, in hope, because no-one can live without a soul.
I search. Have to.

Slipping from Batten's unconscious fingers, the journal bumped to the floor. At 2am he woke in the yellow light of the bedside lamp and switched it off.

At 7.30, head throbbing, he sat in the hotel foyer on a white sofa, amid chandeliers and engraved glass screens, toes tapping on the floor tiles, faster and faster, impatient for the airport taxi.

He hated flying.

But what choice did he have?

PART FIVE

England

Thirty eight

For once, Batten's flight passed in a blur. After the nerve-twisting roar of take-off, a single journal page put him to sleep. He woke to hear the man behind ask his wife, 'is that grey thing down there the English Channel?' To deflect pre-landing jitters, he returned to the page he'd half-read – written by a much older Rose, newly returned to Somerset. He could almost smell alcohol in her words, the ink a black whip.

> *Are all solicitors fat, like fat twat Mr Goodie-Goode? Slobbers across his desk, Mum's ashes barely cold, and dangles her last will and testament. Wants a striptease for the contents, does he? Shouldn't have emailed Mum. Lard-arse Mr Goode would never have found me.*
> *Voice like his, should be against the law. Urrr, I do so believe in <u>convenience</u>, he says. Urrr, you are <u>here</u>. Gina's house is <u>here</u>. The trust fund is <u>here</u>. Urr, the best of all outcomes!*
> *Best for him, he means. Can bill me for his suurrrrvices now!*
> *A house I couldn't wait to leave? In Parminster? What's fucking convenient about that?*

Black doodles scored the rest of the page. Overleaf, Rose added a more sober postscript.

> *In Parminster, no-one knows about the Linnets.*
> *Can gaze at the stars. Can't stop me sleeping under the stars, can they?*
> *And where else am I supposed to go?*

The office of Goode, Goode and Moulde was in Parminster High Street. Once home, Batten knew where *he'd* be going.

*

As he emerged from the baggage claim at Bristol airport, the mineral scent of the Cretan Sea became the smell of England. His parked Ford Focus had been valeted, and Batten was confronted by a car that looked brand new. *If only I'd been valeted*, he thought. When he opened the door, the sickly blast of car freshener merged with the smell of jet exhausts and whiffs of brassicas.

Soon, clean air from the Mendip Hills breezed in through wide-open windows as Batten steered the Ford on back roads towards Somerton, his mind on Doc Fallon: *'no driving and no alcohol, is that clear?'* If the absolute worst came about, he would learn to cope with neither in his life.

But could he cope without *work*? Aunt Daze began her working life aged 15, a trainee seamstress in a Leeds clothing factory, retiring fifty years later as office supervisor at the same firm. When the company went bust, she said, *'it's 'cos I left.'* Daze had raised Batten to work.

When the route south of Glastonbury became a straight road on a high bluff, his thoughts straightened too, Queen Mab seeping into the space Aunt Daze once filled. By the time he paused at the traffic lights in Martock, he had listed the work to be done, the focus on Ray Breeze – or whatever Abe was calling himself.

The red light turned green. What kind of roadmap, he wondered, will help me track Abe Linnet?

Thirty nine

After unpacking, and a back-porch gaze across the valley at Ham Hill, Batten phoned Goode, Goode and Moulde, in hope. Only when he said *CID* did a faux-posh voice concede that 'Mr Goode may see you briefly, after lunch tomorrow.'

Impatient for work, Batten arranged an 'unofficial' post-shift meeting with Hazel Timms in The Orchard. The bistro's pastel-painted tables were a fair distance from HQ, but he still guided Timms to a spot away from early evening punters and shielded by potted palms. He's avoided the pink tables, she noted, when they sat down in blue neutrality.

'On me, Hazel. For whatever you've dug up.'

Timms smoothed the leather skirt she never wore. This morning, late for work, it was the first thing her hand grabbed in the wardrobe. As she hurried into HQ, Nina Magnus was already leaving. 'Ships in the night, eh, Nina?'

Glancing at Timms' skirt, Magnus said, 'mm, black leather, Hazel - seconded to Vice?' and they shared a laugh. Timms stopped laughing when she found another domestic violence case on her desk, a 'gift' from Sergeant Ball. And he was watching, so she couldn't curse.

Hope the boss isn't a black leather fetishist, she thought, but Batten was squinting at the menu, not at her. *At least my hair's clean.* She ran a hand through it, and ordered steak, chips, and a giant glass of Shiraz. Since mum and dad died, she'd barely eaten, so Batten's wallet was a chance to put that right. And when did she last dine out with a *man*?

Mutual pleasantries over, she nudged aside the salt and pepper and slid Ray Breeze's *Safeguard Security* ID onto the table. Batten produced the Alimos Marina mugshot of Abe. 'One and the same, Hazel – unless Abe and Ray are identical twins?'

'I'll settle for one and the same, sir,' Timms said, dealing out six photos - of the six exquisite paintings from Queen Mab's storage unit, where the security guard turned out to be Ray Breeze. 'I guess he was after this lot. Materials pertinent to a serious crime.'

'If they are?'

'If not, I'll eat them, along with my steak. When I loaded the paintings, I thought Breezeblock's nasty sneer was his default expression. Looking back, it might've been fury. And anyway, if…' She stopped herself.

'*If it's not ruled out, it's still ruled in?*' Batten's team aped his favourite mantra behind his back – in a cod Northern accent. He shared a knowing smile with Timms.

The steaks arrived, and Timms shuffled the three 'Ben Nicholson' abstracts into sequence, showing the fake they might have become. Batten was relieved she'd had the photos enlarged, because now he could see what made her suspicious. 'You're the expert, Hazel, but these look good?'

'The third one's way beyond good, sir.'

'After he'd practised?'

She nodded. 'Practice makes –'

A Batten eyebrow and a half-smile stopped her.

'Practice makes a perfect *fake*. And the odd 'lost' Ben Nicholson does turn up.'

'And sell?'

'For big money - if authenticated. A minor pencil sketch, five grand. A full Nicholson canvas, three hundred grand and keep going.' *About what mum and dad's bungalow is worth,* she thought, pointing to the 'best' Nicholson fake. 'This might puzzle the experts. And it's 20th Century.'

'Why's that matter?'

She tongued a chunk of beef to the side of her mouth, wishing the boss would give her time to *chew*. 'Easy to find genuine 20th Century paint and canvas, sir. If you want to fake an 18th Century old master…' She let Batten catch up, forking in a fat chip in the pause.

'Ah. The fake materials would be too modern.'

'Spectroscopy, sir. Tells you exactly when a pigment was made - even where. This one, though…' She tapped the third photo. 'The latest computer technology might struggle. But it's surely by Daniel Flowers. I don't imagine Rose Linnet painted it.'

'Rose? She'd struggle to paint my ceiling.' He stopped himself. 'Oops. Clumsy.'

Batten played with his steak. Hazel gnawed a hefty slice of medium-rare. Work has made me hungry, she realised, pleased with her return to the rhythms of CID and the sin of red meat. 'Fancy being glad to be back at work.'

Another Batten eyebrow pointed out the gaffe *she* had made. 'Oops, again,' Timms said, and their chuckles attracted the waiter, a spotty youth in black and white. Timms said yes to another giant Shiraz. She'd get a taxi home, and certainly not accept a lift from Batten. Sergeant Ball's Somerset burr had let slip, 'that naughty Yorkshire boy, he's not supposed to *drive*.'

When the waiter left, Timms drew two documents from her folder. 'Our Mr Breeze, sir, he's a magician. For this passport to be genuine, he'd need to be grown-up before he was even born.' Pushing forward Abe's National Insurance number, she said, 'Abe Linnet, though, came into the world in the accepted manner. This *is* genuine. Abe got his N.I. number at age 16, automatically, same way you and I did.'

Squinting at Abe's history, Batten saw mostly gaps in the timeline – the fruits of a shady life overseas. But more recent dates confirmed a return to England, and why. 'He came back for medical treatment?'

'At least in part. But he had to revert to Abe Linnet - the NHS struggles to treat you if you don't exist. Abe must have been ill with knobs on, to chance it. Er, I'm afraid I didn't request his full medical records. I thought I'd better not. With you being…'

'Unofficial?' They both smiled. A request would need the signature of Area Superintendent Wallingford – followed by his wrath.

'These bits and pieces from the hospital – they're unofficial, too. I've got a pal there.' She hoped Batten would assume her pal's name was Dirk or Rocky, not Harriet.

'I'm a bad influence, Hazel.'

She didn't feel quite ready to tell her boss he was a good influence, if hard to get to know. Instead, she watched him scan her notes, assuming the few morsels of steak he'd eaten were troubling his stomach. What in fact she saw was the jab of pain he felt when he read, *Musgrove Hospital, Taunton Cancer Ward* and remembered Aunt Daze's failed chemo. 'Abe's been having treatment, these last few years?'

Resigned to talking with her mouth full, Timms said, 'I compared the dates against the timeline of Queen Mab's murder. Abe Linnet first surfaces at Taunton the year before her death.' She ran her fork down the list of dates. 'I can't prove where he was the night she was killed, but he wasn't in hospital, so...' As Batten scanned the timelines, she chewed and swallowed. 'Two months after she's killed, he's back in the cancer ward. In and out is the pattern. Not long been out when I turned up at the storage unit.'

'Delighted to see you?' Batten added a grin.

'A sick and surly ghost,' she said, dismissing Abe's mugshot with a glug of Shiraz, rich, peppery and red as a plum. Batten, she noticed, stuck to plain water.

'Are we thinking the same, Hazel? Abe Linnet's in remission?'

She wiped her lips on her napkin. 'Seems likely.'

Staring down at the expressionless face in the photo, Batten despised the man he had never met, a man 'lucky' enough to be in remission from the clutches of cancer. Pushing aside his steak, he tried getting his ducks in a row.

'Abe could have stuck a pin in a map of national cancer hospitals, Hazel. Why Somerset?'

Timms waved her fork at the six photographs. 'Two birds with one stone? The paintings?'

'Yes, but that was later. Take a look at these.' Batten drew the Hellenic Aviation Authority passenger lists from his document case and spread them out, finger jabbing at the numerous flights. 'Abe - or Ray Breeze - has been flying in and out like a fiddler's elbow, for ages. My guess is he was tracking down Gina - and succeeded.'

'What, so they could go to marriage guidance?' Timms smiled through another glug of Shiraz.

'Tracking her down because she upped sticks from Crete with a pocketful of his readies. She didn't buy her house with Monopoly money, did she?'

'Well, she drank herself to death with it.' Hazel put down her glass, in thought. 'But I see where you're going. *Rose* inherited when Gina died. So Abe sneaked back for treatment, *and* for his cash?'

Batten nodded. 'And later for the paintings, which Rose had locked away. With Gina gone, Rose becomes Jonny-on-the-spot for everything.'

Jenny-on-the-spot, Timms might have said, had the Shiraz kicked in. She savoured her penultimate chip. Alone at home, she might have burped with satisfaction, but not with her boss sitting opposite – and not making complete sense. 'But it's much bigger than cash and paintings, sir. Somebody *knifed* Queen Mab. Are you suggesting Abe slit his own daughter's throat?'

'It's possible, foul though it sounds.'

'I'm not questioning Abe's foulness - I've *met* him. But to knife your own child?'

'Revenge? A powerful motive?' When Timms pulled a face, Batten tapped the Ben Nicholson fakes. 'And these. Abe must have been livid when he found Rose had six chunks of damning evidence.'

'Or livid with Daniel Flowers, sir, for letting Rose get her hands on them in the first place?'

Her mention of Daniel set Batten off on a different track. Abe's boat, *Aura*, sailed into his mind's eye, Daniel Flowers and a cargo of fake paintings stowed below deck. Then, hidden amongst a thousand other boats, *Aura* docked in Alimos Marina, before Abe and Daniel, in cahoots, drove the few miles to Athens – where '*Daniel did some valuation, for the auction houses...*' But what was it he valued?

'Sir? You've gone quiet.'

Steak-fat and charcoal tanged in Batten's throat as forgotten pennies struggled to drop. How broad were Daniel's skills? 'Greek paintings, Hazel, are they easy to fake? Twentieth Century ones?'

On its way to skewer her final chip, Timms' fork halted in puzzlement. 'Sir? Ben Nicholson was an English painter, not a *Greek*. What are you -?'

'Yes, yes, but with all this Abe business, I've taken my eye off the ball. Off Daniel Flowers, at least.' He twirled an explanatory finger at his skull. 'You won't know, but Daniel painted a stunning pastiche of Botticelli's *The Birth of Venus*. Rose was the Venus, but that's not the point.'

There's a point? thought Hazel.

'The point is, our disappearing Daniel was a copyist – an expert copyist. St Ives abstracts and Renaissance classics, yes?'

'Er, yes?'

'Then why not Greek art, too? He knew the market. If he was valuing Greek paintings, what's to stop him passing off top-draw copies as the genuine article? Struth, if the auction houses *paid* him to value his own bloody fakes, then sold them at auction, they'll have paid the sod twice!'

Timms paused, mouth open, pennies of her own beginning to drop. Before she could speak, Batten was off again.

'Abe and Daniel must have built up quite a nest-egg. All from transporting fakes from a locked studio in Crete to the art markets of Athens!'

Down went Timms' fork. The last chip was cold - but her boss was warming up. 'I *think* there was some sort of art scandal in Greece, a few years back. In Athens, at least. I'd need to check.'

Batten's hands asked the question.

'OK. I will. Time permitting,' she said, as laughter broke in, from a birthday celebration at a pink table across the room.

Fizz, a cake, three proud generations, and a beaming youngster blowing out six candles to raucous applause. The Linnets would never be like this, Batten thought. But neither would the Battens - he was the last.

Families on his mind, he stared at Abe's mugshot on the bistro table until, with an imagined crack of broken glass, another penny dropped. The mugshot morphed into the shattered glass of a photo-frame, dumped by Queen Mab over her neighbour's fence in a post-funereal bender. Batten remembered the unsmiling face of young Sue Linnet, standing next to her mother and older sister, staring at the camera as if it was a gun.

'Sir? You've gone quiet again. Something I said?'

'Something *I* said, Hazel, before. *Inherited.*' The framed photo hovered in Batten's mind. All the Linnets were dead or presumed so - except Sue Linnet. She had drifted to the back burner weeks ago - and stayed there. Was she the legal heir to the Linnet estate? 'Sorry, Hazel. Dark thoughts. If Abe cut the throat of his eldest daughter, what if he did the same to the youngest? To stop her claiming the tidy nest-egg belonging to him.'

The final soggy chip curled round Hazel's fork like a question mark. 'And stop Sue inheriting six bits of damning evidence?'

'A double motive for cutting her throat.'

Hazel's last chip was cold as a corpse. 'If Abe killed Sue, there'd be a body.'

Batten shrugged. 'Then maybe she's Abe's unfinished business. We have to find him - before he finds *Sue*'

'Might be difficult, sir. I phoned *Safeguard Security* and Abe - Ray Breeze - doesn't work there anymore.' She glanced covetously at the wasted steak on her boss's plate. *Hardly the time to ask for a doggie bag.* 'He was casual labour in any case, but he left, citing ill-health.'

'Humph, bastard told the truth, for once.'

'Problem is…the forwarding address. It's fake.'

Batten glared at the grease on his plate. 'Hell's teeth! Fake paintings, passports, addresses! Is *nothing* true?' He wanted to smash the plate on the pastel-blue table, on the passing waiter's spotty face, on his own damaged skull. 'I'm sick to the back teeth of disappearing suspects.'

'Sir, I'll get down to *Safeguard Security*, when I snatch a minute.' *Once I've finished checking art fraud in Athens!* 'I'm looking. I really am.'

'And you're good at it, Hazel. I'm not doubting you.'

'But, sir, canny sod Abe doesn't even have a digital footprint. If he's floating round in Somerset, I'll eat another steak.' She could, she thought, glancing at Batten's, she really could. Instead, she dabbed her napkin at a splash of red wine before it marked her black leather skirt. When she looked up, Abe Linnet was a furrow on Batten's brow, as if the rich red meat had bypassed his stomach and gone straight to his head.

Draining the last of her Shiraz, she almost suggested they share a taxi.

No. He's the boss, she told herself. He makes his own decisions.

Forty

Next morning, Batten stood for an age under the hot shower, trying to clear his mind of images of the dead and disappeared. *Finding* Abe Linnet - and Sue, alive or dead - was the priority. He climbed into a rarely-worn grey suit and bland tie. If he soothed his next appointment, perhaps they'd help him decide where to look.

The office of Goode, Goode and Moulde occupied the upper floor of a hamstone building at the expensive end of Parminster High Street. Its huge windows frowned down on the pavement like a magistrate on a felon, the pelmets hung with velvet eyebrows in faded grey – the same shade as Batten's suit.

When an ageing flunkey ushered him into Mr Goode's musty-smelling office, Batten had no idea which of the two Goodes sat behind the mahogany desk, nor if it mattered. The figure peering up at him was no scarecrow, but hardly the 'fat twat' from Rose's journal, whose every other word was 'urrr'.

'Nnn, Inspector, nnn, yes, do sit down,' said the ruddy-faced solicitor, hands resting on a green moleskin waistcoat, fingers steepling together like a metronome. When Goode smiled, evidence of his recent lunch smiled too, from brown teeth. Spinach, Batten guessed - to match the waistcoat.

'Queen Mab?' said Batten. It was enough.

'Ahah! You mean *Rose Linnet*!' said Goode, with a chortle.

'Indeed, sir. You've joined the elite club – those who know her real name.'

'Acted for the family for years, Inspector. Otherwise, nnn, I should be calling her…Queen Mab!' Goode's louder chortle failed to dislodge the spinach in his teeth.

'It's the Linnet *family* I'm concerned with. To be frank, I'm here to borrow your memory.'

Borrow unsettled Goode. His steepled fingers opened like theatre curtains as he mentally totted up the unpaid fee. '*All* of it?'

'Snippets, sir. We know so little about them. I wondered what you might add?'

Goode perked up at 'add'. 'Nnn, nothing about the husband. Never met the man. My involvement was purely legal advice.'

'Advice about…?'

'Oh, well, simple enough. It was Mrs Linnet, Gina, we acted for. She sought a declaration of presumed death. Presumed death of her husband, that is. Abraham?'

'Abe, yes.'

'His family had been religious, apparently, hence the name. Well, it didn't rub off on *Abe* - no, no. Something of a rogue-male, apparently. Drink and *womanising!* And, if you'll allow a professional guess?'

Batten nodded a 'get-on-with-it.'

'Well, something at the darker fringes of legality.'

'You mean *illegality*?'

Goode's fingers tapped back into steeples, defensively. 'Nnn, yes, I suppose I do. But as to what *kind*…' The steeple fanned a 'don't know.'

'But he *was* officially dead?' Batten kept to himself Abe's apparent resurrection as Ray Breeze.

'In the official opinion of the courts, *presumed* dead. As perhaps you know, after a disappearance it takes seven years, minimum, for the courts to rule. Frankly, I struggled to prove much about him at all, beyond his early years in Cornwall. Rootless, a nomad. But *Goode sense* prevailed' - a chortle - 'and we provided Mrs Linnet with legal closure.'

'Seven years? What did she live on, meanwhile?'

'Income of her own, Inspector. She was well-spoken, you know.'

Tempted to roughen his Northern accent while waving banknotes, Batten asked where her money came from, already guessing the answer.

'Nnn, well, one didn't *fully* enquire, Inspector. This was the recent, not the current England. When our clients could be *trusted*.'

If they pay, Batten thought. 'You must have some idea?' asked Batten.

'Gina was a highly private person but, once - with liquid refreshment aboard, alas - she did mention bearer bonds. I assume you know what they are?'

Damn right. Handy ways to hide cash. 'Unregistered money. Doesn't that describe them?'

'Unregistered in the sense that whoever holds them may effectively cash them, yes. Or *could*. The law is tighter now.'

'But still loose when Abe disappeared?'

'Nnn, well, yes, I would say so.'

'Abe was drowned at sea? Wasn't that the verdict?'

'He had a boat, which seems to have capsized, in a storm. Treacherous, the Mediterranean. Boats either turn up or, well, sink without trace. In his case...' Goode's fingers mimed the bottom of the sea. 'And natural disasters do tend to be compelling in the courts because they are, well, natural.'

'This boat? What was it for?'

Green waistcoat drawing closer, Goode became a confidante. 'Now, I asked the same question of Gina, and reading between the lines of *her* account, the boat began as a floating dwelling. For a while perhaps, the Linnets were happy adventurers at sea.'

'Like *Swallows and Amazons*.'

Goode's fingertips trilled out silent laughter. 'A somewhat vaster scale, Inspector, the mighty Mediterranean.'

'But the Linnets? Happy adventurers? Not the impression I'm getting.'

'Moi aussi, Inspector. The purpose of the boat appeared to drift, as boats can' - another chortle - 'till the land beckoned. Thereafter, the boat was reserved for Abe alone, whenever he felt the need.'

'The need for what?'

'Oh, I surmise, to *escape*.'

'Yes, but from what?'

'Nnn, from women? Female voices – so Gina implied. Whatever the spur, he escaped frequently. On occasions, for months. You understand I am merely retailing Gina's version of events.'

Batten guessed the boat helped Abe sidestep much more than the family females. He changed the angle.

'Was this before the youngest daughter, Sue, was born?'

'Poor Sue. She was born in the *post-drifting* period when the boat was reserved for Abe alone. Hardly saw him, poor girl.'

'Sue didn't turn up at Gina's funeral, did she?'

'Alas, no. We had no address. Barely a soul turned up, other than Rose.'

'You had an address for Rose?'

'We - I mean Gina - had an *email* address, an old one. The firm sent an urgent message, and for once Rose replied. Is it uncharitable to suggest *inheritance* was a factor? We delayed the funeral, to give her time to travel up from St Ives.'

'St Ives?'

'Yes. The bright jewel of Cornwall. Do you know it?'

St Ives. Again. 'Not yet,' he said. 'But Sue, no recent contact?'

'Many attempts - because of the estate – but nil success. Now, if no heir turns up, the house, chattels and trust fund become *bona vacantia.*'

'Vacant goods?'

'*Ownerless* goods, Inspector. As you know, if not claimed -'

'They go to the Government.'

'Via the Treasury Solicitor, or representatives thereof, yes. Mind you, the Limitations Act of 1980 does allow late claims against the estate, even after the Government have, well, *snaffled* it. For at least twelve years, in fact.' Goode looked pleased with himself, till he remembered he was working for free. Suppressing a smile, Batten noted the information.

'So, Sue Linnet is the one remaining heir, and could make a late claim?'

'With Abe Linnet officially presumed dead, and Rose *extremely* dead...' Goode's fingers fanned a 'yes'. 'Gina herself -'

'- Died from heart failure?'

Solicitor fingers conjoined briefly in prayer. 'Inspector, as poor Gina is, nnn, with the angels, forgive me for suggesting her death certificate could have specified *any* of her major organs. Not least her liver? Sadly, her romance with alcohol rather influenced Rose. Not that the two ever *got on*. And when Gina dragged young Rose to Somerset - kicking and screaming - well.'

'Did Gina say why? Why Somerset?'

'For the apple orchards, Inspector!' said Goode with a throaty laugh. To Batten's stone face, he added, 'she was in fact from Cornwall, but having discovered the beauty of Somerset - she stayed. Her very words were, *now, I can go anywhere I choose!* A cry of freedom perhaps – freedom from Abe?'

'Doesn't explain why a small place like Parminster.'

'All she said was, '*nobody knows us here.*' The same reason Rose stayed on, after Gina's funeral?'

'Despite previously hating Parminster so much she couldn't get away fast enough?'

Goode's shrug covered a surreptitious glance at his watch. Batten gazed past the window's velvet swags at silvery clouds in the distance, and pictured three silver rings on Queen Mab's fingers, each carved with the letter 'L' for Linnet. Abe. Gina. And Sue.

'Did *Rose* know Sue's whereabouts, when she took on the house?'

'We posed that very question, but persuading Rose to utter one word about Sue… The family bonds were severed, I suspect. When Rose discovered her absent sister had fled the nest, pretty much on her eighteenth birthday, she showed not an ounce of surprise. Poor Sue.'

'Why poor?'

'For too many reasons, Inspector.' Goode's fingers doubled as bullet points. 'An unwanted baby - Gina made comments to that effect – who grew into a dowdy child, three times less beautiful than her older sister. The father an absent rogue, residing at the bottom of the Mediterranean. A sibling, nnn, who escaped from Gina's decrepit dwelling to university, then abroad, when Sue was a whippersnapper.' Goode leaned forward, the spinach still in his teeth. 'And a mother whose favourite beverage was not *tea*?' Goode's fingers recovered by resting on his moleskin waistcoat.

'But people don't just disappear,' Batten said. His inner voice sniped, *oh, really?*

Hands fatigued, Goode shook his ample skull. 'Inspector, when discussing the Linnets, I recommend a moratorium on all assumptions. A worse-for-wear Gina claimed Sue departed on her gap year, 'somewhere in Europe,' an account bolstered by sightings of Sue at Parminster railway station, heavy rucksack on her back.'

'So, you *do* know where she went?'

'Ah, Inspector, a gap year takes place before university. But since Sue never applied to university - couldn't, since she never completed her A levels…' In lieu of his hands, Goode again shook his skull. 'Rather than 'disappear', perhaps Sue - like Rose before her - merely 'escaped'?'

And did Abe find out where? thought Batten, but Goode was still talking.

'The house Sue left was not a happy one, with Gina drained of everything but alcohol. Drained by Abe, by Rose, by a troubled Sue. And by endless *moving*. Shipping up in quiet rurality, she could be at peace.'

'And drink herself to death,' said Batten.

'An unfortunate choice, but hers to make. I suspect in our respective roles, Inspector, judgement is easy, but influence hard?' Batten nodded agreement and asked about the trust fund.

'With the firm's help, Gina set it up when she settled here - a modest monthly return. Gina and Rose drew on it sparingly. But now, in the absence of Sue...'

'It's in limbo?'

'In the ether, yes, awaiting an heir or a claimant. Or the Government's clutches.'

'Are you allowed to mention an amount?'

Goode's pursed lips considered the question. 'Nnn, nnn, one moment, Inspector.' Scuttling across the carpet he disappeared through a door into the adjoining room.

Batten assumed Goode had no use for his legs - or had none. In the silence, he stared through the window at the comings and goings of Parminster folk in the High Street below. Shopping bags, a man wheeling a bicycle, a woman in a red hat pushing a baby-buggy, dogs large and small, sniffing the air and each other. He doubted Gina, Rose and Sue were ever part of this daily parade. What *did* they do all day, apart from uncorking a bottle?

Voices dispersed the thought when, to Batten's surprise, Goode reappeared with his exact facial double - Tweedledum and Tweedledee in person, except the second Goode had a stomach the size of a watermelon.

'Inspector, my sibling, Bertram.'

Batten shook the fleshy hand of surely the 'fat twat' from Rose's journal.

Pointing the fleshy hand at his twin brother, Bertram Goode's throaty voice said, 'Urrr, Digby here, is land and litigation. *I* am equity and trusts.' From habit, he checked his watch, plonked a weighty folder on the desk, and commandeered Digby's chair. It'll do Digby's legs no harm to stand up for a while, Batten thought.

Despite his size, Bertram was brisk. 'The Linnet trust fund, yes. Urrr, already public domain, so no reason not to divulge, urrr, Digby?' A nod of agreement set him off again. 'Including current dividends... approximately £200,000 remains. Records show 'travel money' was paid first to Rose, then later to Sue. For overseas adventures - destination unknown.' In answer to Batten's eyebrow, Bertram added, '£25,000. Each.' Turning to his brother, he asked. 'Urrr, fully sanctioned, Digby?'

'Nnn, indeed, Bertram. Gina *ecstatic* to facilitate the girls' departure.'

Before Batten forgot which twin was which, he intervened. 'And the house?'

'Ah,' said Bertram. 'That's land. *I* am trusts. Urrr, for *land*, you want Digby.' He vacated the chair and Digby, relieved, sat down.

'The size of the plot is key,' said Digby. 'The house may be in disrepair, but as *land*, nnn, at least a quarter of a million. You've visited?'

Batten had seen a jungle and a shell, not the interior. House, land and investments, around half a million pounds. A meaty inheritance - for someone. In his notebook, he underlined Sue Linnet's name in thick black ink, scribbling 'where the hell is she?' 'The trust,' he said. 'Who runs it now?'

Digby's steepled fingers burst upwards, a brief firework, accompanied by a satisfied nod from Bertram. 'Our Goode selves,' they said, in perfect unison.' Bertram added, 'urrr, if no claimant appears, Rose Linnet's remaining assets will, I'm afraid, become what is termed a 'failed trust', succumbing, with the rest of the estate, to the Treasury's clutches.'

'Reward for some,' Batten said.

'Nnn, but dismay for others, Inspector,' replied Digby. 'Urr, yes,' Bertram concurred.

Tweedledum and Tweedledee shared looks of regret. It seemed a Goode moment for Batten to take his leave.

Forty one

The search for Sue Linnet was a steep climb for an unofficial detective. Even Batten baulked at nudging more 'favours' onto the desks of Chris Ball and Hazel Timms. For all he knew, Sue could be five thousand miles away. Cornwall, he reminded himself, was still a warm trail, and a hundred and fifty miles by train. No white-knuckle flight required.

In his Ashtree study, he ran his fingers over hand-built bookshelves bristling with travel literature, mostly vicarious because Batten had little stomach for travel - or so he told himself. He found no book on Cornwall because he'd never been.

But Daniel Flowers had. One of the Goodes - he'd already forgotten which - said both Abe and Gina spent their early years there. And Queen Mab travelled up from St Ives for Gina's funeral – never to return. In the mire of journal pages, Batten at last found an entry suggesting why Rose went to Cornwall in the first place.

Clio wants me out – to make easy cash from the new tourists. I sit near the beach, painting the bay, and the idiots gawp like gargoyles. Can you see what it is, yit? one idiot asks his fat wife. I turn round – oh, look it's a painting of an ignoramus, would you like to buy it? No need to be rude, says the wife. Fuck off! says I. They did, the waiters pretending not to laugh. But quick enough to grab the euros for a litre of wine – and that's gone up!
Clio has thrown away her paints, hallelujah. Sofia's buggered off to Rhodes with her latest shag. Even nice Andreas moved to Thessaloniki - his dad died, left him the house. Never owned a house in my life. What would I do with one? Rather be under the stars. Almyrida – it's dead to me. No artists. And there was only ever one. When men don't return, are women supposed to fetch them?
*St Ives, it said, on Daniel's paintings - is he there? Want them, does he, his secret canvases? Then look for **me**!*
Full of artists, St Ives.

'*St Ives it is!*' Batten said, grabbing his phone. Maybe Sonia Welcome would join him…?

'Zig, you know damn well I can't. I have to book leave in advance.'

Even her 'no' voice soothed him. 'Tell them you'd be acting in a medical capacity – helping a friend convalesce.'

'And see their faces when I told them which friend?' Her silence filled the phone - too soon for rumours. 'Ask me when I *am* able, Zig. Then the question will mean something.'

Now, the silence was his.

'You'll go anyway,' Sonia said, laughing when he pretended to disagree. 'But, Zig, please?'

'Please what?'

'No driving?'

Phone still warm in his hand, he booked a seat on tomorrow's train. Then, with Sonia's voice tutting in his head, rolled his car from the garage. A short drive into Yeovil, to buy a Cornwall guidebook, what's the harm in that?

*

Yeovil was quiet midweek, the multi-storey carpark only half full. Strolling through the Quedam Centre to Waterstone's, between stores old, new or empty, his peace was disturbed by the harsh clang of a burglar alarm. From professional habit, he followed his ears and eyes till he spotted the flash of a warning light above an empty shop. A clothing store gone bust, judging by the bare hangers dangling from forlorn racks bolted to the walls.

As he watched, the warning light clicked off and silence returned. Perhaps a sensitive soul had phoned the security company - he imagined an angry voice yelling over the din. Maybe it was *Safeguard Security*, he mused. Maybe Ray Breeze would roll up to check the premises - their very own casual employee with a double life. The alarm's company logo was one he didn't recognise – not that he would recognise the logo of *Safeguard Security* because he'd never seen it.

But neither had Hazel Timms, he recalled. Her contact had been only by phone…

On his own phone, he googled their website and found an address – a ten-minute walk, past Yeovil Library, in the opposite direction. Trusting his instincts, he abruptly turned on his heel.

'*Oi!*' said a thirty something woman in chubby floral leggings and a cigarette. 'Nearly knocked me over.'

'Sorry,' said Batten. 'Forgot where I was going.'

'Try remembering, then!' the woman shouted. 'And eff off there!'

Watching her back disappear, he mouthed 'Waterstone's' to himself. Then headed in the opposite direction.

His arrival was timely. *Safeguard Security* was housed in a puny office above a cafe, and as bare as the staircase he'd climbed to reach it. A heavy bunch of keys dangled from the open door as he entered.

'Not particularly secure,' he said, pointing at the keys. Without returning Batten's smile, a threadbare man who could be thirty or fifty, said, 'no point. About to hand them back, the keys.'

'Moving, are you, Mr -?' asked Batten.

'Drew,' said the man. 'Might as well be called *Lost*. We're closing. Been wound up. So, can't help you.'

Batten knew when to flash his credentials. Mr Drew winced at the warrant card. 'Oh, great,' he said, 'first the taxman, now CID. Want a second pound of flesh, do you?'

'The taxman? asked Batten. When Drew shrugged and said nothing, Batten sat down in one of two office chairs still gracing the near-empty room and rolled it in front of the door. 'I'm happy to ring them,' he said. 'It'll take all day.'

Flopping onto the other chair, Drew gave Batten the bare bones - a stonking fine, just for a smidgeon of 'off the books' employment activity. From experience, Batten translated the tale as tax evasion, National Insurance fraud, false accounting, and half a dozen other misdemeanours – the use of unregistered employees being one of them.

'You had a security guard by the name of Ray Breeze. Remember him?'

Drew pretended to think. Yes, Breeze was an 'off the books' employee he'd already fessed up to. 'Oh, Ray. Ancient, but reliable. Kept his eyes open. Well, till he got sick.' Drew kept quiet about non-existent sick pay.

'Sick?'

'On and off. He was alright a few years back. Night shift. Drove a patrol van for us. Stopped a burglary, did Ray.'

'Where?'

'Um, over at Parminster. We had a contract there, patrol van, at night. Chased off thieves breaking into the Vet's. Bit of petty theft, but he stopped 'em cracking the drugs cabinet. Bute, ketamine - horse drugs, but humans like 'em. Fetch a good price. Er, I'm told.'

Tingles in Batten's feet egged him on. 'Parminster?'

'I said.'

'When?'

On a long sigh, Drew reached into his coat for a cash book. 'Um…three years back, give or take.' He ran a bored finger down the page. '*Parminster Business Consortium* – didn't last long. Says here they paid us for three months, night patrols. Ray Breeze, mostly.'

'This Consortium, who was in it?'

'Who?' Another long sigh and a flick of pages. 'Well, the Vet's. The industrial estate. Three or four town centre places. Do you know Jake's Bake shop?'

Batten did.

'Used to get free pies, from Jake's. Huh, not anymore.'

'*Comfort Carpets*?'

'Yeh, the carpet shop. And…a pet shop. That's it.'

'Ray Breeze, what did he actually do?'

'Do? Patrolled, in the van, at night, when no other bugger would. Checked the alarms, security lights, grilles, doors. Usual stuff.'

'And ended up as a guard at Camelot Self-Storage?'

'Er, well, a casual.' A Batten eyebrow nudged Drew along. 'He'd been ill, you see, couldn't drive. *He* asked *me* for that Camelot job, said he lived nearby. I only agreed because he'd foiled that break-in at the Vet's, and even an old fool like Ray could lock and unlock a door. Wasted my time, didn't I? Never saw the week out - he went AWOL. Bloody idiot.'

An idiot canny enough to abscond after Hazel Timms turned up and clocked his name and features, thought Batten.

'I wouldn't mind but he buggered off with a set of *our* keys.' Drew jabbed a finger at the now redundant bunch dangling from the office door. 'If he turns up, tell him to stick the keys where I'd like to stick those. Ugly big lump, Ray. There'd be room.'

Back in the Quedam Centre, the signposts, flowerbeds and interlocking paths reminded Batten how much he missed the everyday *structure* of his role. For all his quirks, he functioned best in a team. Compulsory sick leave, light duties, unofficial delving - none of it suited. Perhaps he should visit St Ives just to convalesce?

With Ray Breeze and Safeguard Security on his mind, he tramped towards Waterstone's in a daydream, then tramped beyond it to his car, which somehow drove him home. In his study, bookshelves lacking a Cornwall travel guide reminded him why he'd gone to Yeovil in the first place.

Forty two

For Batten, trains trumped planes, because they were 30,000 feet closer to the ground. After a day staring through different carriage windows, he finally chugged from St Erth station to St Ives in fading sunlight.

Saints figured strongly in the placenames he passed, his phone browser identifying St Erth as a 5th Century Irish missionary, presumably with a mission to sanctify Cornwall. St Ives was named after St Ia, another Irish missionary from the same period – but female, and some sort of princess. He wondered if other surprises awaited.

After a heavy sleep and a light breakfast, he squeezed through the buzzing streets of St Ives, edging past sweaty bodies elbowing themselves into shops bristling with artwork - good, bad, cheap and expensive, but none of it signed 'Daniel Flowers'. His loose plan involved trawling galleries and artists' groups, in search of a memorious St Ives resident - or one with access to records…

'History? Of *course* we have history! An Arts Club has existed hereabouts since 1888 – and not for 'donkey's years', as you loosely put it.'

The Chair of the St Ives Arts Fellowship hadn't warmed to Batten when he'd entered her lair and asked his questions. Nor had Miss Nancarrow risen from her perch behind a table sporting a *Visitors Welcome* sign. He was tempted to raise an eyebrow at it, but she was raising enough eyebrows for the pair of them.

In the white-walled gallery, visitors that *were* welcome muttered polite British euphemisms at the amateur paintings. At the rear, a clutch of local artists fettled works presumably intended, in the fullness of time, for the gallery walls – if they managed to sneak past the horn-rimmed stare of Miss Nancarrow.

'Imagine we do keep membership records going back decades, yes?' Batten nodded, agreeably. 'What would persuade me to *divulge* them, to a perfect stranger, for purposes unclear?' Batten opened his mouth to speak, but she beat him to it. 'Regardless of your attempts at explanation.'

He had no answer, and no official right to be asking, without clearing it with the local police. He kept his out-of-area warrant card in his pocket – Miss Nancarrow would gleefully report him, despite already assuming he was a divorce lawyer or debt-collector. Her nostrils displayed her assumptions with caustic joy. So far, it was the only joy to crack her face.

Short sleeves and sunscreen, and I still behave like a cop! Batten told himself. 'I'm not asking you to divulge anything sensitive, Miss Nancarrow. But a simple confirmation that Rose Linnet was a member of your Society, and when? I see no harm in that.'

'Rose. Linnet.' Miss Nancarrow spat the words like lemon pips.

'That's right. Blonde, slim? Extremely attractive?'

Batten's adversary arrowed two disgusted eyeballs at him. If a debt-collector before, he was a lecher, stalker and rapist now. *You're off your game, Zig,* he told himself. Across the room, an elderly artist and his young companion paused over their work, trying not to laugh at his ham-fistedness. When Miss Nancarrow shot them a Headmistress-like stare, they shovelled their easels into a pair of knapsacks and made for the door. The older man gave Batten a concealed grimace of sympathy.

Batten cut his losses too. There were other ways of tracking down Queen Mab. The St Ives Arts Fellowship, icily mentioned in her journal, proved to be the wrong place to start. Or Miss Nancarrow was.

He muttered, *thank you for being so helpful,* while nudging the *Visitors Welcome* sign from table-top to floor. It landed by Miss Nancarrow's ancient feet like a discarded betting slip. Feeling discarded himself, he stepped out into blinding sunlight and fought his way down Wharf Road, along the St Ives seafront, amid ice-creams, dogs, street musicians and a crush of tourists looking twice as happy as he did.

Every table outside The Sloop Inn, by Harbour Beach, was crammed with drinkers defying the heat and the buzz of passers-by. Batten needed cool and quiet. Stepping inside in hope, a darker world met him, of paintwork black and brown, of walls seamlessly covered in dark drawings and prints, the names of the artists too small to read. Or his eyesight was worse today.

In the cooler air, an empty seat stared up at him. Spreading his discarded jacket over the chairback, he joined a queue at the bar, behind two men, one elderly, one a young buck. Each carried a knapsack, the end of a mini easel sticking out the top. He recognised them from the gallery where Miss Nancarrow had wiped the floor with him. The older man had flashed a knowing smile, he recalled.

And now here they were. Have I somehow followed them, he wondered? Are my Detective Inspector instincts still working? *Then let them lead*, said his inner voice.

'Buy you a drink?' he asked the older man.

'Why'd you want to do that?'

'Pint o' cider,' the young buck told the barman.

'Suppose I'd better have the same, then. To supervise.'

Batten settled for a half, and the three of them settled at the table. The young man sank a third of his drink with a smile made lopsided by a missing front tooth.

'Marcus, my nephew,' said the older man. 'I'm Trevor, by the way.'

'Call me Zig,' said Batten, and they shook hands.

'He's supposed to be learning to paint, like I did. Keep him out of trouble,' said Trevor. 'So he don't lose more teeth.'

Marcus shrugged away his uncle's jibe, and all three sampled the cool, dry brew. Sergeant Ball would approve, Batten thought, as young Marcus scrolled through his mobile phone.

'This is what I'm up against,' said Trevor. 'How can you paint the world if you never look at it.' Eyes on the screen, Marcus tutted.

'You're not the first,' Trevor said, 'to get the wrong side of Miss Nancarrow. Turn a man to stone, her gimlet eyes. Marcus calls her Miss Can-Narrow. Don't you?'

'Not to her face, unc. I'm not *suicidal*,' said Marcus, scrolling.

'She's all frosted up inside, is Miss N. Teetotal, too.'

In the dark silence, Trevor eased his pain with cider. Marcus scrolled through the something or nothing of his digital past. Batten wondered why he'd bothered. Till Trevor spoke.

'Rose wasn't teetotal, though. No danger of that.'

A trombone blared in Batten's chest. 'Rose Linnet? You remember her?'

Trevor nodded. 'Best looking female I ever saw. Kind, too. When sober.'

'Rose liked the sauce even back then, did she?' asked Batten.

Trevor sipped and smiled. 'Police, are you?'

Apparently, Batten said to himself. 'Obvious, is it?'

'Not to Miss Nancarrow. She had you down as a wife-beater, out for revenge. Obvious to me, though. Where'd you suppose I learned to paint?'

'Royal College of Art?' said Batten, over a smile.

Trevor's chuckle returned. 'Channings Wood Prison, down the road, near Newton Abbot. In my carefree days, I got over-involved with exotic substances. Channings Wood set me straight. I'll make sure *he* stays straight, too.' Trevor nudged his nephew's phone hand.

'Oi, watch it, unc. You've had your youth. Still having mine.'

'Have it clean, then,' said Trevor, before turning back to Batten. 'With old Nancarrow, you couldn't have picked a worse subject if you'd tried. Hell's teeth, Rose Linnet? Miss Frosty tried to turf Rose out of the group a dozen times, before Rose buggered off under her own steam. And as a matter of interest, is this official, or what?'

Caught, but trusting his instinct, Batten told the sad truth about Queen Mab. Trevor's response was to drain his glass and stare at nothing for a long ten seconds. Pulling a twenty from his wallet, he nudged his nephew from his reverie. 'Marcus. The bar's over there, not inside your phone. Same again all round - and I want the change.'

When Marcus, phone in hand, joined the queue, Trevor's levity departed with him. 'I've often wondered if Rose still graced the world. She and me...you know, once or twice. She liked older men. But the only reason we...you know, is because of the drink.'

Trevor stared at his empty glass as Batten's scepticism kicked in. Most witness statements contained errors, false memories, or plain lies. He was wondering if Trevor's did.

'Drink. It loosened Rose, and she'd get in your face, or in your pants – no telling which till it happened. God's truth, I struck gold, 'cos for half an hour she made me feel like George Clooney.'

Batten allowed Trevor a few moments of nostalgia, before asking about Daniel Flowers.

Trevor dropped his voice further still. 'I thought I heard you ask old Nancarrow about a Daniel, back there. I never met the man. Nobody called Daniel around when Rose lived here. And before that, I was at finishing school, by request of Her Majesty.'

'Sounds like you knew *of* him, though?'

With a sigh, Trevor stared at the flagstone floor, his voice dropping to a whisper now. 'Only his bloody name. When me and Rose were, you know, in the throes, she called me Daniel, more'n once - in a posh voice from nowhere. Put me off my stroke, to be honest. After, I said who's this Daniel, then? Well, she climbed into her clothes, said not a word, and buggered off. Next time I saw her, there was a lot less between us.'

Trevor pointed to the empty glasses on the table.' I long expected this stuff would kill her. Not…well, what you said.' His face paled, as he relived Batten's sanitised account. 'Would she have suffered?'

More than she had already? 'We don't think so, no.'

'Hope you find the bastard who done it. But you wouldn't be here otherwise.'

Batten didn't admit his search for Queen Mab's past was sandwiched between a 'convalescent' trip to the Barbara Hepworth Sculpture Garden, in glorious morning sunshine, and a planned tour of the St Ives Tate. He'd begun to believe Trevor and wanted him to talk only of Rose. 'What more can you tell me, about her? Even little things.'

Despite his sadness, Trever managed a chuckle. 'I said before, she was the best-looking woman I ever met. Well, she was the worst painter, too. Even worse than Marcus,' he said, as his nephew slopped three drinks onto the table.

Marcus picked up his pint and shook a fag packet at this uncle. 'I'll be outside.'

'Er, Marcus? My change? *Thank you.* Go on, then. Smoke yourself to death.' When Marcus stumped away, Uncle Trevor shook his head and sipped cider, lost in thought. 'Marcus just reminded me of Rose, even with a tooth missing and his mind, if he's got one, hypnotised by that bloody phone.' Seeing Batten's puzzlement, he explained. 'Rose, donkey's years back. She hated cigarettes. The smell, I suppose.'

Batten remembered Rose's Queen Mab years, when she would stop perfect strangers in Parminster High Street and warn them cigarettes were the breath of Satan. 'But when it came to drink?' he said.

'Phuh, she could drink for England. Shoved the booze equivalent of fifty a day down her neck. And had the cash to pay for it, too – not that she wasn't generous.'

'She was selling paintings, maybe?'

Trevor laughed so hard he had to put down his glass. 'Who *to*? Didn't I say she was the worst painter I ever met? Her hands craved holding a brush, like Marcus craves a cigarette. After that, you felt sorry for the canvas. Drunk or sober, no different.'

'But she kept painting?'

Trevor clothed a nod with a sigh. 'I once asked her why she bothered, gentle, you know, but Rose she'd had a couple, so she threw my question back at me. *Why do* ***you*** *effing paint?* she says, feisty. I told her, straight up. Because I've been inside, locked in, and now I paint the blue sky and the open sea, so in my mind I'll never be in prison again. *Well,* she says. *I'm the same!*' Trevor paused to wet his whistle. 'I told her the name of my prison, HMP Channing Woods, near Newton Abbot, I said. Where's yours?'

'Did she reply?'

'Went quiet. I'd maybe upset her. After a minute, she taps her fingers against her skull. Big silver rings, on every finger. *In here*, she says. *My prison's in here.* She gives me a sideways look and wouldn't say another word. If Rose didn't want to talk…' Trevor downed a throatful, wiping his mouth on a hankie so colourful Batten wondered if he'd painted it himself. 'She kept sloshing paint onto canvas, regardless. It'd be charity to say she improved.'

The pub door burst open as a party of tourists flooded the bar, squeezing against the tables, animated voices killing the peace. Trevor leaned closer and said, 'Rose would have hated this.' He waved at the noisy throng, the men like prop forwards, giant thighs pushing at the seams of their summer shorts.

'The noise, you mean?' said Batten, voice ironically raised.

'Noise. Squeeze. Push 'n shove. She needed open space. But summer in St Ives - proper busy. Couldn't abide the squeeze, poor pixie. One of the reasons she left.'

'Left? Do you know where?'

''Course I do.' Trevor pointed over his shoulder. 'South coast, ten miles. Look, here.' He planted his finger on a framed map screwed to the wall behind them. 'See?'

No. Batten couldn't. He went through the palaver of dragging his specs from his pocket and hooking them over his ears, to read the name on the map. 'Marazzion?' he asked.

'Mara-zyyy-on,' said Trevor. 'You've surely heard of St Michael's Mount? Little island in the bay, across a causeway, fairy-tale castle on top?'

Batten had seen a photo.

'Well, Marazion's the little town on the mainland, opposite, where the causeway starts. Arty, but fewer people.'

'More head-space?'

'That's about the size of it. I went over there, to see her. Just the once -'

'What, you and she were still...you know?'

Trevor found the suggestion hilarious. 'You never met Rose, that's for sure. *Rose*? Once she sobered up, she could tell a frog from a prince. Look at me! Even donkey's years ago I looked like this!' He laughed so hard his rainbow hankie had to soak up the splutter. ''Just friends' by then, or so I thought. I went over to Marazion to *paint* her. First time I saw her, I wanted to paint her. When I plucked up courage to ask, she turned purple and bit my head off. *I don't let **anyone** paint me!* she snapped. And when Rose snapped at you...'

Even the ink in the journal snapped, Batten recalled.

'*She* was still painting, though, God help her. In a scruffy studio with a bunch of misfits.'

'Studio? asked Batten. 'Do you remember where?'

'I'm old,' said Trevor, 'not *senile*.' Peeling the Sharps Ales advert from a beer mat, he scribbled an address and a rough map on the blank surface and handed it to Batten. 'That's where Rose was. Don't want to think where she is now.' He closed his eyes and for a moment Batten thought he was asleep. 'No, never let me paint her, never. Lost her liking for St Ives, and since I was from there, lost her liking for me.'

With a shake of the head, Trevor settled his empty glass on the table and pulled his knapsack towards him. 'The one thing Rose cared for was the view in Marazion, across the bay, to St Michael's Mount. When we were talking, in the street, I don't think she looked at me more'n once. Just stared at the island, the sea, the castle in the clouds. Those crazy eyes of hers, searching.'

'For what?'

'Search me,' said Trevor. 'But *I* wasn't it! That's the last I heard of Rose. I mean, until you…'

'She stuck in your memory, by the sound of it?'

'How could she not?' said Trevor, his voice softening. 'How could she not? Cheekbones to sharpen pencils on. Poor Rose.'

Best leave Trevor's nostalgia undisturbed, Batten thought. When poor Rose decayed into Queen Mab, she stuck more in the nostrils than the memory. He pushed aside his own glass, still half-full, head throbbing from a sour encounter with Miss Nancarrow, from raised voices, rising heat, a lack of air. He could understand Rose's hatred of being enclosed.

'Miss Nancarrow, back there,' said Trevor, 'she remembered Rose alright, for the wrong reasons. Too much spirit for Old Frosty.' As Trevor climbed to his feet, the pub door opened again, and Marcus yelled over the noise.

'Dad phoned, says they're eating early so come now, it's pie.'

'Pie,' said Trevor. 'Proper job, a slice of pie…Though I'd rather have Rose.' He shouldered his knapsack and made for the door. 'Whatever happened to Rose, it happened in here.' Trevor tapped his skull with a bony finger, and the door snapped shut behind him.

Everything happens in here, thought Batten, rubbing his own skull. He had something in common with Queen Mab.

And with young Marcus too. Pulling out his phone, he opened the browser, typed in 'Marazion', and pressed *Search*.

Forty three

Batten's room at The Godolphin Arms Hotel looked straight across the beach towards the stone causeway connecting Marazion to the stately island of St Michael's Mount. Below his window, the incoming tide forced white-tipped iron waves across the sand. Mesmerised, he watched the ripples creep across swathes of seaweed, drowning the causeway inch by inch, till all was grey water.

When I go across,' said the receptionist, 'I go when the tide's in, on the early boat, and climb up to the battlements for the wonderful views. Once the tide's out, it's a lovely stroll back along the causeway. But do keep an eye out – the tide comes in fast. We don't want to lose you, Mr, er…' She checked her screen. 'Mr Batten. Table for dinner?'

Batten had barely finished lunch. And St Michael's Mount could wait. In walking trainers, he set off into Marazion, following the rough directions Trevor had scratched onto a beermat. Tramping past art shops selling everything from cheap prints to original works at wallet-crushing prices, he passed East Cliff Lane, and crossed to a narrow road curving out of sight, parallel to the sea.

Trevor had written, 'Number 8' on the beermat and seconds later Batten faced a smart run of three-storey cottages. 'Seaview Holiday Apartments' was emblazoned over the UPVC door of 7, 8, and 9, neat containers of clipped box straddling the entrances. 7 was teal blue; 9 a pale shade of pink. Rose Linnet's scruffy art studio had been reborn as a hymn to primrose yellow, it's proud number 8 set into a wall tile in which enamelled seagulls were trapped.

Batten's cop-eye caught the twitch of a curtain and within seconds the door of number 8 scraped back. The upper half of a fifty-something woman in a paint-stained smock peered round the frame at him.

'Can I help you?' she said - the polite British form of *bugger off*. Her paint-dotted smock carrying artistic hope, he explained his presence.

'*What?* Those *artists?* That was an ice-age ago,' snapped the woman. 'We purchased the cottages here' - she wafted an arm left and right – 'and had a devil of a job with the renovations. I spend my life converting mess into tidiness. And some holidaymakers, you would not *believe* the damage.' Easing open the door, she waved a four-inch brush of beige emulsion at scratches and scrapes on the hallway. 'As for what *you* call *artists. Ugh!* In the end, my husband obtained a court order, to evict them and their unspeakable paraphernalia. Grubby so-called creatives - and using *language. We* had giant bailiffs on *our* side.'

Batten controlled an urge to reposition her four-inch brush. 'I don't suppose you remember a blonde woman? One of the artists? Very attractive?'

Batten's reward was a harder stare.' *None* of them were attractive to *me*,' she said, before pausing in thought. 'Oh, heavens, not the drunk one?'

'It's possible.'

'*She* I wish I *could* forget. I shan't repeat what she called poor Hugo. Screaming at him, 'I won't leave my island, I won't leave my island -'

'You mean St Michael's Mount?'

'Can you see another?' asked the woman, jabbing her brush at the bay. 'When we began boarding up the so-called 'studio', she practically sprinted across the causeway to 'her island' - appearing not to notice the tide was coming in, moronic wastrel. Almost succeeded in drowning herself, but some busybody called the coastguard, or the lifeboat, or the police. Well, *some*body dried her out - in both senses of the word. Was there anything else?'

Batten returned her acid smile with one of his own. 'Do you recall when this was?' he asked.

With a *tuh!* the woman flicked her paintbrush at the information sign Batten was leaning against and slammed the door. Turning, he read the blurb. 'The Seaview Holidays fairy tale began on the first day of Spring, in...'

'Very helpful!' he told the door, half in truth, and headed up the road to The King's Arms. He'd earned an afternoon beer. If the coastguard, lifeboat or police 'rescued' a hysterical Rose Linnet, there would be a report. And Mrs Four-inch Paintbrush had provided the where and when.

*

Sweating over a teeming desk at HQ, Hazel Timms would kill for a red wine. Her herbal tea was clap cold and smelled like compost. With three domestic violence cases done and dusted, she'd begun to feel efficient, till the fourth sent her back in time in search of incriminating 'previous'. The potted plant beside her - a calathea, the label said - was supposed to purify the air. Either she'd forgotten to water it, or the laptop's blazing heat had incinerated the bloody thing.

Feeling incinerated herself, she moved from the screen to old-fashioned paper - piles of it, old records of *domestics,* written up by uniformed officers with too many callouts on their hands. She shoved aside reports not featuring the current victim, ploughing on with the rest.

Which is when, amongst the rejects, she thought she saw the name 'Linnet'. No. Too much of a coincidence.

She looked again. *Linnet, G.* said the heading. Timms read the thin file in seconds. Across the room, Batten's office was vacant, his desk as empty as hers was full.

'Sarge?' she said. 'Where's the boss today?'

Ball narrowed his eyebrows at her and put a discreet finger to his lips.

'Oh. Sorry,' she whispered. Ball comically mimed a phone and wiggled his watch.

Fine. She'd ring Batten later, at home.

If that's where he was.

Forty four

One of reasons Batten was pleased to be in Cornwall was the South-West Coastal Path. The leaflet he'd 'borrowed' from Reception spoke the truth when it said the two-mile walk from Marazion to Penzance was mostly flat, with magnificent coastal views. In sunlight, he breathed in the blue-tinged vista of Mounts Bay - while not envying Queen Mab's encounter with its waves.

But his two mile walk soon became six, as he tramped between Penzance Police Station, the Lifeboat, and the National Coastwatch Lookout. All told the same story, of buildings sold and records lost in the chaos of Government cuts. Thank the lord for volunteers, he thought, with coastal safety leaning heavily on the unpaid and the uncomplaining.

The Coastwatch manager cupped his chin in the palm of his hand when Batten asked his questions. 'Now, that'll be before my time,' he said, thinking hard. 'You'll be wanting old Kenwyn. If anyone knows, old Kenwyn knows. He's an elephant.'

A leg-weary Batten perked up. 'Any chance I could I speak to this elephant?'

'Not today, sorry, no.' Batten perked back down again, fingers coiling to a fist in frustration.

'*Today*, it'll be pub, allotment, grandkids, or gone a-wandering. And Kenwyn won't do mobile phones. But he's on shift tomorrow.'

Batten did do phones. After checking when 'old Kenwyn' finished his shift, he did the sensible thing and rang for a taxi. Back at The Godolphin Arms, he crawled from the shower, muttering a silent thank you to his police team who, in normal times, did much of the legwork, the questioning, the statement-taking that Batten was doing solo. He imagined the meeting room at Parminster, the murder board, the lines of enquiry, and him comparing notes with Ball and the team – even with Eddie Hick, his sharp mind only half-hidden by dyslexia and bumping into things.

Batten bumped himself into bed, in twilight, fell asleep and woke in darkness. One glance at the bedside clock and he decided to stay where he was.

Next day, arriving in Penzance earlier than planned, he sat on a clifftop bench watching boats out at sea and thinking of Almyrida, of Daniel Flowers, and Abe Linnet's *Aura*. Digby Goode said Abe was born in Cornwall. Did he return, to track Rose? And if Batten also tracked her trail, would he find Abe Linnet at the end of it?

When two Coastwatch staff emerged from their lookout it was easy enough to guess which was old Kenwyn because his companion was at least forty years younger. 'Alfie Couch,' he said, shaking hands. 'Our boss says you wanted to talk to the elephant?'

Batten managed an embarrassed shrug. The older man, skin like dried fish, chuckled to himself while pulling on a cracked brown waterproof, despite sunlight gleaming from cloudless blue.

'This elephant,' said Alfie Couch, 'he only forgets one thing - his wallet. That right, Kenwyn?'

'Tell you what, Alfie, I've remembered it 'ent my turn to pay.' If salt could talk, thought Batten, it would sound like Kenwyn. 'See, me and Alfie's goin' across The Turks Head,' he croaked, 'if you fancy a pint?' The hint was not lost on Batten.

The Turks Head reminded him of The Sloop, in St Ives. Searching for Queen Mab was bound to be a journey into the past, but Batten was tired of interviews with dried old prunes or salted fish like Kenwyn. Under this blue sky, the old Penzance coast watcher could have been Andros the fisherman in Almyrida.

As in The Sloop, Batten bought the first round.

And the second.

Kenwyn's struggle to remember seemed like trained opportunism. Batten stuck to halves - and waited, glad to rest his feet. When the second pint arrived, Kenwyn admitted to a past as a lifeboatman. When he'd swallowed a third of it, he remembered Marazion.

'Offen rescued windsurfers, struggling in the bay, out of puff. It's colder 'n they expeck. But Marazion, you say?' Batten nodded. 'Arrgh, I do recall a crazy woman. A looker, despite a fair coverin' of seaweed. Tried to swim to the island – don' ask me why. Frozen solid when we picked her up. But she wouldn't go below – y'know, to get warm. Went crazy when we tried persuadin' her. Knocked back plenty o' brandy, mind. Artist? That her?'

'Sounds like it,' said Batten.

'Humph. Artists, all of 'em, in Marazion.'

'My cousin's from Marazion,' said Alfie. An' he don't know a paint brush from a pint o' Sharps.'

'I was talking about *normal* folk,' said Kenwyn. Batten wondered when Cornwall might produce one.

'What happened to her?' he said. 'The 'artist.'

'Something and nothing, I expeck.' Kenwyn drained his glass and looked at his watch. 'Ooh, I'm late.'

'Forgot your wallet again?' said Alfie.

'No, no. Grandpa duties.'

Batten almost asked for a refund.

With two fast pints inside him, Kenwyn took twice as long to struggle into his battered waterproof. But the beer didn't cloud his memory. 'Now, what happened to her, you ask? We took her to shore, not that she wanted to *go*. Paramedics checked her over while we waits for the police. But a bunch of scruffies turns up, four or five o' them, in an old van. Got a bit antsy, if I recall, soon as we mentioned 'police', and they whisked her off. Nothing we could do to stop 'em, not without fisticuffs – and it's not what we're for, is it?'

'What *are* you for, y'old bugger?' said Alfie, pushing Kenwyn's arm into a sleeve.

'For this,' said the older man, lightly cuffing Alfie round the head before turning back to Batten. 'Small she might've been, that artist woman, but she'd have put up a fight. Great whopping rings like knuckledusters on her hands! One o' the scruffies, woman with more studs than teeth, says to me, "she's upset, she's just lost her mother. An' now she's no place to live. Where can she go?" I dunno, I said. But *swimming* won't get her there, will it?' Something between a chuckle and a sneeze disappeared behind Kenwyn's dirty sleeve. 'Well, they ignores me, and drives her off in the van. Couldn't begin to guess where,' he said, and on an affectionate kick in the pants from Alfie Couch, disappeared through the door.

But Batten knew where, another journey explained. Not long after her rescue from the sea, she turned up at her mother's funeral in Parminster. And stayed there, till her own.

He pondered what else he knew, from the journals, the gut-wrenching crime reports, the flights and favours – and the interviews like the one he'd just conducted, each time pretending it was a conversation. Alone at his Turks Head table beneath the pub clock's tick, he swirled the beery remains in his glass and considered Rose's history. A long series of escapes from… what? Sweeping up the beer mats littering the damp table he flipped them down, a mat for each series, hoping one of them might somehow reveal a motive.

Living off the map in Crete - sea and mountains - because Abe says so.

School and Darren in Chania, and a bleak escape from motherhood.

He flipped down more beermats, for more escapes. Somerset. University. Almyrida, in Clio Demopoulou's rented house. St Ives and Marazion, in search of 'something' of Daniel Flowers.

The failed escape back to Daniel at Leeds University warranted no beermat. He waggled the next, uncertain. Was Rose's near-drowning in St Michael's Bay a welcome rescue - or a failed attempt at the ultimate escape?

Flip went more mats. Gina Linnet's inherited house in Parminster. A rented storage unit. Then the slow decline into Queen Mab, and a land where only the fairies live.

The last beer mat hovered in his hand, redundant. Queen Mab's final escape was permanently sealed in thirty-six crime-scene images. On that last broken night, someone clubbed her about the head and sliced a knife across her throat from one ear to the other - motive unknown.

He tossed aside the beer mat in frustration, pushing away the pale dregs in his glass. Weary, he tramped back to Marazion, legs and spirit leaden by the time he arrived.

Across the causeway, St Michael's Mount, a capsule of deep history, rose dreamlike from the sea.

*

Darren Pope's deep history, by contrast, was on hold. Since they dumped him overboard, he had felt only water. Now, the sea grew warm as he drifted close to land.

The coast, Darren! Over there! said the Voice that was his own.

His arms cleaved the waves, grey-white water trailing behind, sea foam trickling into the thickness of his beard and out again. In, out. Driving forwards, the passport and knife still in his pockets, snug against his hip.

His leg, though. He swam with two strong arms and one strong leg, the other dragging behind, a faint sense of bone scraping on bone. When he made it ashore, would he be able to stand? Could he walk?

He had the knife and was practised. Cut a stick, fashion a crutch. And someone would fix his leg – or be forced to, by the knife. If not, he would crawl all the way to England to finish this business.

Early sunlight dappled the shore. Darren Pope gasped when a wave wrenched his damaged leg but, the beach in sight, he wiped salt from his eyes and put his strong arms to work.

Forty five

How could a five-minute ferry ride from beach to island leave him queasy? The small boat rolled like a deranged dolphin and when Batten's landlubber legs met the solid earth of St Michael's Mount, they were still at sea.

A smiling National Trust volunteer scanned his membership card while her older companion reeled off a history of the island in an over-cultured voice. Despite seeking a different history, he followed her guiding finger, taking in the beauty of the bay, the gardens and walkways, exhibition rooms, café and shop and, snaking above his head, the high castle and its battlements. He thanked both women - before pitching in himself.

'You certainly know your stuff,' he said. 'Worked here long?'

'I haven't,' said the lady with the card scanner, 'but Margaret's been here since the Stone Age, haven't you, Margaret?'

'Stone Age indeed,' said the well-turned-out older woman. 'Shona here tells visitors I started when the Trust came on board, in *1954*. She keeps asking if I've had my birthday card from the Queen!'

Batten joined their laughter and gave his hunch a spin. 'Sounds like you *have* worked here forever.'

'Because I look old?' she said. 'Twenty-nine years next month - and every year a joy. How could it not be? Look.'

Batten followed the sweep of Margaret's arm across the pretty harbour and the grey waters playing tide-games with the land. But once a cop, always a cop…

'I was chatting to a man in Penzance who knew one of your volunteers. He wondered if she was still here. Linnet, I think her name was? Rose Linnet?'

Shona shook her head. 'Before my time. I'm *young*,' she said, cocking a snook at Margaret, who pointed to an approaching group of visitors.

'Responsibility approaches, Shona,' she said. 'Scan those cards. I'm late for my stint up top.'

'I'll wander up with you,' said Batten.

Margaret nodded, saying nothing till they climbed a curving pathway, out of sight of the entrance booth. 'Shona's given to gossip,' she said, 'and it doesn't do. We older folk have standards.' Away from the public gaze, Batten noted that the pride she took in her work came with a tinge of vanity. 'By the way, you are treading in the footsteps of Queen Victoria and Prince Albert, who visited the island in 1846. You'll find the Queen's footprint preserved, just there.' She pointed to an indent in the ground that could have been anything. 'You are also treading in the footsteps of Rose Linnet, who volunteered here, more years ago than I care to remember.'

'Ah. You did know Rose, then?'

'Rather more than *know*,' she said, peering over her glasses at Batten. 'I was her mentor. She and I spent hours in the castle, cataloguing the exhibits. She had a degree in art history - *I* have a Masters. Dear Rose. I suggested she do a Masters, too. It opens doors. She was quite taken with the idea, gave me a bright little smile. All things bright and beautiful, Rose. At first.'

'Only at first?'

Margaret pondered the question. 'Brightness...can tarnish.'

And fall from the air, thought Batten, recalling Professor Merry's quotation games. Before he could probe, Margaret raised a palm to stop him. He wished people wouldn't keep doing that.

'I don't believe for a moment you bumped into 'a man in Penzance' who knew Rose. I'm far too experienced. You have an official air about you. A solicitor, perhaps? Or that programme on TV? *Heir Hunters,* is it, where lost heirs are tracked down? How wrong would I be if I guessed your concern for Rose is inheritance-related?'

In lieu of a gold star, Batten let Margaret's assumption become another private lie, for the public good. Nor was it miles from the truth. 'Very shrewd,' he said, as a self-contented smile curled across her face, 'but I was giving up on Rose Linnet.'

Margaret stopped to get her breath. Batten too struggled with the steep paths and granite terrain, feeling twice as steep when he caught a glimpse of the sea, a distant grey blot frosted with tiny white breakers, way below.

'I used to climb up here every day,' she said, 'in half the time it takes me now. Rose was a mountain goat. But of course, we grow older. And as for giving up on her…well, I shan't pander to tittle-tattle. You may have the facts, as I know them - the key fact being you won't find Rose on St Michael's Mount. Not anymore. She was ordered off…when her brightness tarnished.'

'Ordered off?'

'Drink, I'm afraid. I could smell it. Smell *her*. At first, I said nothing, because I liked her. But we handled delicate objects, valuable artworks, and her physical coordination became… Latterly, she struggled to climb these very paths. More than once I had to see her safely down.' Margaret stopped again, as much to remind herself of the craggy heights as for breath. They were a dozen or so boulder-like steps from the castle entrance.

'Not much fun if she'd fallen from these,' Batten said, waving an arm at the weathered stones.

'She almost did. But that's not the point. You can see how we work - visitors from all over the world, children included. We, the staff, are ambassadors. It couldn't continue. I dislike the American phrase, *we had to let her go*, but that's what happened. Alas, when 'let go', she raged at the manager, screaming that this was *her* island. Non-essential words crept in, as you may imagine. But she left.'

'And that was the last you saw of her?'

'Not so.' Margaret's wise-owl head gave the faintest shake - a power gesture, Batten thought. 'She continued to arrive as a visitor, as you have, with her National Trust Membership card. Mostly, she climbed to the peak, stared at the sea from the battlements and behaved herself. Twice, while I was on duty, drink had been taken and she became abusive. The final time, Security escorted her to the boat back to Marazion. Customer welfare and safety apart, there were concerns for her physical and mental health. Believe me, the Trust did everything possible to help, but Rose, well, too tarnished by then.'

They reached the entrance to the castle. Below, Batten could make out only the tops of trees, trunks hidden from view, so precipitous was the mount. When Margaret paused at a door, he made to follow.

'Staff only, I'm afraid,' she said, once more raising the palm of her hand. 'Your entrance is over there.' With a sigh, she added, 'Perhaps her inheritance will cover the cost of any…treatment. I have long believed in conservation and renewal and I don't see why that can't apply to Rose.'

I do, thought Batten, with a careful nod. For the public good of Margaret's peace of mind, he maintained the private lie, keeping to himself the details of Queen Mab's grisly death. When they shook hands, she pointed at the grey sea below.

'The last I saw of Rose, she was out there, in the bay - in a lifeboat. Can you believe it? A lifeboat! The tide came in strong, that day, but it seems she tried to swim to the island. To *her* island. All I know is they took her ashore. After that…' She threw her hands at the air and was gone.

Gaze fixed on the unrelenting waves, Batten wondered if Rose entered the sea with life or death on her mind. With no stomach for tourist queues and antique furniture, he breathed in the giant vistas surrounding him, from one vantage point after another. In Rose's journal - once only - a well-oiled Daniel reminisced about St Michael's Mount. Disturbingly, Batten remembered every word:

From the battlements, in every direction, the stuff of paintings.
Enough paintings for a lifetime and more. Land, sea and sky.

He imagined Daniel on this very spot, dreaming of a great work of art – a stormy Turneresque seascape perhaps, without people, without Rose. And imagined Rose herself, gazing at the same sea and sky, in hope it was populated with 'something of Daniel'.

Batten shuffled his feet on Rose's castle in the air, its battlements protected by ancient cannon, slowly rusting in shades of amber, salt, and iron blue. Way below, the causeway was a thin granite snake, grey sea lurking on either side, precariously linking the mainland to St Michael's Mount. Staring down at the causeway, he was struck by another reason to search for Queen Mab. Her ingrained silhouette was a tremor of his lost Aunt Daze, but did Rose/Mab and Batten also share a common hope - of a free and constant world, and the fear of disconnecting from it?

As the two little seas on either side of the causeway failed to connect, their waves thwarted by the granite barrier, he saw positives, too. Rose had at least chosen her road. However disastrously, she resolved her crossroads moment – albeit with booze, art-without-skill, and eccentricity - and lived her own brand of freedom, till a knife-blade put an end to it.

Up here, like her curious half-smile, did Rose choose to be half-connected to the world, half-not? A kind of half-bargain with safety, for a soul in peril on the dangerous edge of things?

And you, Zig, still at the crossroads, hanging in the breeze.

Across the bay, he picked out the seaweed-speckled beach, his hotel, and dozens of matchstick visitors blithely journeying to and from the landmark. When they puffed their way to the battlements, would they care that Daniel Flowers viewed the same vista, or that Rose Linnet trod the same granite stones, day after day, in search of...?

If he found what Rose searched for, would it lead him to who had searched for Rose - and might still be searching for Sue? Gingerly, he clambered down the steep maze of steps, laid out below him like a massive jigsaw hewn from the grey granite rock.

Forty six

To top off Batten's fish and chips, the waiter at The Godolphin Arms recommended a zesty lemon posset. It still zinged on Batten's tongue when Timms phoned but, seconds into the conversation, the fizz of lemon faded to a tingle of suspicion. Perched on a chair, he turned his back on St Michael's Mount, picture-framed in the window of his hotel room.

'What? Gina Linnet called the *police*? She was practically a recluse!'

'Well, there's an old domestic with her name on it, sir, and the address fits.'

'When did you say?'

Sergeant Ball had trained Timms to interpret Batten's questions before answering. 'Less painful,' he'd said. She ran a hand through her hair and tried. 'Must've been while Rose was living in Albufeira, sir.'

'Albufeira? Albufeira's in Portugal. You mean *Almyrida*? In Crete?'

Wake up, Hazel. 'Er, Crete, sir, yes. There's a reference to a male adult endangering a minor. No name given, but since Rose was neither there nor a minor, must be Sue Linnet?'

'Must be. But this male adult? Is that *no name given,* too?'

'Sir, the report's thinner than a...' Flustered now, she couldn't remember what.

'A rake? Abe Linnet and Daniel Flowers were both *rakes*. Was it one of them?'

'Don't *know*, sir. I'll read you the rest. 'Householder' - that's Gina - 'reported male adult attempting to gain entry' - *large and bearded* was all Gina would say. 'Female child distressed. Intruder left when householder called police. Officers patrolled vicinity, located no-one fitting description. Checked door and window locks. Premises added to patrol schedule.'

'Big, male and bearded - is that it? Age, dress, accent? Green hair?'

Wish I'd never mentioned the bloody file. 'That *is* it, sir. The report does say Gina was 'confused'.

'Pissed?'

'Likely what they meant.'

'Not a random drunk who mistook Gina's house for his own?'

'*Un*likely, sir.'

Batten agreed. Who, then? Beards can come and go, but large is large. And three large males had links to Gina Linnet - if Gina was the target. Batten wouldn't fancy his chances when it came to punching Darren Pope. But despite never setting eyes on Abe and Daniel, he'd gladly break his knuckles on the pair of them.

'*Sir?*'

'Sorry Hazel, thinking.'

'About Sue Linnet?'

'Thinking Sue was maybe in danger long before you and I began policing Somerset. Who from, though…'

Timms was relieved she wasn't the only one struggling to fill in the blanks. 'Anything else, sir?'

'And thinking about Gina - and that house. A visitor must've been a rare thing.' Could Timms find time to ask Elliot Paine what he'd seen or heard? Old he may be, the Linnet's long-suffering neighbour with the double-thick fence, but his memory was sharp. Best do that myself, Batten decided. 'But good that you rang, Hazel, in your free time - it's appreciated.'

A thank you! And he didn't mention the art frauds she'd had no 'free time' to check. 'You're very welcome, sir.'

'Oh, Hazel, any progress on that art scandal in Athens…?'

Putting down the phone, Batten wondered if he expected too much of Timms. Chris Ball, though, was used to his funny ways. He sent him a text:

Any chance you can open up Queen Mab's house, so I can take a shufty? Be back in 48 hours. Zig.

He could be in Parminster tomorrow if he wished. But another day in Cornwall actually convalescing might keep Doc Fallon off his back. To celebrate, he poured himself a glass of sparkling water from the 'free' bottle by the bed. In the clear night sky beyond his window, St Michael's

Mount was a picture postcard, encircled by dark waters and cloaked in a million stars. For ten long minutes he stood by the window, gazing up at the battlements crowned by a silver halo of light. A single tear trickled down his cheek as he raised his glass to the view.

'To Aunt Daze,' he said. 'And to Queen Mab. And all those who can't see the stars anymore.'

Forty seven

Back in Parminster, on the quiet, Batten arranged to meet Sergeant Ball outside Queen Mab's house at midday. Half an hour earlier, he tapped on the door of her neighbour, Elliot Paine. For a second time, Batten entered Paine's neat kitchen-diner with the same framed photographs of Morris dancers on the walls.

'That's me, there,' said Paine, arthritic finger pointing at a face in one of the photos. 'I was younger, of course.' Batten struggled to see the likeness but nodded politely, still failing to understand why grown men would strap bells to their knees, jump up and down to folk music and wave white hankies, as if surrendering. Erin Kemp used to call it 'one of your cultural blind spots,' and she was probably right. He turned down the offer of tea, sat across the kitchen table from Paine, and asked his questions.

'Being so long ago, Inspector, I wouldn't ordinarily remember. But a night visitor, *any* visitor, hammering on Gina's door? Word had spread, by then. Her drinking and odd behaviour discouraged even the Jehovah's Witnesses.' Caine pulled a face. 'Do you know, I walked young Sue to school half a dozen times when Gina was, well, sozzled?'

Batten perked up. 'How did you know she was, well, sozzled?'

'How? Because a six-year-old, dressed and ready for school, rang my doorbell and said, 'mum's ill, she can't take me.' The first time, in my naivety, I offered to call a doctor. After that, I donned my coat and walked little Sue to the school gates. Come the afternoon, Gina had invariably struggled to her feet in time to collect the poor child.'

'Was she 'sozzled' when this night visitor hammered on her door? The police report describes her as *confused.*'

Paine paused, fingers rubbing his chin. 'Probably. To be frank, I was astounded to hear any voice from Gina's house. Nocturnal sounds mostly involved bottles smashing into the dustbin - in those pre-recycling days. But voices, in that silent house? At night? In winter? Rare. Hen's teeth-rare.'

Batten remembered he liked Elliot Paine - but that Elliot Paine liked to talk. 'The man, then. Did he slur his words?'

'I don't *think* so. I'm not given to lurking in my garden with an ear trumpet. I only know the man was tall because I saw the top of his head, over the fence, and heard his voice because when Gina refused to let him in, he shouted at the door, and she shouted back. Her voice shocked, I would say. Even fearful.'

'And the man?'

This time, Paine's chin-rubbing produced greater caution. 'Shouting to be heard, I think?'

'And you recall what was said?'

'Oh, snatches. I think he said, 'I'm entitled.' And Gina yelled, 'you're entitled to nothing!' After more of the same, Sue joined in, crying - no, no, screaming. Frightened.'

'Frightened by this man?'

Caine's arthritic fingers shrugged an 'obviously'.

'But you didn't see his face?'

'Couldn't. It was winter. Dark, and late. Had things become, well, dangerous, I would have dialled 999. But no sooner did Gina shout 'police' than the man disappeared. I think he kicked the door before making off. Then it was just Sue, screaming at the night. Please don't be offended when I say the arrival of two giant men in uniform did nothing for Sue's distress.'

'This visitor's voice? Age, accent?'

'I'm not good with accents. As to age, best I can say is not a whippersnapper - nor a geriatric like me.' Paine shrugged out a chuckle.

'And when the police left?'

'Blissful silence, Inspector. Which thankfully continued for years, till Gina's death. Until, alas, Rose replaced her.'

'I mean, that night, no further visitations?'

'None. And after the incident, Gina practically hid herself away. Twice as reclusive, if that was even possible. Strangely, I never walked Sue to school again because Gina stayed sober for the school run. And the pace she dragged that child, it almost *was* a run.'

Batten lost himself in thought. A run? Running from what? If 'word spread' of Gina's odd behaviour, did it travel further afield than was safe for her and Sue? In the silence, against type, Paine glanced at his watch,

261

hurrying Batten along. 'Mr Paine, after Gina died, did Rose have 'night visitors'?'

'Not while I was here – which was less often.' Paine pointed to his photo hanging on the wall. 'Stiff joints put a stop to my Morris dancing. I evolved, into management.' With a little chortle, he added, 'those that dance, do. Those that can't - administrate!'

Batten's own 'light duties' came to mind. He flashed a wry smile, but Paine was still rattling away.

'This very morning, two big chaps removed the boards from next door, so perhaps a new neighbour is imminent? I shouldn't say this, but I will have mixed feelings if the new neighbour turns out to be Sue…'

Without admitting he was the cause of the 'two big chaps', Batten thanked Elliot Paine and sneaked next door, to meet Sergeant Ball.

*

'We've had our fair share of smelly ones, Ballie?'

'Smelly what, sir?'

'Houses. Like this ghastly pile.' On the threshold, Batten imagined what lay within.

Ball shrugged. This was his second visit to Queen Mab's house. To his misfortune, he'd been added to the police search team not long after she was killed. This morning, the two burly lads who unscrewed the boarding from the front of the house winced when he told them the address. He forgot to tell them the visit was 'unofficial'.

'At least we didn't need a machete to get past the brambles, sir. Lord knows what poison she used to clear a path through the weeds, but it's still working. If not, you'd be stepping in plenty.'

Batten pushed at the door. A swathe of junk mail and discarded food wrappers littered the open plan interior, dust and grime concealing what might have been carpet. Rotting blankets lay in a dishevelled heap by the front window, amid piles of greying newspapers spread like a sea. The only safe place to walk was through a sinuous, swept track between front door and stairs.

Suited up, for non-forensic reasons, Batten was grateful for gloves and bootees as he waded from a filthy bare kitchen to what used to be a dining room. Now, it contained nothing but an old mahogany table and one hard chair.

'What happened to the rest of the furniture, Ballie? There's hardly a stick in the whole place.'

'Apart from more pigeon shit, it's just as we found it. Otherwise…' He didn't say the place smelled considerably better now, with the passing of time, and of Queen Mab. 'But reserve judgement, sir, till you've seen up above.'

Piqued, Batten gingerly climbed the staircase. The crud of old newspapers, food wrappers and rotting blankets on the lower floor disappeared as he reached the upper landing. Cleanish boards met his feet, which slid unencumbered over them.

'She slept up here?' he asked, imagining an indoor winter-quarters smelling of stale booze and old dirt, and an unspeakable soiled mattress.

Ball pointed across the landing to a closed door. 'That room, sir. Only one in the house with a bed in it.' Jabbing a sausage finger at two other doorways, he added, 'bits and pieces in there suggested they were once Mrs Linnet and Sue's bedrooms. But Queen Mab must have cleared the rest. It's as if Gina and Sue never existed. No beds, chairs or chests of drawers, no clothing. Old dust and sod all else.'

'She threw the sod all else over her neighbour's fence, Ballie, remember.'

'He was lucky she didn't chop up the fence as well. My guess is she chopped up the furniture and burned it, to warm the house. There's a woodstove full of ash downstairs, and we found a pile of old bedsprings in the 'garden'. If the broom cupboard ever saw a broom, it was empty, except for an axe.'

'An axe?'

'For protection, maybe?' said Ball, wrinkling his nose at the bathroom door.

'Any need to look?' Batten asked.

'Nothing to see, sir. And less to enjoy.'

'Her bedroom, then.' Batten pushed open the closed door at the far end of the landing. 'Oiled hinges?'

'Indeed, sir. Gave me pause, too.'

Tensing against the smell, Batten was surprised when the expected foulness became the faintest whiff of herbs. Thyme, oregano, mint, rosemary, basil? He recognised their shapes from the Springtime hills of Crete, where their scent filled the air all day and into the night. He'd planted the same herbs in his Ashtree garden, in homage.

Queen Mab must have bought hers, in quantity. She'd covered every windowsill, every flat surface with a mass of overflowing pots, jam jars and old tin cans, stuffed to the brim with bunch after bunch of Greek herbs, curled and dry now. On the bedside table, the largest bunch stood upright in a battered copper vase. The bed itself was the cleanest object in the house, a pair of pillows waiting for a head that would never lie there. On the floor sat a gin bottle, and a single empty glass.

By the window, paint-spattered dust sheets protected the boards beneath two easels, propped beside an old cupboard. Brushes, rags and tubes of paint peeped out. Batten pointed a question at two racks of canvases by the far wall.

'No idea, sir. But since no-one else visited - apart from Social Services and a once-a-blue-moon builder with wadding up his nostrils - she must have painted them herself.' Ball jabbed a finger at the easels, each holding a canvas. 'Seems she could only paint two scenes. Or cared to. There's twenty or so of each scene in the racks, too,' he said.' All the same.'

Batten peered at the canvas on the first easel. An offshore island in a grey sea, a narrow stone causeway connecting island to shore. A castle, with towers and battlements, sprouting from the island's peak.

Despite Queen Mab's painterly limitations, Batten recognised St Michael's Mount, across the causeway from Marazion. The work was crude, beyond primitive. Would he hang it on his wall? Only as a curio.

He turned to the other. Here, the palette was brighter, a yellow sun blazing from cloudless sky, merging with the warm green of the sea. On the blue crests of a few desultory waves, her amateur hand had daubed naive ripples of white.

'A harbour, islands, a beach and a bay, sir. Same painting, twenty-odd times, and could be anywhere.'

'No. It couldn't, Ballie.' Batten stared at the crude depiction of the familiar view he'd enjoyed from his hilltop home in Crete. Here in Parminster, Queen Mab had painted it twenty times over in coarse yellow sunlight. 'She might have been with the fairies, Chris, but she had enough wit to paint a memory or two.'

'Memory, sir?'

Tapping the first easel, Batten said, 'St Michael's Mount, in Cornwall. Not far from St Ives.'

'Never been.' Ball pointed at the blues and yellows. 'That one?'

Batten had spent weeks looking down on it. 'Almyrida. Can't say she's done it justice, but she's done enough.' He flicked through the rack of Crete canvases, all sporting a harbour – but not one sporting a boat. Scanning the walls for more pictures, in hope she'd painted a Darren, a Daniel, or another 'D', he saw only a framed quotation.

Ball looked over Batten's shoulder and read it aloud. "I paint myself because I am so often alone, and because I am the subject I know best.' It sounded less poignant in his Somerset burr. 'Who's that, then?'

'Frieda Kahlo, Chris. Mexican artist, 20th Century. After an accident, she lived in constant pain. Bit like Queen Mab, I suppose.'

'Except she didn't, sir.'

'Didn't what?'

'Paint herself. These are all seashores and castles. No people, no faces, no Queen Mab.'

Batten recalled Clio Demopoulou's comment about Rose's non-existent self-portraits. *'How can you paint self-portraits if you do not know yourself?'* Instead, Rose had crudely painted the granite causeway connecting workaday Cornwall to her castle in the air. 'I think this room might be her shrine, Chris. A shrine to her sacred places.'

'Pity she didn't have more places, then, sir. Same two, over and over again? Pity she couldn't paint something different.'

'Pity's about the size of it. Do you know Einstein's definition of insanity?'

'I'm big on Einstein, sir,' said Ball, cracking his knuckles in retaliation.

'Doing the same thing, the same way, over and over, yet expecting a different outcome. Are we staring at Queen Mab's road to madness?'

To Ball, the room looked more or less clean and tidy, the bed made, dust sheets protecting the floorboards. 'Dunno, sir. I mean, she kept going, and kept painting, after a fashion, until… Maybe we're staring at her way of keeping sane?'

Batten gazed at the pots, jars and tin cans full of dry Greek herbs, softening the space. 'Could be, Ballie. And this is her sanity room?'

'Could be, sir. Feels wrong, though, to be standing in it.'

The rear of the house still boarded up, Batten peered beyond the grimed hall window at the front 'garden', a rampant sea of blue leylandii and dark green savage brambles. Trying to look through Queen Mab's eyes, he saw a house surrounded by blues and greens, except for a weed-killer causeway slicing through the overgrown sea, from garden gate to entrance. Inside, a second causeway snaked between grey seas of discards from front door to stairs, and thence to Queen Mab's private castle - of sanity or madness - in the clouds.

Ball had his hand on the bedroom door. 'Finished in here, sir?'

'Yes, Ballie, finished.'

But finished with what?

Forty eight

In Batten's Ashtree study, Rose's leather journals poked up from the desk like a pair of hedgehogs, prickly with bookmarks and post-it notes. He pushed aside the niggle of pages and rummaged in the desk drawer for Sellotape and scissors. His hunt for wrapping paper yielded only a thick brown roll, like tree bark.

It would have to do.

*

The length of driftwood, a weathered tree-branch, washed up on the beach at much the same time as Darren Pope. Its bark felt slimy in his hand, but it would serve as a makeshift crutch. He tested its strength, pushing down hard to raise himself upright, leg hurting like hell. On the improvised stick, he dragged himself inland, guessing the bone was broken. When he rested in the palm-tree shade and stared back at his footprints in the sand, he saw only one. The other was a dragged scar, edged by the pockmark of a stick.

What made him suddenly think of *Robinson Crusoe*? Forced to read it at school - but didn't mind. Better than *Zorba the Greek*, which he only pretended to read. Rose read *Zorba* three times and loved it. Well, she would. How can you *love* a book?

A baby. You can love a baby - if you have one. Alone on the beach, he wished someone had loved *him*. Rose said she would, him and the baby, forever. His giant hands gripped the damp driftwood like a throat, her throat, and pushed himself to his feet.

Water. That's what Robinson Crusoe would find. Darren could taste only salt. After water, help - medical and otherwise.

And if help was refused, there was always the knife.

*

'It's for, you know, all the unofficial digging.' Even in the empty CID room, Batten dropped his voice on *unofficial*. 'And for the Athens stuff.'

Hazel Timms was flabbergasted. Her boss, giving her a thank-you present? She tore away the thick brown wrapper, revealing a framed painting. 'A Ben Nicholson, sir. Thank you. I like him.'

Batten did too. 'It's only a print, but…given what you've found.'

Timms scanned the painting: a window view, cubist jugs and mugs on a table in the foreground, chimney pots, harbour and boats beyond. She liked the palette of cool blues and browns, the splashes of deep colour. With a smile, she said, 'it's not a Daniel Flowers, is it?'

'Hope not, Hazel. I bought it in a shop in Martock.'

'Appreciated, sir.' She ran out of things to say.

'Well, back to my 'light duties', I suppose,' said Batten, and the little ceremony was over.

In his cubby-hole office, Batten re-read the fruits of Hazel's digging, despite his eyeballs feeling like a sandstorm. Though unable to say how Rose acquired the Nicholson fakes, Timms did suggest what else Daniel Flowers might have been up to.

'Athens, Art Auctions, 1990s onwards - many twentieth century Greek paintings thought to be faked. Auction houses focused on expensive end of market, so fraudsters pushed lower end, 30,000 euros or so. Lesser-known Greek artists a safer bet. Genuine materials easy to find.'

Batten did the sums. If Daniel and Abe fed, say, thirty or so works onto the market, over a safe period of time, a million euros would rack up. And if greed kicked in… He rubbed his fuzzy eyes and read on.

'Much rumour. Increasing police interest. Finally, 2011, Sotheby's pulled their own Athens auction, fearing many of the works on sale were forgeries. After, fakers had a tougher time.'

Good, Batten thought, as Ball steered two mugs of tea into the office. And a half-eaten wedge of carrot cake.

'You didn't want cake, did you, sir?' he asked, smiling through crumbs.

'Not allowed cake on *light duties*, Ballie.' He didn't even want tea. 'Ta for this though.'

'She did good, our Hazel, eh?' said Ball, nodding at the notes on Batten's desk.

'She did. I guess Rose thought Daniel was leaving *her* when he buggered off - and he probably was. But I reckon the police hurried him along. Abe might be happy to hide himself in the White Mountains, but I doubt it was Daniel's cuppa tea.' Batten idly sipped his, not even sure what it tasted of.

'Which is why Daniel headed for England, instead?'

'For the sleepy corridors of academe, yes. Easy to be anonymous there. But since university pay doesn't make you rich, my bet is he looked to the English art market for bigger bucks. Peddling his St Ives fakes would be a dangerous temptation, but he's always struck me as a chancer.'

Ball finished his carrot cake - in one large mouthful. 'Cocked it up then, sir,' he said, between crumbs. 'They do, sooner or later.'

'Rose cocked it up for him, more like. Wish I'd seen Daniel's face when she told him six pieces of damning evidence were locked away in sleepy Somerset, and she was happy to *dangle* it.'

'Padlock-Woman trounces Padlock-Man.' Proud of his wit, Ball set about his tea. Batten had barely touched his, skull grumbling, eyes stinging.

'Not upset about the cake, are you, sir?'

'*Cake?* I'm *thinking!*'

Looking over his mug at Batten's face, Ball saw only tightness and tension. Had his boss done *any* convalescing in Cornwall? 'Not doing too much thinking, are you, sir? In view of Doc Fallon's advice?'

'Thinking takes three times as long as before! I still don't know where Daniel went, after Leeds University fell out with him. Nor Abe's role in all this, beyond sailing a boat between Crete and Alimos Marina.'

'Playing dead, sir. That seems to be Abe's role.' Cake and tea despatched, Ball started on his knuckles.

'Stop that criminal noise, Ballie, or I'll arrest you.'

'Instead of Abe?'

'If we nab the sod, you can crack *his* knuckles.'

269

'I'd like to crack his medical records - but I doubt our esteemed Area Super would consent.'

'Wallingford? He'd sack me for not being *efficient* and *streamlined.*' Batten sipped tea that didn't even smell of tea. He plonked the mug down on a letter about his next appointment with Doc Fallon, drumming a finger on it, slow thoughts briefly quickening. 'We can't get Abe's records, Ballie. But what about his appointments? What if he's due back for treatment in the cancer ward…?' He peered through the cubby-hole window at the CID room. Timms had left. 'Hasn't Hazel got a pal at Taunton Hospital?'

It was Ball's turn to frown. 'Hasn't Hazel done plenty *unofficial* digging already, sir?'

Batten blew out his breath. Plenty - and some. But he ploughed on. 'No harm in asking, is there? This pal, at the hospital, on the quiet, surely he could help?'

Ball's two-pounds-of-sausage fingers grabbed the mugs. 'No sir. He couldn't.'

'Why not?'

'Because *he's* called Harriet.'

'Well, all the same?' said Batten, to Ball's receding back. Despite an increasing wooziness, he raised himself and his voice. 'I did just buy her a painting!'

When Ball disappeared into the staff kitchen, Batten dropped a surreptitious note on Timms' desk.

Forty nine

For a good five minutes her foot had been tap-tap-tapping on the waiting room carpet. Beige, worn - *like me,* she thought. Realising her feet had picked up Batten's habit, Hazel Timms plonked them squarely on the ground. And waited.

Another characteristic shared with her boss was a hatred of hospitals. In Mum and Dad's decline, she'd spent too many sad hours in grey waiting rooms – like this one, its neon lights doing nothing for her pasty complexion. Where the hell *was* Batten? The message she'd left in answer to *his* message was clear enough. Timms, on a good day, was *clear*.

Pointlessly, she looked at her watch again, as if looking would make the boss appear or time tick forward. The only thing ticking forward was the eye-watering cost of parking at Taunton Hospital. And, sod Batten, she had a *date* tonight. Tony. She met him at a do, at Harriet's. Not a Dirk or a Rocky, no. But *nice.* If Batten didn't hurry up, nice Tony would think he'd been dissed.

Tapping thumbs on her phone as fast as her feet - she hadn't noticed they'd resumed drum-drumming - she texted Sergeant Ball instead. And waited.

No reply from Ball either. She glared at the *Oncology* sign. Given the boss's trips up north, no surprise if he couldn't face another visit to a cancer ward. All the same, it was Batten who'd wheedled on about 'your pal at Taunton' and Batten was the reason she was stuck here, waiting.

With a *schoom*, the automatic doors opened like a throat and CID walked in. Not walked. Lurched. DC Eddie Hick only ever lurched. At least he didn't collide with the information stand as he spotted Hazel and *lurched* over.

'Where the bloody hell's the boss?' she hissed. 'I've been tapping my toes since doomsday! And I do have a life, you know!'

Hick managed a twitch of sympathy. 'Yeh, a DC's life, Haze. I don't want to be here neither.'

'Why are you, then, Eddie? And why's no-one answering their phones? Have I got body odour, all of a sudden?'

Hick sniffed to check. 'No, you'll pass. Y'see, the fork 'n spoon' - Hick's nickname for Batten and Ball - 'they're at Yeovil Hospital.'

'*Yeovil*? I distinctly said *Taunton*! I was *clear*! I'm not an idiot!'

Easing Timms back into her seat, Hick said, 'neither's the boss, Haze. He's at Yeovil Hospital, in a *bed*.'

*

Timms shuddered at the *beep-beep* sound, and its parental memories. Rhythmic, high-pitched, louder when the nurse entered, fading to a backdrop when the grey door closed. The plastic chair outside the little room was rock hard, or maybe Timms was numb from sitting in it.

'Thanks, Eddie,' she said, when Hick returned with paper cups of tea. They sat either side of the closed door. Hick twitched up and down at irregular intervals, peering through the glass at the figure in the bed, at the wires and tubes. Out of loyalty to Laura – she'd be home by now – he resisted a stare at the nurse's curves.

'He's going nowhere, Eddie. You don't have to keep checking.'

'Something to do, Haze. A DC's life, eh?'

She sipped her tea. Too hot. Hick crunched into a shortbread biscuit, crumbs flying. He flicked them onto the vinyl floor and thrust the packet at Timms.

'No thanks. Gone off food.' For something to do, she stood up and peered through the glass.

'You don't have to keep checking, Haze,' Hick said, smiling through biscuit crumbs.

Feelings mixed, she stared beyond the nurse at tubes and wires. The face above the sheets was strained, the grey hair lank on the pillow. Abe Linnet was going nowhere. She and Eddie would make sure of that.

*

Thirty miles away, in Yeovil Hospital, the first thing Batten saw when he came to, was the outline of his left foot covered by a white bedsheet. Why couldn't he see the right, without turning his head? He covered his left eye with his hand. And saw nothing at all. Damp, his palm, fingers claggy. A sweat of fear pricked his brow, droplets seeping down into his eyes.

Eye.

His one good eye.

Batten closed both, though closing the left would have sufficed. Blackness again imprisoned him, then panic, drumming through his bones. In that strange world between eyeball and lid, a lost future flared.

When he forced his eyelids as far north as they would go, the left side of an unsmiling Dr Fallon stepped into focus, his own eyelids raised.

'Bit of a pickle, eh, Mr Batten?' he said.

*

Sergeant Ball finally decided what Area Superintendent Wallingford's phone voice sounded like – the hiss of acid burning into steel. In the empty CID office, Ball updated Wallingford on Batten's hospitalisation.

'Well, I can't conjure up a stand-in, with my meagre resources. Good job he was only doing light duties.'

Ball opted for silence

'You still there?'

'Er, yes, sir.'

'Right. I assume you can cope?'

What in the name of cider do you think I'm doing? 'We'll cope, sir,' Ball mumbled.

'Anything untoward on your desk?'

Thousands of bloody things! Including Abe Linnet. He had no choice but to tell Wallingford about Abe, since two Detective Constable *resources* were sharing guard duty at his hospital bed in Taunton. Knowing Wallingford's hatred of waffle, Ball waffled on about Maud Cotter appearing from nowhere with new information about the unsolved case of Queen Mab who'd rented a storage unit and there's an aging security guard who turned out to be someone else with false ID and who's also hospitalised and waiting to be interviewed –

'Yes, yes,' said Wallingford, cutting in. 'Just keep a check on the *resources*, OK?'

273

'Of course, sir.' *We'll work for free, so you can take the credit.*

When the phone went down, Ball glanced at the clock. Parminster, Yeovil, Taunton, home. Too many miles. One of them would have to go. He picked up the phone, called Di, apologised about dinner. Then picked up the phone again.

An exhausted Jess Foreman might have turned down Ball's quiet request had Batten not figured in it. Generous with cider, was the Inspector, placing him near the top of Foreman's value system. And soon as he heard the words 'Queen Mab' he climbed into his boots, to share the load, to keep tabs on Abe Linnet - or whatever name Abe was going by - because if he turned out to be the man who…

What did bloody Wallingford ask me? Sergeant Ball grumped to himself. *Anything untoward on your desk?* Grabbing his keys, Ball glared at the paper mountain before clomping to the CID car park and a second trip to Yeovil Hospital, this time without a semi-conscious Batten in the passenger seat.

Doc Fallon had beaten him to it. They met in the Head Injury Unit corridor, two neon-lit duellists - both accustomed to Zig Batten's stubborn side.

'Well, Sergeant. Bit of a pickle…'

Too tired for lectures, Ball pitched in. 'His sight, Doc? Is that pickled too?'

To his credit, Fallon drew Ball away from the corridor's public ears to a pair of faux leather chairs at the fringe of the half-empty waiting room. 'Probably…not,' he said quietly. 'A partial loss of vision can occur, in cases such as Mr Batten's. A loss of taste and smell, too. Likely to be temporary. If he takes care.'

Mr Batten, not *Inspector*, Ball noted. 'You mean if he behaves?'

'If he does, we live in hope. If not…Let's say the road to self-destruction lacks roundabouts. I imagine you have tried slowing him down?'

Ball cracked his knuckles, making Fallon wince. 'Like stopping a tanker, mid-ocean,' he said. 'Give him a thread to pull-'

'Yes,' said Fallon. 'Understood.' He climbed to his feet. 'By the way, Sergeant, he's conscious…But there's no-one by his bed.'

Ball had to be in Taunton, by a different bed. He slapped himself on the skull.

'Careful,' said Fallon, pointing at Ball's sausage fingers and the 'Head Injury Unit' sign. 'Not with those hands.'

'I clean forget to call her. Blue-arsed fly, all day.'

'Day has faded into evening, Sergeant. When you find time, look through the window. And speaking of time…'

As Fallon's back disappeared down the corridor, Ball wondered if doctors were trained not to finish their sentences. With one male Doctor gone, he phoned a female version, praying Sonia Welcome's skills in pathology would not be required at Batten's bedside.

*

Abe Linnet watched the nurse scribble on his patient record sheet and hook it over the bed rail. Young and curvy, this one. Previous nurse swamped the room, and Abe preferred firm curvy handfuls to cupboard-loads. Not well enough for handfuls of any kind, he nevertheless ogled trim thighs and hips as the nurse closed the door.

In the corridor outside, Mr Bhatti, the consultant, quietly summarised. 'Lucky the ambulance found him,' he told Sergeant Ball. 'And just as well he was transferred here -' Bhatti jabbed a surgical finger at the *Oncology* sign - 'where he's no stranger. He's stable now.'

'Can he be interviewed?'

Bhatti shook his head. 'Not yet. And even then, the analgesics may produce…'

Another doctor who can't finish a sentence, thought Ball, finishing it for him. 'Lies?'

'I was thinking, moments of dubious coherence.'

Ball found himself thinking of Eddie Hick, who'd lurched home. Timms too. Even if Abe Linnet could lurch, he'd not get past the bulk of PC Foreman, now dwarfing a plastic chair struggling to contain his buttocks. 'What more can you tell me, doctor?' asked Ball.

With a glance at his notes, Bhatti said, 'you know he was found by, er, hikers, in the Blackdown Hills?'

'Wild camping. That's what my colleagues were told.' In search of off-trail nookie, the *hikers* found Abe instead, not far from his half-hidden tent. 'Collapsed, middle of nowhere?'

'Indeed. A devil of a job getting him to the ambulance.'

'His condition's what I meant.'

'We are in Oncology, Sergeant, so... All the same, you're not a relative.'

'When I say I'm relieved *not* to be, doctor, you'll guess why I'm asking?'

Bhatti considered this, before ushering Ball into his office and closing the door. 'We have procedures, and he must rest. Tomorrow morning, after my rounds, a brief interview may be possible.' He paused to tap surgical fingers on the edge of his desk, juggling his professional ethics. 'While I cannot divulge any details, I would advise that, where Mr Linnet is concerned, your questions be posed with a degree of urgency?' On Ball's nod of understanding, Bhatti showed him the door.

Alone in the foyer, Ball realised urgency might be difficult. Beyond a holding charge of false ID and illegal entry, he wasn't completely sure what questions to pose. The case wasn't his. But then, it wasn't supposed to be Zig Batten's, either. Leaving Jess Foreman outside Abe Linnet's room, Ball trudged to his car and yo-yoed back to Yeovil.

*

'You're a sight for a sore eye,' Batten told Sonia. She tried not to laugh, failed, then laid down the law. 'I spend all day with the dead, Zig. Stay alive. Please?'

When Ball arrived, she said, 'he's up to one and a half eyes now,' but not without an articulate tilt of her brow which politely asked why Ball was here.

'Errr,' said Ball, caught.

'He's come for cider,' said Batten, buoyed by Sonia's presence and the slow return of his sight. 'Or cake.'

'In a hospital?' Sonia said, brow still questioning.

Ball was too tired for games. 'Kick me out if you must, Doc, but to help the boss with *his* case' - he jabbed a mitt at Batten - 'I need help with Abe Linnet.'

Eyes met eyes, five and a half in all. In the absence of Darren, Daniel and Sue, dealing with Abe was the one-eyed reality. How often had Batten told his team, *search for what's missing, but don't miss what's already there?* 'You've spoken to Fallon, Chris. I'm stuck here for another day.'

'Or longer,' Sonia said, pointedly.

'And much as I'd like to gut Abe Linnet…'

'I know, sir, but' - smothered in doctors now, Ball had forgotten Bhatti's name - 'matey over at Taunton dropped a big hint about Abe. He might not keep too long.'

Fifty

Next day, Doctor Bhatti was true to his word. 'Ten minutes,' he said, unsmiling. Ball eased into a chair by Abe Linnet's bedside. Both men looked better for a night's sleep. Timms set up the portable recorder and went through the niceties as, for a slow ten seconds, Ball took in Abe's features, framed against white walls. Lank grey hair, long-boned, vague stubble on his cheeks and what seemed like a permanent sneer on his face.

'Speak, do you?' said Linnet.

'I listen better, sir.' Ball had spent all morning with case files, reports and the questions Zig Batten conjured up – against Sonia Welcome's advice. 'Please confirm you have declined the offer of a duty solicitor?'

A grunt of assent rustled from the bed.

'DC Timms here, will take notes, if you don't mind.'

Linnet looked across his nose at Timms. 'Seen *you* before.'

Timms gave the faintest nod. *All you're getting*, she thought.

'You met DC Timms at Camelot Self-Storage, sir. Where you pretended to be a security guard by the name of Ray Breeze?'

'Hmph. Good bloke, Ray. *Secure.*'

'Yet he failed to secure the contents of a storage unit?'

Timms' dry smile earned a sneer.

'Ray might've mentioned it. He said *she* turned up. His luck ran out.'

'In more ways than one,' said Ball, nodding at the medical spaghetti curling from Abe's chest to a monitor by the bed.

'Not going to put me away for a long stretch, then, are you? Ask my batty doctor, I'm dead already. Killed - booze, fags, women and *life*. But at least I've lived one.' Wilting under his glare, Timms wondered how he knew she hadn't.

'It's not what's killed you, sir. It's who you might've killed along the way?'

Killed? thought Abe, his criminal ethics kicking in. 'No comment,' he said, with a sly smile meaning *up yours*.

Ball checked his notes for Batten's advice: 'don't start with Queen

Mab, throw him a curve ball first. Ask about Darren Pope, get him talking.'

'Folk seem to disappear after being in contact with you, sir-'

'Folk like Ray Breeze?' Despite the wires, tubes and police presence, Linnet was determined to enjoy his final rounds. 'Poor old Ray, *he* went missing. Have you not found him?'

'Actually, I was thinking of Darren Pope.'

A tremor disturbed Abe's demeanour. He disguised it with a flick at the bedsheets. '*What?* That little wanker?' 'He's years ago, in the stone age.'

'And currently on the run, *whereabouts unknown*, as it happens.'

The tremor shook Abe harder. 'You must be using blind cops, then. Biggest little wanker I ever saw.'

'Whose lights you punched out, according to our information.'

Bit more than that, Linnet recalled. 'Last I heard he was wide awake, on his way to Australia. I might've given him a tap, as a parting gift,' he said.

'Would you be admitting to assault, sir?'

'Pull this tube off my wrist, you can slap it.' Before Ball could reply, Linnet tried to draw a line under Darren. 'I kicked the little wanker in the crutch, and he went down like a trainee whore, his dad the same. They buggered off, all three. I might have *excommunicated* the Popes, but I didn't kill any of the bastards. As for Darren…' Abe gave a grudging shrug. He'd watched his back for Darren, because Darren was big and angry and dangerous. 'Anyone's guess where the big little wanker went. Maybe in the next room, dwarfing that fat nurse who comes in here to squidge my pillows.'

He's talking, thought Ball. Try Daniel next. 'Your partner in crime, Daniel Flowers. Also disappeared.'

'Who?' said Linnet.

'Daniel Flowers, the artist, in Crete. Often seen on your boat, the *Aura*.'

'Ah, the *Aura*. Lovely boat. Ask Ray Breeze, when you find him. Ray liked the *Aura*.'

'Daniel Flowers liked it, too.'

'Ohh, *him*. That bloke with the fishing rods? I remember now, he used to come on the boat - bigger fish, offshore. His name slipped my mind. It's the medication.'

'But it wasn't fishing rods locked away in Camelot Self Storage. It was fake paintings – the ones you wanted to get your hands on.'

'Puh.' Linnet was almost disappointed with this stubby Sergeant and the mousey bitch with hair like an oil slick. Even the dregs of his energy craved a punchier fight. 'Nothing to do with me. Wouldn't know which end of a paintbrush is which. Why don't you ask this Daniel Flowers – wherever he is?'

A weakness in the case, Ball knew, was the broken link between Abe and Daniel. 'Perhaps he's in Athens, sir? Only a short hop from Alimos Marina, where you used to moor your boat?'

Abe's yawn failed to hide his surprise at the British police tracking him to Alimos. '*My* boat, sure. Hardly knew *him*.'

Sensing the change, Ball decided to throw in Queen Mab - as Bhatti's head ducked round the door.

'Sufficient for today, Sergeant,' he said, scalpelling Ball's angry frown with one of his own. 'First and foremost, this is a hospital.'

Climbing to his feet, Ball leaned over the bed and whispered, 'to be continued.' Did Abe Linnet's sneer have a less triumphant edge? 'Just soften him up, Ballie,' his boss had said. 'I'll be there day after, with a different approach.'

Fifty one

Abe Linnet lay back in the white walls of his cell - he knew that's what it was. When Bhatti closed the door behind him, Abe spotted a twitching figure on guard outside. Abe had just one thing in common with DC Hick: neither of them wanted to be here.

Staring at the grey door beyond his toes, Abe dreamed of better places. *A life on the ocean waves,* snow in the White Mountains, and Athens - many a tasty night in Athens, in the narrow streets off Plaka. How he'd love to be there now...

But when that stubby Sergeant returns, where else will he make Abe go?

*

In a different ward, at Yeovil Hospital, compulsory bed rest and clinical care were doing for Batten what taking Fallon's advice might have achieved weeks ago. Nourished by macaroni pie with kale, topped off by rhubarb crumble and custard, he did what Sonia Welcome asked him not to - pulled on the loose thread still dangling from the red hem of Queen Mab's dress.

If Sonia had peered into his bedside console, she would have spotted the case files and journals smuggled in by a reluctant Ball, on the promise of anonymity and 'much cider'. Batten donned spectacles, checked for blurred vision and awarded himself a fanciful 20/20. With Abe Linnet/Ray Breeze now in a custody of sorts, he went back to the beginning.

Mark Bragg, who discovered Queen Mab's body, said the security light in the alley by *Comfort Carpets* didn't work, negating the CCTV cameras. And on the same night, 'Ray Breeze' was a private security patrolman in the area. Batten guessed the two were linked - and sensed a further connection. Breeze foiled a burglary at a Vet's, not long before Queen Mab was killed.

Brass neck back in place, he texted Sergeant Ball, suggesting he visit the Veterinary practice to sniff out answers. *Put it on my cider bill*, he added.

Moving backwards and forwards in time, Batten covered the white paper of his notebook with fast black ink, scribbling down enough uncertainties to make a journal of his own…Queen Mab's missing necklace, with its ring and cross…an olive wood club…a bleached knife…the paintings in her storage unit…her maybe-baby…her missing silver ring.

'Seeing sense', for once, he stopped to rest his eyes. The water in the beaker by his bed was lukewarm, but at least he could taste it. Somewhere between sleep and daydream, he ticked off names in his head.

Gina, Rose, Abe. Dead; murdered; dying.

Andros Antonakis, Clio Demopoulou. Reliable?

Darren, Daniel, Sue. Wanted; disappeared; disappeared.

When he opened his eyes, swirling reflections in the door-glass reminded him of Edvard Munch's *The Scream,* bringing paintings to mind, and Daniel to mind, and Rose, and the St Ives fakes she'd carefully locked away. *Maybe start with them, Abe,* he told the empty room.

*

Strong medication ensured Abe Linnet slept well, but breakfast was a blur. The lunch now sitting on his over-bed table had neither smell nor taste. He chased it round the plate, chewed a few mouthfuls of maybe fish and decided: *make the situation work for you.* Leaning against the pillows, revising past events, he chose what to tell, what to trade, and what to keep to himself. By the time the slim nurse entered, he'd re-written his personal history.

'The police are back,' she said with a hint of disapproval.

'The buggers never left,' said Abe.

'For an interview,' she whispered. When the DC with oil slick hair sat down, notebook and recorder in hand. Abe wondered where the mousey bitch had stowed her chunky Sergeant. His sneer faded when in walked the *English detective, moustache less good,* a faint grin on his face - but his eyes unsmiling. He gave his name, for the tape. Batten.

282

Batten down the hatches, Abe warned himself, though 'Batten' didn't seem to recognise him in this sterile setting, without the beard, dark glasses and hat. In the warm hospital room, he tried to ignore the cold sweat between his shoulder blades.

'Well, well, Mr Linnet. Bit of a pickle, eh?' Batten doubted Doc Fallon had a monopoly on the phrase. 'Got something to show you,' he said, sliding the over-bed table closer and dealing out six enlarged photos of the Ben Nicholson copies. 'The real ones are at HQ. And when I say 'real', of course I mean *fake*. What did you want with them, by the way?'

'Never seen them before. Why *would* I want them?'

'Oh, to help you continue your life's work, sir – defrauding folk of their hard-earned cash. Or because they're evidence?'

'Evidence? Of *what*?'

'Of your criminality. But we'll get to that. On my way here, I had a phone call about you.'

Phones. Abe avoided phones like the plague - too easy to trace. Letters, though, easy to burn. Go-betweens. Boats meeting at sea, swapping fish - and other cargo. Safer. Till Daniel got cocky. 'The Queen, was it? About my knighthood?'

'Our Head of Forensics, as it happens. Your tent, rucksack, all your worldly goods from your hidey-hole in the Blackdown Hills, they're being processed as we speak. We'll soon have the results. More evidence, eh?'

Abe struggled to recall what he'd disposed of. And what he hadn't. The prickles of sweat turned to ice.

'Refreshing was it, sleeping under the stars, communing with Nature?' Abe's sneer tightened his sallow face. He really does look like a horse, thought Batten, enjoying the animal theme. 'Cat got your tongue?'

'Doc says I need rest. Talking tires me.'

'On the contrary, Doctor Bhatti says you're fit to answer questions, such as, what *were* you doing in the Blackdown Hills?'

Fluid drip-dripped into Abe's arm like a scornful clock, ticking away his options. Oil slick's tape was running. The monitor wires that chained him to the bed might as well be a pair of handcuffs. In the silence, he shuffled truth to the back of his mental rucksack. *I was hiding. While I tracked down Sue. To finish this business.* 'I've always liked the great outdoors.'

'And the open sea? You and Daniel Flowers, setting sail from Almyrida, on your way to Alimos Marina?'

Alimos. The boat. Again. 'Never heard of it.'

'Hard to believe, Mr Linnet. You still owe three months harbour fees, for berthing the *Aura* while you and Daniel hopped over to Athens, with bundles of fake canvases, which you passed off as real. And for good money, we understand.' Batten nodded in appreciation at Hazel, who gave Abe an eyeball. She was growing immune to his sneer. 'Those fake paintings, how did you manage to hide them from the Hellenic Coast Guard?'

Abe remembered the Coast Guard's increasing visits, his nerves on a knife-edge. Once, they opened Daniel's plastic rod case, without spotting the canvases rolled up in the lining. Smooth-talking Daniel, chewing the fat with the sailors, swapping tips on how to catch *lavraki* in his appalling Greek, while Abe did Daniel's worrying *and* his own. 'Told you, don't know one end of a paint brush from the other.'

'You're not being accused of painting them, sir. Just passing them off as real. For gain.'

Abe wanted to snarl but smiled instead. A great little scam, a great big earner. And the snide cop's evidence all pointing to Daniel - Mr Academic Artist, valuing his own fakes for the auction houses and trying not to smirk when they fetched twice the price on auction day. Till the arrogant sod got too up himself. 'Look at me,' Abe told Batten. 'Do I look like a man with a tidy sum to his name?'

'You don't, sir, no. Because when you disappeared, Gina Linnet helped herself to your tidy sum and took flight. Being 'presumed drowned' kept the police off your back - but didn't keep Gina off your bearer bonds, eh? Left the safe door open, did you, and your punchbag wife dipped her fingers?'

Abe's dark sneer sharpened. *Dipped? She gutted the fucking thing.* Too guessable, the safe's combination. *1. 21. 18. 1.* Letters of the alphabet. *A.U.R.A.* 'Nasty, speaking ill of the dead.'

'As is *making* people dead, sir.' Abe's sneer grew darker still. 'Your entire family - a wife and two daughters - dead, murdered, or missing, like your artist-friend and partner in crime. We're wondering which of the four you knifed.'

Wonder away, thought Abe. 'From what I hear, Gina killed *herself*. Pickled her liver in gin, stupid cow, knew she would.'

Batten gave a pretend nod of concession. 'One off the list, then. Three to go.'

'Try asking Daniel Flowers, 'stead of dragging my good name through the mud. Sounds like he's splattered with the stuff. Go on, ask him.' *When you find him.* Abe retreated into his squidgy pillows.

'Tired,' he said, pushing the call button by the bed, and closing his eyes.

Fifty two

'Sarge?' said DC Hick as he headed for his car, 'there's a punter wants you, in Reception.'

Ball dropped his pen. Please let it not be Maud Cotter, the half-dead woman from Camelot Self Storage. I've had my fill of cancer. 'What's she want, Hickie? I'm due at the Vet's.'

'You look well enough to me, Sarge.'

Pinned by Ball's glare, Hick mumbled, 'er, wouldn't say. And it's a 'he'.'

Relieved, Ball scurried to Reception. He couldn't remember the name of the edgy twenty-something perched on a hard chair.

'Mr...?'

'Wade. Henry Wade. We met after...'

'Ah, yes, Blackdown Hills.'

Wade shuffled to his feet, embarrassed. No-one believed the story that he and his girlfriend were 'hiking' off-grid in the woods when they found Abe Linnet collapsed near his half-concealed tent.

'Your girlfriend not with you?' Ball had forgotten her name, too.

'Emily. Em. No. No, she...' Wade looked at the door, the walls, the carpet. 'Er, could we go somewhere private?'

'This way,' said Ball, with a vocal glance at his watch. He pointed a hesitant Henry Wade to a different chair in Interview Room 2.

'She bottled it, you see, Emily. I told her to come herself, but...'

'Bottled what, sir?'

'Well. Owning up, I suppose.'

Ball was too busy for twenty questions. I'm late for the Vet's! Cough it up in three, or you're out. 'Owning up to what?'

Wade rummaged in his bomber jacket pocket and pulled out a grubby brown paper bag. 'I mean, we did help. I told Em to find a coat or something, in the man's tent. To put over him, keep him warm – it was ages before they got to us, you see, the paramedics.'

Just as well, thought Ball. Gave you and Emily time to get your drawers back on. 'And...?'

Sliding the bag across the table, Wade mumbled, 'there's no two ways about it. Em spotted this in the tent. It was shining up at her, she said. You know, gold. And what with the shock, and everything… She can be a bit fly and, well, she pocketed it. 'S'why she wouldn't come. So, I'm here. Handing it in.'

The grubby paper seemed to whisper as Ball shook the contents onto the table. A gold chain, scratched, worse for wear. And dangling from it a brassy something that could have been from a charm bracelet, a brass ring and cross. When he peered closer and saw it was a brass key, he knew which door it would open. 'Who's handled this, sir?'

'Handled it? Just Em. And me, of course. And I suppose he must've done.'

And whoever it belonged to, Ball guessed.

'Is Emily in trouble?'

'We'll see,' he said. 'Theft is theft. But under the circumstances…'

Wade shot to his feet like a dog smelling dinner. 'Can I go, then?'

'I'll see you out,' said Ball, using his pen to ease the key back into its paper bag, and frowning at his watch.

Fifty three

The cops left - again - then Doctor Bhatti came and went. Whatever they were pumping into him, it was stronger now. Alone in his white bed, Abe Linnet stared at the walls, seeing only blurs as his snake-in-the-grass mind dredged up tremors from the past. *It's always the bloody past*, he thought, till the *bleep* of the bedside monitor reminded him of his future.

That twat cop with the moustache had reminded him too. Again. Must be a new police method, get their pound of flesh an ounce at a time. Questions, bloody questions…

… 'Did you know Rose Linnet kept a journal?'

No, I didn't, and who gives a fuck?

'Six hundred pages of evidence, some of it pointing at you?'

Yawn, yawn. Squeeze twelve chairs for the jury round my bed, and one for the judge - if batty Doc Bhatti lets you.

'Perhaps I should read you some choice pages? From Rose's journal?'

Perhaps you should piss off? Got my own journal, in my head. It was cancer put me here, not dementia…

Abe craved a cigarette, had done since the ambulance brought him in. He listened to the monitor's sneaky rhythm drawing him back in time and further back, *blip-pause-bleep, blip-pause-bleep,* till the bleeps became old voices and the square glass panel in the door morphed into a screen, flickering, settling, flashing out past pictures he would rather forget…

…He could almost smell the smoke from Daniel's bloody cheroot, out there on the sea, except his sense of smell had long gone. Wanker Daniel, skinny cigarette bobbing on his lip like a lit pencil, as *Aura* cleaved through the waves, Abe at the tiller, twilight fading.

'What if you could paint, Abe? Might you more appreciate the sheer skill, in these?' Daniel pointed his wine glass at the plastic rod-case concealing a pair of exquisite fake Greek paintings, on their circuitous way to the auction houses of Athens. 'I don't see why we can't double the shipment, to double the take?'

I do, Abe thought, shaking his head at Daniel's risk-taking arrogance.

He thinks I don't know about the extra fakes he's sneaked into the pipeline.
And Daniel had blithely dismissed the thud of Coast Guard boots on the
gangplank when they last moored at Alimos Marina - too busy charming
the sailors with fishing stories while Abe did the worrying. 'The police are
close,' said Abe. 'Stick to the slow Greek way. We're making plenty.'

But plenty was never enough for Daniel. Sex, money, the dream of
fame - Abe could see it in Daniel's eyes, in the louche way he carried
himself. He watched him draw on the last inch of his cheroot, as if posing
for a photograph. Bare feet and shorts, flashing his tanned thighs at the
seabirds, when he ought to be in a tuxedo and patent leather shoes, like
some black and white movie star. Cary Grant, Clark Gable, bloody-
Humphrey-Bogart-with-a-paintbrush. And just as well he *can* paint.
Wouldn't stomach the wanker otherwise.

Before they set out, Daniel showed off half a dozen of 'my other great
fakes'. Abstracts these, some for practice, some the final article. Even Abe
admitted the finished versions were astonishing,

'Not Greek, Daniel?'

'Perceptive, Abe. Where, then?'

'Mm. Italy?'

'Tut, somewhat closer to your birthplace, Abe - Cornwall! St Ives
School, early to middle period. These are Ben Nicholson - who's almost
as good as me!' Daniel's cocky little laugh and posh voice were an
acquired taste. 'Abe, don't you keep saying, 'we won't fool the Greek
auctions forever'? Then why not widen the scope? The English art market
is *huge.*'

And with experts sharper than you. 'I'll think about it.' Abe had, his
'drowning' already planned. *Over my dead body,* he muttered to himself.

'Can't you see the irony, Abe? I paint a fine original work and sign it
'Daniel Flowers'. Well, it brings in a few hundred euros. But I *copy* a
work, sign another artist's name, and it's thirty thousand. Is that justice?'

Will Daniel ever stop whingeing about fame denied? 'Daniel, listen to
me, and listen hard. Justice is what you get *after* the police feel your
collar. They'll not feel mine, and if you help them, God help *you!* Are we
clear?'

And in a sulk, Daniel had stubbed out his pathetic little smoke on the white boat's varnish, while Abe steered *Aura* through near darkness towards Alimos Marina, an iron grip on the tiller…

…The *blip-pause-bleep* half-woke Abe from his reverie, fingers stiff from gripping the bed rail. He stroked the clinical whiteness of the sheets. Am I in hospital, or all at sea? When reverie reclaimed him, the bleeps became voices, the square window again a screen, flashing out different memories now – of raging at Gina, she at him, the rage and fear exploding to a fistfight - but still she wouldn't get rid…

A White Mountains silhouette, two dark shapes against the snow, two pregnant bumps, Gina and Rose…

Human flesh - one living baby, and a dead one. Abe digging a tiny grave, high up in the White Mountains, digging it deep to keep the animals at bay, hiding the unmarked spot with old dry sticks and brushwood, so the tiny grain of himself would never be found…

Blinking to remove the dead baby's waxen face dragged up more memories. Of close shaves with the Greek Coastguard, and Abe severing his partnership with Daniel, then a forced 'disappearance' to a hidden life in Istanbul. Not so bad there, a buzz in the streets, colourful food, the women young and exotic. But Gina's claws had found his stash of bonds by then, in a disappearing act of her own.

At least his new life meant a 'new' boat. A faint laugh shook the bedsheets as beloved *Aura* sailed into his thoughts, white no longer, *Aura* no longer. A repainted dark blue version, *Sea Breeze*, cleaved the waves, its wheelhouse reshaped, its registration fake.

The bed shook harder as Abe laughed at *Aura*'s new name, matching the name on his new passport. 'Ray Breeze' sailed on dubious waters aboard his freshly christened yacht, breezing through a fake life off the shores of Turkey.

Laughter caught in his throat, fingers tightening to a fist on the bedsheet. Breezing through a second life, yes.

Till wanker Daniel reappeared…

'No, no. Not *broke*, Abe, no. Never broke, am I? But shall we say my coffers would benefit from a refill? The life of an academic is rich only in ideas. I tired of it. Of England, too.' He didn't tell Abe his coffers were empty because when Rose threatened to donate the Nicholson fakes to the police, he had to pay well for her silence. 'And, goodness, who wouldn't miss the Aegean Sea?'

Daniel raised his wine glass and swallowed half the contents. Has he drunk my boat dry? Abe wondered. Must've, because Daniel never says anything resembling truth till the liquor flows.

'Your big plans for the English art market didn't pay off, then?' said Abe, tutting at the thought of Daniel planning anything, other than a fake canvas. Might as well squirt oil-paint up his arse. Abe was the planning, Abe the connections, - which is why Daniel was back. 'You showed me half a dozen beauts, as I recall. Ben Nicholson, was it?'

A discomfited look clouded Daniel's face. Abe perked up at the rarity, till Daniel said, 'Ah. Those Ben Nicholson 'beauts' were...acquired. By another party. In error, I'm afraid.'

Abe was afraid too. '*Another party?*' If it's the police, Daniel, I'll punch your lights out, and when you wake up, I'll punch them out again.'

'Goodness, Abe, no, no. Not the police.' Daniel pulled at his glass, spilling wine onto the deck.

'Who, then?' Abe had to ask twice. '*WHO?*'

Daniel's fingers twitched around an imaginary cheroot. The 'new' boat was strictly non-smoking.

'Abe, I cannot tell a lie -'

'*YOU CAN'T WHAT?*'

'Abe. It was Rose. *Is* Rose. I'm afraid she still has them, the Nicholson's. In England. Has them locked away, that is.'

The deck creaked with danger as Abe climbed to his feet. 'You'd better know where, Daniel.'

'I do, Abe. In Somerset. Worry not, I know her new address.' *I had to send more cash there!*

Before Daniel could move, Abe had him by the throat, one arm strong enough to yank his head and shoulders over the rail, sea spray peppering his face. His wine glass spun into the air and shattered on the deck. 'Crazy Rose has evidence that could lead the police to *me*? Is that what you're saying, you fuck-up?'

'*Abe! Please!* See sense! *Please!* The paintings aren't signed with *my* name!' he spluttered. 'And who will believe crazy Rose?'

Tempted to drown Daniel in the blue Aegean, there and then, Abe fell back on his mantra - *make the situation work for you*. He yanked a shaken Daniel back onto the deck and stood over him. 'Locked away, you said?'

'I followed her, Abe. Kept watch. In disguise, of course - I grew a beard, wore different clothes.'

'What a clever little *artist* you are,' snarled Abe.

'Rose is much changed. A recluse. And she's in England, while *we* are here, off the shores of Turkey.' Daniel waved a nervous arm at the waves he'd come close to joining.

Noting the 'we', Abe watched the breakers roll into white then back to blue. He dragged the storage unit details from Daniel, face darkening with every word. 'Why *shouldn't* I dump you overboard, you wanker?'

Daniel licked his lips, from salt, from fear. 'Perhaps because my artistry is still convincing, Abe? What if I were to paint a series of Turkish 'beauts', which you then inveigled into the Turkish market…? Is Athens the only place where art auctions may be found? Handsome profits to be shared? Yes?'

At 'shared', Abe pretended to consider. 'Shared?' he said. 'What d'you have in mind?'

'Well. As before?'

'*Fifty-fifty?* With the risks? You can jump overboard right now, Daniel, save me the trouble of throwing you.'

'Come now, Abe. Surely two old sea-dogs can negotiate?'

And Abe did. They compromised at 70/30 in his favour. Much-needed money. A relieved Daniel dabbed sea spray from his face with a fancy handkerchief as Abe looked on, pretending to ignore their differences.

But not ignoring the dangerous fakes locked away in England. Nor the two fuck-ups who put them there…

'Are you listening, Mr Linnet?'

Abe, in dreamtime, had forgotten Batten was back. Timms resisted an urge to give the grey man a sharp nudge with her elbow.

'I asked you about Daniel Flowers,' Batten said. *For the umpteenth time.*

'Who? What? I'm tired. This drip thing…'

Batten and Timms rolled their eyes in frustration. When the nurse bustled in without knocking, they were almost relieved.

Fifty four

Sergeant Ball was no more convinced by the *Somerset Angels Veterinary Service* sign than by the receptionist. Expecting a female cherub, he binned his casual sexism when an unsmiling male appeared. A male with status issues.

'Yes, Sergeant, I *did* 'happen to be around', then. Seventeen years I've faithfully served the practice. But a petty break-in, an age ago? I'm not an elephant.'

Even through the shiny glass screen, Ball could see that. The man was a stick insect, at best. 'Mr...?'

'Lloyd. With two L's, should for some reason you need to write it down.'

'Well Mr Lloyd, I was asking about your records, not your memory. I imagine after the break-in there was an insurance claim?'

Lloyd's face took on a 'pointless extra work' expression. 'Mm,' he said. 'Perhaps in the files.'

When he made no attempt to *look* in the files, Ball gave him his best ginger stare, and waited.

'I'll see if they're available,' said Lloyd in a grump, and disappeared through a door marked 'Private'.

The empty waiting room smelled of damp dog, the walls peppered with fluffy pet photographs flanked by posters screaming *Rabies!* Not a foot-tapper like Batten, Ball ignored the rabies and thought of cider. Even so, he'd almost adopted a 'pointless extra work' expression of his own by the time Lloyd returned, gripping a thin buff file. He dropped it on the reception desk, spun it round without a word, and folded his arms.

Smug bugger, thought Ball, muttering a 'thank you,' and scanning what little the file contained.

The insurance claim listed a replacement rear door, repairs to a dented drugs cabinet, and a series of random items grabbed by the thwarted burglars as they fled. Perhaps to prove he *was* an elephant, Mr Lloyd saw fit to speak.

'Amateurs, unable to get past the drugs door. It has a triple-bolt system - *my* recommendation,' he said proudly. 'And lacking the wit when disturbed, to make off with items at least saleable - computers, medical instruments and the like. I suppose they grabbed whatever lay in their path as they fled. I ask you, towels, surgical gowns, artificial insemination gloves - bin liners? Pointless imbeciles.'

Hardly listening, Ball clocked the list before flicking to the *Safeguard Security* witness statement, signed by the guard who foiled the robbery – *Ray Breeze*.

'I'll need a copy of this,' said Ball.

Mr Lloyd unfolded his arms. And rolled his eyes instead.

*

When Batten and Timms emerged, glum-faced, from Abe Linnet's room, Eddie Hick was outside, waving a sheet of paper like a chequered flag. When it briefly came to rest, Batten made out typescript and handwritten jottings. He ushered Hick and Timms away from the closed door to a quiet waiting area with chairs and a table. Bizarrely, copies of *Men's Health* poked out from beneath *Food and Drink* magazine.

'Going to keep waving that, Eddie, or might you hand it over?'

'No, sir. Er, yes. Forensic report. Well, a one-page cheat-sheet. From Andy Connor.' Hick handed it over.

'Did Andy have anything to say for himself?'

'Er, yes. He did, sir, yes.'

'Well?'

'Er, he said, nothing to add yet, so don't bother him today, or...'

'Or what?'

Hick looked to Timms for help but got a *dunno* shrug. 'Er, he said, or you can shove this piece of paper up-'

'Thanks, Eddie, I get the gist.' Batten pulled a tenner from his wallet and pointed at the *Refreshments* sign. 'Three coffees. Straight black for me and don't spill it.' Catching the back end of a Timms smirk, he added, 'Hazel will help you carry them.'

At the table, he pushed aside *Men's Health* and studied Connor's notes on the contents of Abe Linnet's half-hidden tent. Dismissing the obvious items - camping stove, sleeping bag - he focused on *'no mobile phone, no laptop, nothing remotely digital. Dinosaur, is he, Zig?'* A canny, hospitalised T-Rex, Batten thought.

Scanning the list of objects 'awaiting analysis', he rubbed the back of his head when 'a walking stick, brass-tipped' appeared. Didn't he hear the *click-pause-click* of one in the street, in Almyrida? Didn't Clio Demopoulou have one?

Next was 'a round piece of wood, heavy, size and shape of a rolling pin.' Connor's scribbles said, *'not tested yet, Zig, but an early guess is olive wood. Ring a bell?'* Batten searched his fuzzy memory till the bell rang and he recalled Connor's earlier notes on the Queen Mab crime scene. *Traces of olive wood* were embedded in her skull.

A loud fanfare announced the last item. 'One medium-sized, wooden-handled knife with curved blade.' *No prints but I'll run tests. Either traces of blood'll turn up, or bleach will. Btw, my clever dick assistant, the arty one who goes foraging, he says it's a mushroom picker's knife. Plenty sharp enough, this one, and a tad besides. Seems gardeners use them. And painters - for slicing through canvas. And Uncle Tom Cobley, when he or Mrs Cobley wants a knife.*

Despite Connor's levity, Batten could almost see a honed blade slicing into helpless Queen Mab's throat. In whose hand, though?

'Thanks a bunch, Andy,' said Batten aloud. 'And Uncle Tom *Cobblers* to you, too.'

Down the corridor, Hick nudged Timms' arm.

'*Eddie!* I nearly spilled the boss's espresso!'

'He might not need it, Haze,' whispered Hick. 'Or us. Look. He's talking to himself.'

*

Years before, alone on the empty shoreline, Darren Pope had only himself to talk to. Impatient for other shores, the shores of England, he gobbed salty phlegm onto the beach with a sound like *Rose!*

What is this shore? Is there fresh water? To left and right, the sand was hemmed in by high rock walls and sea. Ahead, rising land met the sky at a gap in the treeline. Struggling up, he leaned on the makeshift crutch and dragged himself away from the beach.

An hour's painful trek got him to an outcrop of rock, where he was forced to rest. Picking up a stubby piece of driftwood from the ground, he whittled it aimlessly with his knife, to keep in practice.

Sharp still, the knife. He drew it across and back again, stripping the bark, re-shaping the wood, each cut a reminder of his true task, till the rounded club felt balanced and firm in his grip. *Rose*, whispered the knife. *Rose, Rose*, again, again.

When a hairy spider, minding its business, scuttled harmlessly across the rock, Darren Pope raised the stub of wood and brought it down with force, enjoying the wet crunch as club met creature.

Rose, he said, wiping the club against his sleeve, and easing it into his pocket.

Rose.

Fifty five

'At least I bothered to phone, Zig. Not heard a whisper from you since you got back from your desert island. Avoiding your cider debts?'

In no mood for Andy Connor's levity, with Abe Linnet parrying questions like an Olympic fencer, Batten needed fast information. 'You told Hickie today, Andy.'

'And I've told *you*, a thousand times, testing takes resources. My forensics boys and girls, I've got their cogs turning so fast you can smell the smoke. Next thing, they'll want paying, too!'

'Andy, just -'

'Zig. Listen, for once. Gimme another day's grace, eh? 'Cos if you do, I'll tell you the reason I bothered to phone.'

On a long sigh, Batten gave in. 'Fine, Andy. Tell me.'

'Something else turned up, Zig. It was tucked away, right at the bottom of a pocket in the strap of your man's rucksack. The new trainee, he missed it first time, but they've got to learn, haven't they?'

'Andy…'

'A ring, Zig. Silver. Chunky, in the form of the letter -'

'D,' said Batten, to hurry Connor along. 'Shape of a triangle. The Greek letter 'delta', D, yes?' Batten enjoyed the brief silence echoing down the phone.

'Sort of shaped like a triangle, Zig. But the Greek letter 'delta'? I doubt it. Depends which way round you hold it. Two wonky shanks of silver, at an angle. Could be an L. Could be an A…'

Batten's phone went down as Ball squeezed into the cubby-hole office, carrying a puzzled expression but no tea or cake. They shared information, of silver rings and Vet's break-ins.

'Either Abe retrieved a silver ring from Queen Mab's body, after he sliced her throat, or some other bastard did, and it wound up with Abe. Yes?'

'My money's on Abe, sir. But say it is the letter L, why? Didn't Queen Mab already have an L ring for each of the Linnets?'

'Maybe it *is* an A - for Abe?'

'It was in Abe's possession, sir – and I suppose that's nine tenths of the law.' Ball cracked his knuckles. 'But why?'

'Some kind of keepsake?'

'Of what, though?'

'We'll ask Abe.'

'Not sure I'd trust the slimy sod to tell me the time.'

Batten glanced at his watch. 'All the same, you know what time it is, Ballie?'

'Cider time, sir?' said Ball, in hope.

'Musgrove Hospital time. To ask Abe - waste of time or not.'

'Fine, sir. But if you don't mind, *I'll* drive.'

*

'Oil slick not with you?' asked Abe when Ball and Batten eased into their bedside chairs. 'Got used to *her*.'

Ignoring the jibe, Batten played the waiting game, poring over forensic reports and statements. 'Ever heard of Mark Bragg?' he asked.

'Is he the bloke who came out fishing on my boat?' Abe clocked the thicker pile of paperwork in the Batten-bloke's fist but was determined to spar.

'He's the poor unfortunate who led the police to a back alley, by a carpet shop, where they found Rose's body. After you slit her throat.'

'Very public-spirited of him, he should get a reward.'

'He also noticed the automatic light wasn't working. Which meant neither was the CCTV.'

'No pretty pictures, then. Shame.' Abe added a sarky grin.

'Remember Ray Breeze?' Batten looked up from his papers, face unsmiling.

'Course. Good bloke, Ray.'

'Seems he was working for *Safeguard Security* that night. And one of his jobs was maintaining the automatic lights. Seemed he must've forgotten. Coincidence, eh? Or planned?' Abe rolled his eyeballs. 'And this 'good bloke' Ray, he foiled a burglary at a nearby Vet's, not long before Rose was murdered. Another coincidence, I suppose.'

A bored sigh.

'And the dumbest burglars ever. Instead of computers, they nicked the cheap stuff. Surgical gowns. Bin liners.'

'Must've been public-spirited too. Keep Britain Tidy.'

'And what else was it, Sergeant?'

Ball pretended to look at his own wad of notes. 'Artificial insemination gloves, sir. Very strange choice.'

'Me, I prefer straight sex,' smirked Abe.

God, who with? thought Batten, giving Abe's horse-face a dismissive glance. 'Or did you use them to cover your hands and arms - to keep off the blood? It tends to wallop out when you slice through an artery, with the sharpened blade of a folding knife. Would you like to see the pictures?' Batten almost dragged them out to make Abe look.

About to call the nurse, Abe's criminal pride kicked in and he gave a tiny shake of his head.

'By the way, where did you dump the gloves and gown, after you stashed them in a bin liner? Up in smoke, are they?'

Abe licked his lips, craving a different kind of smoke.

'Sergeant Ball and me, we know you ripped Rose's gold chain from her neck. It's in evidence, by the way. So's the key – which didn't do you any good. Fancy an oil slick getting there ahead of you. Oh, and the six fake paintings you were after, they're also in evidence.'

'Told you. *I* can't paint. Try asking that artist bloke. Duncan Bowers, is it?'

Batten would love to ask Daniel Flowers, and Darren Pope – *because if it's not ruled out, it's still ruled in* – but Abe was here, in a white-walled cell, handcuffed to a monitor by wires and tubes.

'Oh, and we found the ring, the silver ring. Your pal 'Ray Breeze', he forgot to ditch it.'

'What ring's that?' Abe said, with less bravado.

'Not *what*, whose?' said Batten. 'My Sergeant here, he thinks it says A for Abe?'

'Wouldn't know. Silver, you say? Make sure you take care of it.' Abe wished *he* had.

Batten's eyebrows waited for a serious answer. Abe kept quiet and

300

yawned. No way could they prove who the ring belonged to. A for Abe, my arse.

If that's what the cop with the moustache thinks, let him.

Fifty six

Ball now winced whenever Reception - or Eddie Hick's jabbing finger – nudged him towards a visitor at the front desk. He dreaded another interview with Maud Cotter, the terminally ill lady from Billingham's Self Storage, having seen his fair share of the dead and dying. 'Folk think I'm immune,' he told Di, at home. 'They think, oh, old Ginger Biscuit, he's seen it all. But that's the point. I *have*. Why would I rush to see more?'

The foul death of Queen Mab, Zig Batten's loss of his beloved Aunt Daze, Hazel Timms burying both parents – and now Abe Linnet, sneering up from a near-as-dammit death bed... He pushed reluctant knuckles at his desk and climbed to his feet. Not a believer in signs and portents, his bones nevertheless seemed to know Maud Cotter was the visitor. He'd be forced to ease her to an interview room, and dutifully listen to whatever words her rasping breath produced - while trying to ignore the involuntary tap-tap of her stick and the pale skin stretched so tight across her cheeks the bones showed through. And wishing to be somewhere else.

With a deep sigh he pushed open the connecting door, to confront his duty. She was squatting upright on the waiting area bench, rain dripping from her coat, staring at him. Dowdy, a rebellious expression on her face, a damp rucksack at her feet.

And about half Maud Cotter's age.

*

'*Who?*' said Batten. '*WHO?* You better not be having me on, Hickie!'

'No, sir, never, sir. Just saying what he said, Sergeant Ball.'

'Sergeant Ball? Thought he'd gone out?'

'No, sir, he's gone in. Said he's waiting. For you.'

'Waiting for me? Where?'

Hick twitched a vague arm beyond the CID room. 'There, sir.'

'Where's *there*, for God's sake?'

'Sorry, sir, Interview Room 1. Fast as you like, he said.'

302

A tight-faced Ball approached the interview room as Batten arrived.

'Bringing her tea, Ballie?' he said, pointing at the thick brown tar in Ball's grip.

'She turned her nose up, sir. This is mine. I need it. She pulls words out like teeth, one at a time, and wants a bloody receipt for all of 'em. Smells better than Queen Mab, but she's done me in. Look at her.'

Peering into the video screen, Batten thought his eye trouble had returned. The woman sitting upright in a hard chair stared blankly across the chipped table bolted to the floor, her body a frozen photograph, thin mouth tight as a zip.

'*Is* it her? he asked.

'No bank cards, no phone. Cash only. And illegal – though she still managed to ship up here. There's an old passport in her rucksack, years out-of-date.'

'If it's fake, she can eat the bloody thing.'

'Her National Insurance number looks genuine, so...'

Batten nodded. So she must have been resident in England at age sixteen. He peered closer at the video display, and rubbed the back of his neck, as Sonia's hands had done last night – along with a gentle reminder to slow down. The frozen figure cemented to a chair could do with speeding *up*. 'Do you know, Ballie, I'm buggered if I know where to start.'

'You do often say, 'begin at the beginning,' sir...'

With a grunt, Batten opened the door and he and Ball sat down, the woman merely flicking an eye in their direction. Ball's sausage fingers tapped against his knuckles, aching to crack them. The hands of the woman opposite were yellow with nicotine and still as the night. Waxed jacket, neither old nor new, cargo pants, walking trainers, lank hair in a ponytail. When Batten took in the thin lips and long bones of her face, she awarded him a silent glare.

Batten got down to brass tacks. 'Sergeant Ball's told me who you claim to be. Why should I believe you?'

Her narrowed eyes turned slowly towards him, experienced, wary. She could have been a lizard, till words emerged like smoke. 'Please yourself. I know what's true.'

Thank God someone does, Batten thought.

'Can I have my rucksack?' she said.

Batten glanced at Ball, who'd followed protocol. 'It should've been checked by now, sir. I'll fetch it.'

'Thought it was a bomb, eh?' she asked Ball's back.

'There are procedures,' said Batten, 'and we're obliged to follow them.' Though he rarely did.

'Procedures,' she said. Neutral, without feeling. Then the frozen stare.

When Ball returned, she drew a reinforced packet from the rucksack, removed a photograph and dropped it on the chipped table. Ball's face was a puzzle, but Batten had seen the photo before. A juiced-up Queen Mab had thrown it over Elliot Caine's fence into her old neighbour's garden. This copy, without the broken frame and shattered glass, showed the same three women staring at the lens. Rose Linnet, head tilted to one side, half-smiling. Gina Linnet, her stretched face unreadable. Sue Linnet, lizard eyes glaring at the camera as if it was a gun.

'That's me,' she said, tapping a younger version of her frozen glare.

Batten saw the resemblance to the photo in her old passport - and the dowdy contrast with the fine cheekbones of sister Rose.

'Who took this?' he asked.

'Some social-worker. 'What about a nice family photograph,' she says, stupid woman.' Sue Linnet nipped the photo from Batten's fingers, stared at it again then flicked her younger self onto the table. 'It's me, don't worry.'

'You'll appreciate we have more checking to do?' She shrugged. Batten slid the photo towards her.

'*I* don't want it.'

'Well, you kept it. And they're your family,' Batten said.

'Huh. *Families.*' She glanced at the bare floor as if in search of a spittoon, flicked the photograph away and resumed her stare at the walls. 'They're all dead,' she hissed.

In his cubby-hole office, Batten pored over the photograph. Ball plonked down two mugs of tea. Batten had asked for coffee, but sipped in gratitude, almost pleased his Sergeant was more distracted than him.

'Do you believe her, Ballie?'

'Starting to.' Ball's eyes searched the desk for the cake he'd forgotten. 'Date of birth fits. You?'

What did Batten believe? He swallowed tarry tea, considering the claims of the woman claiming to be Sue Linnet…

'Dad tracked me down.'

'And Dad is?'

'Tuh. Abe. Always-Absent-Abe.'

'How did he manage it?' Goode, Goode and Moulde had failed. 'He's like you, hasn't even got a phone.'

'There are ways. How do you think I got here?' She left it at that, till Batten nudged her along with an eyebrow.

'You ever read *Hamlet*?'

'*What?*' he said.

'We had to, for GCSE. I took to it straight away. Hamlet, another poor sod with a piss-artist for a mother, and a dad who's a ghost.'

Batten almost smiled at the aptness. Had Sue Linnet also read *Romeo and Juliet*, and Mercutio's speech about the fairy Queen Mab, galloping night by night through lovers' brains? Did Sue know the whereabouts of Darren and Daniel, Rose's lovers? Did she gallop back to England and slit her sister's throat?

A glance from Ball made him plough on. '*Hamlet* is relevant how?'

'Because Hamlet has some tosser friend with a posh name-'

'Horatio.'

'Whatever. Hamlet tells this pal, 'there are more things in heaven and earth than are dreamt of in your philosophy.' Well, there are more things underground than are dreamt of in police stations. That's how.' Ball and Batten shared a knowing look. They spent their working lives digging underground.

'Can we move from how, to why?'

A shrug. Batten was reminded of Grigoris, lifting his characteristic Greek shoulders, palms upturned. Sue Linnet's shrug was closer to contempt. 'Put your brains together, work it out.'

Swallowing a growl, Batten said, 'you arrived voluntarily. Feel free to explain.'

She bypassed the shrug this time. 'You've got Dad, in that hospital?'

Batten enjoyed giving her a silent shrug of his own.

'Well, you have. So you know he's a goner.'

'And if so?'

'*If so*, I'll be the last.' She looked away, the faintest hint of emotion in her eyes. Then her mouth zipped tight again.

Batten nodded at Ball. A change of voice might ease her along.

'Last what?' asked Ball.

With a stare that had 'thicko' written all over it, she said, 'the last *Linnet*,' and clammed up.

A memory of birdsong flashed into Batten's skull, then an image of Rose, singing *Lady in Red*. The more workaday Ball wanted to crack Sue Linnet's knuckles. His retort surprised her - and Batten. 'Wants you to arrange his *funeral*, does he?'

When she blew out her breath, Ball's face reddened. 'Amongst other things,' she spat.

Taking back the reins, Batten said, 'these other things. Could you be more specific?'

'Thought you were the bright one,' she said. When Batten's eyes reflected her words back at her, she added, 'Dad doesn't want you lot having it. Or the Government. He wants it to come to me.'

'It being?'

A bigger sigh. 'The *house*. And there's a trust fund Mum set up. Dad says I'm the heir.'

The two detectives shared a look. If Sue Linnet really was sitting opposite, she'd already inherited Abe's disdain - and turned up to collect the rest of her legacy. Glancing across the table, she yawned.

'Tired?'

'Tired? Yeh, of *you*.'

Batten thought of Aunt Daze describing her dubious brother, Russell. *He's always been a...wanderer.* 'Tired of wandering?' he asked.

She twitched both eyes at him, the faintest hint of agreement on her face. 'Maybe.'

'So. You inherit the trust fund, the house, ditch the rucksack, move in, stop wandering?'

Her look of faint agreement twisted into a sneer. 'Move in? To *Parminster*? And that *house*? Fuck that,' she hissed. 'Wasn't once enough…?'

'There's some good news at least, sir,' said Ball, draining the dregs of his dark brown tar. 'Your chubby solicitor pal, what's his name?'

'Goode. With an 'e'.

'Well, Mr Goode with an 'e', he'll finish our work for us. Make sure she's pukka.'

'After he gets her past a charge of illegal entry, you mean?'

'Indeed, sir.' Knuckles newly cracked, Ball's ginger face looked brighter.

Batten didn't feel bright at all. 'What if she managed illegal entry three years ago, in advance of Queen Mab getting her throat cut?'

Ball shook his head. 'No knife or wooden club in *her* rucksack.'

'Easy enough to get rid.'

'Maybe. Clothes and the usual, all we found. And one paperback, Zorba something, by some bod with an unpronounceable name.'

'*Zorba the Greek*?'

'Er, think so.'

Zorba the Greek. What would Sue want with Rose's favourite book? 'Any diaries, or suchlike?'

'Sorry, sir. Nothing.'

Batten was privately relieved. Sonia claimed Queen Mab's convoluted journals had almost blinded him. He pushed aside Sue Linnet's discarded photograph.

'What are we going to do with her, Ballie? And if you crack your knuckles while thinking about it, I'll crack *you*.'

'No need, sir, plain as day. We've got an old sea dog in Taunton hospital, right? So, let the dog see the rabbit?'

'What if the rabbit doesn't want to see the dog? We can't make her.'

'No, sir. Best ask permission, then.'

Fifty seven

Sue Linnet's permission fizzed out with more disdain. 'About time. Why the fuck d'you think I'm here?'

Batten stopped himself saying, *so Abe can cut your throat? Or you his?* 'There'll be a police presence,' he mumbled.

Once again, the dismissive shrug. 'Knock yourself out.'

I'd like to knock *you* out - and Abe - Batten thought, as Timms ferried him and the rabbit to Taunton to see the dog. Or was 'dog eat dog' closer to the truth? He and Timms set their chairs as far from the hospital bed as the walls would allow. In the small room, it wasn't far enough.

'Made it, then?' said Abe, hooded eyes on his daughter.

Sue Linnet stared at the crisp white sheets and bedside monitor, tracking the wires and tubes that led towards the man with the grey pony-tail, her alleged father. *Be careful what you say* was imprinted on Abe's face. She met his expression with a guarded nod.

How had Malkie McTay described Abe - 'full of strange oaths', forcing a young Rose to keep her effing opinions to herself, and reinforcing his point with a fist? Now, with one look, he was Mr Control again, this time with puppet-daughter Sue.

'I've written a will,' he said. Hazel Timms shifted in her chair. She'd squeezed one of the Goodes into her car and driven him to Abe's bedside, to keep things legal. 'You'll inherit everything, Sue. What passes through me and Rose and Gina, it'll all be yours.'

Batten and Timms shared a look. Without Daniel Flowers, there was little chance of proving Abe a conman and a fraudster – and no chance of confiscating his ill-gotten gains to compensate the victims. From Timms' knowledge of the art world, she doubted a queue of victims would rush forward to admit their vain pricey walls were hung with fakes. Sue Linnet would inherit nigh on half a million.

'Yes. Mine,' she said. Two words, then silence.

In the echo, Abe flashed a look of double-triumph at Batten and Timms. If the cops fitted him up for killing Rose, compensation would go to the remaining victim - and the remaining victim was Sue. Trapped by white walls and duty, Batten stared at the sneering face and wished he was on a plane to Crete. Abe Linnet, Mr Control, to the end.

'Maybe you can settle. Settle down. You know, after,' said Abe. 'A child, maybe? Eh? Keep the Linnet flag flying.' His smile came out as an expectant emoji.

'A child,' she said, without conviction.

'Your legacy,' Abe said. 'Maybe ours?'

How many times had Batten seen vicious people long for their journey's end to have meaning? Abe was no exception. *Legacy?* thought Batten. *Wants Sue to edit his memoirs, does he?*

A hopeful Abe leaned forward in his clean white bed. 'Maybe a grandchild, yes?'

Sue Linnet's tight lips blew out a sigh. 'A child? A grandchild? Don't you *know* how old I am?' she said.

Abe backtracked. 'Well…you'll be able to move on, though?'

'Move on?' she said. 'What, again?'

'In your life, I mean. Move on in your life.'

'My *life*?' Arctic-cold, Sue Linnet's face, the icy silence disturbed only by Timms squirming in her plastic chair to the rhythm of the monitor.

When Sue at last unzipped her mouth, words chilled the air like frozen smoke. 'It's here, is it?'

'Is what here?' said Abe.

'The will,' she said.

'Er, it's with the solicitors. Why?'

'Need to see it. People promise all sorts of guff. They told us you were dead, but you're not. This will, how do I know it's real?'

Batten could swear the monitor beeped doubly shrill and loud as Abe's emoji faded to a weak frowning face in sickly grey. For years, Sue Linnet had borne the inherited burden of Always-Absent-Abe.

The rest of his legacy, Abe saw, would be under Sue's control, not his.

*

'Relieved Hazel?'

What, because you're not driving? 'Relieved to see the back of those two, sir?'

'Indeed. We've earned the respite.' Batten's head felt like a sack of grit. Sonia Welcome had warned him, with disarming medical frankness, what would happen if he refused to slow down. And, worse, what would happen to their relationship.

Endings and beginnings clouded his mind. He pushed away Clio Demopoulou's caustic words: *the moment comes when we must choose how to be remembered.* Trying to relax, he leaned back in his seat, watching Timms' skilful hands steer her Nissan along the A358 back to Parminster. But the compact bonnet and windscreen reminded him of Aunt Daze's little Micra, parked outside her empty house in Leeds, waiting for probate to churn through the system. His suppressed sadness eased when he thought of Timms' unfussy and professional return to duty, despite burying not one parent but two.

Laddering between the falling leaves of roadside trees, a red-dotted mural of hawthorn berries caught his eye. Almost unnoticed, summer was fading into autumn. Dislocations in the human season, he realised, had soaked up his attention. As he watched, the red berries became Aunt Daze's red dressing gown, trailing down the corridor to Chemotherapy - then, against his will, became the faded red dress beneath the dirty greatcoats of the late Queen Mab.

The car slowed as they approached a crossroads. Not *another* crossroads, Batten thought, the imminent, feared appointment with Doc Fallon contorting his face. Timms glanced across, concerned.

'Anything wrong, sir?'

'*What?* No, no, Hazel. Fine. No problem,' he lied.

Fifty eight

When Sue and the police left, frozen silence filled the white-walled hospital room, the *bleep* of the monitor droning on, unheard.

Abe stared at an empty white ceiling, oblivious to the drip in his arm, memory escorting him back from cold Somerset to the warm Aegean sea all those years ago, his hand on the tiller, sailing through darkness to the rendezvous point. At Abe's insistence, for extra safety, the new Turkish fakes were passed to a transfer boat as the two vessels sat broadside, pretending to share fish. Sometimes, they did. Silver sea bass, Daniel's favourite.

Silver fins and silver scales, glinting in the faint moonlight – Abe remembered the shapes and colours. Not the scent of fish, though, his sense of smell long gone. Too much booze, for too many years. The name of his condition had gone too, despite his vengeful memory dredging up everything else that happened that night.

If wanker Daniel hadn't been below, drunk as a skunk in his bunk…Voice like a posh toff but he snored like a docker. If he hadn't been half-cut, if he hadn't been *Daniel*, he might have smelt what Abe no longer could, and might have followed his smarmy nose to the propane tank. Might have noticed the leak, noticed gas swamping the galley, spreading into the cabins, slithering into the bilge.

Abe's second 'drowning' would have been real, he reminded himself, had *Sea Breeze* not been near the rendezvous point - and had he not been on deck, strong hand on the tiller. Daniel must have ignored the boat's 'no-smoking' rule because where the arrogant bastard was concerned, rules were for breaking. Woke up in his bunk below, did he, and lit one of those poncey cheroots? The smarmy wanker surely did, because without warning the explosion blew a hole the size of Daniel right through the bottom of the boat.

A stunned Abe and random pieces of his partner-in-crime erupted from what was left of *Sea Breeze*, littering the gentle waves for a few teasing moments. Human litter, signed 'Daniel Flowers', stained the blue waters then slowly sank as red bled to pink and back to blue.

Fitting, Abe thought. Daniel painted the sea – 'and only the sea, Abe, without pesky people in it'. Now, the sea had painted Daniel.

Plank by jagged plank, the remains of Abe's beloved yacht disappeared beneath the waves, a life jacket with its flashing light keeping him afloat on the empty sea. He remembered the first life jacket he ever wore, learning to sail, ten years old, in a leaky wooden skiff. And swiftly mastering the tiller, gliding along in sole control, feeling the punch of that wonderful boat, the skim of freedom on open water.

His childhood memories sank to the depths when the transfer yacht arrived and dragged him aboard. The amazed skipper gaped at blue-grey waves and nothing else. 'But where is *Sea Breeze*?' he asked.

'It's here,' said Abe, frozen fingers clamped by shock to a stub of olive wood, the broken end of the tiller - all that remained of his beloved yacht, his money-spinning safe haven-home. His freedom road.

As the transfer boat cut a half circle through the waves and headed back to Turkey, a silent Abe slumped below, listening to the swish of the sea. After water, he decided, would be fire. When they docked, everything of Daniel's would go up in smoke. And this time, not a single fake painting would survive.

Smoke. He didn't even want a cigarette. Blanket-wrapped, amid the alien trappings of a stranger's yacht, glass of brandy untouched in his frozen fist, he wished they'd let him drown…

When the brandy glass became the cold metal of the bedrail, Abe realised he was on land, in a hospital in Somerset, two thousand miles from where he'd rather be.

He thought this business done with after Sue arrived at his hospital bed. The will signed, the Linnets living on. *I've dodged the law, I've left my legacy.* And Sue's face carried his features, even her hair was his – though in truth her mother's looks might serve her better because beauty opens doors, no key required. Horse-faced Abe kicked doors down to get *his* way.

But when a stone-hard Sue departed, unease was Abe's bed-mate. Why couldn't she breathe a simple 'thank you' to a dying man? And say, yes, yes, the Linnet line, it's safe with me?

Abe stared at the wires and tubes, at the winking lights on his bedside monitor – more alive than he felt right now. Do we only rise so we can fall again? he asked himself, as his life history sank, like *Sea Breeze*, to the depths. If Sue fails me, will I be remembered at all?

He considered telling the moustached cop everything, so his under-the radar past might at least be recorded. *No,* he thought. *Make the situation work for you.* Those who tell everything have no secrets left, and secrets are power. The trick, he knew, is tell just enough.

Wanker Batten, could he still be of use - despite looking like *he* should be in hospital? Closing his eyes, Abe sorted grain from chaff, and eased aside most of the grain.

Then his fingers found the red button and called the nurse.

*

Zig Batten shuffled 'light duties' paperwork from one side of his desk to the other. A sack of grit before, his head was a bag of random gravel now, the swift response of the Crown Prosecution Service ringing in his ears. Don't bother with a full dossier, they decreed, not with Queen Mab three years dead and the chief suspect about to join her. Even if the overworked Courts ever saw Abe Linnet in the dock, your evidence is circumstantial. If you have other suspects, where are they? And where are your witnesses?

Elbows on his CID desk, chin in his hands, Batten imagined Area Super Wallingford's acid voice: '*resources, resources!*' For the Wallingford's of this world, the only true justice was *efficiency*.

Batten was left to ponder how Sue Linnet might use the money she'd inherit. Paying a shrink, he hoped, to penetrate the frozen sea entrapping her. Malkie McTay remembered an unsmiling Rose tilting her head sideways 'to keep one eye on the vultures.' By contrast, her sister Sue froze bolt upright in a cold steel cocoon. Might a paid professional help her emerge, into something finally tasting of freedom?

Families, he hissed, thanking his lucky stars for thirty-seven years of nurture with Aunt Daze, whose compact silhouette - the spit of Queen Mab's - had triggered his long journey into Rose Linnet's past. And in some ways into his own.

He ticked his fingers like an old clock on the piffle of paper. Here I am, he thought, at journey's end - a filing clerk. Through the glass sides of his cubby-hole office, he watched Ball, Timms, Hick and a newly returned Nina Magnus pore over statements and delve into real crime.

Journey's end? his mind hissed. *You're not even sure who killed Queen Mab, let alone why!* A proper detective would dig up the *why!* Piston fingers beating *why* into the desk, he barely noticed when a shuffle of aimless paper slithered to the carpet. Grabbing his keys, he squeezed from his tiny office and slammed the door.

'I'm going to Taunton, to the hospital,' he told the room, with what unofficial authority he could muster.

Ball, on the phone, raised a 'one moment' finger before replacing the receiver. 'Hazel will drive you, sir.'

Timms looked up from her screen, horrified. *What, a chauffeur now, am I?*

Batten shook his head. 'No, no, Ballie. I need to talk to Abe. I'll-'

'Yes, sir. But that was the hospital. Seems *he* needs to talk to *you*.' Ball nodded at Timms. 'To both of you.'

'Abe? To us? Bloody hell, *why?*'

Shoulders and palms pointing upwards, Ball aped the Greek shrug Batten had picked up from Grigoris.

'I'll need to *pee* first,' Timms muttered, wrenching her coat from the back of her chair.

Watching them disappear, Ball was glad he kept Abe's verbatim message to himself. 'Wanna talk to oil slick and that Northern twat with the moustache.'

Then he groaned. A week's paperwork leered up at him, and all he had was a day.

Fifty nine

'*Truth-weather* - that's what my Aunt Daze used to call Autumn skies like this,' said Batten. A crisp, clean light seemed to draw leaf-fall through the windscreen into Timms' car. Beyond the glass, the tree-lined stretch of the road to Taunton danced brown and gold with leaves plucked from dry branches and tossed into the air on a blue wind.

When she'd driven from the CID carpark, Timms' tyres crunched over banked-up Autumn debris, blown into piles like speedbumps. All she'd thought about was the dirt on her car. Now, she glanced at the passenger seat in surprise. Her boss never reminisced, to her, about his 'mother'. She only knew Batten had lost his real mother as a two-year old, because Sergeant Ball had filled her in.

'As a youngster, when the weather was like this, if I'd told a fib or wouldn't own up - you know, when my football smashed a window, or I'd nicked rhubarb from Mrs Yeadon's allotment - Daze would say, 'today's a truth-day, Zig. You're not going to waste a lovely blue sky on fibs, are you?'

Timms thought she'd better say something. 'Er, and did you, sir?'

'No. She could always tell. Always.' Batten smiled at the blue, clear light.

Perhaps the boss is getting over his grief? Hazel thought. Perhaps 'truth-weather' helps. Does talking about loss move you from darkness into light? Deep down, she knew she must talk about hers. But who with? And this was hardly the moment, Abe Linnet twenty minutes away and, as far as she was concerned, immune to truth.

Doctor Bhatti met the two detectives outside Abe's door. 'I must make it clear, Inspector, this interview is entirely against my wishes, a fact I have formally recorded.'

'We're here because of *him*, Doctor,' Batten said. Timms rolled her eyes. She'd watched her father die in this hospital, and now she'd be watching Abe. But in they went, the room feeling tiny, a strong scent of medication in the air.

Bolstered by drugs, voice as grey as he looked, Abe said, 'made it, then?'

The same first words he said to daughter Sue, Batten recalled, after God knows how many years. Timms humphed herself into a plastic chair. Batten would have preferred to stand. 'We're waiting,' he said.

Abe looked across his nose at Timms. 'No tape recorder, oil slick?'

'No *point,*' she snapped.

'Mr Linnet-'

'Yeh, yeh. Humour a dying man, can't you?' Abe paused, an uncertain look on his face, till words oozed out like cold treacle over rocks. 'I need a favour. Any chance?'

Timms' face was pure horror. Batten said, 'a *favour*? What do we get in return?'

Abe's fingers ticked on the white bedsheet. 'A bedtime story. Mine,' he said. 'For grown-ups. Isn't that what you police do, collect stories?'

'Here's the deal,' said Batten. 'You ask your favour and tell your story, then me and DC Timms decide what's next. That's the only deal you'll get.' As Abe considered, Batten folded his arms, pretending he was comfy in the plastic chair.

'Favour first, then,' Abe said, looking at Batten, then Timms. 'It's a favour for Sue. She'll soon have no parents.'

'*Soon?*' said Timms, free of the tape recorder. 'She's had no parents for a lifetime.'

Batten cut in. 'What *about* Sue?' he asked.

'You've seen her,' sighed Abe. 'Cold. Like she's carved out of stone. It's Gina's fault. But Gina's dead and I'm pending.'

'Gina's fault?' said Batten. 'Not yours?'

Abe ignored the question. 'Sue could still have a life,' he said. 'With help.'

'Oh, you want *us* to be her mum and dad?' asked Batten, shocked that any hint of humanity could emerge from the grey sneering figure in the bed. 'We're CID, not foster parents.' Timms nodded, with relief.

Abe's face began to harden till he remembered he wanted a favour. 'You've got contacts, welfare, counselling, all that.' For the briefest moment, his self-control cracked. *'I don't have anyone else, dammit!'*

Disquiet clouded Timms' face - neither did she. Batten felt a reluctant sting of compassion, as Abe's weak finger pointed at him. 'If you were a bit of male support, in the background, and she was the female side?' When his finger dipped towards Timms, her eyebrows climbed to the ceiling. 'Just at first, I mean. She'll have money. That balloon-belly of a solicitor-'

'Mr Goode.'

'Him, he says she'll inherit, give or take. But fat-lot-of-Goode, he's only the legal side.'

Sergeant Ball had already been in touch with the relevant agencies on Sue's behalf, and PC Foreman - Sue's childhood sweetheart - was itching to help. But no way was Batten telling Abe. All the same, would an extra eye on Sue be much of a burden? He glanced across at Timms who gave the slightest flick of her head.

'This bedtime story of yours, for grown-ups,' Batten said. 'Better be a good one.'

With Timms and Batten squirming on their hard seats, Abe said, 'if you're sitting comfortably, I'll begin.' Voice just louder than the monitor's *bleep*, Abe told his story, avoiding any part with a whiff of evidence.

'I suppose I've lived a life of sea and mountains. The Aegean Sea, the White Mountains - my freedom roads. Not that *Rose* was freedom. Crazy from day one, and when she learned to talk, sweet Jesus. Whingeing, whining. *The boat's too small*, she says. *The roof's too low*. I said, huh, let's swap it for the QE2. And if I said, do X, she'd do Y.' When Batten made to speak, Abe added, 'Yesh, yeh, I might have shut her up a time or two, kept her in hand.'

'Hand? You mean *fist*?'

Abe twitched his shoulders. 'Different world, different times.'

'Same old excuses,' Timms sniped.

'Do you want my story, or not?' said Abe.

The two detectives leaned back in their painful chairs as Abe blew out his breath. 'Maybe if I jump ahead, to down the road?'

'Down the road?'

'*Parminster*. Buggered if I know why Gina ended up there. Bloody poky-yokel-town.' Batten worked in Parminster. Timms' parents had lived in its suburbs. 'Took me an age to trace Gina but I paid her a visit, one dark night. Huh, her face when I turned up, for the bonds she'd thieved – I'm entitled, I said. She snarls at me, *you're entitled to nothing!* Threatened to call the police.'

'Which got you off her doorstep sharpish, I'll bet.'

'We must've woken Sue. Little Sue.' Abe's eyes glazed over, and Batten couldn't tell if the tears were real or fake. 'I could see her, through the glass in the door, coming down the stairs, a scruffy ragdoll in her hand. But she saw me, and screamed – at me, her father. Because she recognised me, even with the beard? Or because a stranger on the doorstep frightened her? To this day, I don't know which.'

Timms could hazard a guess. She controlled herself.

'I swore to myself I'd be back, for little Sue. For my daughter. Give her some sort of life.'

'Took your time,' said Timms, her self-control snapping.

'On the other side of Europe, oil slick. I could hardly just drop in, could I?'

'But years later you managed to,' Batten said. 'Or 'Ray Breeze' did. Dropped in to Parminster more than once. Drove a nightshift van for *Safeguard Security* and scuppered the automatic light in the alley where Rose slept. Handy, getting paid for patrolling the area, to *protect* people. And you faked a burglary at a Vet's, and stole what you needed to keep Rose's blood off you? Rose, your *other* daughter. That key to her lock-up, on the gold chain round her neck – did you grab it before you cut her throat, or after?'

Abe's hands on the bedsheets twitched, for the briefest moment, before his control returned. 'Who's telling my story, you or me?'

'Tell all of it then.'

'Twat,' hissed Abe. Before Batten could react, he added, 'I never killed a daughter! *Sue's* my daughter, you wanker. *Rose* isn't.'

Timms and Batten did an eyebrow dance. 'What do you mean, Rose isn't your daughter?'

'Cuh, don't they teach biology at schools *up north*? I'm miles away on business - let's call it that - I'm away for four months. Four and a bit.

318

When I come back, Gina's two months pregnant, and even my dick's not that long. She was young, tasty, a bit free up there.' Abe flicked a hand towards the faraway White Mountains. 'And it's not as if Rose looked like me, is it?'

'Small mercies,' muttered Timms, as Batten squeezed a horrified duck into a row. 'You'd better not be saying *Daniel* helped himself to Gina when you were away on 'business'. That would make him Rose's *father!*'

Batten thought a look of indignation was beyond Abe, but Abe managed it. '*Daniel?* Do you think I'd let that poshed-up wanker anywhere near Gina?' Abe could still feel his fingers tighten on Daniel's windpipe till Daniel turned blue. He'd seen the arrogant bastard cast an eye over Gina, and Daniel was a rat up a drainpipe at the sight of female flesh. 'And for Christ's sake, do you think I'd let him shack up with Rose if she'd been his own daughter? Who do you think I am? Bloody Oedipus?'

'Oh, I think we've established who you are, *Mr Linnet.*'

'Establish all you like. Had to give Gina a slap or two to *establish* who Rose's father was. And you want to know the truth?'

In a world of fakes, Batten wondered if he'd ever know 'truth' again.

'Truth was, she hadn't the foggiest! Best she could do was narrow it down, the drunken slag. If I say I 'did the right thing' when I took her on, her and someone else's kid, I expect you'll laugh. So, pause for laughter?'

Batten and Timms stared back, as stone-faced as Sue Linnet.

'Humph. Gina was useful, I suppose. I pretended to forgive her. But I never did. *Never.* I pretended Rose was mine, and Gina raised her. When she wasn't pissed. Some mother, eh?'

And you were a better 'father'? Batten was about to ask, but Doctor Bhatti's knuckles rapped.

'Treatment time, Inspector. If Mr Linnet *again* ignores my advice, try again in an hour.' Bhatti pointedly held open the door, which gave Timms and Batten an excuse to leave.

*

Musgrove Hospital's coffee bar was pleasant, but the high walls and ceiling seemed to amplify the myriad voices and clattering cups, the noise

319

grating in Batten's head. He finished his black coffee and climbed to his feet. 'Fresh air, Hazel?'

The label on Timms' herbal teabag claimed it soothed and harmonised. She pushed away her cup of failure. 'Gladly, sir.'

In the sprawling hospital grounds, they strolled aimlessly past ambulances and Ear, Nose and Throat, hardly speaking. Only when they arrived, perhaps by chance, at the multi-storey car park did Hazel breathe a question-mark sigh. Batten's face asked the same question. *Get in the car? Let cancer deal with Abe?*

Timms reached into her bag and weighed her car keys in the palm of her hand, as if about to toss a coin. Nodding at the keys, Batten was struck by the wavelength he and Timms had developed. When he caught her eye, she said, 'If the CPS won't touch our foul 'wanker', sir, why can't I just drive away?'

'You know why, Hazel. 'Our foul wanker' made one verifiable claim: the police collect stories. We haven't finished collecting his.'

'Even if it's fake?'

'I've never met a crook able to lie *all* the time. What if a grain of truth sneaks out?'

With a glance at the cloudless sky she said, 'let's hope the truth-weather lasts, then.' Dropping the keys into her bag, she headed back to *Oncology*, and Batten followed.

Sixty

'Couldn't keep away, eh?' said Abe, when Timms and Batten reclaimed the plastic chairs in his white room. 'My magnetism, I expect.'

'Your *story*, Mr Linnet. If you still want this 'favour', we need an ending.'

'Huh.' Abe raised the arm attached to the bedside drip. 'I'm hooked up to the ending. Not good enough for you?'

Batten stared Abe down. '*Rose*'s ending. The full story, or no deal.'

Looking away, Abe wondered if he could trust the stronger medication to keep his head clear. But Sue, his only daughter, she needed him. Didn't she?

'Talking about Gina and Rose, was I? Well, what do you do with a kid at that age? In the commune, someone was there when I wasn't - or when Gina was finding fairyland in a bottle. I remember the day I dug out her stash of gin, hidden behind the nappies. Gina tried to stop me pouring it down the sink. When I did, she threw an empty bottle at my head. Glanced off, just here.' Abe touched his temple with a grey finger. 'Could have broken my skull. It was her started the fisticuffs, not me.'

Timms couldn't zip her lip any longer. 'A fair fight, was it - her huge muscles outgunning yours?'

'Whatever it was, we stayed together-'

'After a fashion!'

'I couldn't care less what you think, oil slick. Do you want the story?'

Batten dabbed a reassuring hand in Timms' direction. She folded her arms, tighter.

'We stayed together, *after a fashion* or otherwise. Adventuring - sex and booze and sea and mountains.' He looked across his nose at Timms. 'You should try *adventuring*, oil slick – might loosen you up. Sure, a bit of *business*, here and there, to pay the bills, including Rose's posh school, in Chania. Where she met that little wanker, Darren Pope.'

Soon as he said the name, Abe's medicated mind conjured up a big unfriendly giant bursting into the hospital room, wrenching the drip from his arm and finishing him off with a pillow over the face – the two cops looking on, not lifting a finger. But when Abe shook away the image and stared at the door, it was firmly closed. *I'm losing my thread*, he thought, as the liar's problem muddled him, the liar's need for a good memory. His was slipping. Ring for the nurse? *No, no. I can fool the cops all day, any day.*

'Rose was at the school, in Chania. And me and Gina must have had our moments because she falls pregnant again, but this time I know it's mine, because I was keeping tabs. She wouldn't get rid, and I wouldn't let her drink *my* kid to oblivion before it was even born. So I packed her off to dry out. Some pricey clinic. And while she's away, Rose gets herself up the duff, too. Like mother, like daughter, same old story.'

Batten didn't have all day. 'We know about Rose's pregnancy. We know about Darren Pope. Cut to the chase.'

Darren Pope - that name again. Abe shuddered and checked the door. Still closed, no giant pressing a pillow over his face. But the Northern twat thinks he knows about Darren, does he? About Darren Pope the patsy? Huh.

'Let's say Gina and Rose were getting a bit *conspicuous*. We went deeper in the White Mountains and I hired an old hag midwife. Made sure she kept the pair of them out the public eye.'

'And kept out of it yourself, with the Greek police on your trail?'

Abe barely heard Batten's snipe, his mind struggling to focus on a faulty brick in his story, a fuzzy-headed brick, floating just out of reach... 'She gets a bit heavy-handed with the knock-out drops, the midwife. Pumps Gina and Rose full of stuff...And Gina gives birth early. Hag midwife's next to useless. Before you know it, sodding Rose is giving birth too, and the hag can barely manage one birth, let alone two...Bloody chaos up there, by the time I get back. Gina and Rose half-blotto, close to cuckoo-land. And there's these two babies. These two girls.'

Abe saw their tiny faces again, one twitching and mewling with life. But the other cold, whiter than his bedsheets, lips a dark shade of blue. One live Linnet and a dead one. And Abe had to have a child, a child of his own. Had to have a future.

'I switched them,' he said.

'Switched what?'

'Tuh. The *babies*. Bribed the midwife.'

'Bribed?'

'Well, offered to rearrange her features, useless cow, if she didn't keep her mouth shut. And she was ugly enough already. I buried the dead one. Tiny little grave. Buried her deep, up in the White Mountains.' Abe stared blankly at the white ceiling, remembering the spade in his hands, the hole in his gut, and the dark dirt beneath his fingernails.

Batten recalled the journal. *We buried your baby. In Nature.* Isn't that what Gina told Rose? 'Buried whose baby? Gina's? Or Rose and Darren's?'

This time Abe heard the Northern twat's voice, saw his lips move, made out the words as they floated through the air towards the frosted glass screen in the door. Then the screen cleared, and a shard of the faulty brick hovered in the glass and spoke. *Gina's,* it said. *Gina's baby died. Abe and Gina's baby. And you buried the tiny corpse, yes. Then filled the empty space with Rose's child. And told Gina it was hers. Hers and yours. And Gina called her Sue, but...*

A medicated Abe lost sight of the rest. He found himself answering Batten's question. 'Gina's,' he mumbled. 'She was half-blotto. I buried Gina's baby, our baby. Told her I buried Rose's. Then I gave her Rose's baby instead. Gina called her Sue...' *Without asking **me**! And I hated the name!*

Timms and Batten swapped stares of horror. 'Hold on. Sue's mother is *Rose?* That what you're saying?'

With a flick of his shoulder, Abe assented. Despite Batten's shock, his thoughts flashed back to the journals and to Elliot Caine, who said he'd walked a neglected Sue Linnet to school, half a dozen times, when Gina was too sozzled to bother. A further question clicked into place. 'Gina wasn't fooled, was she?'

The grey figure twitched in his white bed, uncertainty returning. 'New-borns. Lumps of plasticene. They all look like Winston Churchill. And what with the midwife's story, and the drugs...But when Sue began to grow... Poor bitch. Instead of looking like Gina or Rose, she began to look like me.'

Eyebrows in the air, Timms stared at Batten, he at her. A bog-eyed grimace of disgust filled Hazel's face. Batten broke the silence, refusing to believe what he'd heard. 'Looked like *you*? *You*? Not like *Darren*?'

Abe's medicated mind said, *careless fool!* as the faulty brick slotted into place in the wrong wall of lies, the echo booming out as *DARREN* - the patsy Abe thought he'd done with. He stared in confusion, at a crossroads of truth and lies. Run with the lie, and a vengeful Darren, wherever he was, might burst through the door and claim Abe's only daughter. And share Sue's inheritance. And register Sue Linnet as…Sue *Pope!*

'*Shove over that beaker!*' Abe snapped. But sucking water through a straw only brought childhood to mind. *My life will not end like this! The Linnets will live on!* When his fake wall cracked and crumbled, one brick remained: Sue. His only child. *His.*

The two cops had twigged – he could see the disgust on their faces. *Fuck them both.* Sooner or later, they'll know what dying is.

'Darren *Pope?*' he spat. '*Darren Pope?* That thick wanker? Even on a starry night, he couldn't tell a virgin from a whore.'

'Oh, you foul sod, calling your own daughter a whore!'

'*SHE'S NOT MY DAUGHTER!* How many times? Rose was *Gina's* daughter! And the cow had no idea who the father was!'

'Your luck's in, then!' said Batten, ignoring the ironies, throat rasping with anger. 'You could've got seven years for incest! But for *RAPE*, you can get *LIFE!*'

This time, Timms put a restraining hand on Batten's sleeve, alarmed by his scarlet face and clenched fists. Raised voices alerted the slim nurse who burst through the door without ceremony, eyes like daggers. Before she could speak, Timms gave her daggers of her own. '*OUT!* she hissed, and the shocked nurse closed the door behind her. 'She'll call the doctor,' Timms whispered to Batten. 'We won't have long.'

With the ruin of Queen Mab in mind, Batten turned his anger back on Abe. 'You never forgave Gina – *never*, you said. So when she was away 'drying out', you got your revenge, didn't you, you bastard, by raping her daughter?'

Abe tried to lean forward in the bed. '*Rape?*' he snapped. 'Bollocks to rape. You think you *know* Rose, eh, Mr Detective? Think she was fucking

Joan of Arc? She was sampling the sauce before she reached fourteen. No surprise with Gina for a mother - she had bottles stashed all over the house. And that night - sure, Gina was at the clinic - Rose sampled more than was good for her. Maybe I'd done the same. It gets cold up there.' Once more, Abe flicked a weak hand at the faraway White Mountains. 'Next thing I know, half-pissed, she's climbed in bed with me. Maybe thought I was Gina. She sometimes snuggled up to her for warmth when I was away. Cuh, warmth, from Gina, that's a laugh.'

'Nobody's laughing,' hissed Timms.

'No, it might crack your face, oil slick.' In the pause, a flash of clarity almost made Abe fall back on Darren Pope. But once the truth is out… 'Yes, I'd had a few, maybe thought for a minute Rose was Gina. Both curvy. Rose, wow, curvier still. Unpolluted beauty, was Rose, that night.'

Abe's anaemic wolf whistle, barely audible, still punched the walls. Timms clamped her eyes shut and covered her ears. Batten was almost sick at the thought of Rose galloping through the lover's brain of horse-faced Abe. He swallowed instead, as Abe boasted on, energised by the memory of his prowess.

'She'd been sniffing round that little wanker Darren for weeks, plucking up courage. Well, I gave her courage, that night. Gave her a sex education.' Before Batten could open his mouth, Abe snapped, 'don't you come all moral with me, chum, with your *rape*. Rose was a willing learner. And when she found she was up the duff, she was canny enough to initiate Darren. Darren the patsy - to cover her back.'

A remembered line from the journal niggled in Batten's head - *I shall need Darren, to protect me.* Was there a hint of calculation in it? Malkie McTay depicted Darren as a cauldron of rage, with Rose his target – *he would have had her by the throat.* But did Darren have his suspicions, even at sixteen? And, duped, did he bide his time, make his journey of rage, destroy Queen Mab's throat with a well-used knife? Batten shook with rage of his own, needing Abe to be the culprit, not Darren. He couldn't speak.

Timms spoke for him. 'You covered *your* back, too. What did you use, to keep Rose's mouth shut – your fists?'

Abe curled his lip at Timms. 'Puh, Rose didn't need much persuasion.

She almost believed Darren *was* the daddy. Convinced herself, as well as him. Daddy-Abe-Daddy not good enough for *her*.' He leaned towards Timms. 'But I'll tell you something about Rose, oil slick. That first time, your innocent little Rose was a goer. And I didn't charge school fees for the lesson.'

Timms shot to her feet. '*No,*' she said. 'You impregnated a fourteen-year-old *child*. How virile!'

'Always been virile, us Linnets.' Abe leered at Timms and weakly tapped his bedsheets. 'Climb in, why don't you?'

Timms would have slapped Abe - and lost her job - but for a rap on the door. Batten confronted an irate Doctor Bhatti in the doorway. 'Go ahead, ask our Mr Linnet what he wants. If he says we leave, we leave. If not, there's unfinished *business!*'

Recoiling from the anger on Batten's face, Bhatti threw a questioning glance at Abe, who batted away the Doctor with the back of his hand. 'I shall be outside,' Bhatti said. 'And I shall report this.'

You don't know the half of it, thought Batten, needing the rest. He sat down, the chair's hardness forgotten. 'You let Gina believe the dead baby was Darren's, didn't you?' A shrug. 'And told the school, told Darren's parents, told the whole bloody world she'd had a miscarriage.'

'Course I did. What was I supposed to do, admit it? To *Gina*? It was her fault - she wouldn't let Rose get rid. So, yeh, I told *the whole bloody world* Rose had a miscarriage. Handy, too, the Popes doing a bunk. For their own safety, of course.'

'With your boot up their backsides.'

Abe ignored Batten's glare. 'I couldn't give a monkey's tit what you think of me. But don't assume I'm stupid.'

Batten remembered Malkie McTay's angry description of Abe: '*crook* written on one eyeball, and *cunning* on the other.' 'You were clever enough to disappear. Or did Gina kick you out?'

'Gina? Like to see her try. Let's say 'business pressure' encouraged me to drown.' The memory of salt water on his face and *Sea Breeze* sinking below the waves shocked Abe back towards clarity. The white walls of his 'cell' reminded him how close he'd drifted to evidence-land. *I'm saying too much.* Over Batten's shoulder in the glass door-panel, Bhatti's head flailed like a deranged metronome. 'I think my Doctor is concerned for my welfare,' Abe said.

No you don't, thought Batten. *Not yet.* 'Cut to the chase! Rose - Queen Mab - a harmless drunk. Why would even a shit like you slice her throat from one ear to the other? If the crime scene photographs were here, I'd rub your foul nose in them.'

'Haven't a clue what you're talking about. Wasn't there.'

'Ray Breeze was.'

'Well. Ask Ray. *Abe* has said enough.'

He reached for the call button, but Batten grabbed his arm. 'The ring, in your rucksack. From Queen Mab's body. Shape of an A? An L? A Delta? Why bother with it?'

Abe yawned. 'A ring? Yeh, someone donated a ring. Silver. Can't remember who.'

Then Doctor Bhatti's white coat was in the room, almost before Abe's finger pressed the bell.

'*Out!*' he said.

*

Batten had no idea how he and Timms found their way from *Oncology* to the car park, such was their fury. And Batten's fickle mind kept replaying the one entry from Rose's journal that burned him the moment he read it and burned him doubly now. He could see the young Rose in her hospital bed, could see the ink-black words, as crystal clear as if he held the open journal in his hand.

Here, everything is white - white pills and walls, white sheets and uniforms - like I'm living inside somebody else's soul. Because souls are white, aren't they? But what I truly want is a soul of my own. My soul went missing. It went missing when the baby died. I search, in hope, because no-one can live without a soul.
I search. I have to.

How many years did Rose Linnet live a broken, hollow life without a soul? And how many years did she live unwittingly in the same house as Sue, her stolen child, her unknown daughter - the very missing soul for whom she searched?

Batten clenched his fists against the thought, and against all the wasted searches of the dead Queen Mab. The search for a worthless Daniel. For the repetitious daubs of a dream of art. For a fairy-tale island with its castle in the clouds. And the wasted life inside a bottle, in the hope her lost stars might somehow dazzle through the glass.

When Batten contemplated his own wasted searches, the remembered stare of Abe's doomed face, grey against the white pillow, triggered a stab of guilt. Unprofessional, the words he'd used. But, for God's sake, how much longer can I dance the policeman's jig? This dark tango - justice for the tragic dead, partnered with a required compassion for the Abe Linnets of the world? Will I end up like Wallingford, swapping justice for *efficiency*?

About to share his thoughts with Timms, he saw her fumble angrily in her bag for the parking voucher. It slipped from her numb fingers, and in a fury of her own she flung her handbag after it, keys, coins and hairbrush crashing to the ground and spinning across the foyer. When he knelt down to retrieve them, he saw her tears.

'I'm sorry, sir, I...' Sobs replaced words, her hands and shoulders shaking in an earthquake of grief for parents and for daughters. 'That foul man...I watched my father *die* here!' she said, before the tremors consumed her. Batten thought of his grief for Aunt Daze, and Sonia Welcome's tender arms wrapped around him in comfort. He did the same for Timms, all sense of rank thrown aside as he held her close, and she sobbed into his chest.

A mumsy-looking nurse trotted up to the pay machine to validate her ticket, as if Batten and Timms were invisible. When Timms broke away, dabbing her eyes in embarrassment, the nurse whispered to Batten. 'I'm so glad she has a close relative to comfort her. With pain and grief, people shouldn't be alone.' Gently patting his arm, the nurse ghosted away, a bemused Batten staring after her.

Timms regained enough composure to find her keys, but when they reached the car she hesitated, hands still a-tremble.

'Sir,' she said, 'I know it's not my place to make demands. But I refuse to go back there' - she waved in Abe's direction - 'and *never again* will I sit in the same room as that man!'

Batten nodded, his dark tango resolved for now. 'Hazel, I'd rather sit next to Hitler.'

She shook her trembling car keys at her boss. 'One more demand,' she said. 'You'll have to drive.'

*

Darren Pope's fingers shook as he wiped the cold steel blade of the knife and slid it into his pocket, next to the club. A pair of handy tools, to rid the world of Rose. His legacy.

Determined still, he struggled to his feet on the makeshift crutch and dragged himself up the rest of the scrub-covered slope towards the sky. Another slow trek beneath unrelenting sun brought him to the sharp hill's peak, dotted with stunted eucalyptus and acacia. No water, no streams or pools, here or on the way. Salt lips now thick with thirst, Darren Pope leaned against the only tree strong enough to support his giant bulk, scanning the horizon, lord of all he surveyed.

And slid down the dry bark to the ground.

Tiny, this empire, for a giant like Darren. Tiny.

And completely surrounded by sea.

Sixty one

Doctor Bhatti was angry with the nurse, the police, Abe – and with himself, for not exercising more authority. He checked Abe's bedside monitor and left his patient in respite from the pain that would return, till it no longer needed to.

Alone in the darkened room, Abe drifted in and out of consciousness, with nothing but a *blip-pause-bleep* for company. Half in dream, he totted up the ways he'd made 'this business' work for him – and the waste. Hanging back in Parminster's streets, tracking the shambling figure, a distant flash of dirty red and foul grey – but so pickled in drink she wouldn't spot him if he popped up in front of her. And carefully clocking the places she went, when any Parminster resident could have told him which alley she slept in.

This *creature* had given birth to Sue, his only child. Each time he tracked her his disgust festered and swelled. A whole month he'd watched, in daylight and on night-patrol, the disguise of his uniform redundant. And night after night, disgust gave way to rage, to fury.

Thank God his child, Sue *Linnet,* made it home. Wherever home's supposed to be.

He'd never forget the 'home' where he found Rose - and the *thing* she'd let herself become. A scruffy skip outside a carpet shop, in an alley sticky with piss and lord knows what. Though he couldn't smell it, couldn't smell a thing anymore, he could *see* and *feel* how Rose must smell. One hard blow on the back of her skull with the club would've done it, yes, but when he saw the stinking state of her, in close-up…*Unpolluted beauty?* She almost made him vomit into his surgical mask.

One dirty pocket, that's all his gloved hands had searched before the tiny light from his pencil torch fell on the gold chain round the foul bitch's neck. And dangling from it that pathetic key, a puny brass cross on the end. *Could've opened her bloody storage unit with a nail file!*

In the pencil light, beneath the dirt and decay, he could just make out her cheekbones, the fine bones inherited from Gina - but not from *him*.

330

Gina and Rose, two crazy beauties, their curves gone, their own fucked-up livers polluting them. *Trouble. Wombs and trouble.* That's all they were to him.

He'd brought the knife, 'borrowed' from Daniel, a handy folding thing, sharper now, bleached clean. Who magicked the knife into his hand - was it Gina, or was it Rose? When he pulled back the decrepit cow's neck and sliced into her throat, it was the pair of them. Despite the long gloves and surgical gown, he convinced himself he hadn't come prepared, that this was not rage and revenge. *It's my good deed. I'm clearing the rubbish. I'm putting out the bins.*

A *bleep* from the monitor stirred him, but the memories spewed on. *Before the blood flowed, you took the ring, the silver ring. For Sue.* He pushed away the snitching thought that Sue would inherit the ring anyway, with all the 'the effects of the deceased'. And inherit the 'effects' of Rose, too. *Home,* he mumbled. *It all comes home.*

The White Mountains were a home of sorts. Silhouetted against the mountain snow, he saw images of Rose and Gina, two balloon bumps - both belonging to *him.* And remembered the day he gave Rose the silver ring.

'Not *another!*' said Gina, who hated rings. *Prisons,* she called them.

'Rose collects rings,' said Abe. 'A silversmith made it.'

'Needs glasses, then. What is it?'

'It's another L,' he lied. 'L for Linnet. To go with her other three - for me, you and her.'

'Wonky sort of L.'

'It's for a Linnet baby,' said Abe. He didn't say whose.

When Rose wore it as an L, he chose not to correct her - for once. Let her and Gina believe it. But Abe knew it was a V. *V for Verity.* As a ten-year old, Abe learned to sail in a skiff called *Verity.* On the water, his fist squeezing the tiller, power and freedom had fizzed through his veins. Abe's secret child would be free and powerful too, she would sail on, she would be a *Verity.* And Abe always got his way.

His hand formed a fist on the bedsheets. After he switched the babies, Gina named her Sue - a short name, she said, because the baby might not live. Then told everyone the thriving Verity was a *Sue!* Abe's fist hardened, Gina his fancied target now. *And she had the gall not to ask me!*

In Abe's mind, it was *Verity*, not Sue, who came home. *V for Verity,* Verity Linnet. The Linnets, living on.

But to Abe's dismay, when he punched the sheets in triumph, his once-powerful hand could only flop, barely disturbing the drip that dangled from his arm.

Oh, but in my youth, how I could punch…my fist crunching home. The power in my veins, like a drug…

And I dodged the police, to the end, he told the empty white walls.

Not a bad way to go, landing punches, dodging theirs.

Sixty two

When he emerged from his dreaded appointment with Dr Fallon, Batten's face was ghostly white. Sonia Welcome expected nothing else. 'Seatbelt, Zig?' she said.

'What? Ungh. Sorry.' He stared through the windscreen at nothing.

They drove in silence for a mile before she dared hazard the question.

'No. He didn't. He flatly refused to sign me off.' Batten re-lived Fallon shaking his head, firm fingers screwing the cap on his fountain pen and clipping it in the acid-white pocket of his coat. Beyond the windscreen, bare branches, tarmac and puny clouds blurred by. 'Well, no. He *did* sign me off. He signed me off the *Force*.'

Sonia said nothing. Privately, she'd predicted the outcome, because she was a doctor too.

'I'm plain Zig Batten,' he said, screwing up his eyes to stop the tears. 'I'm...not anything.'

After another mile, she said, 'you're alive.' This was not the time to remind Zig of the generous pension he would draw, at barely forty. 'You're alive, with choices.' She leaned across and softly touched her fingers to his cold cheek. 'Would you prefer the alternative?'

Plain Zig Batten shook his head, a long sigh sending his career into the clouds. When he stared through the window, an unfamiliar road stared back. 'We're going the wrong way.'

'We're going the *right* way,' said Sonia. 'I've something to show you.'

*

Eddie 'Loft' Hick said *see you* to a departing Hazel Timms and re-read the letter on his desk. Was his career warming up? Lately, he and Laura's evenings were spent working on their competence portfolios for Sergeant rank - or in bed. The letter in his hand ratified only the Sergeant part, and he was about to speed home to Laura to ratify the rest - when his dratted phone rang. Mind elsewhere, he almost didn't hear the Australian accent, almost called him the Wizard of Oz.

After sharing niceties with Brad, the Australian liaison officer, and jotting down fresh info, Hick tidied up his dyslexic scribble, mis-correcting the odd word here and there.

Darren Pope found. Body disvocered by island rangers. Not much left of him. Teeth. Detnal records. Had carved 'ROS' into a hunk of wood with a knife. Oz police no record of a Ros Pope. Maybe his wife or duaghter? Says can we check for her whereabouts?

Hick slid the note onto Sergeant Ball's desk beneath a glass paperweight claiming, *There's Always Time for Cider*. Might be a Sergeant Eddie Hick desk, he thought, before too long.

On the way out, he swerved round the filing cabinet, and gave it a friendly pat as he danced through the door.

*

Half a mile before they arrived, Batten knew where Sonia was heading.

'I didn't know pathologists went in for exorcism,' he said, when they parked outside Queen Mab's empty house. 'Training for a new career, are you?' Then he thought, *no, I'm the one who needs the new career.*

Sonia flashed an impish smile. You needn't face the future alone, it said, unless you choose to.

Despite feeling bleak, he tried to smile back. 'Is this the bit where I re-enter the victim's environment, to flush Queen Mab out of my system?'

'That's pretty well it,' she said, taking a keyring from her bag. 'And the victim's environment has certainly been flushed out, if the garden is anything to go by.'

Batten remembered the jungle of brambles and leylandii from his last visit, replaced now by bare ground and a 'For Sale by Auction' sign. Sonia took his arm and they strolled unencumbered down the path to the front door, the boarding removed, the porch washed clean. Her key turned smoothly in the lock and they entered, mixed scents of woodworm fluid and disinfectant in the air.

'It looks better without the ton of crud,' said Batten. The filthy carpets, curled newspapers and old food wrappers were gone, exposing clean wide floorboards ripe for sanding. 'Goode, Goode and Moulde didn't waste any time, clearing the place to sell. Think of the commission they'll earn.'

In fact, Batten was thinking of Queen Mab's shrine of sanity or madness, her bedroom in the clouds. Was it cleared now, the dry Greek herbs discarded, her canvases burnt?

Sonia walked him towards the rear of the house. 'It's this I really wanted to show you.'

'The back was boarded up last time, thank God,' said Batten. 'The front was bad enough. A sad place.'

'It needn't be,' she said, unlocking the rear door and stepping into early evening sun. Batten followed, still feeling this was 'Queen Mab's house'. Till he saw, on the near horizon, the vast Iron-age earthworks of magnificent Ham Hill, its golden stone dressed in a coat of autumnal red.

'Wow,' he said, despite himself. 'Some surprise.' He took in the vista, struggling to connect Rose Linnet, whose back garden framed this real and beautiful view, with the gin-soaked Queen Mab – sleeping rough in a dark alley and painting the same dead dreams over and over.

'I think the garden has what Estate Agents call 'potential',' said Sonia, pointing at the stripped ground, scarred by tree stumps and the remnants of weeds. 'But they've made a start on the roof.' Scaffolding climbed up one side of the house and a stack of reclaimed tiles lay beneath.

'Bit premature,' said Batten. 'Not had the auction yet.'

Sonia wandered back inside. 'There won't be an auction,' she said. 'I've already bought it.'

Batten stared at her, dumbstruck. '*What?* Have you forgotten who the last owner was? And lord knows, the one before?'

'Of course not. But I've no time for ghosts and omens. The Linnets have flown away, Zig. This is a solid house, with a future.' Smiling at plain Zig Batten, she ran her fingers along the exposed hamstone wall. 'This house needs to be lived in,' she said.

Acknowledgements

A huge thanks to my test readers for their patient response, and to all who helped during the writing, editing and publishing of The Killing of Queen Mab. I won't list names - you know who you are and know you're greatly appreciated.

Any misunderstandings are mine.

To the reader

Reviews are an author's lifeblood. If you enjoyed *The Killing of Queen Mab*, please do tell others by leaving a review on Amazon.co.uk, Amazon.com, or on Goodreads.

Inspector Zig Batten first appears in Book 1, *A Killing Tree,* where he struggles with his enforced move from urban Yorkshire to not-so-sleepy Somerset. Before he can blink, hikers discover a dead body slumped against a tree on a lonely hill...
www.smarturl.it/akte

A January Killing sees Batten and his new love-interest at a traditional cider 'Wassail', in a pitch-black orchard on a winter night. Celebratory shotguns are fired into the trees, to deter 'evil spirits' and spark a fresh crop of apples. But not every shotgun fires blanks, and next day it's a dead body that has blossomed in the orchard...
www.smarturl.it/ajk

Crown of Thorns Hill overlooks the sleepy village of East Thorne. But on Good Friday morning, the village wakes to a malign vision at the hill's peak – a sight which catapults a flu-ridden Inspector Batten out of his holiday bed to a scene of desecration...
smarturl.it/AnEasterKilling

We live life forwards, but understand it backwards. In these "beautifully poignant and funny stories", minds old and young journey through half-shaded landscapes of memory. Why not take the journey too, and see what they discover?
www.smarturl.it/avwm

The novels can be read in sequence or standalone.

Printed in Great Britain
by Amazon